GENEVA
ACCORD

GENEVA ACCORD

BY JOHN WHITMAN

Crown Publishers, Inc., New York

Copyright © 1985 by John Whitman
All rights reserved. No part of this book may be reproduced or transmitted
in any form or by any means, electronic or mechanical, including
photocopying, recording, or by any information storage and retrieval
system, without permission in writing from the publisher.
Published by Crown Publishers, Inc., One Park Avenue, New York, New York 10016,
and simultaneously in Canada by General Publishing Company Limited
Manufactured in the United States of America
Library of Congress Cataloging in Publication Data
Whitman, John T.
Geneva accord.
I. Title.
PS3573.H4984G4   1985   813'.54   84-9583
ISBN 0-517-55551-4
10 9 8 7 6 5 4 3 2 1
First Edition

FOR CAROL,
STEVE,
MARTITA,
TONY,
AND CHRIS

The name *Inigo* is stressed on the first syllable.
Both *i*'s are pronounced short, as in *sin*.

GENEVA
ACCORD

1

The American was jumpy. It had been a critical meeting, and it had not gone well. He wished now that he had stuck to his resolution to refuse the usual after-dinner brandies. They hadn't calmed his nerves at all, nor had they warmed his belly against the chilling drizzle of the winter night.

He couldn't imagine, trudging alone up the hill to the Vieille Ville, why he had prolonged the evening so. His companion had been more disagreeable than ever. When he had told him in the restaurant, in a hoarse whisper, that his side was prepared to drop its demand for the destruction of obsolete missiles, the Russian had been disdainful.

"When?"

"At tomorrow's plenary meeting."

"How wonderful!" It was scornfully said. "Twelve hours from now we shall all be hearing it officially from the American ambassador. Such valuable information you bring me!"

There was nothing he could reply. Over the past month, their exchanges had become steadily more uncomfortable, even tense at times. The surreptitious quality of their meetings was getting on his nerves. Whenever the Russian sneered at the triviality of his offerings, he felt guilty and defensive. What he needed was a source in Washington itself, where the issues were debated and decided behind closed doors. Here in Geneva, all they got was the final product of those debates, cabled out to them along with instructions to present it to the Soviet delegation. In recent weeks the Russian had become more openly impatient, and his own information, as if in retaliation, had gotten thinner, more nebulous and gossipy. But for some reason he had not felt able to complain. He had a sense that he was in over his head. He had known from the start that he was an amateur working with a professional, but somehow he had not expected that to count for so much.

Theoretically they had identical aims, shared the same mutual ob-

1

ligations, and were at equal risk. How then had the Russian managed
to gain control of the situation? When had it happened?

"I'll be on the secure phone to Washington tomorrow afternoon,"
he offered. "Maybe I can get some advance word on the telemetry encryption issue."

The slight tremor in his voice frightened him. The Russian, giving
no sign whether he had noticed or had even heard the words, gazed
silently at the two remaining waiters stacking the chairs at the other
tables. Tall, lanky in their black suits, they looked like elderly twin
crows. He seemed to feel no tension, to be prepared to sit there all
night. He didn't speak when the American signaled for the check and
paid, nor while they moved toward the door and collected their coats.
Only on the sidewalk outside did he break the silence.

"May I give you a ride to your apartment?"

The American declined. It was a short walk, and he could not bear
the thought of even a brief ride beside this silent, contemptuous companion. They parted with a brief farewell.

Living alone in Geneva for many months, away from wife, children, and friends, he was losing his routine and roots. He had begun,
for one thing, to get fat. His breath came short as he plodded up the
hill past the cathedral. An old familiar ache, revived by his sedentary
ways, started to throb quietly in his right leg. He would have stopped
to rest, but a vague menace in the wet, deserted street drove him on.

When he gained the old square that marked the center of the Vieille
Ville, the ascent eased. The Rue Etienne Dumont was empty and cold
as he turned into it. Halfway up on the right, the street door of number sixteen, leading through a short tunnel into a courtyard shared
by half a dozen apartments, was unlocked. Although this was
strange—by some unofficial custom one or another of the inhabitants
locked it at ten each evening—he barely noticed. The medieval creak
of the heavy door sounded down the tunnel. Wearily he climbed to
the first landing, at the end of which his apartment lay.

A voice, quiet but distinct, spoke his name.

Two men, one tall and the other short, stood in the half-light by his
door. Their hats and the shoulders of their coats glistened with rain-
drops. Despite the dimness, he was sure that he had never seen them
before.

He bolted. With no plan in his head, he rushed back down the steps,
praying to God that they were Swiss. Russians would be no better

than Americans, he thought wildly. In the courtyard he nearly slipped on the rain-slick bricks. He raced into the tunnel. With only a fifteen-yard head start, he was still fumbling madly at the street door when the two men reached the courtyard. By the time he got it open, they had entered the tunnel.

The first shot tore into his knee, felling him immediately. Thus it was that the next bullet, also aimed low by the shorter man, struck the back of his head just as he tumbled out onto the sidewalk.

The tall man cursed bitterly as they ran toward the body. There was no need to inspect it. Still cursing his partner, the tall man pulled it back into the tunnel. Lights began to show in the courtyard as they slammed the door and locked it from the outside. In thirty seconds they were around the corner and gone.

2

Flying into Geneva, the view is stupendous. All night long Inigo's plane had drilled its way through the black sky over the black Atlantic, its passengers irritable from cramped seats and stale air. Since sunrise there had been nothing to see but flat French farmland far below. Then the plane began its descent and, reaching Lake Leman, banked right for the twenty-mile approach into Cointrin Airport. Suddenly there it all was.

Inigo, on Peters's advice, had gotten a window seat on the left side. From the right nothing could be seen but the Jura, marking the border, no higher or more dramatic than the Appalachians. Everyone crowded and craned to the left; even those in the aisle could catch brilliant glimpses.

There they were, the Alps. Rough and random, white even through the summer, jagged, cruel. The last wildness in a continent tamed long ago, they filled Inigo's entire view, except for the dazzling strip at the bottom that was Lake Leman, transformed into ribs of dancing silver and black by the morning sun. The mountains sit implacably in the very center of Europe; they are its heart. They can be climbed, hiked, skied, even built upon, sparingly and at the lower reaches. But they can never be taken, made over, used, shaped. They are not man's land, they stand over against him, terrible in their grand, indifferent existence.

They seemed to go on forever and out of sight except in one quadrant, where Mont Blanc heaved high above its neighbors, broad-shouldered, blocking Inigo's eye. Lord of the Alps, it struck him like the final crescendo and climax of a Beethoven symphony, filling the heart, driving out everything small and petty. Inigo looked away from it only to be pulled back. Something in him wanted not to believe in Mont Blanc; it was too overwhelming, too much itself, but there was no possibility of disbelief. It was there, it would be there forever, and the snows upon it would never melt.

4

He kept his gaze fixed upon Mont Blanc until it was blotted out by the Saleve, a low, rock-ribbed mountain just outside the city, Geneva's trademark. Then the lake was gone behind parks and hotels; then there was the sudden empty space of airport runways, finally the gentle bounce of the touchdown. The poetry was abruptly torn away in a screaming of brakes and the frantic grip of deceleration. They were a quarter mile from the terminal, which they reached on foot through a long underground passageway decorated with huge illuminated banking advertisements. Inigo felt a psychic jolt from the change—too quick—from the glory of the Alps to the the banal, characterless airport.

Two days earlier, on a dull October morning, the guard had routinely waved him through the entrance drive at CIA headquarters. Inigo had a familiar, easily recognizable face. Not actually a nondescript face, George, a colleague had solemnly intoned once in the late hours of a boozy in-house party, but a far from memorable face, if you don't mind, George. Strong lines flaring down and out from the lower nose foreshadowed the bags and folds that would be his in old age. In his mid-forties, his hair was thin and silvering everywhere, already white at the temples. It was a face that, narrowing in its lower half, might have benefited from the frame of a short beard, had Inigo paid more attention to his appearance. As it was, the total effect was passable, comfortable, disarming. In a taut world of rivalrous tensions, even the tiny holes that spotted his clothing, burned there by vagrant cinders from his loosely packed cigarettes, were somehow reassuring.

Only a few of his colleagues—Cornett was one of them, and Elton another—had seen beyond the presentation of himself that had long ago become second nature to Inigo. On the tennis courts, Cornett, himself a methodical player, had taken note of the desperate quality of Inigo's strivings to reach unreachable balls. Elton, on a Canadian vacation with him, had been struck by the contrast between the bureaucrat, whose composure and patience acted like a focusing magnet to his peers, and the skier, whose recklessness was a menace to himself and everyone on the mountain. Separately, for they had never talked to each other about it, each of them sensed a tamed competitiveness, a curbed defiance. Inigo himself was only dimly aware of this turbulence; he thought of himself as one of the steady ones who kept the place going—as, in truth, he was. Cornett and Elton, separately, appreciated the paradox.

Walking in from the parking lot, Inigo was overtaken by Cornett.

"Harry. What's new?"

Inigo reminded himself too late that this was a question Cornett always took seriously. He prided himself on an ever-renewed supply of underground political information and office gossip. He seemed to be the central switchboard for a dozen grapevines, mostly within CIA but also extending into the White House, the Pentagon, and the State Department.

"Hickok's being relieved, I hear."

"Oh, what for?"

"Hard to say. The DDO's clammed up about it. They say Shambler's involved."

That meant Counterintelligence. Inigo didn't pursue it. He didn't want to hear Cornett's wild theories. Instead, he asked, "So who's replacing him at SALT?"

"No decision yet. It's up for grabs. How about yourself?"

Inigo made no answer as they entered the building and fished out their badges. At the guard's nod they slung the small plastic cards around their necks on a chain. They would not take them off again until they passed out through the guard post that evening. Well, and what about it, Inigo thought as contact with Cornett dissolved in the little crowd waiting for the elevator. How about myself?

The thought faded away as the crowd in the elevator pressed him up against a trim young secretary. It returned when he reached the office and found a message from Peters proposing lunch. Guy Peters ran the SALT account for CIA, and Inigo heard from him every few weeks when Peters wanted advice on Soviet policy attitudes. Today's invitation, however, fell into a new context. By the time Inigo returned the call, Peters was already at the first of his day-long series of meetings, and his secretary relayed an invitation to lunch today in the executive dining room. Fine.

The morning had been set aside for work on the annual estimate on the Soviet leadership. For Inigo, it was the seventh time around. "The septuagenarian Soviet leadership shows no signs of purposeful planning for a rejuvenation of the Politburo as it moves into . . ." *Septuagenarian:* It was a word he had never heard in conversation. It seemed to exist only in the written language. Every year he had to look up the spelling. As he did again today, he noticed that it was a noun; the adjectival form was different. Oh well, who cared; it had gone unnoticed for so many years that a correction now would only make trouble.

From nowhere came a vagrant thought: You don't kill time, it kills you. For a moment, he mourned Khrushchev again. There was a worthy foeman, that shrewd, coarse, imaginative peasant. Sovietology was fun in the days when Nikita was around. And now Brezhnev, who seemed to go on forever. He recalled the report of a Western diplomat: "When I called on the first secretary a year after his installation, he impressed me as the manager of a very large and important factory. Yesterday, seeing him four years later, he struck me as the owner." For Inigo, that summed up Brezhnev's dull pomposity.

Not that it was much better on the American side. Inigo had been through too many presidents, too many administrations. Each came to town knowing the answers. One would see the Soviet Union as implacable, impatient, ready to exploit any opportunity, heedless of the normal calculus of risks. Inigo would write reams about Soviet caution, Moscow's pragmatism, its long-headed approach, its aversion to risking the future on one throw of the dice when history was already in its favor. All to no avail. Then along would come the next, convinced that the Soviets were insecure, defensive, misunderstood, anxious for acceptance and agreement. More reams from Inigo, this time about the USSR's expansionist impulses, its trickery, its confidence in its strength, its steady outward pressures. Again to no avail. He had given up hope that the United States could hold to a steady, long-run, unexcited course toward the USSR. Especially "unexcited." It was the emotions, the exaggerated hopes and fears, that wrecked policy after policy.

What both kinds of presidents wanted from CIA was the exciting secret from the mysterious, infallible covert source. The implication being, of course, that there actually is an ultimate secret.

Inigo was plagued by the usual interruptions that morning as he honed his paragraphs, weighted and counterweighted his arguments. Current Intelligence sent around for his approval their report on yesterday's speech by the Soviet foreign minister. With uncharacteristic impatience, he scrawled in the margin: "For God's sake, there's not a nugget of novelty in that speech. Why not say so in one sentence and shut up?" Been on the job too long, he murmured wryly as he sent the draft back through the pneumatic tube system. Now there was a marvel. One set of plumbing for "Top Secret" papers, another for "Secret," another for "Unclassified," all snaking through the walls of the whole building, coyly winding past one another, never intersecting. Like ideas that never meet in argument. Or colleagues that never connect in friendship.

Around ten-thirty his secretary brought in another draft report: "A Review of Sino-Soviet Relations." The tone was bland and cautious, the effect boring. Inigo sighed, remembering the days of discovery and excitement. Back in the mid-1950s, he had been one of a trio of analysts caught up in the initial indications of the split between Moscow and Peking. For three years they amassed a growing body of evidence, but few listened. Finally, when the Soviets pulled out all their military and economic advisers, it dawned on the policymakers that a profound change in international alignments had taken place. By then, a schoolboy could see it.

"Laura, do I really have to comment on this?"

"No sir," his secretary's voice came back on the intercom. "But the author is sitting out here waiting. He seems like a very nice young man."

Training, Inigo thought with a sinking heart. It's our obligation. Someday we'll be gone. Successors will be needed. Turning points will approach. They have to be ready to spot them, broadcast them. Whether anyone listens or not. Oh hell.

"I was once a nice young man myself, Laura. Tell him his piece is fine. Tell him to consider it agreed. He doesn't need a signature." Pushing away a vague feeling that he had just shirked a duty, Inigo turned back to his own prose. Forty-five minutes later, when Laura buzzed him for lunch, he shook himself out of a stupor of pleasure. Scanning his paragraphs, forgetting for a moment that he was merely updating last year's estimate, he decided that the old warhorse still had the stuff. His earlier grumpiness dissolved in satisfied reflections on a long and successful career. For a man without a family, he mused, he'd been lucky to find such absorbing work. It was just getting a bit boring lately, that was all.

The executive dining room, along with the large office and the close-in parking space, was one of the perquisites of rank at headquarters. To pass from the great, noisy cafeteria to this quiet sanctum where waiters hovered was a graduation into a world of privilege. No one knew how staffers officially qualified for it. Inigo, two promotions ago, had simply gone in one day and sat down. No one questioned him. He wondered how others had managed the problem.

Peters was late. As he bustled in and grabbed the menu, he gave the impression of a man who never had time to do any single thing properly. Others, Inigo knew, carried more weight with less fuss. Himself, for example.

"Sorry, Georgie, but I've got to rush. You've heard about Hickok?"

"I heard something just this morning." So Cornett was right.

"He's been canned. Effective today, in fact. The cable goes out tonight. I can't get a word out of the director about why. He just told . me to find a replacement right away."

"What about yourself?" Inigo sparred for time.

"Me? Hell no. I did it for three years. The family wouldn't stand for it again. Besides, let's face it, George, Washington is where the action is on SALT. No, I was thinking about you."

So there it was. Inigo wondered how pressed Peters was, how quickly a replacement was needed, how much time he had to mull it over. His instincts were already saying yes, and he wanted time to fight them down, to achieve a state of calm contemplation.

"Me? You think I ought to put in for it?"

"Look, if you apply, you've got it," Peters told Inigo. "Hands down. I could promise to fix it with Lormack, except that it doesn't need fixing. He'll jump at you. The only question is whether you want it."

Inigo had the familiar sense that his mind had already made itself up. But he needed to talk it out, if only to discover his reasons. Perhaps there was an unconscious pro or con that he'd missed. Or one decisive argument whose potency he needed to understand. Offers like this seemed to come his way every three or four years, and he always took them. He spoke of new challenges, of learning and growing, but was it anything more than restlessness?

"How long would I have to figure on being there?" Not that it made a big difference to him.

"Couldn't be more than a few months. Half a year at the outside."

"Really?" The negotiations were in their seventh year and Inigo, who did not specialize in SALT, had come to think of it as a permanent process.

"That's right. We know that the Soviets have four or five new missiles in development. Two or three will be ready for testing before the year is out. Once that happens, the cat's out of the bag and the treaty loses half its value to us. You see, the way it's written, only one new missile can be flight-tested after SALT is signed. But anything flown before that date is cleared for deployment."

Inigo frowned. "How did we manage to get in such a dumb situation? The United States won't have anything new to test for years."

"That's just it." Peters looked keenly at him. "It's not dumb at all; it's one of the big advantages of the thing for our side. They have to cancel all but one of their new birds as soon as SALT is signed, while the U.S. gets to proceed on the only project we've got going. But the offer's not good indefinitely—anything tested before the treaty is legit. That's why we've got to get a move on in Geneva."

"So it's a race. Diplomats against engineers."

"Nicely put," Peters agreed. "And we're entering the final lap. You could be in on the finish."

"Well, do I want it?" Inigo smiled at him. "Tell me about it. What's involved?"

Peters was a small, neat, methodical man. Given a sizable subject, he liked to deliver a lecture.

"Okay. There's five things. No, six. First is intelligence support to the delegation. Those guys in Geneva need all the details they can get. In SALT we're not trying to limit weapons in general. We're limiting real Soviet missiles and submarines and bombers, those in the field and those being developed. We don't want treaty language that sounds grand and sweeping but in fact doesn't cover the Bison bomber or the SS-16 ICBM. So you'll be fielding questions every day on Soviet weaponry, what's the accuracy of the SS-19, how sure are we of how many SLBMs the new sub will carry, that sort of thing. You'll inherit loads of files on this in Geneva, and we can dig up fast answers for you here in headquarters. Remember, don't shoot from the hip. If you don't know, just tell them you need to check it out. We're only a cable away here, and the commo is terrific. Use the scrambler telephone whenever you have to. It's totally secure.

"Second, monitoring. CIA is responsible for that here in Washington, and you'll play the same role on the delegation in Geneva. Nothing goes into the treaty that we can't monitor ourselves, by our own technical intelligence. Maybe not one hundred percent, maybe not every day. Maybe without much confidence in some cases when a Soviet violation wouldn't be strategically significant anyway. But on the big ones, monitoring has to be a high-confidence job or the U.S. won't accept a treaty limitation. Nothing taken on trust. So the delegation needs to understand the monitoring implications of every proposal.

"Third, protection of intelligence sources and methods. You guys are up against the Soviet delegation at plenary session every week, sometimes twice a week, with lots of other small meetings in between. And those guys are plenty smart. They've got all kinds of questions, direct and indirect, designed to smoke out our intelligence capabilities. So they can figure out precisely what we can and can't do, shut us down with countermeasures where it hurts the most, steer their weapons designers into areas where we can't follow. Maybe even cheat on SALT where they know we're weak. You're the delegation policeman on all this. You tell them what they can and can't say to the Sovs about monitoring. If you're uncertain, fire a cable back to me. And tell the delegation that anytime the Sovs challenge them on how such and such a limitation could be monitored, all the answer they need is, 'By national technical means.' That, plus a sweet smile, is plenty."

Peters's fourth point had to do with briefing visiting senators. As he started in, a woman entered the dining room, searched them out with her eyes, and came up to their table.

"Mr. Peters, the White House has called. They've moved your meeting up to one o'clock. The car should be waiting for you when you get down to the main entrance." Patricia Simpless said it all just right—quiet enough to be professional but loud enough to be heard at several nearby tables. Inigo watched Peters turn extra serious to refrain from beaming.

"Hell. I'll have to go back by the office first to get my papers," he said, matching her tone.

"I've got them right here, Mr. Peters." In the office it was "Guy" and in Geneva, where they had spent three years together away from Peters's wife, who knew what it was. Except for a little too much heaviness in the calves and ankles, Patricia Simpless was the kind of secretary every senior bureaucrat was looking for. When they found one, they took her with them from assignment to assignment. All that devotion and loyalty and intuitive understanding. But when the boss retired, she was left high and dry. Often there was nothing to do but follow him out.

"Thanks, Patricia. George, I'm sorry. I'll get back to you as soon as I can. In the meantime, be thinking it over. You'd be perfect for it. And don't forget the Alps. I know you're a skier."

He bustled out, demurely followed by Simpless. They left by the main door, reminding Inigo that Peters was far from the worst of the lot. Some of his colleagues entered or left the dining room through the other door, the one leading to the director's suite, implying that they were just leaving or going to a session with Lormack himself. Inigo grinned to himself wryly. It would be nice to get away from headquarters for a while.

Back in his office, idly wondering what Peters's remaining points were, he asked Laura to make an appointment with the director.

In his twenty-two years at the Agency, Inigo had seen seven or eight directors come and go. In the beginning, down in the lower ranks, they were invisible to him, mythical figures, clothed in power approaching that of the president. As he climbed the rungs, he came into increasing contact with them. A mixed lot, of course; how could it be otherwise? A general, a corporation executive, a senior spymaster, a politician, an admiral. But there was a trend, and it was not encouraging. More and more, the job was offered to men devoted more to the interests of the administration than the country. More and more, it was sought by men who saw it as a stepping-stone, another credential, a ticket to even higher office. The original principle of an independent Agency, a source of disinterested analysis, was fraying.

Lormack was Inigo's favorite. When his predecessor suddenly quit to run for the Senate, a storm of criticism broke, with charges that intelligence was being corrupted by politics. An embarrassed president stilled the uproar by naming Lormack, a career intelligence officer who, as number two, was known in Washington for the sensibility that he had imposed on the would-be senator. The Agency was back in professional hands, and Inigo and his colleagues found themselves put to proper use. To complete his satisfaction, the ex-director was severely trounced at the polls.

Inigo and Lormack's secretary were old acquaintances. She gave him a midafternoon appointment.

"George. Good to see you. Is it about Geneva, I hope?" Lormack had left his desk at the far end of the big office and was facing Inigo across a coffee table.

"You guessed it, Jim. What do you think?"

"I'm all for it. You know, Hickok really put us in a hole. I'll never understand that man."

"What happened?"

"Don't ask. I will tell you that he's being brought back for interrogation. The cable has already gone out. He may face charges. That's up to the president and how much of a scandal he thinks he can afford."

"It's that bad?"

"It's that bad. George, you know me as a man who thinks the operations types are too suspicious of you research guys. They think you're naïve, careless, therefore dangerous. Well, I must say Hickok proves their point, and they're letting me know it today. All right, enough of that. Are you interested in the job?"

"I'm interested. But I also want to hear how you look at it."

Lormack grimaced and shook his head; a shock of hair fell over his forehead. He put his feet upon the table, then abruptly got up and began to roam up and down in front of the long window overlooking the Potomac.

"I guess I'd better fill you in, George. The truth of it is I'm on my way out. Tomorrow's my last day."

"Damn." Inigo felt a surge of anger. He sat still, waiting while Lormack circled his desk.

"Well, just look at it. You know as well as I do why I'm here. I got the president off the spot. That's the long and short of it. But I'm not their man, and they know it. They don't want my back talk. I'm dragging my feet, they say. Lord"—Lormack swung around in a sudden burst of emotion—"if you knew some of the crazy operations those guys have proposed. I've become the great Refusenik. That's what they've made me into."

He sat down and calmed himself.

"So you'll be getting a new director, George. I won't tell you who it is." A long silence.

"Maybe I ought to call it a day too." Awkwardness invaded Inigo. He felt outraged, but he heard a tinge of insincerity in his own words.

"Nonsense. Our situations are entirely different. In the first place, you're ten years younger. And I got to the top. Did you ever want to be director, George?" Inigo shook his head. "I always wanted it. From the very beginning. And I made it. Against all the odds, and with lots of luck." Lormack was a big man; it was hard to see him so

13

vulnerable. "What I didn't realize was how exposed that would make me. Because now there's no place to go from here. I'm not a board of directors type, you know. Or a book-writing type. James Lormack tells all! Oh no, not me. You understand that." His voice shook.

"I understand that." Inigo was frozen with pity. There was nothing more to say. He and Lormack were not personal friends; they had never been in each other's home. This sudden intimacy stirred up anxiety in him.

"Okay. Enough of that. Geneva." Abruptly Lormack planted himself in a chair. He gazed quietly at Inigo for a moment, taking himself in hand. "I regard SALT as our biggest task. The biggest contribution in the Agency's history. I don't need to tell you that without our resources to verify it, arms control would be impossible. You wouldn't trust the Sovs to observe a treaty voluntarily, would you?"

"For a week," Inigo replied. "Maybe a month. Then some smart weapons designer would come along with a nifty proposal for a really knockout new weapon. It would be irresistible."

"Well, you're more optimistic than most. Everyone else seems to think they'd intend from the start to violate any provision they choose. I confess that once or twice I've swung way over to the opposite pole. I can't believe Brezhnev doesn't see how utterly crucial this is. But that's neither here nor there. Nothing will sell in this town unless CIA can monitor it. And that puts us smack in the middle."

Lormack went over to his desk and returned with a sheet of paper. As the two men hunched over the coffee table, he started drawing boxes.

"Here we are." He put a box in the center of the page, labeling it "CIA." "Over here are the State Department and the Arms Control and Disarmament Agency." Into two boxes on the left he wrote "State" and "ACDA." "They push me constantly to overstate our monitoring abilities, so as to justify a treaty with lots of limits. And over here"—on the right he drew two boxes and labeled them "JCS" and "OSD"—"are the Joint Chiefs of Staff and the Office of the Secretary of Defense. They push me the other way. They oppose lots of provisions on the grounds that we can't monitor them effectively. That leads to a lesser treaty, fewer limits and"—Lormack looked up wryly—"more room for new U.S. weapons programs. Surprised?"

Staring down at the paper, Inigo murmured, "So they try to pull us into every fight that comes along."

"Precisely. Which means that our objectivity has to be above suspicion. Above all, we can't afford to have a man in Geneva who is playing games with the Soviets. Or is even thought to be. There, now you know a little more about Hickok. But if we're distrusted for any reason, we're no use to anyone. Then the whole undertaking collapses in a shambles. Now I don't want to exaggerate too much," Lormack went on. "In a general sense, everybody in Washington wants a SALT treaty. But when it gets down to specifics, guts take over. Wishful thinking from one side, deep suspicion from another. And I tell you"—he suddenly grinned—"when it dawns on a three-star general that his own government's proposal would kill off his favorite program, that's a touching sight to watch."

Something clicked in Inigo's brain. He realized that he had decided. He kept still and Lormack went on.

"Of course Geneva's not the center of all this. Washington makes the decisions. The delegation's kept on a very tight rein. But everything that goes on here is reflected there. All these agencies"—he tapped the boxes with his pencil—"are represented on the delegation. They fight, they watch each other like hawks—and doves." He chuckled. "They'll be watching you the same way. So when headquarters says we can monitor a certain provision with eighty-five percent confidence—and there's an arcane calculation; Guy Peters can explain to you how it's done—it won't do for our man in Geneva to shade that up to ninety or down to eighty. Intelligence calls it as we see it, eighty-five percent and then it's up to the policymakers to decide whether the risks are worthwhile or not. We stay out of that."

"But why accept anything less than one hundred percent?"

"Oh, lots of reasons. Maybe a Soviet violation wouldn't be strategically significant. Maybe we could spot it early enough to call them on it, or have enough time to take countermeasures of our own. But the real question is, how would the Soviets figure the odds on their getting caught in a particular violation? That's why it's so crucial to keep them uncertain about the Agency's capabilities. They're obviously not going to set out to be caught. Uncertainty keeps them honest. Look, George"—as Inigo continued silent—"I have to head downtown in three minutes. I don't need an answer today. Think it over. Any last questions?"

"How long would I be signing up for?"

"No longer than six months. Peters can tell you about the new Soviet ICBMs coming downstream that we're trying to head off. My concern is what's developing here at home. The presidential election is just two years away, and the campaign will be getting started long before that." Lormack glanced at a wall calendar. "Less than a year from now, in fact. Already the opposition is starting to grumble about SALT. Can't trust the Commies. Codifies a Soviet lead. American giveaway. If the treaty can't be finished and gotten through the Senate in the next six to eight months, it'll land smack in the middle of the campaign. And then good-bye SALT. So I'd hope you could leave right away, before Hickok's empty chair starts to complicate things."

"What does 'right away' mean?"

"Tomorrow night. I know it's awfully short notice, George. But frankly, there are a number of things I want to nail down before I go. One of them is to get Hickok out of Geneva. Another is to get you in there. I don't want to take the chance that my successor will leave the job unfilled, or send an inexperienced man. If I can get you in place before he takes over, I'll feel a lot better."

"Will I have any overlap with him out there?"

"Can't tell. I don't know exactly when he's flying out. Just tell the delegation a family crisis came up, a child at death's door, whatever you think will serve."

"What can you tell me about the new director? I'm not asking for his name."

"Very little. No intelligence background. Too bad." He paused. "He's a two-star general. Air force. Please keep all this to yourself for the moment. First-rate political connections. Has a reputation for playing his cards right. Ambitious, but who isn't? Don't prejudge him, George. Military officers have been surprising me all my life, often pleasantly."

Lormack got to his feet and Inigo followed.

"One more thing. If you take the job, be sure to establish a good personal connection with him. It won't be easy, with you in Geneva. Make as many trips back as you can. Peters won't like it, but don't let that stop you. Sooner or later the unexpected usually happens, and when it does, you and he will both need to know who you're dealing with. Don't let yourself be just a signature on a cable when a crisis comes along."

They walked toward the door. Inigo said, "Jim, this is really rotten."

16

"Oh, about me? Don't let it get you down. I'll survive. After all, I did make it. Of course, I hoped for more than eight months. But think of all the guys who wanted it as much as I did and didn't make it."

Each managed a smile at the door. Lormack put an arm around his shoulder as they shook hands. Inigo went out. Stupid males, he said to himself.

Although it was only four o'clock, he told Laura to clear his desk and lock the safe. In the parking lot, Inigo's reason finally hit him. He suddenly realized why, waiting for the elevator this morning with Cornett, his mind had silently, beyond his hearing, said yes. He knew that he badly needed a change, a challenge, and negotiating with the Soviets was certainly that. Besides, in Geneva he could escape all the anguish of helping to break in a new director. The skiing counted for something too.

He went back into the building, borrowed the guard's phone, and called Lormack's secretary.

"Jane, this is George Inigo. Please tell the director I said yes."

"He'll be very pleased, Mr. Inigo."

"Yes. So am I. Tell him that too."

Inigo was still pleased about it when he emerged from Passport Control and, one of the last passengers, entered the big glassed-in customs hall. A woman stood apart from the crowd, facing the arriving passengers, quickly scanning faces. When her eyes met his, she stopped. She was of medium height, dressed with quiet smartness, with stern wrinkles at the corners of her eyes that in other circumstances, one could see, would be crinkles of merriment. A mane of thick, rich brown hair was uncovered. She looked to be in her mid-thirties.

Seemingly satisfied with her inspection of Inigo, she turned and shouted a brief phrase to two men just outside the far exit of the hall. She spoke in Russian, and Inigo, his mind set on English and French, failed to catch the words. Then, as the men watched, and without looking at him again, she walked calmly past Inigo, turned, came back on his other side, and marched away. It was as though she had drawn a chalk circle around him. When Inigo looked again for the two men, they had disappeared. Turning back, he saw that the woman was gone as well.

He was half disappointed, half relieved at not being met by Hickok.

17

He could have used even a few hours of overlap with his predecessor, asking about the inner workings of the delegation, learning how the meetings with the Soviets were conducted. But there would have been the overhanging awkwardness of Hickok's disgrace and recall. Hickok and he weren't close friends, but they were not distant enough to ignore the mysterious circumstances of the turnover. Not with any comfort, at least. Well, Peters had given him the Washington duplicate of Hickok's apartment key, just in case their planes crossed over the Atlantic. After one last reconnaissance, he pushed through the big glass doors of the terminal.

The cab ride down through the modern quarter, across the Rhone, and up into the Old City to Hickok's former apartment took less than fifteen minutes. "We have company, monsieur," the dour Swiss driver remarked casually as they passed through the ancient walls.

"What do you mean?"

"The car ahead. And one behind. They've been with us since we left the airport."

It must be the men from outside the customs hall, Inigo figured, although he hadn't gotten a clear enough look to be sure and couldn't imagine why. It was all very unsubtle; they were making no effort to conceal their interest. One of them had even led the way. As the taxi halted in the Rue Etienne Dumont, the escort cars continued up the street and around the corner.

When he tried Hickok's key in the door, Inigo discovered that the lock had been changed. It took him the rest of the morning to track down the rental agent. An officious young clerk, whose perfect English condescended to Inigo's accented French, gave him new keys but, despite the persistence of his questions, no explanation.

3

Smirnov was unmistakable as he moved down the receiving line. Every handshake, every smile managed to convey both servility and contempt. As he bobbed down the row of Americans, each of his hosts seemed to shrink back imperceptibly, to accept his plump hand, which felt like a damp sponge, to turn with relief to the correct, dour Soviet officer who followed. The colonel's hands at least felt dry; the colonel was a straightforward soldier, a man.

Inigo, standing halfway down the line, almost felt sorry for the little Russian. Round of face and body, he couldn't be more than three or four inches over five feet. At each greeting, he stared straight at the American with an expression that said, "Yes, you have to shake my hand. No matter how much you despise me. Now we have nuclear weapons too," his eyes said, "and bigger ones than yours." Inigo had determined not to hate him, but now he felt this resolve turning to sand.

Everyone had warned him about Smirnov, but he resented being required to dislike anyone. Disliking Smirnov, he saw, was one of those little common threads that held the American delegation together, like complaining about the airline connections between Geneva and Washington, or the beer and darts after work at the Britannia down the street. If you wanted to avoid the beer and darts, you'd better join the Sunday hikes. His new colleagues had established the reviling of Smirnov as one of the qualifications for being admitted to the club. Inigo saw in an instant that he would qualify. Later on, when the American side met privately to discuss today's plenary meeting, he would make some vicious, witty remark about Smirnov. Everyone would laugh and say to himself, "Yes, Inigo is going to be all right." The foreknowledge made him angry. But the man really was odious.

Now Smirnov was before him. He stopped, took Inigo's hand in both of his, and turned up at him a self-satisfied smile. Silently and

19

uneasily, the Russians behind him adjusted to the break in the rhythm of the line.

"Ah, you must be Mr. Inigo. Welcome to our negotiating labors."

"Thank you, Mr. Smirnov. I'm glad to meet you."

"Your predecessor, Mr. Hickok, left quite suddenly. I enjoyed my talks with him. Will you be staying longer?" It was amazing how much the man could convey in three commonplace sentences. He probably knew, as Inigo did not, exactly why Hickok had been abruptly withdrawn and replaced, and he enjoyed baiting the American about it. Furthermore, on another level his words carried a criticism of the American habit of rotating and exchanging members of the delegation, so as not to separate men too long from their wives and children. We Russians, Smirnov was saying, are here for the duration. That is true seriousness.

"That remains to be seen."

"Has Mr. Hickok returned to Washington already?"

"Yes." Inigo, who had no idea where Hickok was, realized that he was reacting to the interrogation.

"Perhaps he took the return flight of the airplane on which you arrived?"

"Welcome to the American mission, Mr. Smirnov."

"Ah yes. You are telling me that I must not hold up our important plenary meeting any longer. Our side will present some interesting ideas today. You should pay close attention."

"Indeed I shall."

"After the plenary we will get better acquainted." As Smirnov moved on down the line, his patient colleagues put themselves into motion behind him.

So that's my partner, thought Inigo as the last Russian, a submarine commander, gave him a firm handshake. We are paired. The CIA and the KGB, condemned to each other. Till death do us part?

The two delegations moved into their seats, eleven on a side, at a long polished table. The Americans, reserving for themselves the better side, faced a long window-wall. From here on the ninth floor, Inigo could see the nearby single massif of the Saleve, bound by long, bare granite stripes tilted from the horizontal, that marked the French border a few miles away. Beyond lay the Alps, peaked with snow and climaxed today by Le Dôle. The air was rarely clear enough to see Mont Blanc, rising nearly sixteen thousand feet, farther off in the same direction, improbably huge, like a god. At his first glimpse of it, Inigo had felt reverential and pagan. But in normal weather tourists who had been promised a view of it had to be satisfied with Le Dôle. The Genevans and the local Americans, in a kind deception, often reassured visitors that they were gazing upon Mont Blanc itself. Hence Le Dôle's nickname: the American Mont Blanc.

The room was large, spare, flooded with light from two glass walls. It had been intended as a magnificent seduction chamber. Here the international financier who built the building had planned a bedroom of extravagant splendors. Surely the views alone would have overcome all but the most chaste, and who could resist the true Mont Blanc? But the empire had collapsed before the room could be put to use. Its creator was on the run, hounded by extradition orders. Where soft voices were meant to murmur, now the talk was of intercontinental ballistic missiles—long, pointed, hard, prodigiously explosive.

"Mr. Ambassador, on behalf of the American delegation I welcome you and your delegation to this plenary meeting of the negotiations on strategic arms limitations. Before we begin, may I introduce Mr. George Inigo, who has joined our delegation." Ten pairs of eyes swept rapidly over Inigo's face. Smirnov gazed calmly at the wall. "Does the Soviet delegation wish to make a statement today?"

At the center of the table, Lebedev created a solemn pause. Picking up his first page, he paused again, then began to read in a voice of weight and formality. Just as Inigo had oriented himself to the growling Russian cadence, Lebedev stopped. The man on his right spoke in flat, bored English.

"Mr. Ambassador, today the Soviet side will present its views on the question of the definition of a heavy bomber. We have given full consideration to the views expressed by the American side in previous meetings, most recently at the plenary session of seventeen November 1977. The Soviet side is convinced that the proposals it will present today represent the views of both sides and correspond to the principles of equality and equal security that, as has been agreed, guide our work in these negotiations."

At the far end of the table, a Soviet official quietly passed two documents across to his American counterpart. These, Inigo knew, were the official Russian text of Lebedev's statement and its unofficial English translation. Later, these would be studied closely, but it was hardly necessary to listen now. Inigo had read the cable traffic and the biographical files. Now he set to studying the Russians in person.

Lebedev: a large, barrel-chested body topped by a bald head in which were deeply set the eyes of an iguana. He punctuated his statement with fierce, intimidating stares and occasionally interrupted his interpreter to substitute an English word that better suited his meaning. With the Americans, however, he conversed only in Russian. Lebedev ranked sixth in the Foreign Ministry and was best known for the ruthlessness and finesse with which he had engineered the Communization of East Germany in the late 1940s. Not a man to meet in a dark alley, Inigo thought. He would have dominated the Soviet delegation wherever he sat.

On Lebedev's left, his deputy Pavlovsky: big, fleshy, wide-mouthed. Behind that broad forehead lay, by all accounts, a brilliant mind. Among the Russians he alone flaunted his ease, slouching in his chair, gazing at the ceiling, flashing occasional broad smiles across the table when Lebedev said something that he was sure the Americans wanted to hear. When Inigo had been introduced, Pavlovsky had had the boldness to wink at him with a grin. He knew every word that was in the draft treaty and every word that was not, and why they were and were not. He could eat you up in argument. When he was sober.

A movement outside the window distracted Inigo's eye. A marine was patrolling the balcony while the plenary met. Against whom, Inigo wondered; the Soviets are already inside.

Beyond Pavlovsky, Rublov: a face ruined by age, the oldest man in the room. He was a living link, one of the last, between the ruling classes of Imperial and Soviet Russia. Emigrés wondered, as they did about all such survivors, how many betrayals and executions he had connived at or acquiesced in during the awful years of Stalin's terror. Courtly and deferential in the receiving line, he now sat quietly composed, only his lively eyes indicating his perpetual alertness. Decades ago, he had been a key physicist in the Tomsk Project, which, in that first astounding detonation, had exploded the American nuclear monopoly. He turned out to be a scientist who could communicate with politicians and generals, and they put him at the center of weapons development. More than anyone else on the Soviet side, it was his classified knowledge that the Americans thirsted for. He never made a slip as he charmed American visitors, in perfect French, with persuasive explanations of the rightness of Soviet negotiating positions. Inigo guessed that for all his wiliness, Rublov, at the end of a long life, wanted a treaty more than any other Soviet negotiator.

Beyond Rublov, Starovsky and Otchinnikov: two mid-level diplomats from the Foreign Ministry. Otchinnikov was big, blond, friendly in a relaxed, American way. The two years he had spent as an exchange student at Stanford stood him in good stead here in the negotiations. In sharp contrast, Starovsky was slight, dark, full of nerves. These were the men who, after all the drawn-out policy decisions in Moscow and Washington, worked the words of the draft treaty with their American counterparts. They were tough, expert, deeply involved in the details, adamant about pronouns and commas. In the American delegation they were referred to as Starsky and Hutch. One of them, Inigo presumed, had written the first draft of Lebedev's statement and shepherded it through several revisions by the Soviet delegation. Now they listened, the one calmly, the other tensely, as though hearing the words for the first time.

Lebedev was done. He laid down his last page and gazed across the table into the eyes of Ambassador Jenkins, all fierceness gone, while the interpreter finished up. The Soviet statement was short and had broken no new ground. Inigo remarked to himself that none of his colleagues had jotted down notes for the post-plenary conversations. Jenkins gravely thanked Lebedev and assured him that the Soviet statement "will be studied with the attention it deserves." Next to Inigo, his ACDA colleague Morgan chuckled softly at the in-joke. When Lebedev said something of interest, Jenkins's formula was that his statement "will be studied with full attention." No one knew whether the Soviets noticed the difference.

"Today the delegation of the United States will discuss the question of multiple independently targetable reentry vehicles. Its statement will respond to several questions raised by the Soviet delegation and will propose revised language on this subject for paragraph 2c of Article IV of the Joint Draft Treaty." At the end of the table, papers were passed in the opposite direction. The American interpreter began in sonorous Russian on a text that had been revised four times in the tank. Inigo resumed his study of the Soviet delegation.

To Lebedev's right, Nechenko: the senior Soviet interpreter. Two other Soviet interpreters sat behind him. They would be needed after the plenary, when the two delegations broke up and paired off—general with general, scientist with scientist, colonels with colonels, diplomats with diplomats, Inigo with Smirnov. The chiefs of delegation, the generals, and the colonels used interpreters. The scientists conversed in French. All the others worked in English. Russian language competence was not a strong point among the American negotiators.

Next to Nechenko, Mardirosian: the general. Although the name was Armenian, heavy eyebrows suggested a junior version of Brezhnev. In his solemnity, he reminded Inigo of a Soviet marshal in heavy greatcoat, pictured by TASS atop Lenin's mausoleum, reviewing the October Revolution parade (down at their feet, out of sight, were electric heaters). Mardirosian took copious notes on the American statement. He wanted to be ready to do battle with General O'Rourke of the U.S. delegation in the informal negotiations that followed the plenary. Mardirosian had one star less than O'Rourke, but even without that inequality they would have despised each other.

Next to Mardirosian, Smirnov: For the moment Inigo passed him over. Beyond Smirnov: two mid-level Soviet officers. Tolstikov was a blond, with the most Slavic face at the table. Before Geneva, he had commanded a Y-class nuclear submarine. Ryabin was a colonel in the Strategic Rocket Forces, which he refused to discuss, unlike Tolstikov, who happily swapped innocuous stories of life under the North Atlantic with the American officers. Oddly enough, Ryabin's name had popped up in clear text during a brief breakdown in Soviet military encryption. Radio-direction finding had pinpointed him in Derazhnya, one of the major ICBM complexes. Inigo guessed that he had been deputy commander there.

Both Ryabin and Tolstikov had arrived in Geneva only three months ago. Their predecessors, after two years on the job, had become too free and forthcoming in the post-plenaries. Probably their interpreter had reported them. At any rate, they had left Geneva abruptly and together. According to the American military, Ryabin and Tolstikov were careful men.

Finally, Smirnov. Hands folded on the table before him, he had moved only once during Jenkins's entire statement, to incline his head and nod in response when Mardirosian whispered something to him. Proud of his self-control, Inigo thought. His file was voluminous, filled mainly with reports on his eight years with the Soviet UN mission. In New York, Smirnov had not run agents. He was a spotter.

Mixing easily at receptions, inviting other diplomats to lunches and small dinners, freely acknowledging small criticisms of Soviet policy, asking questions. Always asking questions. When the time for serious business arrived, Smirnov brought the target and a Soviet recruiter together two or three times, then stepped quietly aside. He was too valuable to risk expulsion if a recruiting pitch misfired.

This left him free for his primary job. Smirnov was an influencer. Inigo had been warned that he specialized in persuasion, thrived on dialogue and debate. Especially was he a master of the vocabulary of peace. And war too, for that matter; he knew the strategic jargon as well as any American expert. He was a familiar figure at the Pugwash meetings, the Dartmouth conferences, and all the other occasions when articulate Soviets and worried Americans came together to explore solutions to the nuclear arms race. For these purposes he was equipped with a variety of titles, such as section chief in the Soviet Peace Council and special assistant to the presidium of the Academy of Sciences. The latter was the cover for his present assignment to Geneva, although he spent no time on the pretense.

And of course there were the traditional KGB functions. Moscow was uneasy about having such a large Soviet delegation, in an attractive West European city, in close contact with Americans, over a number of years. So Smirnov was the watchdog within the delegation. He also had a private reporting channel to KGB Moscow, through which his superiors got a regular, independent view of the proceedings from one of their own. For the KGB regarded itself as the equal and more of the Foreign Ministry in matters of foreign policy. Diplomats might deliver the speeches, but Comrade Andropov sat on the Politburo, and on most of its subcommittees, where the real decisions were made. Indeed there were rumors, fostered by the KGB itself, that Comrade Andropov aspired even higher.

Jenkins was finishing. He put into the record the date of the next plenary, already agreed with Lebedev. "If there is no further business, I declare this plenary meeting adjourned and invite the members of the Soviet delegation to join us in refreshments."

The two delegations rose, collected papers, exchanged pleasantries across the table. Slowly they began milling toward a corner, where a panel had slid back to reveal a counter and a smiling young woman offering coffee, tea, juice, and cookies. Liquor was never served. Jenkins was determined to take no chances that a journalist, or a visiting congressman, could report even a hint that the American delegation was boozily being taken to the cleaners by the wily, hard-drinking Russians of popular legend.

Inigo turned to Morgan as they rose. "So that's the way it goes."

"Right. That's the easy part. Off you go now. To meet your fate." And Morgan joshed him with a nudge toward the coffee bar.

Smirnov was making his way toward the same corner. He chatted briefly with one American, held another in a handclasp. Then he looked around for Inigo.

"Ah, there you are, Mr. Inigo. The formalities are over at last. Thank goodness, yes? Now we can begin to get acquainted."

He opened his arms wide. Inigo, stiffening against the feeling of being swallowed up, extended his right arm. They shook hands.

4

*The testing began as soon as he arrived, even before his first plenary. In-
igo was aware of some of it: the pushing and probing that Smirnov himself carried out. Other parts he never recognized at all.*

The three toughs in the bar, for example. It was Inigo's third evening
in Geneva. He and Colonel Michaels had been sitting there side by side
for an hour when a heavyset man in his twenties moved between them
from behind and turned to face Inigo.

"That's my seat you're in." He spoke a menacing German.

"Really? I've been in it all evening. So buzz off."

"The hell you say. I was here five minutes ago. I go to the can and
come back and find you and your ugly friend. Now get out!"

"Hey George," Michaels put in. "What's he saying? If he wants trouble, let's give him some."

When Inigo leaned back to look over the German's shoulder at Michaels, he saw another muscular young man moving in behind Michaels.

"Bartender!" he shouted.

The bartender had disappeared. The blonde barmaid looked at him
coldly, wiping glasses.

"I said that's my seat, you bastard!" Inigo felt the pressure of a third
body behind him and smelled a candied breath near his neck.

"Time to go, Bert." He slipped off the barstool. Between the two large
bodies was about eight inches of space. Inigo jostled through sideways,
grabbing Michaels's arm as he emerged. The Germans didn't budge, nor
did they lift a hand.

Michaels had had no more to drink than Inigo, but he carried it worse.
He had to be pulled across the narrow floor, prevented from planting his
feet, especially when jeering erupted at the bar behind them.

"Goddamn you, Bert, can't you see the fix was in?" Inigo hissed as he

27

hustled him out onto the street. "A provocation. We had everything to lose in there. You may be in great shape, but I'm too old for those babies."

The night air sobered Michaels.

"First time I've ever seen that in Geneva," he muttered as Inigo propelled him down the street.

5

Well now, Smirnov said to himself, let's see what this one is made of.

"Would you like coffee, tea, or juice, Mr. Inigo?" He had slipped past the American and gotten to the refreshment counter first, usurping the role of host.

"Please, you first, Mr. Smirnov."

"And how are you this morning?" Smirnov leered at the young secretary who was doubling behind the refreshment counter today. "Unfortunately"—he turned to Inigo—"we don't have such pretty girls at our mission."

"Miss McClellan is an excellent secretary." Inigo smiled at her. "Our secretaries like to arrange the refreshments at plenaries. It gives them a chance to see some real live Soviets."

"Ah yes, the bears. But at your zoo in New York it says 'Do Not Feed the Bears.' So she is disobeying orders." He helped himself to cookies. "See, no claws." He waggled his pudgy fingers at the young woman.

They moved out into the conference room. Smirnov pointed with his plate to a small coffee table with two armchairs. "Shall we sit over there?" And he led the way. Since all other groups were larger than two, it was obviously reserved for them. Indeed, Smirnov had sat in just that corner dozens of times with Hickok. But it interested him to see how this new partner would react to his assertion of leadership.

Most people, he had learned, were slightly afraid of short men. There was an air of oddness about a truly short male that was faintly alarming. In his teens, he had come to understand this much himself, and the KGB psychologists had taught him more. A short man who is also forceful and aggressive, they told him, could be quite intimidating, especially to dependent personalities. It had to do with the confounding of expectations, which threw the other party off guard and could overawe him permanently. Look at Napoleon, they told him and, in a whisper, look at Comrade Stalin. The KGB had the best psychologists in the Soviet Union.

"So welcome once more to Geneva, Mr. Inigo. You prefer that we speak English, I suppose. How are things in Washington?

"Things are just fine in Washington. They are eager to have us complete this treaty quickly."

"Ah, no haste, please. One cannot move too fast in these matters. That makes people get nervous. But, on the other hand, not too slowly either. Then they become impatient and irritable. Even hostile. Timing is very important, Mr. Inigo. We are actors on a stage, and on the stage timing is everything."

"I agree. But lately, I believe, the delegations have been moving too slowly. I have the feeling that Washington is becoming impatient, not nervous, over the pace of our work. How is it in Moscow?"

"It is difficult to tell. Moscow is far from Geneva. Very far. Farther than Washington. I do not speak in a geographical sense."

"In what sense, then?"

Smirnov smiled. "In a metaphorical sense, of course." He leaned back and stared calmly at Inigo. It was the famous Soviet style, which he had learned in the training course of the Foreign Ministry. Delphian utterances, elliptical references, obscure metaphors, proverbs. Actors on a stage, timing, a dim and distant Moscow. It all suggested that the speaker was in touch with a deeper rhythm of events, was connected to some higher wisdom. Ambassador Lebedev was a master of this style. Smirnov imagined that Lebedev's private remarks, transcribed by the U.S. interpreter and sent back to Washington, caused many a young analyst to spend hours searching for hidden meanings. They might never realize that Lebedev, who was the grandson of an Orthodox priest, was simply practicing befuddlement.

"But even geography can be a metaphor," Inigo said good-humoredly.

Smirnov pressed him quickly. "What does that mean? Are you speaking nonsense now?" The attack seemed to fluster Inigo, but only momentarily.

"Perhaps we are both speaking nonsense after all."

An interesting man, Smirnov thought. He might suit my purposes quite well. It was, however, much too early to tell.

"Let me ask you about my friend Mr. Hickok. Has he left Geneva already?"

"Yes, he's gone."

"A splendid man. Devoted to his country. A skillful negotiator too. He put me in some very difficult positions during our conversations. I think we came to understand each other quite well. It is a shame that he had to leave this work. Perhaps you can tell me why he returned to Washington so suddenly."

"Didn't he explain it to you?"

"Not a word. He didn't even tell me he was leaving."

"Family reasons."

"Ah, I am very sorry to hear that. He told you this himself, here in Geneva?"

"Yes. We overlapped here for a short while."

Excellent, Smirnov told himself. The man lies well.

"It is most regrettable. But of course families are very important. Families come first, even ahead of state interests. Don't you agree?"

Inigo seemed to hesitate, as though it didn't seem so simple to him. "It can become a real problem. I don't think one can make a hard-and-fast general rule."

"But surely," Smirnov pounced on him, "each family has only one husband, one father. He is indispensable to the others. Whereas the state, it has hundreds of functionaries to move around in the jobs that need doing. Just as you, Mr. Inigo, are a more than worthy replacement for Mr. Hickok, I'm sure." He sat back, pleased with himself.

For the first time Inigo seemed a little rattled. A trace of anxiety flickered briefly in his eyes. Smirnov considered his opponent's position. Inigo must know that Hickok was dead. Because of the tight security barriers within CIA, however, he probably did not know who had killed him. If that were so, he was bound to suspect the Soviets. Including myself, Smirnov thought. He pushed on.

"In recent days Mr. Hickok was concerned about his health. You say that you spent some time with him here in Geneva. Was he in good health?"

Inigo's body seemed to tighten, but it was impossible to be sure. After a moment, he replied in a calm and natural tone.

"He didn't mention any health problems of his own. It seems one of his sons is gravely ill."

"How terrible." One last thrust of the knife. "Is it a matter of life and death?"

"So I gather."

He waited, but Inigo seemed to have nothing further to say. The

American scooped up a handful of peanuts and began to chew them thoughtfully. Smirnov changed the subject.

"I think Ambassador Jenkins's statement today cannot serve as a basis for negotiations."

"Why not?"

"Ah, Mr. Inigo, we have a long history of such statements from the American side. A whole filing drawer of them. We think there must be someone on your delegation who busies himself solely with this topic of MIRVs, these multiple-warhead missiles that obsess your side. We often wonder who it is who writes these statements. But even though the words may change, the meaning is always the same. Your Mister MIRV is not clever enough to conceal that. And so once again we tell you, your position cannot serve as a basis for negotiations. You must change it."

Inigo looked around the room, and Smirnov followed his gaze. In one corner the generals, O'Rourke and Mardirosian, were drawing rough graphics to illustrate their arguments. In another the diplomats were bent over the text of the draft treaty, each side searching for a reference that would support its position. Rublov and Dr. Boroz seemed to be conducting a civilized chat; they too occasionally sketched a drawing to clarify a point.

"In the Soviet statement today, on the other hand," Smirnov went on, "there are some interesting nuances. Significant nuances. Our side is moving forward on this question, and yours should respond."

Inigo stared at him with distaste.

"What nuances?"

"You have the text. Study it carefully. You will find them. After all"—he grinned—"we cannot do all your work for you."

At last he seemed to have gotten under the American's skin. Hotly Inigo asked, "Then perhaps you'd be good enough to tell me precisely what the Soviet side finds so objectionable in our proposal today."

"But we have! A dozen times or more. You can find it in our plenary statement of three weeks ago and a number of earlier statements. Since you repeat yourselves, we are forced to do the same. I'm sure Mister MIRV, whoever he is, can explain it to you in most complete detail."

"Mr. Smirnov, it seems that we will be talking together like this every week. How do you propose that we spend our time?" Inigo's voice had risen, and the Soviet and American colonels, sitting closest to them, glanced over in surprise.

"Spend our time?"

"Yes. We can, if we wish, devote ourselves to attacking each other's statements. We can insist that the other side must alter its positions. Or we can speculate on what our masters in Washington and Moscow are up to." He was gathering energy. He pointed out the window. "We can discuss the beauties of the Alps. We can talk about the weather."

"The Alps, no," Smirnov interrupted. "I never go there. They lie in France, and the French government does not issue visas to Soviet diplomats stationed in Switzerland." He was pleased. Things were going well.

"Very well. Not the Alps. We can discuss the merits and defects of socialism and capitalism if you wish. But we do have this time together. We are bound to it, even condemned to it, if you like. How do you propose that we use it?"

"Ah yes. I sense that you have a proposal."

"I do."

"And it is?"

Inigo let a little silence fall between them.

"I propose that we work." Another pause. "On arms control. That we negotiate seriously on the treaty, the words of the draft treaty. The actual language of the commitments we are prepared to assume. Just as our colleagues"—he gestured around the room—"are doing at this very moment."

"Naturally. That is precisely why we are here in Geneva."

"Good. I'm glad you agree. So let us leave the generalities behind. You must refrain from uttering Soviet platitudes, and I will control my impulses to utter American platitudes."

" 'Platitudes'?" It was Smirnov's first admission of inadequacy in English.

"Broad general truths. Satisfying to the ego, but of no use whatsoever in writing a treaty. Everything lies in the specific details. And incidentally, allow me to congratulate you on your English and to thank you for your courtesy in allowing it to be the language of our discussions."

Smirnov frowned. "You are welcome. I had the opportunity to live for eight years in your country. For an American official to spend eight years in my country, it is not in the cards. So how shall we negotiate this treaty, you and I?"

"Why, like any negotiation. We shall explain our positions in detail. We shall listen carefully to each other's explanations. We shall ask very precise questions, and we shall try to give precise answers. And when we cannot give precise answers, it shall be understood that we cannot, even though we would like to. For we shall bear in mind that each of us is acting on the instructions of his government." Inigo, who had been leaning forward, sat back and smiled pleasantly.

"Of course. It is impossible to act on any other basis. Otherwise one would be disavowed." Smirnov wondered if the name Hickok had flashed in Inigo's brain. "I accept your proposal. In return, you must accept one of mine. In the name of equality and equal security. My proposal is that you be my guest for lunch next Tuesday. At which time we may work, as you suggest, or not, if we choose. I remember an American saying that all work and no play makes Jack a dull boy."

"English, not American," Inigo retorted. "But I accept your invitation. You will not find me a complete workaholic."

"Yes, I know this word. We do not have it in Russian. Perhaps we do not have such a thing in Russia."

"I see our ambassadors have finished their discussions." Jenkins and Lebedev were reentering the conference room from the smaller chamber where they conducted their post-plenaries. Throughout the hall, the little islands of delegates stood up, collected their papers, handed over or reclaimed their sketches. The two ambassadors moved together from group to group, shaking hands, not lingering. When they reached the intelligence officers, Lebedev extended his hand without saying a word. As Smirnov looked on approvingly, he gave Inigo a long, hard look of appraisal. Big men also had ways of intimidating.

They merged into the small crowd milling toward the door, Smirnov shaking American hands and Inigo Soviet ones. In the hall the Soviets collected and waited, under the watchful eyes of two marines, for the elevators that would carry them down through the office floors of the American delegation to the parking garage below. The elevators were programmed to skip all the intervening floors, avoiding the possibility of an embarrassing encounter between Soviet officials and American secretaries carrying classified documents.

The Americans headed for the tank.

On one of the mid-floors, inside a steel-sheeted room with a combination lock on the door, a unit of army engineers had built a long room. Guaranteed to be proof against the most modern sensors, auditory, optical, electrical, what have you, it was a structure as secure against the advances of intrusive intelligence devices as American technology could build. Containing only a long conference table and two dozen metal-frame chairs, it was utterly without decor, windowless, sheathed in oatmeal-colored drapes. Telephones were forbidden. No sound penetrated or escaped from it. Inigo had never seen a room of such sterility, so harshly devoted to nothing but grave affairs.

Like monks arriving for services in a bare chapel, the delegation filed in. In this severe chamber, there was an almost desperate need for humor, and the continual joking served also to relieve the tensions of the formal encounter with the Soviets. For those who had not been there, Jenkins recapitulated and dismissed Lebedev's statement, noted that he had delivered the American statement as prepared, and went on to the post-plenaries.

"Lebedev was pretty hard on me today. They really don't like our MIRV limit. He kept pressing me on how we could possibly verify that a MIRVed missile tested with only four warheads wasn't actually deployed later with six or eight." He looked inquiringly at Inigo, who asked:

"And you said?"

"By national technical means, of course. He didn't like it."

"He doesn't have to," put in General O'Rourke. "No military commander is going to accept a weapon that hasn't been tested in its full potential. It's just a question of whether CIA is sure it can observe the whole test."

"Not the whole test," Inigo responded carefully. "But we can follow all that portion of the trajectory during which warheads are released. With high confidence."

"What does 'high' mean?" It was Smeiser, one of the ACDA experts.

Inigo consulted a chart. "Ninety-five percent. Nothing in the treaty is rated one hundred. You know, professional modesty."

Jenkins recounted the rest of his conversation. It was uneventful. Lebedev had defended his own statement in a bored, perfunctory way and then pointed to a slight change in the wording of the U.S. proposal on MIRV limits. The delegation had made a clarification in the language, and now Jenkins remarked that if the Soviets wanted to regard it as a concession, well and good.

"And that was it. No, he asked about you, George."

Eyes turned to Inigo, who asked, "As the new boy on the block?"

"Yes. And said that he hoped you were in favor of a treaty. Odd. He's never commented like that on a new member before."

Sounds like Lebedev is giving me a hard time, Inigo thought as Walt O'Rourke launched into a long account of his discussion with General Mardirosian. Trying to put me on the defensive. They must really miss Hickok. He began to speculate on how to confront Lebedev when they met at the next delegation reception. He could insist on his devotion to SALT. Or perhaps it would be better to play it cool and undecided, generate a little anxiety, try to make them more forthcoming. Perhaps this would become clearer to him when he finally made up his mind about where he personally stood on SALT. His mind returned to the meeting, where Jenkins was interrupting O'Rourke.

"You went a little far with him there, Walt," the ambassador interjected mildly. "Our instructions are a bit more positive than that."

O'Rourke grinned. "The way I hear it, Washington will be toughening up those instructions in a day or so. I may have been a little beforehand, but that's all." For another two minutes he recited his rhetorical victories over the hapless Soviet general, then concluded soberly, "But I didn't make a dent."

The meeting began to move along faster. Paul Boroz and Rublov had repeated official positions for a while and then fallen to trading news of favorite restaurants and menus in Geneva. The men from the State Department and the Arms Control Agency had continued a long linguistic struggle, begun at the previous plenary, over conflicting translations of the agreed wording of the Fourth Common Understanding to paragraph four of Article VIII.

"George?"

"Well, I can't say I wasn't warned." Several persons smiled, but the slashing, witty remark refused to come to mind. "Very difficult man, Smirnov. A sneaky sort of bastard. We sparred, I guess you'd say. Nothing to report." Inigo fell silent.

"You should understand, George, that your contribution to the plenaries is keeping old Smeary occupied, out of the hair of the rest of us. We appreciate that deeply"—Jenkins smiled wickedly—"and I think his Soviet colleagues appreciate it even more. When it's all over and you get your medal, that's what it will be for."

That produced the laughter, in which Inigo joined. Jenkins called on Colonel Michaels to report and the meeting moved quickly to its end, leaving Inigo in a complex mixture of doubts about the merits of the treaty, his standing among his colleagues, and what he had to deal with in this man Smirnov.

6

The streets of Geneva were deserted as Inigo walked out of Old Town on Sunday morning and took up his post at the bus stop. The occasional automobile, windows closed against the cold, was filled with athletic-looking couples, skis on the roof, headed for the Alps. The silence contrasted eerily with yesterday's Saturday bustle of pedestrians, shoppers, street performers, café-goers in the same quarter, which lay on a flat strip of lakeshore under the hill crowned by Old Town and the cathedral. In the stillness, the sober stone buildings formed canyons channeling a bitter wind in from the water. The sun was bright, but its warmth was still about two hours away.

Far down the street a red bus entered and moved quietly toward him. Inigo checked his watch and peered at the schedule. It was 7:13; the first bus of the day was exactly on time. This was indeed Switzerland. He put his franc into the box attached to the bus stop pole and took the little time-dated slip that the mechanism pushed out. Tickets were not taken on the bus, but they were randomly checked by a plainclothesman, and woe betide the passenger who lacked a valid one. Public humiliation, ignominious hustling off the bus, a huge fine. Inigo had seen it happen the day before to a lovely, well-dressed grandmother. No excuses.

An admirable country, Switzerland, he thought. Everything was so well arranged, so carefully thought through. The wheels of dump trucks, Michaels had told him at dinner last night, were hosed down with water each time they left a construction site, lest they carry mud into the streets. Furthermore, Morgan had added, stores that held a going-out-of-business sale were required, after thirty days, to really go out of business. The safety approval of automobiles, Michaels chimed in, was revoked when body rust appeared. When too much money flowed in, interest was charged, not paid, to foreign depositors. Officials were incorruptible. Everyone had a job, with Yugoslav and Turkish guest workers doing the manual labor for far more than they could earn at home. The city was full of parks, little and big; this very morning Inigo had awoken to find that, even though it was November, all the geraniums had been replaced with anemones, overnight, as if by elves. Traffic flowed smoothly, police were never far away, accidents were rare. To a newspaper reader, crime seemed nonexistent. Reading the wall posters, one would think that the entire population busied itself with self-improvement and the mastery of economics. And cleanliness everywhere. It was as though bums and slums were illegal.

Unhampered by traffic, the bus turned onto the long bridge crossing the Rhone. The river rose eastward in the Alps and followed a long glacial valley until it came into gentler land near Montreux, where it spread out into Lake Leman, a long stunning lake framed by mountains on either side. Forty-five miles later, crowded in again by the Alps to the east and the Jura to the west, it became a river once more and flowed out toward Lyons, southern France, and the Mediterranean. On the spot of its constriction the Genevans had built their city. It might have become a great inland metropolis, a Berlin, except for the mountains hemming it in and defining its borders, for in all directions except the northern lakeshore, the French border was only a few kilometers away. It had found its vocation, and its prosperity, in international diplomacy, the League of Nations and all its successors and offspring. It was a pocket; no, better, a gem embedded in a pocket.

At the first stop on the other side, Inigo shouldered his skis, picked up his heavy boots, and got off. Round the corner he came upon a little burst of life. Skiers were milling about, a bus was loading up, a second bus was backing in to the curb. Lithe figures moved about in the early-morning air, their breath forming little clouds like cartoon balloons. Friends greeted one another softly as though quieted by the silence of the city. Three men collected around a tall pretty blonde who seemed to know everyone. Inigo felt a pang of isolation.

He suddenly realized that he was looking for a woman.

There were plenty of them along the short stretch of sidewalk beside the buses, and they all seemed taken. Bursting with health, faces colored by the cold, they were chattering gaily with friends. Their young bodies, in tight-fitting ski pants and bright jackets, were constantly on the move. Inigo's heart sank as he realized everyone was speaking a rapid French. His own languages were Russian and German; his French was rudimentary. He peered about, looking for some disconsolate beauty, a little older than the average, who had no one to toss her skis and poles into the luggage compartment for her. And can't speak French either, he snorted derisively at himself. She failed to appear. Inigo clambered into the bus and settled into a window seat and a foul mood.

The bus moved easily out of the empty city, was waved through at the French border, and sped up along the open highway that followed the Arve upstream from its confluence with the Rhone. Mountains loomed on either side. Inigo's spirits improved as they turned off short of the Mont Blanc tunnel and began the ascent to Flaine. The valley had been brown and bare, but soon light snow appeared in the fields, deepening as the bus labored up the long switchbacks. It also helped his mood to notice that some of the girls were not so pretty after all. His excitement grew as they mounted above the timberline and the road became a trench between high banks of plowed snow. The whole world was white now. They passed through the last village and he thought, there's absolutely nothing ahead but skiing.

Flaine was a shock. Inigo had skied only once or twice since his college days, and that in the low green mountains of New England, where a fresh snowfall was skied off in a day or two and ice was the normal surface at the turns. They had stayed in little hotels or funny rooming houses, motels not having been invented, and put their ski boots on early to wade through the slush at the bottom of the runs. The bowls of Flaine looked as though they bore a meter of snow year-round and got fresh supplies of powder each night. Seven high-rise buildings at the foot of the lifts must have housed a thousand apartments, each with a balcony facing the broad panorama of lifts, trails, and peaks. Shops and restaurants crowded the base. On the big map outside the rental shop, the network of lifts and runs looked like a diagram of the New York subway system.

Inigo skied all day long. He knew that he shouldn't, that he was not in condition, that he ought to take it easy. But passion overcame him. Perhaps this was what it was like in the Rockies, but he had never been to the Rockies. Every trail was perfection. Whatever lift he took—J-bar, T-bar, chair, *telecabine*—the wait never reached two minutes. Although only an intermediate, he kept finding himself on the expert trails "by mistake." It was an intoxication. Riding up the lift, he would promise himself to be reasonable this time. Dismounting at the top, he would find himself on the roof of the world, a world of brilliant sunshine, breathtaking cold air, and endless white ranges stretching in all directions. Throwing over all his self-promises, he would look for the best skier around and take off after him.

It was, Inigo knew, a kind of madness. He followed an expert through six turns when his leg muscles screamed, his knees turned watery, and he fell, as he had all day, especially among the high moguls. Struggling to his feet, he watched the control skiers move smoothly and carefully down from above, vowing to follow them. Still, he knew that exhilaration would overtake him once more. It was strange, he thought, that a man so careful and guarded in all other ways could not bear to ski except at the very edge of control, always at the rim of danger. The mountain was like a mistress with whom he, an upright churchwarden, repeatedly lost his head.

As a skier, Inigo was an expert faller, and he had not yet truly frightened himself. Now when a band of boys swooped down the slope past him like swallows, he shoved off and gave chase. Roaring around a corner, he suddenly knew he hadn't the strength for the next turn. He went down hard in a heap, slamming into a bush, which saved him from the trees beyond. His release bindings snapped free, his poles went flying, the impact knocked his goggles off. As he lay in the powder, aching in every limb but content to be alive and still for a moment, he heard a *whoosh* and crunch of skis coming to a stop above him.

"Are you all right?" came a feminine, accented English. Inigo struggled to turn his body, but couldn't manage to see her.

"Oh yes. Just another little catastrophe." He waited for her to leave before beginning the long awkward struggle to his feet.

"I will get your poles. Your goggles are just uphill from your head, if you reach round." She glided into view at his feet, turned crisply, and fished his poles out of the deep snow.

"Are you certain you are all right? It seemed a nasty spill." She tossed the poles up to him and waited. Enormous dark goggles covered three quarters of her face. Concern was in her voice, or was it amusement?

"Thanks very much. I'll just catch my breath a minute here." He didn't relish being helped.

"Well, if you are sure." The black goggles fixed on him for a silent moment, then a smile grew below them. "You should take it more gently, you know. Well, good luck." And she pushed off. He watched her traverse across and down the steep trail at three-quarters speed, never lunging or faltering. Goddamn Swiss, Inigo thought. Always in control.

A minute later he was a hundred meters down the mountain and drunk again. Somehow he kept it up the rest of the afternoon, until the shadows under the trees turned blue and the snow, slapped and slammed by a thousand pairs of skis, began to harden and ice up. Finally, with only enough time for two more runs, he began to lose his fire and slow down, like a racing car coasting for the pit after crossing the finish line. Exhaustion overcame him on the last run. Taking broad, shallow traverses across the trail, stopping with every other turn, he finally picked his way to the bottom. The bus was only fifty meters away, but Inigo couldn't imagine carrying his skis that distance. He plodded across the mixture of snow and gravel, arriving with his last breath, too tired to bend over and release his ski bindings, panting and fishing out a cigarette.

"Well, I see you survived after all." The voice was cheery and energetic. As he turned, she lifted her goggles to her forehead and looked quizzically at him.

If this is the woman I'm looking for, he thought, it's just too damn bad. I don't even have the strength to answer.

"Here, take an orange. It will do you some good. The way you kept skiing, I imagine you skipped lunch."

He managed a smile and, still in his skis, began to peel the orange. Suddenly he felt ravenous. She turned away toward the door of the bus. With the first sharp taste of orange, Inigo found his voice.

"Excuse me." She stopped. "I didn't see you on the ride up this morning."

She turned to face him and he fell silent again.

"And now you want to know whether I'm with somebody." Her smile was as direct as her words.

"Well, yes. I'm not with anybody myself."

"I will save you a seat." And she disappeared into the bus.

Still moving slowly, Inigo packed away his skis and hoisted himself up the high step. He wasn't at all sure he would recognize her. She was slender and medium height, but that wouldn't help him spot her sitting down. He lurched along the crowded aisle, looking for a single woman. As he neared the back, she hailed him. He collapsed into the seat beside her, thinking that having someone to talk to was nice but that not having to talk would be even nicer.

"You are tired, no? Rest a little." But one task remained. Feeling eighty years old, Inigo bent over and laboriously unfastened his heavy boots. When he could finally ease his feet out, it was like a final blessing, an amen to weariness. The driver started the engine and the bus quietly throbbed.

"You are American or English?"

"American. Can't you tell?"

"The difference is not so obvious to us. Is it to you?"

"Unmistakable. And you?"

"I am German." The voice was strong, with a strong lilt. She sounded content with herself.

At another time, he might have responded in German, but just now it seemed too much of an effort. Inigo had lived two years among the Germans. He was not charmed by them, although there were exceptions. Perhaps he had too many Jewish friends.

"But you live here in Geneva?"

"I am *en poste* in Geneva since two years. One more to go."

The bus rumbled into motion and the driver turned off the interior lights. Immediately the hubbub subsided, as though skiers were day creatures who tucked their heads under their wings at nightfall. Outside the window, cars were starting up in the parking lot, their headlights coming on like little lighthouse beacons.

"And what about you?"

Inigo turned to reply and, seeing her face in shadow, realized he still hadn't had a good look at her.

"I too. I'm at the SALT negotiations with the Russians."

"I see," she said slowly. "I am from Leipzig."

East Germany. She waited for a moment but Inigo made no response. "I am assigned to CERN."

"CERN?"

"Centre European pour Recherche Nucléaire. They have three good reactors."

"I see. Were you skiing by yourself today?"

"No, with some friends. They are sitting in front of us." As if on cue, from the seat ahead a hand stuck up, waggling a wine bottle. Inigo took it and paper cups followed. "I ski often with this club. And you?"

"My first time. I've just arrived."

"But you have already skied a lot. I saw you twice starting down an expert trail."

"Then you must have seen me on my can a lot."

"Your can?"

"My *popo*."

"You speak German?"

"Like a child."

Another bottle of wine came by, this time from the rear. It was warm in the bus, but the thought of struggling out of his ski jacket was not to be entertained. He was bone tired and, along with the weariness, more contented than he'd felt in a long time.

"My name is George Inigo."

"I am Erika Hartke."

They felt no pressure to talk. Outside the light was fading; one could no longer see the snowfields on the slopes across the valley. The bus crept cautiously around the switchbacks, a little island of warmth and light moving through a cold, dark world. Across the aisle, someone began to snore softly.

"How do you like Geneva so far?" she broke the silence in a low voice.

"Marvelous. I like the scale. It's just the right size for me. Parks, flowers everywhere. I can walk to work. And the Swiss seem very nice."

"Do you think so?"

"Yes. Everyone has been friendly and helpful. Don't you find that?"

"Frankly, no. The city is attractive enough, especially in Vieille Ville, the Old Town. The lake is beautiful. Yes, and the parks too. And of course the mountains are splendid, in summer as well. I spend every weekend in them. But the Swiss—bah!" she finished sharply.

"Sssh, not so loud!"

"Oh, most of these people are French. Or diplomats. And I do not care what the Swiss think of me." She lowered her voice and rushed on. "The Swiss are cold, cold, cold. Polite, yes, amiable on the street, but just try to make a friend. And did you know that it is practically illegal to be poor in Geneva? For the Italians and Yugoslavs it is all right. In fact, it is mandatory; they get sent home if they start to accumulate some money. But if you are Swiss! The police harass you. The police are everywhere, and most of them are not in uniform. I am an East German, and still I say this!"

"But at least it's very clean everywhere," Inigo put in.

"Dirt is illegal too! It is a crime to bring it into the streets. It is a crime to have a spot of rust on your car. Do you know what lies behind all this cleanliness and order? A boring emptiness lies behind it. The Swiss have arranged everything perfectly, and they are bored to death. So they drink. Not in the streets, where the police are, but in their homes and their private clubs. You have been to Paris? To Rome? Those are cities, full of dirtiness and noise. Poor people with big families. Fights and kisses, life. The Swiss, they do not live. They just grow rich!"

Listening to her, Inigo caught a glimpse of his own mental stereotypes. What would have been vivacious in an Italian had begun for a moment to seem vehement in a German.

"Listen, I will tell you a story. All the foreigners here know it. When the Lord God had labored for six days, everyone began to complain. The Africans said, look at those beautiful mountains that you gave to Switzerland! It is not fair! The Chinese and Indians said, look at those lovely lakes! It is not fair! The Scandinavians said, look at that marvelous climate in Switzerland! And the Lord God thought about it until he realized that he really had been unfair. He would have to make it up somehow. So just as the sixth day ended, he created the Swiss."

The bus rolled slowly across the border at the wave of the frontier controllers and picked up speed toward the city. As the streetlights multiplied, Inigo stole a closer look at her face. A long jaw, high cheekbones, a full-lipped mouth. When she caught him staring, she smiled lazily.

"Will you be skiing next weekend?"

"On Saturday. They plan to go to Verbier."

"Could we ski together?" he asked.

"I will go with my friends, but join us if you like."

They had made their way off the bus, plodding in their heavy boots. Inigo momentarily forgot he was not in Germany and shook her hand. Then he lost her in the crowd gathering up equipment. He thought he glimpsed her getting into a car. With a groan, he shouldered his skis and headed for the bus stop.

7

Although there was no necessity, Smirnov locked his office door before sitting down to read the cable.

Per your Geneva 1653, following data are in our files.

Name: George Leonard Inigo
Date of birth: 2 May 1930
Place of birth: Dayton, Ohio
Class origin: Petty bourgeois
Education: No information
Marital status: Widower
Children: None
Foreign travel: Geneva, Switzerland, October 1978. No travel to Warsaw Pact states
Occupation: CIA, Soviet analyst
Present assignment: CIA representative, U.S. Delegation, Strategic Arms Limitation Talks, Geneva

Other information: Subject has worked for CIA since 1954. No record of operational assignments. Published scholarly articles on Russian history in 1950s; content conventional. Subject does not attempt to maintain cover. Washington embassy reports he wore name tag identifying employer as CIA at academic conferences at Columbia (1975) and Stanford (1977). Presented paper at latter conference on Soviet position in Eastern Europe. Embassy officer obtained copy (being pouched Geneva) and in conversation found subject to be conventionally anti-Soviet but not rabidly so. On this occasion subject attached great importance to arms control.

Smirnov read the cable a second time. Then grunted in disgust. Nothing from KGB Washington or New York, and this on a key U.S. official who specialized in Soviet affairs and did not maintain cover. It wasn't much help. With a weary sigh he scrawled a note instructing his secretary to file the cable and send a copy to Rudenko.

8

With the grace of an athlete, Lark scissored himself neatly out of his low-slung sports car in the airport parking lot. The movement was a pleasure to him. Getting his 210 pounds in one easy motion from a semi-recline, his bottom inches above the roadway, to a standing position towering over his sleek red Triumph gave him a satisfaction known only to those who pay attention to their bodies.

Lark took good care of his. At thirty-seven years, his weight was still compactly distributed up and down a frame of seventy-five inches. He spent fifty Sundays a year in the Alps, skiing while the snow lasted and hiking when it was gone. He played tennis after work three days a week, whatever the load of paper work that had to be scooped off his desk and jammed back into the safe at five o'clock. Saturdays belonged to his wife, a chubby, vivacious producer who had already presented him with three boys and a girl in seven years of marriage. Sundays she stayed home, alone or with whichever child was ill, while her husband made men out of his sons, and his daughter too, in the high rocky reaches.

He checked the Arrivals board and planted himself just outside the customs hall, off to the right where he could see all the incoming passengers. Meet a woman and be nice to her. It was the kind of assignment he was used to. Don't tell her anything. Easy, since he didn't know anything.

A decade and a half ago, Lark had been a good enough tight end at a small midwestern college to be picked in one of the late rounds of the professional football draft. Instead, he had chosen graduate school and a white-collar career. Now finishing his eleventh year with CIA, he had recognized long ago that while he was far from stupid, most of his colleagues were smarter than he. It showed in his career pattern, which had made him third man in the small Geneva station at a time when his entering classmates were becoming deputies or even running their own show in one of the smaller African states. Lark didn't much mind. He was steady, reliable, equable. Occasionally his size and strength were called upon in the line of duty. Always he was a comforting presence.

The woman wasn't hard to spot. Alone, anxious, a little mussed, she came out of the customs hall with two suitcases and headed for the taxi rank. Evidently she didn't expect to be met. He went up to her.

"Ms. Hickok?"

The woman stopped in awkward surprise, still holding her suitcases. A puffy residue of tears swelled her already round face. Early forties, he decided, a cute blonde who was holding her looks fairly well. His wife would like her. She looked up at him with a mixture of appeal and suspicion.

"I'm Robin Lark." Like everything else, he had gotten used to the name. "From the local station. We got a cable that you were coming."

Wearily, carefully, she set down her suitcases. Passengers circled around them, sober Swiss business travelers, an elderly lady with two grandchildren, a pack of noisy American teenagers on their first ski vacation. She continued to look at him, saying nothing, the appeal fading, the eyes narrowing in suspicion.

"I'm here to help in any way I can. Do you have a hotel reservation?"

She burst into tears.

In the car she said hardly a word. Lark began a laconic travelogue as they drove into the city, but she cut him short. "I've been to Geneva several times." He took her to the Beau-Rivage, where he knew the manager. Expensive, but he guessed she needed the comfort. She stared blindly out of the window during the entire ride. There was one last single room on the lakefront side, on the twelfth floor. As Lark dug for change to tip the bellboy, she walked over to the french windows and pulled the curtains.

"It's only the American Mont Blanc, isn't it?" she said without turning around.

"I believe so. The station chief wants to come over once you've settled in. I'll give you my card. It's the same telephone number."

She turned slowly back into the room.

"I want to see George Inigo."

That evening Inigo sat at the bar of the Beau-Rivage, where Lindy Hickok had asked him to wait. All his bones ached from yesterday's skiing, aggravated by a long sedentary afternoon in the tank. He had emerged at six to find a telephone message from a Mr. Lark relaying her request. It was incomprehensible to him that she should be in Geneva. Lormack had told him that Hickok was being relieved in some kind of disgrace, but he couldn't fit that together with her presence here.

Something else added to his uneasiness. Years ago, in the depression that had followed his wife's death, Inigo gradually realized that he had become something of a tragic figure to his colleagues. And in particular to several of their wives. Lindy Hickok had been the most solicitous and, eventually, the most inviting. He brushed aside her overtures with less gentleness than he usually showed, never letting her know how tempted he had been. Hickok was not a close friend, and Inigo had often recoiled at his too boisterous ways. But still. There had been an awkwardness between them ever since, a forced gaiety when they met at parties. Now she was here in Geneva alone, asking to see him. And where was Allan Hickok?

"George." A hand tapped his shoulder.

He turned, stood up, and seized her by the shoulders. "Lindy! What in the world?" His smile faded as he caught sight of her grim mouth. An afternoon nap had restored some of her color, but the blue eyes that had once rolled merrily at him were hard now, almost cold.

"Order me a Scotch, George. Straight. What happened to Allan?"

The voice was clipped, demanding. Jammed at the crowded bar, bewildered, sparring for time, Inigo gave her his stool, then stood beside her and waved at the bartender. She waited quietly, gazing at him without changing expression.

"Allan? Is that what you're here for?"

"What happened to him, George?" she insisted.

"Lindy, I don't know. He was pulled out very suddenly. There was some kind of disgrace, I understand. That's all I know."

"Did you see him here in Geneva?" Narrowly peering at him over the edge of her glass, she downed half her drink.

"No. No, I didn't. Nor in Washington. We didn't overlap at all. Hasn't he said anything to you?"

She gave him a long, appraising stare, then finished her drink and signaled herself for another.

"Sorry, George. I figured you had heard." A pause, then her face began to crumple. With an effort she brought herself under control.

"He's dead, George."

"No!"

"Yes. They let me see the body in Washington."

In the midst of shock, Inigo's mind registered the queer expression. *The* body, not *his* body. Was that easier for a fresh widow?

"The top of his head was smashed. By a small bullet. Just a small bullet. And another one through his knee." Her control was wavering again.

Somehow they ended up in her room. There was no question of using the hotel dining room, or even of eating. Lindy had a bottle in her suitcase.

"All I get from the Company is the runaround." She had only two moods, despair and cold fury, and Inigo couldn't tell from one moment to the next when one would give way to the other. "It happened here. In Geneva. Just as they were pulling him out. Which is another mystery. They won't say who did it. The Russians? Some jealous husband? Suicide? Nothing but a goddam runaround, George." And later, bitterly, "They say they're investigating. Investigating! Sometimes I think they did it themselves."

"Good God, Lindy," Inigo said for the fourth time.

"So here I am in Geneva, still trying to find out. I thought you'd know something. But obviously you don't. Unless"—her suspicion was searing, pitiable—"unless you're a damn good actor."

Wounded by the sudden distrust, Inigo didn't answer. He needed time, facts; he still couldn't sort anything out.

"I'm sorry, George. I know you're not acting. It's just that . . ." She walked across the room and moved into his arms, the tears racking her body again.

"Please, George. I know it sounds horrible, and I remember what happened before. But please, George!"

So, unhappily he took her to bed. Dazed, undone by her despair and his own, not really wanting it but unwilling to refuse her. Frantically she begged him to enter quickly. As he did so, she gave an enormous shudder, then lay still and began to sob brokenheartedly. He moved silently and slowly within her for a minute or two, but nothing more happened to either of them. Finally he stopped, lying quietly upon her, his mouth at her neck, until she fell into an exhausted sleep.

Only after he had ridden down the elevator, passed through the lobby, and reached the street did he allow himself to perceive the new question. If someone had thought it important to shoot Hickok, then what about his successor?

9

The Rue de Lausanne, a boulevard utterly without character, begins at the main railway station in the heart of town and runs eastward toward the ceremonial end of Geneva, which is anchored by the Botanical Gardens and the Palais des Nations on the hill above. A double row of modest shops, laundries, auto agencies, plumbing houses, and second-rate restaurants fills the street level, while a series of undistinguished hotels and humdrum office buildings looms above. It could be a street anywhere in Europe, including any of the charmless rebuilt cities of Germany. At the end of the commercial strip stands the U.S. Consulate, sheathed in dark glass. A mile farther on, at the end of the bus line and just where the boulevard turns into the superhighway that races along the lakeshore to Lausanne, is the U.S. SALT mission.

The consulate had little diplomatic business with the Swiss government. It was the mother ship to the fleet of delegates who represented the United States at the various international organizations scattered about Geneva. It supplied, at a lackadaisical pace, office furniture and cleaning contracts, it paid rents and utilities. It sold duty-free cigarettes and alcohol, cashed checks and changed currencies. It also housed, on a secure floor from which local employees were barred, the CIA station.

Inigo had not been in a hurry to make contact with the station. The operational side of the Agency bored and exasperated him. They were forever recruiting trivial sources, seemingly just to run up recruitment totals. In Inigo's experience, studying the spy reports, a recruitable source was rarely a useful source. And so their reports were usually trivial, but they poured in at a pace that could only mean that the case officers were being graded by quantity of information, not quality. He resented the mystique with which they surrounded their work, their inflation of its importance, and most of all the bad name they gave to the Agency he loved, with their amoral excesses and spectacular public failures. The CIA was to Inigo a first-class collection of researchers and analysts, not a bunch of guys cowboying around in foreign lands.

After Lindy Hickok's revelation last night, however, there was no time to lose. If he had to miss the morning delegation meeting, so be it. At the secure floor he identified himself to the secretary and asked to see Mr. Carson.

"The station chief will be free in just a few minutes. Please have a seat."

When a young man came out of the inner office, the girl got on the intercom. "Mr. George Inigo from the SALT delegation to see you. I'll send him right in."

Inigo followed her gesture through the inner door. A middle-aged woman was sitting at a coffee table at the near end of the room. The desk at the other end was empty.

"Excuse me, I was told this was Mr. Carson's office."

"We caught another one, Ellie," she sang out through the door. Then to Inigo: "Mr. Carson is on the golf links right now. I'm Emily Carson, the station chief. I've been expecting you to drop by." She grinned directly in his face.

Inigo stood where he was, flustered, not knowing what to say. He felt himself foolishly grinning back.

"It's all right! Have a seat. It's George, isn't it? Call me Emily. I gather no one told you."

"Not a word," as he sank into the other armchair.

"Well, forgive Ellie and me for our little game. Actually, it serves a purpose. The way people react tells me a lot about them." Another grin. "Would some coffee help?"

"Thanks. Are you the first of your kind?"

"Not quite. Monrovia. Copenhagen. Today Geneva, tomorrow the world! No, actually, it's slow going. Not because the Agency's backward, although there is a bit of that. But you know that outside the Communist countries practically all the station chiefs in the world are declared to the host government. They spend most of their time on liaison with the local service. And the locals have to be reasonably ready for it. Can you imagine the Saudis confiding in a lady station chief? Or the Brazilian junta? Now some of my sisters, as I'm supposed to call them these days, insist we should protest against all that, override it. Not me. I'm a Company woman."

"So I'm to conclude that the Swiss are in the vanguard of the enlightened."

"No, but somewhere in the top twenty percent. More important, they happened to owe us for a few things lately, and I'm the payoff. But when the right candidates come along, we'll be putting women in India, Israel, wherever female politicians have made it big. After that, who knows?"

"Is there a husband?"

"A retired banker. The genuine article, never been a spook. But he's terrifically useful to us here, of course. One of the best Agency wives we've got, I tell him." Her grin was infectious. She offered him a cigarette and accepted a light.

Carson was a bit short, a bit plump. Her face was a bit square, and honest. She was in sensible brown tweeds. Inigo's first impression was maternal, someone to rely upon, to confide in. But now he was noticing as well the keen eyes, the brisk speech. The combination must have made her a formidable competitor in the operational hierarchy. No wonder she was a success as a pioneering female. As a male, Carson would have made station chief eight years ago; as it was, she was simply overqualified.

Just as Inigo was beginning to feel impatient, she got to the point.

"Normally you and I wouldn't have much business together, George. I'm just supposed to give you some commo hours and administrative support. But I guess we need to talk about your predecessor."

"His wife says he was shot."

"That's right. Late at night, outside his apartment. Apparently he died instantly. It was just a couple of days before you arrived. The local police say someone saw two men running away, but they don't have any leads."

"What do you know about it?"

"Damn little." She fell silent as the secretary brought coffee in. When she had gone, Carson gave Inigo a sharp glance.

"Was Hickok in some kind of trouble?" she asked.

"Evidently. Lormack told me he was being pulled back. Some kind of scandal, and he might face charges. That's all I know."

"Well, it fits. All I knew on this end was that he was going back to Washington, and that Counterintelligence was involved somehow. They're the ones handling the investigation into his death now."

"What are they coming up with?"

"Are you kidding? Sorry, I forgot for a moment that you're from the overt side. Counterintelligence tells nothing to nobody until they're finished. I did get as far as finding out he had dinner that night with his opposite number on the Soviet delegation. Smirnov, is it? Then Washington shut me down. I've been ordered to keep my nose completely out of it. All I could do was ship his body home. And keep it out of the Geneva papers. No problem there; the last thing the Swiss want is for diplomats to get worried about their safety."

Inigo hunched forward in his chair, elbows on knees. He gazed a few moments at the floor, then looked up.

"Emily, don't you think I deserve a little more than that? I'm taking over his job. Is there danger in it? What kind, from where? It's not what I bargained for, you know."

Carson regarded him sympathetically. "Yes, of course you deserve more. The point is that I can't give you any more, and Counterintelligence won't. Welcome to the underworld, George."

"Thanks a million," he answered glumly.

"Well, as I see it, you've got three choices. You can refuse the assignment. No dishonor there. As you say, mysterious deaths aren't what you bargained for. Or you can stick it out and resolve to do your damnedest to keep your nose clean. Hickok didn't, I gather. Or you can demand more information, which means going straight to the director."

"Go to the director? I don't even know the man, Emily." They chatted awhile about the new director, about the politics involved in picking him. Inigo began to feel better, trading gossip again with an Agency colleague. Even the sight of the standard U.S. Government furniture was comforting; he had seen it on visits to the stations in London, Rome, Madrid, and a half dozen other capitals. The only novelty was the photograph on Carson's desk. Instead of a wife and two children, it showed a husband and two children.

Finally Carson broke it off. "I've got to go see the consul general in a few minutes. As for keeping your nose clean, let me give you the scoop on Geneva from an intelligence angle. It's a grand operational playground. Every service in the world is here, mostly because they're dazzled by the idea of buying on the cheap some young diplomat who'll eventually make foreign minister back home. Everyone madly keeps tabs on everyone else. The Soviets and their allies lead the pack, of course. But if you sashay around in the right way, that is to say foolishly, you might get a pitch from some surprising quarters."

"Then there's the Swiss," Carson went on. "This is a police state, make no mistake about it. They say every seventh adult is on the payroll in one capacity or another. Simple informers mostly. As long as you stay in line, you'll never see them. But whoever messes up will find that they already know an awful lot about him. And they're tough. I'm talking about the domestic as well as the Foreign Service. Your average Swiss citizen has plenty of respect for these fellows. You've seen how clean this city is, all those parks and flower beds. Well, the Swiss police are efficient gardeners too, in their way. Very good at weeding."

"Should I be scared?"

"Normally, no. You obviously know how to take care of yourself, how to behave. I just want you to realize that you won't have any privacy here. It's the easiest place in the world to attract surveillance. The Soviets, the East Europeans, both kinds of Chinese, the Libyans, the French, the Cubans, the Israelis, they're all here. Money flowing in all directions at once. The North Koreans, my God, you wouldn't believe how active those bastards are. And never forget about the Swiss.

"But there is this business about Hickok. Until that's figured out, I'd say, yes, you should be scared. Was he a friend of yours?"

"Not close. And knowing what I do—and not knowing what I don't—I'd just as soon not have to deal with his wife again."

"No sweat. She's my problem. I'll see her again this evening and she's ticketed for tomorrow morning's flight."

On the way out Inigo quietly asked the secretary to run a file check on an Erika Hartke, a German national living in Geneva. East or West German? He didn't know, he said. It took little more than a minute.

"Nothing on her. Want me to check Washington?"

"No, that's not necessary. You've got no file on her?"

"None."

But we'll start one tomorrow, the secretary told herself as he left. Because you asked about her.

10

"All right," Rudenko's voice came out of the telephone. *"You can come down now. We've got it all ready."*

As Smirnov replaced the receiver, he thought idly about the old times. Both he and Major Rudenko could remember the days when someone had to sit through hours of silence until a conversation finally appeared on the tape of a telephone tap. In those times, a subject could often avoid intercept by making his call at three in the morning, when the monitors had given up. Now, with voice-activated equipment, the bug lay dormant until a phone connection occurred, setting the cassette spinning. No more dead air.

There were few conversations on the Inigo tape. A call from Jenkins, confirming a restaurant date. One from Morgan about the papers needed for the next day's meeting; both parties carefully refrained from identifying the topic. Michaels at 9:00 P.M. suggesting a drink. Then a female voice.

"Hello?" Rudenko nodded meaningfully at Smirnov.

"Erika? This is George." Inigo was speaking German.

"George, how nice of you to call."

"I wanted to confirm the ski trip this weekend. It's Sunday at seven-thirty isn't it?"

"Yes, that's right. The bus is going to Verbier."

A pause, then Inigo in English.

"You'll be on it, won't you?"

"Of course."

"Good. I hoped so. I need someone to dig me out of the drifts."

"You will do fine. I wish I could ski as fast as you."

"Ah, but the price I pay."

The conversation meandered on for another minute. When it ended, Rudenko switched off the machine. He and Smirnov smiled at each other.

11

"Six years!" said Inigo. "How can you keep it up?"

"Yeah, it gets pretty tiresome at times." Morgan took a short swig of his coffee. "All those plenaries and post-plenaries, lunches and dinners with Pavlovsky and his boys. Always the same old arguments. After you've taken an issue through two or three of those sessions, there's really nothing more to say about it."

They were in Inigo's office, relaxing during the coffee break that Jenkins had just declared.

"But you go on saying it. What for?"

Morgan put his feet on the coffee table. Inigo had immediately found him an attractive man. He was ugly to the point of lovability. Big ears jutted out of a heavy cluster of reddish hair that clung to his head in tight curls. An improbably large nose seemed to crowd his mouth and eyes toward the edges of his face. He could set all the secretaries laughing with just one of his big grins. But Morgan didn't play around. He saved every dollar he could out of his overseas allowance until he could buy his wife another airline ticket for a four-day weekend. Sometimes it was only three days. But however long her visit, no one caught a glimpse of Morgan until after she had left.

"You just go on playing the game. It's called 'dictating his memcon.' "

"Huh?"

"Yeah, his memorandum of conversation, his memcon. Starsky or Hutch has to write one up and cable it back to Moscow, just like we have to send our memcons back to Washington. We all know that no matter how good one side's arguments may be, no one can change positions here in Geneva except on instructions from home. So I force them to repeat our points to Moscow, in the memcon, over and over again. What I'm hoping for, working toward, is that after eight or nine times they'll finally put a comment at the end of the cable. Like 'Americans are wholly convinced of their position and warn that

57

treaty cannot be signed without resolution of this issue.' " And eventually, if I'm lucky: 'Recommend Moscow review Soviet position on this matter."

"And they're doing the same thing, I suppose."

"Sure. Trying to dictate our memcons. They all do it. Except Smirnov." He cast a shrewd glance at Inigo.

"Except Smirnov?"

"Yeah. Oh, once in a while he'll do his homework and give you a real substantive argument. But mostly he's pretty flaky on the treaty. Didn't Hickok tell you?"

"No." Inigo was instantly alert. The mere mention of Smirnov and Hickok in the same breath made him uneasy. "We didn't have time for any overlap."

"What took him out of Geneva so fast, anyway?"

"Family problems."

"Too bad. Well, I guess Smirnov doesn't bother much with the treaty because he's got other jobs here."

"Like what?"

"Well now, I guess you'd know that better than I, George." A sly smile. "Best we get back now. Coach Jenkins doesn't like his players being late for practice."

Today's meeting was Inigo's baptism of fire in the American delegation. The issue was MIRVs, the acronym mercifully coined for multiple independently targetable reentry vehicles. A missile equipped with MIRVs could fire each of them with incredible accuracy at a separate target, which meant, among other things, that the side that fired first might be able to knock out four or six or even ten of the enemy's missile silos with just one missile of its own. To limit this tempting advantage, Moscow and Washington had agreed that out of a total of over 1,300 ICBM launchers, only 820 could be equipped with MIRVs, but it remained to define those launchers in a way that enabled the United States to count them accurately. Photoreconnaissance satellites could not peer into launchers to see whether the missiles they contained were equipped with single or multiple warheads. In fact, even a clear view of the missile would not answer the question, because the USSR had tested its newest types of ICBMs with single warheads on some occasions and with MIRVs on others.

In the face of this dilemma, CIA had constructed a set of special counting rules that would give the United States the benefit of all doubts about Soviet launchers. First, all ICBMs of a type that had been flight-tested with MIRVs, even if only once, would be counted as MIRVed. Second, any launcher of ICBMs that had been developed and tested for MIRVed ICBMs would be counted as a MIRVed launcher under the 820 quota. But how to determine whether a launcher had been developed or tested for MIRVed or unMIRVed missiles? That led to the third rule: If a given launcher had in fact ever once contained or launched a MIRVed ICBM, then all launchers of that same type would be considered as having been developed and tested for MIRVs and counted under the 820 sublimit.

It was complicated enough, God knows; it had taken Inigo two days and a night just to master all the connections himself. Jenkins and Rappaport, the State representative, complained that it was far too intricate, that it was impossible to negotiate, that it would drive the Soviets up the wall.

"George," Rappaport complained when they got back to work in the tank, "isn't there some simpler way? I'm going to have to defend this against Pavlovsky and company and I can't remember your arguments for more than ten minutes."

Patiently Inigo ran through the whole problem again from start to finish. Rappaport sighed. The whole instruction, he knew, had been worked out in Washington and signed off by all agencies, including his own, before being sent out in a cable that itself took six pages to explain the matter to the delegation. Still, he needed Inigo to convince him personally before he could effectively carry the case to the Soviet delegation.

The debate went on all morning and far into the afternoon, amid grumblings that CIA was being too demanding, before everyone finally understood the proposal well enough to argue it with his Soviet counterpart. Jenkins assigned an ACDA expert to draft a plenary statement on the issue. When it appeared next morning, it was the longest formal statement the United States had ever proposed. "If a launcher has been developed and tested for launching an ICBM equipped with multiple independently targetable reentry vehicles," said some of the fine print, "all launchers of that type, except for ICBM test and training launchers, shall be included in the corresponding aggregate numbers provided for in Article V of the Treaty, pursuant to the provisions of Article VI of the Treaty."

"Hey," exclaimed Jenkins, "it says all launchers of that type.

What's a 'type'? Launchers of the same diameter? Same depth? Identical support buildings and equipment? Hadn't we better draft a definition of 'type'?''

An appalled silence fell.

"Better not," Paul Boroz finally said. "That would just give the Sovs a blueprint to play games with. They could change the length, say, by three feet on half their launchers and claim they were a different type and didn't have to be counted as MIRVed."

Inigo glanced gratefully at Boroz. That was the right answer, the reason why Washington had avoided a definition of '*type*' in the instruction. He was glad that at last someone else was sharing the burden of defending that instruction.

"Let's go, men." Jenkins finally pulled the delegation together.

Morgan grinned. "Sock it to us, coach!"

"Right. Big game today, team. A tough fight on our hands. But we've got the stuff. Now let's go out there and win one for Washington!" Amid general laughter everyone headed for the garage and the ride to the plenary.

The Soviet mission was a huge fenced compound housing all the USSR's delegations to Geneva's international agencies. Most of the Soviet personnel lived there, and only the higher-ups like Smirnov were allowed to rent outside apartments or hotel suites. Tough-looking plainclothesmen idled about as the cavalcade of black American sedans moved slowly through the gate and up the hill. In front of the SALT building at the top, Lebedev and his delegation were lined up on the porch in protocol order. The Americans shook hands down the line and then chatted in the hall while Lebedev and Jenkins worked out the date of the next plenary. The Soviet conference room was small, and it took some time for the two sides to maneuver to their chairs in the cramped space. As Inigo wriggled into place, he wondered if he heard the whirring of a camera or a tape recorder in the wall behind him.

Jenkins went first. "Mr. Ambassador, the United States delegation will present today a set of interrelated proposals for counting the launchers of ICBMs equipped with multiple independently targetable reentry vehicles, or MIRVs. These proposals ensure that each side, using its national technical means, can verify compliance with the agreed limit of 820 such launchers." The Soviets looked alert. Several of them picked up their pencils. As Jenkins read on, the note-taking began. When he reached the five-minute mark, frowns began to appear. General Mardirosian, impassive as ever, tore a sheet of paper off his pad and began to fill a second page. Jenkins droned on, reading wearily now. Pavlovsky ostentatiously put down his pencil, grimaced across the table at Rappaport, and closed his eyes. Smirnov gave Inigo an impudent wink.

At last Jenkins and his interpreter stopped. Lebedev gravely thanked the American delegation, paused, then launched into his own statement. It was short and blunt, a flat denial of an earlier American presentation on the Soviet missile test center at Tyuratam. Test launchers, including all those at Cape Canaveral, were not counted in the SALT totals. CIA had determined, however, that eighteen of the launchers at Tyuratam were different from all the others and were, in fact, part of the Soviet operational force. Therefore, the United States had told the Soviets they had to be charged against the allowable treaty number.

Lebedev was adamant. All the launchers at Tyuratam were test and training launchers; there were no operational launchers there, nor had there ever been. It was not helpful to the negotiations to raise such unsubstantiated assertions. Such behavior cast doubt on the intentions of the American side. The matter was closed. When he finished, Jenkins demurred mildly but firmly. "I am sure that the matters addressed today in the statements of both sides will be fully discussed between us."

The delegations got their coffee and juice, poured by a woman who bore out Smirnov's comment on the lack of pretty girls at the Soviet mission. They headed for an adjacent lounge, sparsely furnished, with a quiet fountain in the center. Smirnov guided Inigo firmly to a corner where two chairs stood.

"Mr. Hickok and I had many an interesting chat in this corner."

Inigo stared at the fountain. Hickok was the last thing he wanted to discuss with this man. When he finally looked at Smirnov, the Russian's face was relaxed and smiling. Quickly he led off in a business-like tone.

"Well, I imagine you have some questions about the American proposal today."

"I imagine you have no questions about Ambassador Lebedev's statement," Smirnov shot back.

"On the contrary. I would like to know why he called our assertions unsubstantiated. We took pains to supply you with considerable evidence that eighteen of the launchers at Tyuratam are operational, not for testing like the others."

"Evidence? How can you claim that there have been no test-firings from these launchers? Are you watching twenty-four hours every day of the year? It will take more evidence than that to convince me."

"In winter the snow is removed regularly from these launchers. That is not the case with true test launchers. Only with operational ones."

"An extremely silly argument. It in no way justifies the artificial creation of an issue here. I cannot believe you are serious about it."

"Indeed we are!" Inigo declared hotly. "Furthermore—" He halted in a sudden panic. Snow removal! Was that one of the pieces of evidence that was safe to tell the Soviets? He suddenly couldn't remember. The American side had made its official presentation on Tyuratam the week before he arrived. He thought he had memorized it, but now he was flooded with confusion, unable to recall which data were releasable to the Soviets and which were not.

Smirnov observed him with calm amusement. "If you are not prepared to make your case, Mr. Inigo, you can hardly expect to be taken seriously."

"Your own Ministry of Defense has all the evidence." It was, he knew, a lame response. Smirnov made short work of it.

"Ah, but our delegation is negotiating a treaty with the United States of America, not the Soviet Ministry of Defense."

Inigo covered his retreat as best he could. "As Ambassador Jenkins said, we shall have to return to this matter. Now, tell me your reactions to today's American statement on the subject of MIRVs."

But Smirnov would not allow him the last word. "As Ambassador Lebedev told you, the matter of Tyuratam is closed. As for today's American statement, it is an example of how your side constantly puts obstacles in the path of our work." Now all amusement vanished; Smirnov spoke rapidly and aggressively. "An essentially simple issue is made as complicated as possible. Your Mister MIRV has outdone himself this time. The language already in the treaty covers the problem in a completely satisfactory way. The profound distrust of the USSR shown in these proposals is offensive to us." He sat back and glared.

There were no peanuts at the Soviet mission, only small dry cookies. Inigo crumbled a few in the plate, still shaken by the fear that he, the watchdog of sensitive information, might have provided the USSR with classified data. He took a long sip of orange juice and, recalling Morgan's words from the previous day, launched into a detailed recapitulation of Jenkins's statement. MIRVs could be adequately verified only if three counting rules were agreed in the treaty. The three rules were interlocking and interdependent; each was as necessary as the others. First, if an ICBM launcher of a given type had been test-fired with MIRVs, even if only once, all ICBM launchers of that type would be counted as equipped with MIRVs. Second, any launcher that had been developed and tested—

"Mr. Inigo, allow me to interrupt you. I listened carefully to Ambassador Jenkins's statement on MIRVs this morning. I have already given you my reaction. In addition, I will study the text and inform you of any further reactions after that time."

Not knowing what to say, balked by confusion and anger, Inigo gazed at him wordlessly.

"I must also tell you," Smirnov went on coldly, "that I rarely report my conversations about the treaty to Moscow. So it is pointless to try to use me as a channel for conveying your views to my superiors." He paused, then added, "Mr. Hickok understood that very well."

In the face of such bluntness, Inigo still found nothing to say.

"In that connection," Smirnov went on in a changed, affable tone, "have you learned anything further about the reason for his departure? I believe you said family reasons."

"Yes."

"As I recall, he told me he had a wife and two children. Two girls, I believe. Have you any details?"

"No. No details."

"It's a pity. Well, then, perhaps I may ask you how you are enjoying your life in Geneva."

Inigo seized on the topic with relief. Smirnov kept up his end of the conversation in a desultory way. After ten minutes Inigo had regained enough composure to launch a belated, small counterattack.

"The weather was beautiful last weekend," he said. "A group of us took the *telecabine* up Mont Blanc—stunning. Did you get into the mountains?"

A thin look from Smirnov. "As you know, Soviet diplomats need visas to enter France, and the French government does not issue them."

"Ah yes, I forgot." Inigo pushed the needle further in. "Is the same true for West Germany? For Italy?"

"All the NATO countries," Smirnov said shortly.

Inigo made sympathetic sounds. It was a weak revenge, but a revenge nonetheless. Smirnov seemed undisturbed.

"Please do not forget that I am expecting you for dinner tonight," he said as the ambassadors reappeared and the post-plenary discussions began to break up. "I should like to bring my wife, if you have no objections." Inigo had none. Indeed, the evening might pass more easily if they were a threesome.

They met in an elegant French restaurant in the suburb of Carouge, where the duke of Savoy had founded a rival city to Geneva, only to have it swallowed up by the Swiss. Vera Mikhailovna was a faded beauty, small and slight, anxious, intimidated by the elegant dining room and the impressive waiters. Her red hair was done in the artless ringlets of a young girl. Smirnov vetoed her order of oyster bisque, reminding her that shellfish disagreed with her, and she pouted happily. "I don't suppose you'll let me have a drink either." Of course he would. The bullying tone reappeared in his voice as he instructed the waiter how to make his wife's Bloody Mary.

"She always drank them in New York," he informed Inigo.

"He makes it sound as though I were always drunk in New York," she complained. Her English was tentative but good.

"Was that a pleasant time for you? It was eight years, wasn't it?"

"Oh yes, pleasant enough." Her voice was unenthusiastic. "And of course it was an important time. Our daughter was born there."

"So I understand. So she can be an American citizen if she chooses."

Smirnov cut in on her reply. "I think our daughter would not mind that at all. She lived the first six years of her life in Brooklyn. She talks about America all the time."

"But become an American citizen, Victor? Surely not. It's just that she remembers a happy childhood." She turned to Inigo. "I had no friends there, of course. So I took her everywhere with me." There was something fervent in her stare.

"You had plenty of friends, Vera. There was our diplomatic mission, and all the others at the UN. You met quite a few nice Americans, too. It's not correct to say you had no friends."

She gave Inigo a conspiratorial look. "He's right, of course. We met a lot of people. And New York is a fascinating city."

"My wife means that she missed Moscow. Her parents are there."

"Yes. And all my real friends. My old friends. From school days and the university, most of them. Don't you miss your family and your friends, Mr. Inigo?"

It had the air of a familiar game. She tugged at the leash, he pulled her in, she pouted and played the coquette to the bystander. See how meanly he treats me. See how much she depends on me. Inigo suddenly had an image of an evening, many years ago, when Smirnov suddenly ordered her to marry him. No, not quite that abrupt: He simply told her it was time she did. She was the daughter of a deputy minister, Inigo knew from the files, so Smirnov clearly did himself no harm by his choice. Yet there was no weariness or indifference in the playing; the comfort of their rituals spoke of affection.

"And how do you spend your time here in the small city of Geneva, Mrs. Smirnov?"

"Oh, I take lots of walks in the beautiful parks. I sew. I have lunch with Madame Lebedev." She paused, as if before some guilty secret. Then, "And I have my work."

"Your work?"

"Yes, my literary work. I am a translator."

"Really!" She had him interested. "What are you translating?"

"Oh, just some minor works. I think you call them entertainments." She gradually let him draw out of her that she was translating the novels of John O'Hara, that three of them had already appeared in Russian, and that she was late now with the fourth, with the publisher threatening to reclaim her advance. At last she reached into her handbag and gave her husband an imploring look. He nodded and she drew a thick novel out of her handbag. It was studded with paper clips.

"Would you mind if I asked you for a little help? You see, I don't have many dictionaries here, and so few of our Russian friends know English really well. Sometimes Victor has the answer, but we know pretty much the same. If this is an imposition, please say so." She made as if to return the book to the bag.

"Not at all. What's the first problem?" It suited Inigo perfectly to find a way to pass the evening with this strange couple, with their variety of provocations. The idea of seducing the wife of a KGB officer had no appeal for him, even though it might be a first in CIA annals.

Besides, he disliked Smirnov, but not to the point of being rude to his wife. So he explained the meaning of *a pig in a poke* and *so's your old man* and *three will get you five*. He even dredged up out of his memory that a Delaney card was a New York public school attendance form.

"Now here one young man says to another, 'Your mother has banged every officer on the base.' " Her look was all innocence.

"Yes. Um. That's difficult to translate."

"Perhaps I should leave it out?"

"I think that might be best." Her husband was arguing with the waiter. A small smile slowly grew upon her mouth. Inigo kept his smile small too.

"In the Soviet Union we have everything," she told him, "but we do not write everything."

The evening passed quickly. "I still have some paper clips left," she said gaily as Smirnov settled the bill. "But next time I will not ask you to work for your dinner." Inigo wondered whether there was a string of small, needy affairs behind her, or whether she was too timid to proceed beyond flirtation. It seemed more likely that she was content to be girl-wife to her authoritative husband.

During the next post-plenary, Smirnov was unusually agreeable. Yes, he could understand the American concern over MIRV counting rules, even though it was excessive. Yes, Moscow was studying the matter of the Tyuratam Eighteen, despite Ambassador Lebedev's statement declaring the matter closed. You know how diplomats talk. When they had exhausted the discussion of the plenary proposals, he refilled Inigo's coffee cup and said, "May I ask you a linguistic question?"

"Certainly."

"Please, my wife would like to know the meaning of" he fished a card out of his pocket and read it slowly, " 'he ain't got a pot to piss in.' "

12

Meanwhile, in the mountains the snow continued to fall.

Surely there had never been such a winter for skiers, Inigo thought. Not so, Erika's friends told him; it was excellent, but such winters came along every three years or so. They were three men and a woman, all French, except for the Pole Jerzy, who was assigned to the International Labor Organization and lived near Inigo. The rest worked in Geneva and lived across the border in Ferney-Voltaire. The town had been Voltaire's home in later years; his printer had had his shop on Inigo's street. Legend had it that the sharp-tongued writer, who created a sort of personal court there, had wanted to be in a position to nip over into Switzerland quickly if, back in Paris, the king someday ran out of patience and sent his officers after him.

They were younger than Erika, whom Inigo judged to be in her upper thirties. It was not clear to him why they skied together. Claude was an expert, tall and willowy, who danced gracefully down the runs. Charlotte, almost as good, had a more intense style. "Claude plays with the mountain; Charlotte takes possession of it," said Jerzy. He himself was a breakneck intermediate, like Inigo. Several times a day they would both find themselves spread out in the snow, defeated, laughing, tripped up by the same mogul. Henri skied like Erika, never falling, but having to work a little all the time to maintain a steady control. It seemed that no matter how many years he skied, he never intended to get any better. They skied as a loose ensemble, usually waiting for one another but not always, reassembling in the lift line at the bottom, arranging to meet for lunch. It was not clear to Inigo why they had chosen one another.

"Charlotte and Jerzy sleep together," Erika explained. They were sitting together on the bus to Verbier a week after their first meeting. "Henri is her brother, and Claude works with him at the Red Cross." And herself? She smiled. "They just found me skiing alone and let me join them." He wondered, but no more explanations came. Nor were any required of him. Erika had simply introduced him to the others in the gray dawn at the bus depot before they left. He was welcomed easily, and when he proved he could get down the mountain at Verbier as fast as Jerzy, he seemed to be accepted as a regular member. French was the group language, but everyone had English and, out of courtesy to him, used it most of the time. They did a lot of laughing as well. His age seemed to make no difference.

It made a difference to him, however, when the sun moved slowly down behind the peak at Verbier. The snow turned blue-gray, and the cold advanced like a hostile climate of an enemy country. He noticed how Erika and the others easily mounted the high first step of the bus, envying them as he grasped the handrails on either side and wearily pulled himself up. Clearly he was the one who was sighing to himself, I made it. And he was the first to break out a bottle of wine from his bag and start it around.

Erika noticed his tiredness. "Would you like a ride home in my car when we get to Geneva?" He would. He would like much more. He would like to be helped out of his clothes, to have a hot bath drawn, to have a whiskey brought to the tub, to have her sit in his bathrobe on the toilet lid and tell him little jokes while he soaked. And then. And then. And then he would like this strong, healthy, cheerful woman to turn back the covers of his bed and slip under them with a giggle, while he gingerly lowered himself onto the other side. And then.

And then horns blared, snow flared past the window, the bus lurched sharply. Thudded sideways into the snowbank, and stopped. A chorus of gasps went up, as at a murder on a stage. Erika had grabbed Inigo as she was thrown against him. Now she giggled and held on a moment, then let him go and righted herself. They had swerved to miss a little skidding Renault, which had plowed into the opposite bank. Speeds were slow, no one was hurt. After a moment, a cheer went up in the bus.

Skiers clattered into the aisles to make noise, pile out, and help dig. When Inigo rose to join them, Erika put a hand on his arm. "There are more than enough of them. You are not used to these long hard skiing days." He leaned back gratefully.

He didn't wake up until she spoke in a low voice to him as they crossed the city's main bridge over the Rhone. People were beginning to stir in the quiet bus, gathering together equipment and wine bottles. Inigo had forgotten the accident. Exhaustion had given way to mere tiredness. It was chillingly cold in Erika's car. Old Town was only a few minutes away, and the heater had hardly made itself felt when they reached Inigo's building. As he unfastened his skis from the car roof, he imagined his bathtub upstairs, filled with hot water. He came around to the driver's side, and she put her right hand out the window. For some reason, they gently butted together the tips of their bulky ski gloves, smiling at each other. And then. And then she drove away.

It had been a long time since Inigo had been close to a woman. He had been a husband for only four years, in a marriage that lay two decades in the past. When it had ended, there was first a long period of grief, depression, and guilty relief. Then came a sowing of wild oats, a frenzied year of conquests and disgust. Since then he had gone out with fewer women, sleeping for a time with still fewer of them. They tended to make demands, to intrude on his privacy, to crowd his life. They found him strongly attractive at first, but emotionally careful after a while. He gave compliments, gifts, confidences with reluctance, as though at some obscure cost to himself. They didn't understand; neither did he. They drifted away; he let them go.

He rarely thought about his wife these days, and when he did it was with increasing doubt that he ever had been really close to her. In his young twenties, Inigo had married the first woman who said she loved him. He hadn't noticed the desperation behind her fascinating energy. He was not the first man to receive a declaration of love from Penny, nor the last. Indeed, he received more confidences and confessions than he could handle in those strained, tearful nights. What she called sharing contained far more hurt than love for him; what it taught him was withdrawal. When she died, in a car accident that had a fearful but unprovable look of deliberate impulse, he felt like a survivor.

His mother hadn't come to the funeral. "Should have had it at eleven o'clock, son," his father told him with his usual flatness after the service. "Your mother's not up to much after lunch these days." It was no surprise to Inigo, though he blamed himself for forgetting. When he started high school, the drinking didn't begin until she went into the kitchen to prepare dinner. By the time he graduated, she wasn't meeting his eyes when he arrived home after school. No wonder Penny's intensity, her passionate there-ness, had entranced him.

And now this new woman, this skier, this Erika. Fixing his supper, Inigo smiled wryly to himself as the familiar pattern emerged in his mind. Sexually attractive, cheerful, athletic, unattached. A suspicion took shape briefly—why was she unattached?—but he pushed it away. A lot of fun, good companionship, weekends in the mountains, a little love, all in the right mixture. And after six months, good-bye and an ocean between them. He would tell her that in advance, of course. It might suit her just fine, exactly as it suited him.

13

Colonel Michaels let himself down heavily in the seat next to Inigo as the big plane jolted through a pocket of turbulence.

"How's it going, George?"

"Not bad, Bert, no complaints. No, as a matter of fact, I do have a complaint."

"What's that?"

"This recess. Only three weeks after I get here, and right in the middle of the ski season. Who needs it?"

"I do, that's for sure. The general has been running my ass off. So why didn't you just take leave and stay in the Alps?"

They were an hour out of Geneva in the big air force plane that General O'Rourke had obtained to bring the delegation home. A cargo aircraft converted to passenger use, it was roomy and windowless.

"I thought about it. I imagined I'd get too lonely. Have you managed to meet anyone in Geneva?" And besides, Erika was on holiday in Italy. She had ignored his casual hint that she might like company.

"None of the Genevois. Plenty of foreign types, though. Lots of girls around here. Try having lunch at the cafeteria up in the Palais des Nations. Share a table and you're off."

"I suppose that with the local Swiss being so aloof, it throws all the foreigners together faster."

"Right," said Michaels. "Did you hear the one about the Lord making the earth in six days, and then everyone started to bitch?" He didn't tell it as well as Erika.

"So O'Rourke keeps you running?"

"You wouldn't believe it. Five or six cables a night to the JCS. Researching out every question that comes into his head. Written critiques of every paper prepared by the boys from State or the Arms Control and Disarmament Agency. Or yourself for that matter. Drafts of plenary statements for Jenkins. Alternatives to State and ACDA drafts. Plus travel orders, tickets, reservations. You don't see him much around here on the weekends."

"You know, a newcomer," Inigo mused slyly, "just listening to what goes on in the tank, would begin to wonder whether Walt really wants a treaty."

"He'd be wrong, then." Michaels grinned back. "O'Rourke wants a treaty all right. But not this one."

"Which one, then?"

"The one in his head. The one in which the Soviets scrap half their ICBM force and we promise not to deploy more than two hundred new bombers if we can ever get their design right and their cost doesn't drive Congress into revolt. The one in which we get the right to station inspectors throughout Moscow's strategic forces to make sure they're not cheating."

"Well, that's a fine idea, I must say."

"Well, I'm exaggerating, of course. And lots of his ideas are good. I'm for all the inequality we can get, so long as it's in our favor. There's just one problem. Negotiability."

"So I've noticed," Inigo said. "He seems to think that we really are the good guys and that, deep in their hearts, the Sovs know it."

"And they should give up their evil ways and weapons, while we keep ours because they're virtuous. Sometimes he gets confused about whether it's us or our weapons that are virtuous. Or both."

"Are you old enough to remember that newspaper cartoon from the Korean War?" Inigo asked. "General MacArthur is sitting beside General Marshall. Marshall has a globe in his hand, but MacArthur has a cube showing nothing but Asia. And Marshall is saying 'Actually, Doug, we've been using more of a round one.' "

Michaels chuckled. "Yes, something like that. All blacks and whites, no shades of gray. I wouldn't mind it so much if he wouldn't look at me as though I were a traitor every time I explain the Soviet point of view."

"So why put up with it? Can't you get reassigned?"

"Listen, I'm as anti-Soviet as that bastard O'Rourke is, just not in such a dumb way. And SALT is the only battlefield we've got. Just think, out of the whole enormous U.S. military, only about half a dozen of us get to engage the enemy face to face. It's hand-to-hand combat in Geneva. No sir, I worked hard to get this assignment. I'm not letting any fool general screw me out of this. And we're winning!"

"We are?" Plunged suddenly into SALT, Inigo had been bothered by the general enthusiasm for the treaty within his delegation, the insistence on its virtues, the urgency everyone felt about finishing it.

"For Christ's sake, George, read the treaty! I admit it's a pretty modest piece of arms control, but all the restrictions fall on them, not us. And more than that, imagine if it fails. That'll create the kind of atmosphere in which each side blames the other. Then we both arm to the hilt, buying every new weapon that the designers can dream up."

Michaels twisted toward him in the narrow seat, gripping the armrest. "It's a process, George, and a long one. This treaty isn't revolutionary. We'll need five or six of these agreements to really start reducing the danger. But it's a fragile process, too. Some big crisis between us, some change of leaders on either side, and we've had it. Maybe only with this treaty, but maybe with the ones to follow as well. That's why we can't afford to waste time."

"Well, okay. But if we show the Soviets how badly we want it, they're just going to hang in there forever and wait for our concessions."

"I know, I know. That's always the objection. All I can say is, read the treaty. All the limits are on their programs. And you can thank us military types for that. State and ACDA would be selling the farm if we weren't here. But O'Rourke wants the moon, and he's capable of scuttling the whole thing if he doesn't get it."

That seemed to be enough of that for both of them. They fell into a companionable silence. Soon drinks appeared, followed by steaks, and they chatted about Geneva's restaurants as they ate. Later Michaels wandered off to join a poker game, leaving Inigo to stare at the closed door of the VIP compartment, where O'Rourke rode in solitary comfort. After all, it was his plane.

It was dark and rainy when they touched down at Andrews Air Force Base. The lights made ragged strips of shiny wetness on the runway. A huddle of wives and a few children waited in the terminal building. Inigo hitched a ride into town with Morgan and his wife and took a cab to his apartment. He was used to always being the lonely one.

Although the jet lag put him five hours ahead of everyone else in Washington, Inigo took his time the next morning, not leaving for headquarters till ten. There wasn't much for him to do during the recess. He needed to discuss in detail with Peters how much information they should provide to the Soviets to back up the U.S. claim on

Tyuratam. He wanted to spend a morning with the telemetry analysts; their subject was starting to become a hot topic in Geneva. And
he needed to meet and talk with the new director. It was not a heavy
schedule at all.

His badge was upstairs in his safe, but the guard at the main gate
recognized him and waved him through with a "Welcome back!"
He'd lost his close-in space when he went to Geneva, so he had to park
in the general lot, among the secretaries and junior analysts. After a
phone call from the main desk, Laura brought the badge down to
him. Headquarters seemed a strange place, thousands of people
doing very little, mostly making complications for the handful overseas, who did everything. He smiled at himself, a veteran headquarters man, caught up so quickly in the prejudices of the field.

Inigo no longer had an office here; he was a floater. Peters had
found a desk for him to use during the recess, but he still felt like a
transient. He had to borrow Peters's phone to call the director's office
for an appointment.

"Is the director expecting to see you?" The voice on the line was unfamiliar. Of course, Jane left with Lormack or had been found a place
somewhere else. Every new director brought in his own secretary.

"I'm his personal representative at the SALT talks in Geneva. The
delegation is back in Washington on recess, and I need to see him before I return."

"I see. Let me talk with the director and get back to you later." She
was clearly unconvinced. "What number can I reach you on?"

Inigo read her the number off the instrument. "I'm only here for
two days," he invented. "I hope we can meet today or tomorrow. Ten
minutes should do it."

Dialing from his old list of phone numbers, he found that Cornett
was in and had some time. Cornett was an odd duck and his own man.
A bachelor, he played the oboe and spent two nights a week at choir
practice. He had two passions: devotion to China and hatred of communism. Inigo, who had parallel but much less intense feelings about
Russia, wondered how Cornett maintained his equilibrium in that
riptide of emotions. But his papers were invariably calm, balanced,
objective.

"Well, you're the toast of the town around here," Cornett greeted
him from behind a cluttered desk.

"How so?"

"You got out, you clever devil. Just in time. Everyone's jealous.

People are saying Lormack must have tipped you off. Did he?" Cornett was an expert at direct questions, perhaps because he was always willing to give direct answers himself.

"Oh, you mean the new director. Is it that bad?"

"Look, you know how people are around here. Ready to see disaster every other Friday. But yes, it is pretty bad."

"Come on, Harry, you're an old hand. You've survived as many directors as I have. It's never as bad as it seems at first."

"You didn't answer my question. Did Lormack tip you off?"

"He gave me a hint. But I had already decided to take Geneva."

"Smart fellow. Lucky fellow. Probably both." Cornett came out from behind his desk and closed the door. He wrinkled his nose at Inigo's cigarette but said nothing. A sea of parked cars blazed outside the window.

"Have you seen him yet?" Inigo shook his head. "Nor will you. He doesn't need us. Knows everything already. Here he's got a whole stable of Chinese experts." Cornett's voice underlined the word, "and does he listen? Not him. He calls up some businessman he knows who lived three years on Taiwan and asks him. Meanwhile, he seems to think that an intelligence appraisal of a foreign country's position is an apologia for it. Look at this."

He picked up a typescript from his desk and tossed it to Inigo on the sofa. "Chinese Policy Toward the U.S. in the Current Stage" was the title. At the bottom of the first page were vigorous scrawlings in heavy red ink. "Sounds exactly like Peking's line." And "What about U.S. interests?" And "What are the Chinese *really* after?"

"Well, why don't you tell him, Harry?" Inigo teased. "What are the Chinese really after? Come on, out with it!"

"Don't play games, George. Just help me find an overseas post, thousands of miles from here." Overseas assignments for Sinologists were scarce, and Cornett knew it. He flopped down in a chair. "And accept my congratulations. You're the only one who's escaped. Just keep out of sight, and out of Washington, for as long as you can, that's my advice. Got to go now."

Reentering Peters's office suite, Inigo was hailed by a secretary who was just hanging up the telephone.

"You have an appointment with the director at eleven-thirty tomorrow. They said to tell you his schedule is very tight, so don't be late."

Peters's head appeared from his inner office. "Going to see the boss, are you? That's more than the rest of us can manage. Got a minute to talk?"

Closing the door behind him, Peters in his wordy way recapitulated Cornett's account of the new director. As the CIA man on the interagency SALT working group, he needed top-level policy decisions every other day. Matters that used to be decided on the phone with Lormack now had to be put in memorandum form. The written replies came late and usually asked for further information. "Half the time they don't make any sense," he finished.

"Give him time, Guy. He's got a lot to get on top of in a hurry."

"Sure, I know, but in that case he could at least trust us, let us move things forward. Look, I don't know why he's agreed to see you, but if you get a chance, put in a plug, will you? That decisions need to be made quickly, that his experts can make them, that we're anxious to give him an in-depth briefing on the Agency's role in the SALT process. They're getting fed up with us downtown, George, and if we don't get moving, they'll just go without us."

"I'll do my best. Now, what about Tyuratam?"

Peters was a first-rate summarizer when he was in a hurry. "Test launchers," he began, "are not counted under the ICBM launcher limits. We have about a hundred at Cape Canaveral and on the West Coast; the Soviets have about a hundred at Tyuratam. As you know, however, among them are eighteen launchers that have never been used in test-firings. They are part of the operational force." Peters ran quickly through the evidence. The conclusion was quite firm. "Furthermore," he added, "we've briefed the congressional committees on it. There's no way the Senate is going to ratify a treaty that lets the Sovs sneak away with eighteen extra launchers."

"Why'd you tell the Congress?"

"No holdbacks there, George. We tell the committees everything we tell the White House. They'd find out anyway, so it's much safer to volunteer it." He went on. "Now your problem in Geneva is how to press the Soviets on this without jeopardizing our intelligence sources and methods. The fact that they've never been test-fired, that snow cover isn't removed, that the major equipment around the site is different, all that's okay to use. But this other stuff is too sensitive, too vulnerable to countermeasures if they catch on. The delegation will be getting an instruction on this after the recess. You can brief them on all the evidence, but make damn sure they understand what's releasable to the Soviets and what isn't.

"And remember, it's CIA's issue. That means mine here in Washington and yours in Geneva. Lots of SALT people would prefer we'd never raised it. To them, it's just another complication."

"Not Walt O'Rourke," Inigo grinned. "I get plenty of support on Tyuratam from him. Almost makes me wonder what I'm doing wrong."

The buzzer sounded on Peters's phone and his self-importance glowed faintly. "Right. I hadn't forgotten. Two o'clock in the west wing. Is the car ready?" Rising to leave, he looked earnestly at Inigo.

"And let me know how it goes with the director, will you? Don't forget."

Inigo walked the halls, depressed. Everyone had variations of the same story. The director was uninterested in South America; people paid too much attention to it. For Middle Eastern intelligence he relied on what the Israelis told him. There had been one disastrous session with the economists. And as for military intelligence, he made no bones about his belief that it should be left to the Pentagon.

"It won't last," Inigo told his dispirited colleagues. "They'll teach him."

"Who'll teach him?"

"The boys downtown. The White House. State. All he needs is to make a fool of himself in a few high-level meetings. Preferably one including the president. You see, right now he's afraid of us. Scared we'll capture him, take him into camp. He'll find out he needs us soon enough."

"Meanwhile you're off skiing in the Alps."

"Well, there is such a thing as foresight. Some have it, some don't." But teasing did nothing to lift the gloom.

Toward the end of the afternoon he went round to Elton's office. Slow-spoken, thoughtful, unflappable, Elton was one of the last of the old-timers. He'd joined up in 1948, when everyone was an amateur, surviving by avoiding bureaucratic passions and making steady, sound judgments. He shrugged off his coat and got them coffee.

"Just back from the wars, eh, George? You should try some of the battles around here."

"Rough going, is it?"

"Well, take just now. I've come from a two-hour meeting at State, where I tried to explain why all the intelligence estimates are being held up. The NSC staff was there too. Everybody had a wonderful time beating up on me."

"What did you tell them?"

"Finally, the truth. That the director isn't satisfied with the way we do estimates. That he has the entire process under review. That until he's finished, they'll just have to wait."

"And is he really reviewing the estimates process himself?"

Elton rubbed his mouth and gazed at Inigo. "How should I know? But I doubt it somehow. My guess is that Colonel Blom is doing it."

"Colonel Blom?"

"You don't know Blom? Very mysterious character. Been with the director since birth, it seems. Taken along on each new assignment. Reads all the incoming. Sits in all the meetings, in the back."

"Any intelligence background?"

"How could he, riding the director's coattails for his whole career? Next you'll be asking me whether he is intelligent, and I have no idea. He says next to nothing. Just sends out little memos saying the director wants a complete review of such and such by next Tuesday. My fantasy is that when I'm fired, it will be by memo from Blom."

"I'm seeing the director tomorrow. Blom, too, from what you say." Inigo leaned forward. "Any tips?"

"Well, you could fall ill and cancel. No, I'm only joking. Don't expect him to know much about who you are or how the Agency has organized its SALT work. Don't cross him directly; he's got no tolerance for that. Try to suggest that you're there to help him, and that the rest of us are too. Just answer his questions and report back anything that the rest of us would find helpful. And try not to be put off by his martinet manner. Remember that actually he's afraid of us. Good luck."

It was midafternoon. Inigo went down to Administration and helped them find a regulation that would cover the cost of renting a car in Geneva. On an impulse, he asked them to reserve a return flight for tomorrow afternoon. There was nothing more for him at headquarters after the interview with the director, and the place was too depressing for him to hang around. He would spend the rest of the recess touring Burgundy.

Going up in the elevator next morning, he felt happy and expectant. Before seeing the director, he was going to spend two hours with the telemetry specialists. Talking to the analysts always cheered Inigo up. Here were the troops, the fellows who knew the facts, the foundation on which the Agency rested. They were eager and expert; they loved to respond to interest from above. And thorough: They knew how to distinguish between what they were certain of, what was a probability, and what was informed speculation. They made him remember himself in the early days, when he was the reigning American expert on a small corner of the Soviet economy. None of the jobs that followed, as he moved up the ladder, had been so thoroughly satisfying.

Telemetry analysis was only one of the many tools with which the United States monitored Soviet weapons programs and checked on possible SALT violations. But it was important and, worst of all, acutely vulnerable to Soviet countermeasures. The word itself was a modern invention, adapted from Greek roots and meaning "measurement from afar," just as the word *television* had been coined to represent "vision from afar." Every rocket had hundreds of components, each of which had to operate perfectly to ensure a normal flight. Thus the engineers needed a continuous record of the performance of each component, particularly in trying to track back from flight deviations and disasters to discover exactly what had gone wrong. In theory the data could be recorded and stored aboard the missile, but in that case not much of it would survive the final impact. So it was all radioed back to earth continuously during the flight, an enormous stream of numbers reporting on the performance of each component in terms of such variables as pressure and temperature.

What the Soviet missile engineers needed to do their job, the U.S. intelligence analysts also needed to do theirs.

But the Soviets controlled the telemetry. If a code machine aboard the missile encrypted the numbers before they were radioed out, they could decrypt them later on the ground. The Americans, lacking the keys to the encryption, would find no meaning in the numbers they had intercepted. They would be blinded.

Encrypted telemetry had already begun to appear in a few Soviet test flights, threatening the U.S. capacity to monitor SALT. Washington was pushing hard for an agreed ban on encryption in the treaty, and CIA was warning loudly that without such a ban, it could not verify Soviet compliance with a number of its provisions. Moscow was resisting, just as hard. The United States, it said, had no "right" to such information.

For two hours, Inigo and the telemetry experts immersed themselves in the details. Then it was time for him to report to the director's office.

"It's Mr. Inigo, isn't it? Please have a seat. The director will be with you shortly." The outer office was strangely bare; Jane had taken a lifetime collection of plants with her. A tall, stooped man emerged from the director's private office, looking weary and discouraged. Inigo recognized Stewart Marcus, chief of the Operations Directorate, but Marcus looked straight ahead as he trudged out.

A slight, slightly ridiculous figure appeared in the doorway. A crew cut, of all things, Inigo thought. A redheaded crew cut!

"George Inigo?"

"Yes."

"Come in please. I'm Colonel Blom." No handshake was offered. Blom marched Inigo the length of the room to where the director sat behind a massive desk, correcting a memorandum. They stood silently waiting for him to look up.

The director was a strikingly handsome man. Regular features were organized around a strong thin nose. Black eyebrows contrasted with nearly white hair. His concentration was total; he seemed to feel himself entirely alone with his memorandum. When he finally slapped down a red fountain pen and snapped his head up, his eyes were a piercing blue.

"Mr. George Inigo, sir," Blom intoned. "Back from the SALT negotiations in Geneva." He discreetly indicated a chair at the corner of the desk, and Inigo sat down in it.

The director gave Inigo a long stare.

"How did I get you as my personal representative on the delegation, Inigo?" The voice matched the blue eyes.

"Inheritance, sir. Your predecessor appointed me. You merely inherited me." He knew better than to smile as he held the director's gaze.

"Well, report. You have eight minutes."

"The negotiations are moving along slowly." Inigo, entirely uncertain what the man wanted to hear, went on. "So far the Soviets seem to be coming our way, very grudgingly." He paused, but got no hint.

"The intelligence issues seem to be in fairly good shape." He stopped.

"That's all?"

"I'm not sure I know what you want me to address, sir."

His eyes never leaving Inigo's face, the director leaned back in his chair and put his fingertips together in front of his chest.

"Well, perhaps you would summarize the state of the negotiations for me."

"Not in eight minutes, I'm afraid. You see, the draft of SALT Two is already forty—"

"Why not?"

Inigo pushed his temper down. "The draft is forty-one pages long and still growing. That length is at American insistence. We're determined to define every term and close every loophole, which wasn't done in SALT One. To our subsequent regret."

"You think it's a good treaty?"

"It's a modest treaty, sir." Inigo sensed a trap. "It's not up to Intelligence to make policy judgments about it. We simply supply data on Soviet forces and our monitoring capabilities."

"Walt O'Rourke doesn't think much of it." The trap sprung on empty air.

"Yes, that seems to be clear. The rumors in the delegation are that he'll resign and oppose it."

"He seems to feel he's entitled to a little more support from you."

"It's not my job to support a policy position."

"Then what am I supposed to think? You're my personal representative."

"If I may say so, I think the negotiations are going to be one of your main priorities, sir. There are a lot of important intelligence issues, such as the range of the Backfire bomber, the telemetry encryption problem, the data base. There's the whole question of the confidence with which we can monitor Soviet compliance with each provision."

"And you can't explain these to me?"

Inigo looked at his watch. "Not in four minutes, sir. Guy Peters has an excellent command of all these matters. You might want to let him brief you in detail." He ceased and held his breath.

Without moving his eyes, the director waved a hand at Blom, who made a note. "When are you going back to Geneva, Inigo?"

"This afternoon, sir." He prayed that the director didn't know that the recess still had five days to run.

"Then you'd better get cracking. Thank you." His eyes dropped to the memorandum on his desk. Blom stood up and Inigo followed suit. Together they moved toward the door. As they reached it, the director called across the room.

"And Inigo!"

He stopped and turned. The gaze was upon him again.

"Next time you want an appointment with me, have a better reason."

14

The day after he got back from Washington, Inigo picked up a rented Renault. It took only a little argument to get the diplomatic discount. He was working late at the delegation that evening, developing the counterarguments to the Soviet objections to the MIRVed launcher counting rules. When he finished his briefing notes, he meant to go straight home to bed, but as he emerged from the building, the warmth of an unseasonable winter night excited him. He decided to go for a slow drive along the north side of the lake.

The highway was empty for the first few minutes. Then headlights appeared in his rearview mirror. The distance between them collapsed rapidly; the fellow must have been doing 120 kilometers an hour. Inigo edged over to the right as he was overtaken, but instead of completing the passing maneuver, the big black car adjusted to the speed of his little Renault and began to crowd sideward toward him.

Inigo swore, floored the accelerator, and glanced across the narrow space between the two cars. Two men sat in the front seat, staring fixedly ahead behind the darkly tinted glass of the side window. Effortlessly the car—it was a Mercedes—matched Inigo's burst of speed; inexorably it drifted rightward toward him. A bridge loomed ahead.

He jammed on his brakes and the Mercedes bounded forward, swerving into his lane a foot beyond his left fender. He saw the black car's brake lights come on. Sweating, he circled in a U-turn and raced back toward Geneva.

He was not pursued.

15

Erika awoke, as always, two minutes before the alarm was set to go off. She needed only ten seconds to be fully returned to the world. Was there a prealarm, she wondered, some thin, very high note above the normal threshold, that woke her subconscious mind and was the real start of the day?

The thought itself was only half-conscious, and it skittered away as she stepped into the shower. A mild erotic warmth spread through her body as she soaped it, first vigorously, then gently. Men aren't the only ones who enjoy you, she told it, caressing her belly and breasts. When she switched to the cold water, she would have liked to dig her fingertips into her scalp, but a few hard rubs through the shower cap were all she could have. Hair-washing was for evenings; her thick roan mane took over an hour to dry.

Today was going to be tedious and tiresome. Her team had finished its three weeks on the reactor, firing short, invisible bursts of neutrons, seeking out little particles of bombardment on the plates. Now their allotment of reactor-hours had run out. They had nearly all the data they wanted, but Erika would have liked to spend another day or two chasing isotopes. Instead it was time to array the results for computer processing. It was the part of the work that she liked the least, since she knew the least about it. The big CERN computer, with capabilities far beyond those that had been available to her at home or in the USSR, intimidated her. Although she was deputy team leader, she always turned into the student of her Western colleagues when the computer stage was reached.

And she would have to deal with Chandaree. Zubin Chandaree, the team leader, was an Indian only a little older than she. Erika had been assigned to his team when she arrived, and sometimes she wondered whether he hadn't somehow managed to arrange that in advance. "Just call me Zoobie," he had smiled at her when they first met, white teeth shining in a dark face. When the deputy position became vacant a few months later, he had put her into it, overbearing the objections of others and her own doubts. "I need you there. Someone I can rely on as my number two." But she knew she didn't deserve it; there were others more qualified.

It was clear that by number two Chandaree meant woman, not physicist. Erika had no objections of principle to a married man. She had had several such affairs and had discovered that it was men who worried about the principle of fidelity. She practiced fidelity herself—the alternatives were too confusing—but without its being an issue for her. In her experience, infidelity was to men first a terrific stimulus, then a complication, and, finally, if the affair lasted long enough, an unbearable sin. Chandaree, she thought, might prove to be an exception, but only because his unshakable arrogance left no room for guilt feelings.

It was pleasanter, as she finished an orange and downed her coffee, to think about the American. Inigo had no arrogance, as far as she could see. The problem was more of shyness, which had a certain charm and was usually, in Erika's experience, temporary. It meant that she might have to exert herself more at the beginning, but that didn't violate any principles either. It was of course always nice to be pursued, but the feeling of control that it gave her never lasted. Shyness didn't mean weakness, she knew, and once it was gotten past, it often gave way to strong and demanding. If it took some initial pursuit on her part to reach that stage, and the man seemed worth it, she was willing. This one, so far, seemed worth it.

They were going out to dinner for the first time tonight and she could find out what he was like when he wasn't tired. She knew him only from three ski Sundays, which had taught her that in the mornings he was amiable but sleepy and, after a day on the slope, exhausted but still amiable. His skiing amused her. It seemed to express something very American, headlong, ungraceful, courageous, exciting. A thought struck her as she pulled her apartment door closed and heard the lock click: I wonder which way he makes love, tender or crazy?

"You chose very nicely," Inigo said as the waiter tucked them into a windowside table. They were in a small, stylish restaurant on the lower slopes of the Jura. A fine mist blurred the lights of Geneva lying below and beyond. "You know, I never would have expected to find such a fine restaurant in such a plain little village. We don't have such things in America. We hardly have villages, in fact."

"We are in France," she replied. "The French eat well as often as they can. This food is better than in Geneva, and the price is lower too. It is easy to find such places here, if only you ask."

There was a long discussion of the elaborate menu, with Erika interpreting the culinary vocabulary between Inigo and the waiter. Then a shorter study of the wine list, which she left to him. Most men, she had learned, didn't welcome a woman's help in certain things: starting a log fire, mounting a horse, choosing a wine.

"So." He finished and looked at her. "A German and an American living in Switzerland and dining in France."

"It is not so unusual. I am sure it has happened before."

"Not to me."

"But to other Americans surely. Only perhaps not so often with a German who is an East German."

"Yes, I've never met an East German before. Except for a couple of defectors."

She frowned. " 'Refugee' is a nicer word. It is different for us, you know. East Germans do not become exiles in Paris or the United States. If they want to leave, they have another Germany to go to."

"And the same with West Germans?"

"Please do not make fun of us. You know that West Germans do not move to East Germany."

"You misunderstand." He seemed on the point of denying he had meant to tease, then stopped. "Excuse me. I'm sorry."

"One should always be sincere," she said. Hearing her own words, she was dismayed at their priggish sound. Couldn't one also be lighthearted at times? Yes, one could and one often was. She had shown him that in the mountains. So why was she being so boring now?

He took off the glasses he had used to read the wine list. In the candlelight the brown of his eyes was darker than it had been on the slopes.

"I know a little of West Germany, but I'll probably never get to your country. What is it like?"

Erika was accustomed to the condescension of Westerners, but this one might really be interested.

"Not much different from the other Germany in most respects. A little less of some things, a little more of others." She waited to be asked again.

"Less of what, more of what?"

"Less of the material things, of course. Good things are harder to find: clothing, furniture, cosmetics. Apartments are small with us. It takes a long time to buy a car. Years."

"And more of what?"

"That is hard to say, since I have never been to West Germany. More security, I suppose. We do not worry about losing our jobs. There is competition among us, of course, but I have the impression that it is not so nervous and intense as in the West. And we are spared many things. The pornography, the warmongering, the exploitation by the rich."

How had they gotten into such a political discussion? She was talking a silly mixture of belief and official propaganda, not at all in line with her statement about always being sincere. Politics always bored her. But he seemed to be genuinely interested. Best to let him talk.

"And I also shall probably never visit your country. Tell me about it."

"Not to be understood. Much too big to be explained. Full of contradictions. I can show you in terms of skiing. We have New England, with not much snow, where the trails turn icy every week or so. We have the area around Washington, where I work, Pennsylvania and West Virginia, where the snowmaking machines try to stay ahead of the sun's warmth and fail most of the time. You find yourself skiing on wet grass down small mountains with ten thousand other people. Only some of them are skiers. Then we have the Rockies, big as the Alps and running way up into Canada. Deep snows, room for everybody, and they complain when there's no fresh powder for two days."

"I have only met some Americans. They seem quite different from Europeans. In your movies, too."

"How so?"

She paused to think. How to put it without seeming to be insulting? "They think that it is all right to want everything. That they will succeed in having everything. They expect everyone to like them, without their having to try."

"Well, yes, it's our history, you see." But she didn't let him go on.

"They do not understand that it takes time to build personal relationships. They are extremely friendly and easy to meet—we are a little jealous of that, you know—but one wonders how good friends they will be in the end."

She stopped. This time Inigo waited. Am I saying something about him? she wondered. About the two of us?

"It is as if they do not know about tragedy, as if they do not have it in their bones as we do. They are not ripe." She searched for English words. "Not seasoned, do you say?"

"I think I know what you mean. It's what makes Europeans seem so cynical to us. Tired. As though they always expected the worst. I guess our optimism just seems silly to you."

"Oh no, it is a very attractive quality."

"But childish?"

"A little. Childlike, I would rather say. It makes us feel older, wiser. I suppose that allows us to feel superior. But I think that feeling of superiority also hides our envy. You are envied, you Americans."

Back at her apartment, she went into the kitchen to fix drinks. A nice man, she thought. One can speak openly with him and he does not become offended. But what had she been saying about Americans being impatient, wanting relationships too quickly? Surely he must have felt that she was pushing him away. Was she?

"Do you want ice?" she called out.

Instead of answering he came into the kitchen. She was standing at the counter, her back to him. She felt him move quietly up behind her and touch her upper arm.

They stood silently for a moment, without moving. Then, still facing away from him, forcing her voice to be calm, she spoke.

"How long did you say you will remain in Geneva?"

"About five more months. Maybe six."

She turned into his arms.

"And I only a little longer than that. So perhaps we should get started now."

"I slept with Claude a couple of times last year," she told him a few weeks later, when they had become comfortable with each other in bed. "Somehow we did not succeed. So we stopped."

Inigo lifted his mouth from her lightly curved belly. "Do you see him during the week?"

"Oh no, just on our ski trips. We are good friends in the mountains, that is all."

"But we succeed, you and I, don't we?" He grinned at her. "Yes, darling, we succeed very much. We have a big success." She tugged him up across her breasts and pulled his head down. She stuck her tongue into his ear, and as Inigo squirmed in delight and pulled away, she whispered, "We are a hit. I think you say that, no? A big hit."

She had become one of the poles of Inigo's life in Geneva. They skied together every weekend of that wonderful winter, usually with the friends on one-day bus trips, but sometimes alone together on a two-day trip to some other distant resort. There was a magical weekend at Zermatt, where they awoke on Sunday morning to see the Matterhorn towering over the village, the bulk in shadow and only the famous hooked peak wreathed in golden sunshine, surrounded by small pink clouds; it looked simultaneously like a bad postcard and a Renaissance masterpiece. Not knowing whether to gasp or laugh, they did both.

Their lovemaking was, to Inigo, a revelation. He had little experience with a woman other than his wife, and he sometimes winced when he recalled how young and ignorant they had been. He had only read, not really believing it, of women who became as readily aroused and climaxed as continuously as Erika did. By turns quiet and tender, then vigorous and demanding, she utterly destroyed his old conviction that sex was a favor granted by women to men. Inigo's hands and mouth made expeditions that were new to him, absorbingly thrilling. He marveled at himself, at forty-eight years, virile several times a night. The freedom that he felt was overwhelming. Sometimes their caresses floated him into a long, slow hypnosis, drunk upon her intoxicating body, scarcely able to tell leg from arm, or indeed woman from man. When this went on too long, she had to shake him out of his trance, frightened at the total anesthesia of his mind.

"George," she murmured.

"Yes."

"It is very good, is it not? For you, I think."

He rolled toward her with a dreamy smile, fitting his exhausted body to hers.

"It's very, very good."

"For me too," she said.

"I'm glad."

"Does it not worry you that it is so good? Because it is also crazy, you know. An East German physicist and a American diplomat."

Silence.

"It will turn out to be dangerous somehow. Do you think so?"

But Inigo had fallen asleep.

16

There were other bits and pieces, but they didn't change the picture much.

The Australian journalist who lived one floor above Inigo had invited him to one of his parties. He reported to Rudenko's man that the American held his liquor well. Inigo had easily repelled the advances of a semi-attractive and thoroughly willing young lady from the Canadian consulate. He had made himself popular as a conversationalist and piano player. He had left before the orgy began.

Inigo was an easy subject to tail. He took no precautions and seemed oblivious to street surveillance. This was not particularly bothersome to Smirnov; countermeasures could easily be taught. He was somewhat more worried when the surveillance revealed that Inigo had abandoned Hickok's practice of visiting his office briefly on Saturday mornings. It bespoke a certain lack of thoroughness. His anxiety dissolved, however, when the telephone taps revealed that Inigo called in every Saturday to ask whether there were any nonroutine cables for him. There never were; Hickok's visits had been unnecessary, a sign of the man's vanity.

The time to move was approaching. Rudenko was beginning to press him, albeit circumspectly, since Smirnov was a colonel and Rudenko only a major. It was a regrettable complication that Rudenko was involved at all, but he was the Geneva KGB resident, and there was no chance of operating behind his back. Besides, he controlled the local resources. Rudenko would have to be handled with the utmost care.

17

Someone had shot Hickok. Killed him, in fact.

There was no getting away from it. *Someone had shot Hickok* pulled at Inigo's mind once more as he snaked out of the traffic headed for the Lausanne freeway and began to maneuver through Versoix, the first of the lakeshore villages on the way to Coppet. *Someone shot Hickok* brought back the old familiar bafflement as he edged around a small truck and passed the little sign to Mies. Carson was insisting that she was as much in the dark as ever about it, and Inigo was inclined to believe her. Neither Cornett nor Elton had volunteered any rumors when he was back at Langley. Indeed, they hadn't mentioned Hickok at all, and Inigo for some strange reason hadn't either; evidently they hadn't heard he was dead. But the fact remained: *Someone shot Hickok* and killed him.

Lindy had been full of possibilities. Suicide? That sounded absurd, a product of hysteria. A bullet in the head, yes, but not another one in the knee. A jealous husband? Sheer speculation; no evidence. Our own people? It was true that Hickok had been in some kind of trouble with headquarters. Lormack had made that clear. But enough to be executed? In the tunnel to his own apartment courtyard? Not to be believed.

That left the Soviets. That's where my train of logic always ends up, Inigo thought. But again, what could have been the motive? Carson had told him repeatedly that the KGB, like the CIA, considered it very bad form to murder a member of the opposing service. No one knew what that might lead to. They would do it, she assured him, only if the target was on the verge of blowing one of their top-priority operations, something absolutely vital. It was hard to fit Hickok into that role. And even then, they would have proceeded with the utmost care and subtlety.

An idea occurred to him, and not for the first time. Smirnov knows. That's why the bastard keeps after me about those "family reasons."

He wants to know how much I know, whether I've found out something since the last time he inquired.

Inigo pulled into the parking lot, turned off the motor, and sat quietly for a moment, trying to think. If Smirnov did know, that was powerful evidence for the idea that the Soviets were the killers. Carson had said that was rare, but not impossible. And if that were the case, then the reason surely involved SALT. It was ridiculous to imagine that Hickok had gotten involved in some other, unrelated secret operation. A hypothesis began to take on a dim shape in his mind. Some sort of espionage had been taking place between Hickok and Smirnov. It could have been that Hickok was the traitor, although he couldn't imagine why. Or Smirnov, though that seemed even more fantastic. But whatever it was, maybe Hickok had threatened to expose it. To torpedo the negotiations, perhaps.

It didn't make any sense.

Nevertheless, *someone shot Hickok.* Smirnov kept pressing him about it. Should he tell him that Hickok was dead? But if Smirnov already knew that, wouldn't he be stepping into some sort of trap? The same trap, perhaps, that Hickok had stepped into? And ended up getting shot.

The Hotel du Lac proved to be a cavernous nineteenth-century pile, probably originally a town hall, directly on the main square. He feared for the cuisine; none of his delegation had ever eaten there. With time heavy on their hands during the evenings and weekends, the Americans were avid restaurant-seekers. Discussing the treaty among themselves, they never took notes, but let someone mention a newly discovered restaurant and out came the notebooks and pens. It was a bad omen that no one had tried the Hotel du Lac.

The great dining hall was darkened by curtains against the brilliance of the afternoon. At first it seemed empty, but then Inigo spied a couple in the far corner, chatting quietly with an aged waiter. A movement in the opposite corner drew his eye. It was Smirnov, waiting.

"I took the liberty of choosing a table, since I arrived ahead of you." He rolled to his feet as Inigo approached. For a moment his round, short body looked like one of those bottom-weighted dolls that can be knocked over but always bobs back up. And he is a bit like that, Inigo thought. He's taken a lot of insults from me and never shown real damage; he's never withdrawn or lost his temper. He behaves better now; I guess I've knocked a few sharp corners off him. He does his job, enjoys it when he can, doesn't fret when he can't. There's a sort of durability in him that has to be respected.

The lunch was uneventful. Inigo had filet of perch, always a safe bet around Lake Leman. Smirnov inquired, as he often did, about the mood of the Senate about SALT. He seemed to be responsible to his delegation for U.S. politics or perhaps he just liked to make political chitchat. Inigo took the opportunity to tell him that three senators visiting Geneva had discovered that the Tyuratam Eighteen alone were capable of annihilating all the inhabitants of their three states. They would certainly be reading the treaty carefully to discover the disposition of these launchers. Smirnov smiled and congratulated him on the ingenuity of his argument, wondering aloud who had raised the question with the senators and done the computation for them.

The only unusual thing was that Smirnov declined dessert.

"I would like to introduce a new subject into our discussions," he said after the waiter had brought the check.

"Yes?"

"It is a difficult and complicated theme." He paused. His aplomb suddenly deserted him and he flushed deeply. "Today I will merely raise it. I would like you to think about it and pursue it with me further tomorrow night at dinner, when I hope you will be my guest." Another pause. "Mrs. Smirnov will not be joining us."

Inigo was completely bewildered.

"I begin by telling you that I have been making observations of you. Conducting an assessment, you might say."

A warning light flashed on in Inigo's head. "And now you are going to present me with an analysis of my personality?"

"Of your character, it would be better to say. And please, this time allow me to ask you the favor of not interrupting." Inigo sat back, all attention.

"You are a strong man, Mr. Inigo. You assert yourself firmly and do not allow yourself to be bullied. At the same time you have a sympathetic mind." Smirnov spoke with slow deliberation. "I feel that you have a good instinct for understanding the concerns of others. I believe, for example, that you understand me, although it may be that I will surprise you in some respects.

"Your political views are sensible and moderate, in the American context. You are clearly devoted to the success of SALT. We have not spoken before about our mutual profession. In terms of its requirements, I find you quite conscious of security considerations but perhaps not sufficiently suspicious. It helps, you know, to be a little paranoid. But I understand that your experience has been in analysis, not field operations.

"You have a temper, Mr. Inigo. That is good. It is even better that you always keep it under control. When situations of danger arise, you are neither cowardly nor rash. You are realistic. This is good in our profession, and it is good in life as well."

Smirnov gazed for a moment at the wall.

"Your relationships with others seem to be honest and steady. There is a stubbornness in you"—he swung his head and looked intently into Inigo's eyes—"that is a worry. It goes with strength of character, but it may be excessive. None of us, however, is perfect. Certainly including myself." A smile, and he leaned back and stopped talking. He seemed to be finished.

Inigo was outraged. What did this man take him for? Was he really about to make a proposition? Was this how Hickok's doom had begun?

"Do you mean by all this that you are proposing to recruit me?"

"No." An absolute seriousness suddenly came over Smirnov's face. "You have it precisely wrong. I told you that I might surprise you.

"It is you, Mr. Inigo, who shall recruit me." And then, with a strange formality, "I wish to defect to the United States of America."

18

Inigo could scarcely remember driving back to Geneva. He had already passed the U.S. mission and was halfway across the bridge heading for the Vieille Ville when he woke up to his surroundings. There was no question of returning to the office. He maneuvered the Renault up the hill, through the gate, and into a parking space near his apartment. He was not ready to go home yet; he needed the reality of strangers. Walking down to the picturesque old square, the Bourg de Four, he found a tiny table at the outdoor café.

Smirnov had told him nothing more. He would explain his motives, he said, tomorrow night at dinner. Also the specifics of his proposal. Each would want certain things from the other. It would be a negotiation, like a treaty, serving the interests of both sides. Yes, he would explain how he had come to learn so much about Inigo. For now, his only request was that nothing be said to anyone until they had talked again. "No cables, no conversations with your Mrs. Carson." Soon, others would have to be involved, but for the moment absolute secrecy was required.

The thought of Carson led his mind further. At their first meeting, she had mentioned a tacit Soviet-American agreement that the KGB and CIA would not tamper with each other's delegation. What did that mean, a tacit agreement? Was it, Inigo wondered, merely an American presumption? Maybe the KGB had no such compunctions. Smirnov's offer could be the first step in a complicated plot to recruit Inigo. Perhaps Hickok had become ensnared in just such a plot.

There was also the opposite possibility, he thought, the opposite route to the same result. Smirnov might be posing as a genuine defector in order to create a body of evidence—contacts, tape recordings, exchanged documents—that the KGB could later use to charge CIA with an attempted recruitment.

His most insistent thought now was of Hickok. Was this the sort of thing that had led to his predecessor's disgrace and death? He recalled Lormack's hints. The man was naïve, careless, therefore dangerous. That had been easy for Inigo to disregard as typical spy talk until Lindy Hickok had arrived. From the Agency he had heard no more of Hickok's fate. Presumably Counterintelligence was still investigating. At any rate, he had to keep the Hickok story in mind as the gravest of the dangers surrounding Smirnov's proposal.

Apart from that, Inigo could only speculate on that astonishing offer and other motives that might lie behind it. Smirnov was in trouble with Moscow and had to bolt? Some past transgression had come to light? Or he was a secret anti-Communist who had reached the limits of his endurance. His father, like the father of Colonel Mayorsky, the famous spy, had been murdered by Stalin, and the son burned for vengeance against the Soviet state. He was greedy; he wanted a million dollars. He had come upon his wife's infidelities and needed to put his whole past behind him. There was a woman waiting in New York. He was driven by such narcissistic ambition that if he could not achieve fame in the Soviet Union, he would compensate with notoriety in the United States.

Suddenly a clear thought emerged. None of the speculations made any difference. Whatever the KGB thought, the Americans had forsworn recruitment efforts against the Soviet delegation. To accept and work with a defector was tantamount to recruitment. If he went forward with this crazy idea, Jenkins would put him aboard the next plane out of Geneva. That settled the matter.

But the moment Inigo fastened onto this conclusion, new questions arose. How had Smirnov come to know so much about him, to have such a confident judgment of his character? Perhaps he was under surveillance; despite Carson's warning, he had never paid much attention to the possibility, here under peaceful Swiss skies. Perhaps his apartment was watched, his telephone tapped. But there was nothing in all this with which to coerce him into treason.

Suddenly, Erika.

The idea struck him like a palpable blow.

An East German. On assignment in the West. Frantically he tried to recall exactly how they had met. She had helped him up after a fall. Yes, she had spoken first at the bus when the day ended. It would not have been difficult to discover that he was a skier and, that before he got a car, he would be taking the weekend ski bus. In fact, he'd talked about it on the phone, to Michaels or Morgan or someone.

Well, there was nothing to do but have it out with Smirnov. He could sit here and get furious with him, with Erika, with himself for being such a fool, and then flip over to attack himself as distrustful, paranoid, unworthy of her. None of that was going to help. He had to maintain an open mind. Moreover, if the worst were true, there was nothing in his relations with Erika that would make him vulnerable to blackmail.

Only vulnerable to deception, to treachery. To outrage and pain.

Inigo ordered another coffee and forced his mind to become a blank. The square was filling up as the afternoon waned. Students began to crowd the café, his second chair was commandeered, standees stared at him in hopes that he would leave. The small Bourg de Four had two levels, five entrances, and a big fountain in the center, providing a maelstrom of traffic that was comfortable to contemplate. It was like watching riptides meet off a complicated shoreline. The sunlight marched slowly up the faces of the buildings opposite, a chill grew in the air, and behind him the cathedral bells slowly tolled a sonorous six notes.

Inigo heaved himself up and plodded across the square, daring the crawling automobiles to hit him. He had not once, he admitted wryly to himself, stopped thinking about Erika at all. She stood at the center of his present life, nearer than anyone else, an essential part of his hopes, his image of himself in Geneva. He could give her up, of course he could give her up. But what a great loneliness stood beyond that.

Well, he thought bitterly, as he reached his street, if they are together, they seem to have screwed up on one detail. I have dinner dates with each of them for the same night. The irony of that helped a little, until he imagined Erika appearing together with Smirnov in the restaurant tomorrow evening. No, he refused to believe that. But no, he couldn't dismiss it as impossible either.

His apartment was only a hundred paces from the square, up a narrow street four meters from curb to curb, flanked by sidewalks one person wide. The sun penetrated between the five- and six-story buildings only twice a day, at noon along a southerly cross street and later from the western end. It had always been full of charm for Inigo, with its tiny ground-floor shops and heavy pedestrian traffic, for which one constantly had to step off the curb. Now it seemed hostile, full of menace. There was the bar of the near-fight. Here was a doorway that would make an excellent observation post. He wondered if someone had earned an afternoon's pay today watching him sit motionless at a café table. Mounting the stairs, he remembered Harry's apartment, one floor above his; was Harry's party a part of it? Across the courtyard, where a large window faced his living room, the lights were almost always off. Angrily he pulled the drapes.

He went to the phone. No point in waiting.

"Hello?"

"Erika, it's George."

"George dear. How are you?" Pleasure in her voice.

"Fine. Listen, I'm not going to be able to make it tomorrow night."

"Oh, that is too bad. Is something the matter?"

"No, I just have to work very late tomorrow night."

"What a pity." A little coldness.

What if I'm wrong? "Could we make it the next night?"

"The next night? That would be Wednesday. No, I am not free on Wednesday evening." He was sure now that he could hear a little coldness.

"Thursday then?"

"Thursday? I cannot be sure about Thursday. Call me tomorrow and I will be able to tell you."

"All right. I'll call you about this time tomorrow. I'm sorry, Erika." He was not sorry, he was miserable.

"So am I, George. Good-bye now." The line went dead.

Smirnov, you bastard, I hope you enjoy hearing that little conversation.

19

Smirnov was sitting alone when he arrived, but Inigo could not refrain from a radarlike scan of the restaurant as he came in. There were no return blips, no Erika, no German thugs, no one else from the Soviet delegation. They greeted each other gravely. Inigo put down the menu that Smirnov handed him, folded his arms on the table, and unceremoniously began.

"Mr. Smirnov, I have to tell you that what you have suggested is completely impossible."

"What would you like to drink, Mr. Inigo?" Smirnov sat back and smiled. "You are being a workaholic, I fear. Even in the most tense of times, one must live well. Surely you agree?"

"Surely. Scotch on the rocks. But you have my answer."

"You are behaving like a Soviet diplomat," Smirnov teased. "Or rather the Western caricature of one, with absolute demands and blunt rejections. But in fact a Soviet diplomat is trained carefully to listen to the proposals of his partner. And in this case I say 'partner,' not 'opponent.' "

Inigo gave him a frustrated stare, then picked up the enormous menu. Smirnov had chosen La Reserve, one of the most expensive in Geneva, patronized mostly by stupendously wealthy Arabs. Upstairs, it was rumored, there were elegant private gambling rooms where incredible sums passed from their indifferent hands into those of a motley band of European and Lebanese experts.

Inigo ordered oysters and *rognons de veau* while Smirnov plodded through the pages of the menu. He fancied himself a gourmet, but every time it came to a choice, his confidence deserted him. He's really searching for those barbecued spare ribs he loved in New York, Inigo thought maliciously. The silent joke calmed his nerves a bit and he took up the wine list. Smirnov had long since abandoned to him the task of selecting the wine.

"Now," Smirnov began when the waiter had carried off their order, "why do you find my suggestion so unacceptable that it cannot even be discussed?"

"Because it would destroy our negotiations."

"Do you really think so?"

"Of course. You are aware that there is an understanding between our two governments, and our two services, to refrain from such operations against SALT delegates. There is much hostility between our countries, and a scandal here could easily cause one side or the other to break off the talks."

"Not the Soviet side, I assure you. We take espionage for granted. But are you really so devoted to the success of SALT?"

"Extremely."

"Excellent. That is the chief aim of my proposal. I think we shall reach agreement." He gave Inigo a self-satisfied smile.

"That seems unlikely. But go ahead, if you want to explain." Inigo cautioned himself about possible hidden microphones and recorders; he must be careful of what he said.

"Very well. I see you are ready to listen. I will begin by explaining my motives. I wish to be quite methodical and thorough with you.

"As I said, my chief concern is precisely yours: the success of SALT. I do not know how you judge my sincerity on this matter, but I assure you that to me nothing in present world history is more important than this. Perhaps a Russian who fought the entire war on his native soil as a boy among the partisans can understand this even better than others." His voice checked before the last word; he had been about to say "an American."

"These negotiations have been going on here in Geneva for six years, Mr. Inigo, and still we are not finished!" His voice rose. "The Great Patriotic War lasted only five, and your part of the world war only four! I have been here for that entire time. I have seen our two sides bury themselves in trivial details while the Chinese stockpile their nuclear bombs, while the Indians and the Pakistanis and the South Africans master nuclear technology. You and I are forced to argue about eighteen launchers at Tyuratam—and by the way you are correct, they are operational launchers—while Iraq may be working toward a nuclear attack on Israel. Do you think our two countries can stay out of such wars? All of them? If the Chinese launch a nuclear missile against Taiwan, for example? Our two countries may produce sane leaders, but we are not alone in this world, Mr. Inigo, and someday even one of our leaders may make a fatal mistake."

Inigo moved to speak, but Smirnov waved his hand.

"Yes, I know, these are the thoughts of everyone. They even appear in the statements of our leading politicians. But are they acted upon? No. We behave as if we had endless time at our disposal. Your government constantly makes complicated new proposals on minor issues, and my government constantly resists, drags its feet as you say, and feeds your suspicions with our passion for secrecy. I see nothing to choose between Moscow and Washington on this matter, my friend, nothing at all. When the bombs start to explode, each will be equally guilty, although by then it won't matter how anyone assesses the blame.

"One more point, and then I shall be finished with this first theme. It is no secret that many of your countrymen, including influential persons, are opposed to this treaty and to improved Soviet-American relations. You may imagine that something of the same sort goes on in Moscow. If you do, you are correct. There are not a few marshals and ideologues who would be glad to seize upon some unfriendly American act to sabotage our efforts here. Suppose Washington signs an agreement for military cooperation with China? Do you think such people will not welcome the opportunity to withdraw the Soviet delegation from Geneva, or to stiffen our terms so as to prevent an agreement? Just as, if we should be forced into another police action in Eastern Europe, or do something that would arouse your overly acute sensitivities about Cuba, the American opponents of SALT would be delighted to inflame public opinion and reject our work here. This treaty is a terribly vulnerable thing, Mr. Inigo, perhaps a fatally fragile thing.

"There is another thing," Smirnov continued. "It is clear that President Brezhnev does not have much more time left to him. Your service perhaps knows more about his health than I do, but my friends in Moscow wonder whether he will last beyond this year. In the entire Politburo, he has always been the strongest supporter of SALT. After he is gone, who can say what will happen?

"But what worries me the most is the possibility that my own service is planning some operation that will sabotage the negotiations." Smirnov had lowered his voice and was leaning forward. "I say this carefully, since I know that you imagine my proposal could turn out to be exactly such an operation. But during the last recess"—his eyes narrowed and his voice dropped to a whisper—"I picked up hints from some colleagues in Moscow that we in Geneva might receive an unpleasant shock, from an unexpected direction. It was, they implied, a matter of weeks. They would not say more."

Smirnov stopped to rest a moment. Sweat had appeared on his forehead, and his round face was flushed and exhausted. An impressive performance, Inigo thought, waiting for him to go on.

"Please excuse me, my friend. I am making long speeches. It is necessary to do so now. These things will not have to be repeated later."

"Your sentiments do you great credit."

"But can you believe them? That is the question in your head right now. Am I not right?" He broke off and gazed at Inigo, who sat motionless and silent. "Of course I am right. Nothing I have said to you in our meetings has prepared you to believe that I attach such historic importance to the treaty. I have seemed not to take these negotiations seriously. In fact, I have worked hard to create that impression. It is important that no one on the delegations, particularly my own, should suspect my real feelings. It is much safer for me that way. And as you shall see, it is I who will be bearing the heaviest risks."

Except it was Hickok who got killed, Inigo thought. The waiter arrived; they fell silent.

"My proposal," Smirnov continued after he had gone, "is that you and I should arrange to complete SALT as soon as possible. On terms favorable to America."

Inigo slapped his palms on the tabletop and was about to speak, but Smirnov was faster.

"Hear me out. My government has already worked out, for the remaining disputed items, the concessions it is willing to make if necessary. I believe you call them fallback positions. These are the basis of my proposal. Please listen carefully. I offer to tell you what these concessions are. I will give you the fallbacks."

"And in return?"

"Why, you must use them to hasten the negotiations. You will be able to present to us our own proposals, proposals that our delegation is already authorized to accept!"

Inigo grasped instantly the significance of his companion's offer. With the Soviet fallbacks in hand, they would no longer have to grope blindly toward agreement. The talks could be concluded within a few weeks. He fought down his excitement.

"And that is all?"

"No," Smirnov said shortly. "I have some personal requirements. But now I would like to stop for a while, to let you think it over."

"I understand one thing already. You are talking about treason. It is punishable by death."

"Yes," said Smirnov calmly, and began to eat.

Halfway through his salmon, he peered up at Inigo and asked, "Well, are you ready to discuss the details?"

"You talk as if I had already agreed to this idea of yours."

"Oh. I thought perhaps you had by now." And he returned to his meal.

When they had finished the entrée and ordered dessert, Smirnov gave Inigo a questioning look.

"So?"

"Perhaps you'd better give me what you call your personal requirements."

"Quite right. That is proper procedure. First, I require asylum in the United States after our work is finished. As you say, we are speaking of actions that under Soviet law carry the death penalty.

"Second, I require the means to live well. When I lived in New York, my pay and allowances were equal to an American income of forty-eight thousand dollars a year. I would not expect to need that amount indefinitely, for I would intend to earn my living. I want to work in the field of arms control. But I am abandoning not only my country but my pension and other benefits, which are substantial in my service."

"That's a very large sum. Nearly half a million dollars over ten years."

"Mr. Inigo"—Smirnov looked at him with a lordly expression—"at enormous risk, I am offering your country an opportunity that, among other things, will lead to the saving of billions of dollars in strategic weapons. I could have asked for a million dollars without deserving a reproach."

"Anything else?" Inigo checked his temper. Nothing was going to make Smirnov lovable.

"Secure and secret transportation from Switzerland to the United States for me and my wife, at the proper time, of course. And there is one other thing.

"You have heard me speak of my daughter. Ever since she left New York at the age of six, she has never stopped speaking of her desire to return. Indeed, it has been an embarrassment and even a danger to me. She presses me constantly to get another assignment in America, even though I tell her that with what is known about her sentiments, she would never be allowed to visit us.

"You are not a father, are you? I do not know whether you can understand the strength of a father's desire to make his daughter happy. As they say of us, in Russia, when a child is born, it's 'up against the wall!' for the parents. And for the father of a daughter, it goes on forever.

"So there you have my second motive. And my last personal requirement. You must bring my daughter from Moscow to America."

"And how am I to do that?"

"It will test the resources of your service, I am sure. But you have done it before. I know of at least one case myself."

"Oh? And how was that done?"

"We don't know even yet. It was several years ago. But this is what I require of your service. And now you know my entire proposal."

Inigo leaned back, signaled to the waiter, and ordered coffee. Smirnov waited for him to speak, but he remained silent.

I half believe him, Inigo thought. He really seemed sincere about SALT, and it's plausible that he despairs of it; I do myself sometimes. But what about a trap? He could have a recorder running right now. If I say the wrong thing, he can blow me out of the water tomorrow. He felt acutely the need for advice. And more than that, for authority to back him up. From no less than the director. There was a lot to suspect here. But the demand about the daughter, he thought, does make it seem more credible, since Smirnov must know that could be a sticking point for the Agency. Better keep my mouth shut, Inigo decided.

"I think you will need the approval of your new director," Smirnov cut in on his thoughts. "What sort of man is he? Have you met him?"

"Briefly."

"We understand that he is capable and ambitious. You will be offering him the chance for a major success at the very start of his work. My proposal may have a great appeal for him. But of course, I do not know his views on arms control. What are they, may I ask?"

Smirnov was pushing again. Inigo decided that it was time to take the initiative. And to find out what he had cooked up with Hickok.

"Did you make this proposal to Mr. Hickok?" he demanded.

"You don't know about that sad episode? Your agency is to be congratulated on its compartmentation." Smirnov leaned forward, forearms on the table. "With Mr. Hickok the situation was reversed. To begin with, I soon found him quite unsuitable for the purposes I had in mind. Too impetuous, too careless. This, by the way, explains some experiences that may have been puzzling to you. On occasion you have seemingly been placed in danger here in Geneva. In a bar one night, for example, and another time on the road to Lausanne. You were actually quite safe. The men who were dealing with you were well trained and carefully instructed. I arranged such episodes in order to discover how strong your nerves are. I hope you will forgive me. It was imperative that I be satisfied about you before I could risk putting myself, so to speak, in your hands.

"To return to Mr. Hickok, one day he suddenly surprised me with a proposal almost identical to the one I have put to you. We were to exchange secret information in order to speed up the negotiations and ensure their success.

"Naturally I was interested. I reported his offer to my superiors in Moscow, not only to obtain approval but to protect myself later on when, as I thought quite likely, things went wrong. I gave Mr. Hickok some trivial information about our side and he supplied me with documents on the American position. Unfortunately, these documents were almost useless, since your masters in Washington do not provide you with what we want—their fallback positions.

"As I had feared, it ended badly. Mr. Hickok became quite excited. He tried to move too quickly, failed to take precautions. As a result, he was discovered by your people."

"What happened?" Inigo was transfixed.

"Your people set out to arrest him. As it happened, he and I had dinner together that very night." Smirnov leaned back, holding Inigo's eyes in his own. "When he got back to his apartment, which is now yours, they were waiting for him.

"He made the mistake of trying to run away. It was typical, if I may say so, of his impulsive nature.

"I am sure that they intended only to wound him, not actually to kill him. But it was very badly handled. Such blunders occur from time to time, in our service as well as yours. One of our people who was assigned to watch Mr. Hickok saw it all from the far end of the courtyard. He says the man died instantly. I hope he was not a close friend."

Disbelief was written across Inigo's face.

"Again, you find it hard to believe me. I quite understand that. It is an improbable story, and I have no way of proving it to you. Perhaps on this occasion the truth is not so important. Whether he was killed by your service or mine, it shows the dangers we will have to run. But I assure you that our man witnessed the whole thing. Maybe someday you can satisfy yourself that I speak the truth."

It was no more implausible, Inigo admitted to himself, than the other possibilities he had come up with himself. It would also explain the silence, within and outside the Agency, about Hickok's death. Still, it was a monstrous idea.

"My proposal is quite different from his," Smirnov continued, "in that it puts all the risks on me. You will be the one who informs his superiors and obtains approval in advance. But Mr. Hickok's fate shows how extremely careful we must be."

Inigo was sunk in thought for a long moment. When Smirnov spoke again, he lifted his wineglass.

"It is a terrible story, George—may I call you George? The man shared our determination to make these negotiations succeed. I propose that we toast his memory."

Dazed, Inigo raised his glass and clinked it against Smirnov's. The Russian went on.

"You must understand that Geneva is a playground for the services of the world. You can imagine why. We will need to take careful precautions in our work together. One should always assume that recording instruments are about, planted in apartments, on telephones, in automobiles, even in restaurants. I checked this table before you arrived. There is also a great deal of surveillance, not only by the Swiss police, but by others as well. Major Rudenko, who heads our Soviet Residentura here, has three men whose task is simply to roam about the city freely, reporting anything of interest. Naturally a good deal of trivial nonsense is collected. But one must always assume the worst. If you and I did not have legitimate reason to meet frequently, my plan would be impossible. But even we must take great precautions. For one thing, we should never discuss our plan in either of our missions."

"You seem to be assuming that I have agreed."

"Forgive me. You want more time. You see, I have imagined this discussion so many times that I forget that it is quite new for you. Just now I overlooked what I said earlier about creating trust between us over time. I have been making observations of you from that standpoint since you came to Geneva. You are a competent person and an honest person, and I feel that we can work well together."

Even at a time like this, he's a pompous, condescending bastard, Inigo said to himself.

"My real concerns are less about you than about your service's competence and its ability to keep secrets. A leak would be disastrous. And, as you know better than I, CIA's record for security is questionable, to say the least."

There seemed to be no more to say. Smirnov spent five minutes over the bill, demanding explanations from the waiter for each item and laboriously checking the arithmetic. Fortunately, a standard tip was included. In the parking lot outside, he stopped Inigo at a distance from their cars.

"Now I give you our first fallback. It is what you call, I believe, a token of good faith." He peered up at Inigo's face in the dark and said quietly and slowly, "If the United States repeats its demands concerning your beloved Tyuratam Eighteen in two more plenary statements, the Soviet delegation is authorized to agree to the disposal of those launchers."

He couldn't have chosen a better hook, Inigo smiled to himself. Smirnov walked him to his car and opened the door for him. When Inigo was inside, he lowered his round face to the window.

"Good night, Mr. Inigo. And remember, it is not necessary for you to like me."

Then he was gone.

20

Inigo fared badly in planes, and this hurried flight back to Washington was worse than most. There was the usual cramped seat and unsatisfying food. The young American beside him had started off as a promising seatmate, but after fifteen minutes of comparing ski resorts, they found themselves with little more to say. Disengaging, they had spoken less and less, with longer pauses. Now, four hours over the Atlantic, Inigo had moved through dislike and totally erased him.

He had slept little and badly since the dinner with Smirnov, but even now, two days later, he couldn't manage to doze off for more than fifteen minutes. Dinner with Erika before the flight had been an awkward affair. Inigo had been unable to concentrate on what she was saying as his mind kept returning to Smirnov's proposal, worrying over its feasibility, looking for traps, trying to measure its worth against the dangers. It would be wrong to describe it as a calculated risk, for who could calculate the odds? But a clear and conscious risk, indeed it was that. Either the risk of provocation and entrapment or, if Smirnov was on the level, there remained the risk of failure, exposure, scandal, and, despite what Smirnov had said, the breakoff of SALT.

But the gains! Smirnov was offering to turn over the highest state secrets, the entire Soviet SALT hand. Knowing Moscow's fallbacks, the United States should be able to complete the negotiations in five or six weeks, largely on its own terms. True, some of the fallbacks might not be acceptable, but the United States could concentrate all its energies on precisely those items and perhaps get further concessions. Smirnov was right, of course, in calling the remaining difficulties trivial when measured against the awesome stakes of the arms race. Except for the telemetry issue, which was crucial to verification, their importance was symbolic: Which side would prevail? Moreover, it was precisely as symbols that they had become vital to those on both sides who hoped to drag out the talks until something happened elsewhere, as Smirnov had warned, to overwhelm and destroy them. Indeed, in the person of Walt O'Rourke the United States had one of these on its own delegation.

Inigo ordered another Scotch and thought about the cable he had sent.

TOP SECRET
DIRECTOR EYES ONLY FROM INIGO
UNEXPECTED MAJOR DEVELOPMENT HERE URGENTLY REQUIRES YOUR PERSONAL GUIDANCE. RETURNING TO WASHINGTON TOMORROW. REQUEST APPOINTMENT THURSDAY MORNING.

THIS TIME I HAVE A BETTER REASON.

That, he thought, should get him into the director's office. He was glad he had followed Lormack's advice and wangled a meeting during the recess. It had gone badly, but trying for a first visit now, as a faceless name from Geneva, would have been harder.

He'd been in his apartment no more than half an hour when the phone rang. Funny, no one knew he was back in Washington.

"Hello."

"George, what the hell?"

"Guy?"

"That's right. What's this about you meeting the director tomorrow?" Peters's voice quivered with anger.

"Been reading his personal cables, have you, Guy?"

"Damn right. All SALT cables come to me. No exceptions. He doesn't know a MIRV from a MARV, for Christ's sake."

"Well, Guy, it's like this." Inigo spoke slowly but invented rapidly. "In the first place, he asked me to communicate directly with him in certain contingencies." That was an invention, but in fact he was the director's personal representative. "In the second place, what we have to discuss has nothing whatsoever to do with your responsibilities." That was true. "I promise you that."

Silent heavy breathing on the line. It's like an obscene call, Inigo thought irreverently.

"Flying a little high, aren't you? But it's not going to work, George. I can really screw you out there in Geneva. You need me more than I need you. If you can't play it straight with me, I suggest you start looking for a new assignment."

Peters did not have a reputation for making idle threats. He was a good man to work with and a bad man to cross. More to the point, however, Inigo realized that as bits and pieces of a possible Smirnov operation slipped across Peters's peripheral vision in the future, he might be clever enough to see a jigsaw puzzle and put it together. It was important to steer him away from it at the start. He invented some more.

"Guy, when I met with the director during the recess, he gave me a task to perform personally. He swore me to secrecy. I swear I'll tell you all about it as soon as I can. But in the meantime, I'm sworn. And"—invoking the hoary principle—"you don't really have a need to know."

Peters blustered and threatened some more, but Inigo held fast and he finally hung up. Must remember to notify the director about this, Inigo thought, and to work out a secure cable routing to him for the future.

Next morning he called the director's office from his apartment and asked for Colonel Blom, guessing that was how things worked now.

"Blom," came a dry voice on the line.

"It's George Inigo. Good morning, Colonel."

"Back without orders again, Inigo?"

"Without orders is correct, Colonel. 'Again' is not. Last time the delegation was home for a recess."

Blom ignored the distinction. "What's this cable of yours all about?"

"Can't say on the phone. I can be there in thirty minutes."

"I think that would be a good idea."

"Does the director have some time free this morning?"

"We'll look into that after you've explained yourself."

"Okay. In the meantime, Colonel, I'd like to keep my visit as quiet as possible. You'll understand why when I explain. Could you have one of your secretaries pick up my badge from my old office? Have her put it as routine."

"I guess I can do that," said Blom laconically. "See you in thirty minutes." He hung up.

From Blom's tone, Inigo expected to be kept waiting. But Blom evidently didn't feel the need to teach lessons like that. Inigo was called in immediately. As he entered, Blom stayed seated, waving him silently to a chair. Preliminaries obviously were not in order, so Inigo began directly.

"Victor Smirnov is the KGB representative on the Soviet SALT delegation. As opposite numbers, we see a lot of each other on official business. Two evenings ago he offered to defect in place and give us their SALT fallbacks in return for asylum after the treaty is signed." He stopped for a reaction; none came. Blom went on staring at him coldly, not changing expression. He continued, sketching briefly the details of Smirnov's proposal. In two minutes he was done.

Blom remained expressionless. For a terrible instant, Inigo feared he had brought his story to the wrong man, that it was all over before it began. Then, "What do you think of it?" Blom finally asked.

"Don't know for sure," Inigo replied. "Could very well be a provocation. But if he's on the level, it's a really big deal. I'm inclined to think he is, but I'm an analyst, not an operator."

Blom picked up an appointment calendar and studied it. "The director's morning is completely full." Inigo's heart sank. Without looking up, Blom went on. "I can cancel his ten o'clock and ten-thirty appointments. Once you've briefed him, he can decide about the eleven o'clock himself. Be back here at ten, please."

It was only as Inigo left Blom's office that the comedy of his immediate situation struck him. He had to hide out for twenty-five minutes. The director's waiting room wouldn't do; too many acquaintances might chance on him there and ask why he was back. He didn't even dare go to the cafeteria for a cup of coffee. A fugitive inside CIA headquarters! At last he remembered the barbershop in the basement. Draped in sheeting, Inigo felt almost invisible.

When he returned at ten, he found Blom waiting for him outside the director's door.

"I'll speak to him first and then come back and get you. Wait here, please." The colonel opened the door silently, slid in, and closed it without a sound. Thirty seconds later he was back, to escort Inigo down the long room to the chair at the director's desk.

Whatever the magic words are, Inigo thought, Blom knows them. The director was alert and smiling. "Colonel Blom tells me you have an interesting problem, Mr. Inigo." Not a word about returning without orders.

After the rehearsal with Blom, Inigo had his presentation tight and ready. Smirnov's proposal, the gains, the risks, the demands for money, asylum, and exfiltration of the daughter. The chance of a trap. His own tentative estimate of Smirnov's trustworthiness, plus the need for careful testing. The tacit agreement not to tamper with the delegations, which brought the only interruption.

"Agreement? No one told me about any hands-off agreement! Where is it? Lormack filled me in on everything, but he never mentioned this. Joe?"

"First I've heard of it, sir." So Blom did have a first name, Inigo thought.

"Well, get on it, find out if it exists."

"May I suggest," Inigo put in, "that a lot of questions being asked is going to alert a lot of people to the idea that someone in Geneva has been recruited. On our side or theirs. That won't be helpful."

"Right!" the director barked. "I never agreed to any such thing. If nobody told me about some tacit agreement, then as far as I'm concerned it doesn't exist."

"Except," remarked Blom quietly, "State believes in it and ACDA too. If we get SALT information from Smirnov, they can't know where it's coming from."

"Right again!" The director was pacing the floor, trying to master a high tension. "No one is to know about this except the three of us. And the president, of course."

"The president?" Inigo asked.

"Of course the president! This is the biggest thing that's happened since I took over here. Do you think I'm going to hide it from the president?"

"I can't see any good coming of it, sir," said Inigo. "He sees a lot of people and he's not the most security-conscious man in Washington. The fewer who know, the better."

"Good God, Inigo! If we can't trust the president, whom can we trust?"

"It's not a matter of trust, sir. It's a matter of need to know. He hasn't got a need to know."

"Dammit, I've got a need for him to know."

"You spoke of the three of us, General," Blom cut in deftly. "I see problems in that. Inigo here may at times need instant cable responses on technical matters. That could be difficult when you're out of the country or testifying on Capitol Hill."

"Umm."

"Also we'll need the operational boys and their resources to get the Smirnovs out of Switzerland. Particularly to get the daughter out of Moscow."

"True." The director looked like a disappointed little boy. He wanted to play case officer, Inigo realized, to run the operation personally.

Blom went on in the same flat voice. "Perhaps you'd like to have the operators come in on this at, say, two o'clock. Carlton could take the meeting at State for you."

"Okay." The director seemed to draw on new sources of energy. "Bring Marcus in. But no one else." Blom looked calmly at him, saying nothing. "Except maybe his Soviet and Western European chiefs. They'll have to do the exfiltrating."

"Shambler?"

"That idiot? That saboteur? Haven't we replaced him yet?"

"We're working to offset his connections on the Hill, General. In the meantime, there's an obvious counterintelligence angle to Inigo's operation. Later on, it might look bad to have excluded him." He means in case I screw up, thought Inigo. No, he realized with a flush through his whole upper body, he means in case I defect.

The subject needed changing.

"What about Guy Peters?" Inigo asked.

"He's got nothing to do with it."

"I agree. But I should tell you that he got a copy of my cable to you and is asking what it's all about. I thought I should throw him off the track, so I said it had to do with a personal task for you."

"Good. Fix the cable routing, Joe. Keep all of Inigo's SALT cables going to Peters except those relating to . . . we need a code word, don't we?"

Everyone thought for a silent moment. Then Blom spoke.

"Redbird?"

"I like it! Redbird. Inigo plus his Commie buddy equals Redbird. Okay, George?"

"It's fine. He even wants to sing."

"Then it's settled." The director walked him to the door. "Great job so far! See you at two."

Inigo went into town for lunch to avoid encounters and questions. It was an odd way to start an espionage career. He felt more covert, more concerned about being spotted, here at headquarters in Langley, Virginia, than he did among the spies of Geneva. He began to comprehend the mentality of the secret agent, who had to be ready to improvise without notice, to lie spontaneously, to avoid the warmth of friendship, to never forget that he was of a different species, not as other men. Suddenly it came upon him that if he could feel this alienation, here in the safety of home territory, where the risks were nonexistent, how deeply it must by now be affecting Smirnov, who stood on the brink of treason, preparing to plunge in, abandoning all his roots and connections, sure of vilification at best and annihilation at worst. He began to imagine what Smirnov's feelings toward himself must be. A mixture of love and hate, with no possibility of indifference. A terrible need to trust, and behind that a need to love. A terrible awareness of dependence, and behind it a hatred born of that dependence. An enormous relief each time they met, for Inigo was the only man in the world with whom he could drop the pretense of normality. Yet at the same time a fierce determination to confess none of this, to hold himself together before Inigo, to maintain his pride, lest he be pitied, or rejected, or scorned and manipulated. For the first time he became aware of the abyss beneath Smirnov's feet, and a sympathy and understanding was born in him, even a nascent admiration of his courage.

If, that is, Smirnov were on the level.

He knew the other men in the director's waiting room in varying degrees. Marcus was the deputy director for Operations, a close friend of Lormack's, whom he had followed up the ladder. Rumor whispered that the director saw him as a rival, to be disposed of at the first opportunity. Marcus carried himself as though such an idea had never crossed his mind. Relaxed and humorous, his manner conveyed that working with this director was as agreeable as with any of his predecessors.

Sloan, who ran the Soviet Division, was an old friend of Inigo's, dating from the days when they had learned Russian together. He was a man without vanity or pretense, in whose company the vanities and pretenses of others tended to wither and fall away. Inigo was glad to have Sloan's good common sense in the game.

Petrocelli, the West European chief, he knew less well. Dark and intense, the man had a reputation for erratic brilliance. Carson, who belonged to his stable, had summed up Petrocelli once to Inigo in Geneva: "Louis is good at remembering all of our successes and forgetting all of his failures." Petrocelli was not much disposed toward cooperating with analysts like Inigo, who he felt did not appreciate the continuing value of human agents in the increasingly technological business of intelligence collection. He seemed surprised and disapproving to find Inigo among those summoned to this meeting on an unknown subject.

Last of all there was Shambler. Tall, cadaverous, grave, he sat aloof and apart from everyone. He had been in charge of counterintelligence at CIA for twenty-three years and was a power unto himself. Few were admitted to his secrets, and none to all of them. Many thought his work had crazed him. Shambler had his own truth, his own world view of an enormous Soviet conspiracy that reached into every corner of the globe. The most widely separated and disparate events were secretly coordinated. Egypt's Nasser was not merely a crypto-Communist; in Shambler's mind he was actually a full-fledged although secret member of the Soviet Politburo. The Soviet-Yugoslav split was a fake. The Sino-Soviet conflict was a sham from start to finish; the two sides had jointly concocted, among other things, evidence of military clashes on their border in order to delude the West.

If all this were true, if the USSR had such powers of penetration and deception, if the West were so easily blinded and misled, then it stood to reason that more than one CIA turncoat must have been recruited into the service of the KGB. It was Shambler's job to find them. He agonized over his inability to do so, to find the proofs to back up his suspicions. It was a grave responsibility, on which the future of the West might well depend, and he was failing to meet it. He was an unheard voice crying in the wilderness, a gloomy, guilty man.

Inigo felt the coolness when Blom ushered them in. There was no love lost between Shambler and his three colleagues, but the director was crisp and distrustful with all four of them. Trying to take hold of the Agency, he felt these men to be constantly eluding his control, slipping behind barriers he couldn't penetrate. It seemed to gall him that he needed them at all for Operation Redbird.

For the third time that day, Inigo told his story. No one interrupted. When the director asked for comments, there was a thoughtful silence.

"Quite a proposition," Marcus finally began. "Isn't Smirnov that slippery character who used to be in New York? And then snookered friend Hickok? What's your personal impression of him, George?"

"As a man, he's very unlikable," Inigo replied. He spoke carefully, as though he were on trial. "As to his sincerity, it's hard to be sure. It could be a provocation to torpedo the negotiations. Or he could be on the level." The latter was his hunch, but he kept it to himself.

"Well, it's not out of the question. It certainly ought to be explored." Sloan smiled at Inigo. "Looks like you're going to start a new career, George."

"Frankly, that's what gives me pause," said Petrocelli. "It looks to me like Smirnov has deliberately picked an amateur. No offense"— he nodded to Inigo—"but a pro like him knows how to get in touch with a pro on our side if he wants to do this kind of business."

"But he already knows George," the director objected. They squabbled for a while, with Petrocelli arguing that the case be turned over to an experienced operator and Marcus straddling the fence.

"Inigo is the only person whom Smirnov can meet freely," Blom put in quietly. "That's why he was chosen."

No one countered that, so the director happily made a command decision: Inigo would remain the Redbird case officer.

"Ever been to the Soviet Union, Inigo?" The question was put by Shambler, who had been silent till now.

"Yes. Lormack sent me last year. For a month's observation."

"Ummm."

That was all. Everyone knew what Shambler was getting at. Counterintelligence could never trust a man who had been on Soviet territory, at the disposal of the KGB, vulnerable to their persuasions, coercions, blackmail. Everyone understood, that is, except the director, who was merely exasperated at the irrelevance.

"Now, how do we test this Smirnov?"

"Well, that's standard procedure," Shambler answered. "We ask him for the names, ranks, and biographies of all the KGB officers he knows. Especially those stationed abroad. Then we check his names against our files. Most of them should check out, but there should be a few new ones. If there aren't, that means he's holding out on us. That would be bad news."

"Now wait a minute," Inigo objected. "I told you his motives, at least what he said. He's pro-SALT, and of course pro-Smirnov, but he's not actually anti-Soviet. I don't know whether he's willing to blow the cover of all his buddies."

"I thought you said he was a pretty unlikable article," Petrocelli countered. "I'd be surprised to hear he had scruples like that."

"Look, Smirnov's bona fides are the Soviet fallbacks. They're the test. If it works out as he says, if the Soviets accept proposals based on his information, then we know he's on the level." Inigo stopped, fearing he had spoken too hastily, too heatedly.

But the director was on his side. "That's right," he proclaimed. He enjoyed a chance to overrule the operators. "We'll test him by the fallbacks. Now listen, no one outside this room is to know about this. Blom here will hold the cables; you can read them in his office. No deputies, no secretaries. Is that clear?" He was in full stride now. "I'll table Smirnov's fallbacks myself with the boys downtown, without telling where they come from. I'll call them personal suggestions. The only man who'll know the truth will be the president." He was enjoying himself hugely. "Anything else?"

No one spoke. Inigo looked up to see Shambler gazing at him with an appraising air. He was reminded of Lebedev's look when Jenkins introduced them after the first plenary.

"By the way, Art," the director intervened. "Ever found out who did Hickok in?"

Inigo froze, but no one noticed. All eyes were on Shambler.

"Still working on it, sir. A few leads, but nothing solid yet."

As they left, Sloan took Inigo aside.

"Free for lunch tomorrow?"

"No, I'm flying back this evening."

"In that case come along to the office for a few minutes. We should talk a little."

When they were settled in with coffee behind a closed door, Sloan began.

"George, you've stumbled into something big here. I get White House pressure all the time to come up with a source on SALT. Smirnov is just what's wanted. But this Operation Redbird"—a wrinkle of distaste for the codeword creased his nose—"is full of troubles. I think we ought to talk about them."

"Please do." For the first time that day, Inigo felt comfortable. With Sloan, he didn't have to be on guard.

"In the first place, security. Don't imagine this is going to stay among the people in that room today. Petrocelli is certainly going to fill in Carson, out in Geneva, whatever the director says. And he should. You never know when you're going to need some local help, maybe even emergency help. And I'm certainly going to fill in the Moscow station. Does the director think I'm going to personally fly into Sheremetovo Airport and bring Smirnov's daughter out?"

"Yes, what about that? We never did discuss it."

"It can be done," Sloan said simply.

"How?"

"Let's just say we worked out a contingency plan for something like this several years ago. It's not foolproof, but it's worked once already."

"And you won't tell me what it is?"

"George, it's not just that you don't have a need to know. You actually have a need not to know. Smirnov is going to press you on it, and I'm certainly not going to expose it to him. If you don't know, I can be sure he won't either."

It made sense. "What do you need from me?"

"Everything about her. Addresses. Telephone numbers. Nicknames. Habits. Routes of daily travel. She's at Moscow University?"

"Yes."

"Her courses, her professors, her classrooms. Contacting her is going to be very delicate. If Smirnov is setting a trap for us, my guys will be stepping into it right along with you."

"I hadn't thought of that."

"You're not supposed to; you've got no experience in all this. Petrocelli made a lot of sense when he said Smirnov should be turned over to one of our officers. But I agree with the director in keeping it with you. I just want to emphasize how much help you're going to need. We'd never dream of letting a junior case officer, even with two or three years' experience, handle a man like Smirnov. I suggest you take Carson with you every step of the way. She's experienced, has good judgment.

"George, there's no way we can really be sure of Smirnov, right up to the end. If he's running a provocation for Moscow, he can compromise himself with you every which way and still be safe. The fallbacks can be phonies, or things Moscow wants us to have. The only real test is the one Shambler mentioned. To have him blow his colleagues in the West."

Sloan stopped. Inigo stared silently at him. He was afraid Smirnov wouldn't do it. And he didn't want to administer a test that might be failed. Suddenly he wasn't sure he really had an open mind about the possibility of a provocation.

"Think about it, George. The director won't insist with you; he's too gung ho on Smirnov as his meal ticket to the president. But he's an amateur too."

"Would you like to put Smirnov on the polygraph?" Inigo asked savagely.

"Take it easy, friend. As a matter of fact, I would. But that takes a lot of time. He might have trouble accounting for where he'd been. Also, he'd probably refuse, and it's just possible that at that point he'd run out on us. Look, George, I'm trying to help you see what you're up against. In a perfect operation, we'd do all of these things, so as to push the risks as low as possible, to depend on trust as little as possible. But we don't always have the luxury of all these safeguards. So we have to decide whether to run a few risks or just forget the whole thing.

"Shambler obviously thinks the risks are extravagant. Petrocelli probably leans that way. Marcus I don't know about; sometimes he takes hellish chances. Myself, I'd probably have a go, but watching Smirnov like a hawk all the way. Anyhow, you've got the director's go-ahead. He'd probably can you if you tried to back out now. I can just see him sending Blom out to Geneva to take Smirnov over from you." Sloan grinned.

"So what are you telling me?"

"Don't get exasperated, George. Just some friendly advice, plus a few ins and outs of the business. And good luck. You may end up a hero. But if we get burned on this, you'll be the first to be shot down in flames. Along with your beloved treaty."

21

"I assume everyone has read the new instructions. Oh, and welcome back, George. Any news from Washington?"

Full of energy, Jenkins neither wanted nor waited for an answer. The delegation had waited in the doldrums for two weeks while the Washington bureaucracies did battle over the remaining disputed items in the draft treaty. Each delegate had been on the secure telephone to his home office, trying to find out what problems were holding up agreement. All of them reported that the Joint Chiefs of Staff were withholding concurrence. Everyone knew what that meant: The JCS, taking their guidance from O'Rourke, who was backed in turn by his Senate connections, was demanding further study. Finally, however, the logjam had broken in Washington, and Geneva could get to work.

Inigo sat patiently as Jenkins read aloud the first instruction, drafted to resolve the Bison problem. The Soviet Bison bomber force was aging but still effective; it had to be counted in the total limit of weapons. But the Soviets had objected that thirty-one of the Bisons were tankers, incapable of carrying nuclear weapons and therefore not subject to counting. CIA confirmed this, but added that it was impossible to tell precisely which aircraft were bombers and which were tankers; furthermore, the tankers could probably be converted to bombers with little effort. Now Washington was proposing that it would exclude thirty-one tankers from the treaty count if the USSR gave them "functionally related observable differences which indicate that they cannot perform the mission of a heavy bomber."

Michaels had assured Inigo before they entered the tank that O'Rourke had already accepted the language in his own channel to JCS. The general nevertheless carried the fight to a bitter end.

"How come we're accepting thirty-one? I thought CIA said there were thirty-three tankers." He glared a challenge at Inigo.

"That's right," Inigo answered. "It's also an estimate we're not too precise about. Could be plus or minus three aircraft. The Defense Intelligence Agency carries twenty-nine, with the same caveats. So when the Soviets claim thirty-one, both agencies are willing to accept it."

"Why are you so unwilling to fight for your own estimate? Suppose the Sovs know about the spread between CIA and DIA. They could have thirty-five or thirty-six and just pick the midpoint of our numbers."

Inigo was weary of O'Rourke's harassments. "My guys signed off on thirty-one back home, Walt, and I do the same."

O'Rourke looked at him in disgust and then turned to Jenkins. " 'Functionally related observable differences.' What the hell is that supposed to mean?" he demanded. Jenkins patiently explained that the Soviets would have to modify the tankers in a way that U.S. intelligence could observe and that also prevented them from dropping bombs.

"Like what?"

"Sealing up the bomb bay doors, for example."

"Then let's put that in the treaty. Why pussyfoot around?"

"Walt," Paul Boroz objected, "those are their aircraft, not ours. We can't order them what to do with them. What this language says is, that if we're not able to see the frods and aren't satisfied that those tankers can't drop bombs, we'll count all thirty-one in the treaty limits."

"The 'frods'?"

"Yeah. Functionally related observable differences. 'Frods.' Time to learn another new word, Walt."

O'Rourke complained for another five minutes before allowing Jenkins to go on to the second new instruction. It authorized the delegation to repeat the U.S. demand that the Tyuratam Eighteen be destroyed or counted against the Soviet weapons total.

"My God, we did that two weeks ago! If we come back so soon on it, they'll figure we're anxious for a compromise. The ball's in the Soviet court. Let's leave it there."

"I talked to Peters on the phone last night," said Inigo. "He says Washington knows that, but they want us to repeat it this week anyway." He didn't add that, according to a puzzled Peters, the director had made a strong pitch for this, which had carried the day.

O'Rourke was unpersuaded. "I'm all for pursuing the Tyuratam

Eighteen, but what's the hurry? I notice that Washington has 'instructed' us to go on the tanker question but only 'authorized' us to return to the Tyuratam launchers. We're ordered to do the first but permitted to do the second. They're asking the delegation to make a tactical decision on timing. I say we should wait."

"George, I know you push this one a lot with your buddy Smirnov," Jenkins noted. "Do you get any sense from him about where it stands?"

"On the surface he holds the line. But he did mention that the General Staff had been asked to look at the question again. I think it might be a good time to renew the pressure."

It turned out, when O'Rourke demanded a vote, that everyone else did too. Jenkins commissioned draft statements on both topics and adjourned the meeting. O'Rourke stayed behind to make a note in a small black book he carried to all the meetings. Michaels called it his "Treasons, Treacheries, and Transgressions" notebook. Inigo figured that he had earned a few lines in it, but that it was filled mostly with the sins of Jenkins, Rappaport, and Boroz.

"Was Pavlovsky high today, Abe?" Jenkins began when the delegation had gathered in the tank the following day to discuss the just-completed plenary session.

"Was he high?" snorted Rappaport. "You didn't smell that breath?"

"I wondered," said Jenkins. "I expected him to get really charged up on the idea of frods. But just as I was finishing up on the Tyuratam Eighteen, he gave me the broadest wink and the biggest grin I've ever seen at a plenary."

"He never mentioned Tyuratam in the post-plenary with me," Rappaport replied. "But I did see that grin. Whatever it meant, it was a real whopper."

"Mardirosian had a lot to say about the Tyuratam launchers. All of it bad," O'Rourke put in. "He as much as told me to go fly a kite."

"But did you notice Lebedev's response to my statement at the table? That the Soviet side 'took note' of the American position? That's a far cry from last month, when he tried to declare the subject closed. What's the word from the KGB, George?"

"It never came up. All Smirnov wanted to talk about was his boat trip to Lausanne." Inwardly he was holding his breath. The Soviet response would be the first test of Smirnov's fallbacks.

At the next plenary, Lebedev launched into a tirade against the American proposal on Tyuratam. The U.S. position was totally without foundation and had been adopted for reasons inimical to the success of the negotiations. As he railed on, Morgan passed a note to Inigo.

"So much for Smeary's hint about the General Staff."

"Wait. He's about to give in." Inigo scribbled back.

"... devoted as it is, however, to the completion of the draft treaty," intoned the interpreter, "announces its willingness to assume a formal obligation to destroy twelve of these launchers and to convert the remaining six into test launchers for missiles undergoing modification." Pavlovsky, sober as a judge, remained impassive. So did Smirnov. So, with considerable self-restraint, did Inigo. Later, there was jubilation in the tank.

Dinner with Smirnov that evening, however, was a disaster.

Inigo had chosen for this evening Le Chandelier, a local restaurant near his apartment in the Vieille Ville. It was a quiet, modest place, never very full, where the mussels were well prepared and the waitresses, in black skirts and severe hairdos, were prompt and discreetly formal. As he waited for Smirnov to arrive, a tall man entered, looked around, and came straight to his table.

"It's Mr. George Inigo, isn't it?" he asked in American English.

"Yes."

"I'd like to join you if I may." Without waiting for an answer, the stranger pulled out a chair and sat down.

"Excuse me," said Inigo, "but I'm expecting someone. And I don't know you."

"Pete Gonzales." When Inigo ignored his outstretched hand, he picked up a menu and began to study it.

"What the hell do you think you're doing, Gonzales? I'm expecting a guest!"

The stranger looked up briefly. "I'd like to meet him myself. How are the veal kidneys here?"

Suddenly it dawned on Inigo. "You're from Art Shambler's outfit," he accused. "Counterintelligence."

Gonzales looked him full in the eyes. "Well, I was on a European trip anyway. Art sent a cable suggesting I drop by to meet you and your friend."

"Get out of here, Gonzales. Get out of here this instant before I have to—" But he was too late. Smirnov stood in the doorway, looking for him. When he spotted Inigo with another man, he froze. Their eyes met. Inigo, trying to maintain a calm gaze, saw terror suddenly suffuse Smirnov's face. After an agonized moment, the Soviet turned abruptly on his heel and disappeared out the door.

"So that's him," said Gonzales, swinging around and catching a final glimpse of Smirnov's back. "Well, we'll have to get acquainted another time. I've got some questions for him. But I can wait."

Inigo was furious, but he knew he couldn't afford a scene. He reached in his pocket and Gonzales started, but then relaxed as Inigo pulled out a notebook. He wrote in it slowly for two full minutes of silence, then ripped out the page and tossed it at Gonzales's place.

DCI/Eyes Only Redbird.

Man calling self Pete Gonzales, claiming to be assigned by Arthur Shambler to interrogate subject, imposed himself on me tonight in restaurant. Subject bolted on arrival when he spotted the unexpected third party.

Please confirm Gonzales's identity and details of his assignment. If his involvement not authorized by director, request he be instructed to depart Geneva immediately.

Subject badly shocked. Anticipate difficulty in reestablishing rapport and cooperation.

"Anything you want me to add?"

Gonzales tossed the message back.

"It's your cable, Inigo. It's fine with me if you want to document your refusal to cooperate. And as for the director, Counterintelligence would never accomplish anything if we were scared of the front office. I'll hang around and stay in touch." His long, challenging stare was only a fair imitation of Lebedev's. When Inigo gazed back contemptuously, Gonzales smiled, shrugged into his overcoat, and left without another word.

Son of a bitch! Inigo's mind raced. How many players are there going to be in this game? If we still have a game, that is. Smirnov had been stunned, and this bungle would surely play into all his fears about CIA's incompetence. Smirnov's loneliness might be grueling, but at least he could play his own hand. And if he threw it in now, Inigo couldn't blame him.

He ordered dinner and ate it, wondering all the while whether Smirnov might return and whether he even wanted him to, hard on the heels of this disaster. Finishing his coffee, it struck him suddenly that the Soviet's reaction, so spontaneous, so frightened, was an important piece of evidence. A double agent constructing a provocation would not have been so terrified. A provocateur would have welcomed the chance to identify Inigo's companion and perhaps weave him into his net. It was not a decisive proof, but it counted for something with Inigo, who was coming to conclude that he could never get decisive proof. It was up to him, he saw, to make his own best judgment.

Best judgment, yes, but surely now it was time to call in Carson. He dialed her from a pay phone, congratulating himself on remembering not to use his own. I'll make a spy yet, he said to himself. It was the only carefree thought of a grim evening.

"May I speak to Ms. Carson, please?"

"Just a minute." It was a deep male voice. Inigo wondered what it was like to be the husband of a CIA station chief. Driving her to the office at one in the morning to read priority cables, taking nighttime calls from men who declined to identify themselves. Unexplained trips. Promises not to ask her questions about her work. Worry and doubt when she denied that the job held any danger. Rather like being a wife, Inigo realized.

"This is Ms. Carson."

"Emily, it's George Inigo."

"Hello there, George. I've been expecting to hear from you."

"You have?"

"Yes. Petrocelli sent a cable." On the phone, nothing more. A sweep team went over the Carsons' place regularly, but still one couldn't be too careful.

"Good. I need to talk to you. Are you busy now?"

"Not at all. Come on out and I'll give you a drink." She gave him directions to their house in the suburb of Eaux Vives.

Mr. Carson was discreetly out of sight when he arrived. Emily ushered Inigo into the living room. The house belonged to the familiar old world of spacious parlors, big kitchens, luxurious sofas, french doors giving onto gardens. In his small apartment in the Vieille Ville, he had begun to forget about all that. Emily brought him a Scotch and pulled two armchairs close together.

"Troubles?"

"Well, yes. I'm glad Petrocelli filled you in. I'm going to need you in carrying this off. But tonight is something different." He told her about Gonzales's appearance and how Smirnov had bolted.

"He's one of Shambler's boys, all right, George." From Inigo's description—tall, lanky, narrow-nosed, thin-lipped—Carson had recognized the man at once. "He's on a roving European assignment. Comes in and out of Geneva without letting me know." She paused, remembering that Lark had reported sighting Gonzales at the railroad station the day before Hickok died. It was the kind of suggestive but inconclusive information that Carson was trained to keep to herself. Did Inigo have a need to know?

Yes, she decided.

"He was seen here shortly before Hickok's death."

They stared at each other in a long silence.

"Are you thinking what I'm thinking, Emily?" She nodded. "If we're right, that was a murderer at my table tonight."

"And in that case we'll never hear a word from Shambler's so-called investigation," she added soberly.

"Well, you'd better hear Smirnov's version of it." Briefly Inigo recounted what Smirnov had said of Hickok's approach to him, his carelessness, his death as witnessed by a KGB watcher.

"Unproved, but it fits," she commented. "I know Gonzales to be a violent man. These are passionate people, George. They live in their own world. To them, their peculiar brand of patriotism justifies anything. So watch out."

Inigo stared into his drink for such a long time that when at last it seemed that he was never going to speak, Carson asked a quiet question.

"Do you want out?"

He stirred then, put down his glass, and looked seriously at her. "Nope." His tone was matter-of-fact. "No, I don't want out. So let's get on with it. What do I do next with Smirnov?"

Merely asking the question brought Inigo some relief. Except for his short visit back to headquarters, he had been playing a lone hand, and the stress was beginning to wear him down. He didn't think he'd made any big mistakes yet, but making all the decisions by himself, with no input or reactions from anyone, had begun to take its toll. The worst part was having to second-guess himself by himself, with no one to reassure him that he'd done the right thing. It was like

126

trying to conduct one's own psychoanalysis. Carson was going to make a big difference.

"Well, let's start by imagining what sort of shape he's in right now," she began. "I gather he panicked. Probably still shaking. Full of fears and uncertainties. What might they be? That you're a fool? That you want to betray him?"

"Perhaps. He hasn't talked like that, though. Apparently he spent a lot of time investigating me before making his pitch. But he knows I'm an amateur."

"Good. You can use that to explain things away. What else?"

"He says he's more worried about the Agency's incompetence than he is about mine. Its bungles, its leaks. That's what he's afraid of."

"You know, in a day or so he may actually hit upon the truth. The rivalry between Shambler's crew and the rest of us is no secret. But he never even met Gonzales, so that could only be a suspicion for him. What else might he think? Assuming he's not finished with you forever. What was supposed to happen tonight, before Gonzales blew it?"

"I was going to tell him the director has given us the go-ahead."

"How much does he want?"

"Forty-eight thousand a year till he finds work. He wants to come to the States. And to have his daughter exfiltrated out of Moscow."

"That's a tall order." Carson frowned. "You'd better figure on forty-eight thousand a year for life. And getting someone out of Moscow, what did Sloan say to that?"

"He says it can be done."

"So is Smirnov's SALT stuff worth it?"

"Are you kidding, Emily? Why, we'd be happy to spend half a billion on a satellite that would intercept just those fallbacks alone."

"Okay, okay, keep your shirt on. Tell me how people reacted at headquarters?"

"From the director, a green light. A complete green light, with sirens and bells. From your buddies, warnings about provocation. Suspicions of Smirnov and, in Shambler's case, of me. Therefore our friend Gonzales."

"All right, so you've been warned. What that means, operationally, is don't give him any papers. Assume he's recording you. Assume surveillance, and a tap on your phone. Want me to have your apartment swept?"

"No, thanks. It might encourage me to be indiscreet."

"Right. Ready for a refill?"

"Let me get it."

"It's in the first lower cabinet on your right as you enter the kitchen. None for me, thanks."

When he returned with his drink, she was ready to move on.

"All right, hypothesis number one is that he's on a provocation. I assume you've been told that the only way to check it out is to ask him to blow his buddies' cover. And that you're debating inside your head. We can talk about that if you like." She waited.

Inigo felt himself shrinking from that topic. "Let's explore hypothesis two." And, to cover up, "This is really very helpful, Emily." He wondered whether she noticed.

If she did, she gave no hint of it. "Hypothesis two says Smirnov is on the level. So we go back to the restaurant, where he comes in and spots you with Gonzales. Or rather, with a stranger. He knows you've been back to Washington to try out his proposal, this Operation Redbird." She frowned the same frown that Sloan had. "What does he imagine? Why does he bolt?"

"Sheer surprise, I suppose. He's jumpy, and he had no warning from me of a third party. Better to get the hell out of there."

"You realize, don't you, George, that that tells us something? A provocateur would have walked right in, found out what was going on. Unless he was the nervous type, which provocateurs aren't. Could it have been an act?"

"He turned white."

"Good. Score one for hypothesis two. Okay, now he's wondering who Gonzales was. The worst possibility is that he recognized him. Was our friend facing the door?"

"No, I was. Gonzales had his back to him."

"So we have an abstract stranger. Who turns up with you after you get back from Washington. He didn't see you two quarreling? No. Then Gonzales is an emissary from Washington. He has a message for Smirnov. Maybe straight from the director—whom you must tell me about soon. Could it be that at this very moment he's blaming himself for panicking, and wishing he'd joined you?"

"Could very well be. And also mad as hell at me for not giving him forewarning."

"Yes, that fits. First he blames himself, then puts it onto you."

"So what do I do with that?"

"I don't know yet." Carson got up and wandered over to the french doors. She pulled the drapes absentmindedly. "What's he like? Tell me about him."

"Disagreeable, for starters. None of the American delegation can stand him. Sarcastic, superior, a bully."

"And what do you suppose lies behind all that?"

"Insecurity, I imagine. Some of it would be generic, the old Russian peasant sense of inferiority before the cultured West. But more than that is his body. Five feet three or four, I'd say, and roly-poly. I can imagine the other kids knocking him around as a child, and him having to use his wits to establish someplace for himself. No shortage of wits. He loves to be in control of the situation, on the offensive. He seems to need that badly. Maybe that had something to do with his going into the KGB. That and the chance to settle some old scores. That may be a little too vicious, but certainly he'd want to have other people understand that he could settle scores if he wanted to."

"Anything else? Is his wife in Geneva?"

"Yes. She's been to dinner with us a couple of times. As small as he is. It was a great marriage up for him—her father's a deputy minister. They seem to have worked out a game; he's the firm parent and she plays the flighty daughter who always obeys in the end. It makes me uncomfortable, but it seems like a mutually satisfying arrangement."

"So," Carson summarized thoughtfully, "an undersize, bright, ambitious type. I imagine he experiences life as a question of where the power lies. Sees people as divided into those who control and those who are controlled."

"I should think so. It's one of the major Russian personality types, accentuated by Communist rule. And heightened in his case by that ridiculous body."

"Well, George, it's not hard to see why defection would be a crisis for him." She was back in her chair. "It's a crisis for anyone, of course, but most of all for men like Smirnov. There's a dream of power in it, of changing the course of history single-handedly, of revenging all the slights, real and imagined. But alongside that, a feeling of powerlessness that must be excruciating. Under hypothesis two, he's putting himself in your hands. He may trust you at the surface level, but deeper down he's got to feel that no matter how careful he is, basically he's at your mercy."

"And from that," Inigo put in, "it's a pretty short step to panic."

"Right. We're getting somewhere, aren't we? Just now he needs a big dose of reassurance, a conviction not only that you won't betray him but that you know how to control events. Since he no longer can." She gave him a long look from under lowered brows. "I think you're going to have to come on pretty strong for a while, George."

"Yes, I agree. I'll bawl him out for bolting. Tell him that Gonzales was the director's personal emissary. That he came to Geneva to convey the director's personal blessing, but now he's gone back to Washington with a bad report. That I'm going to have to work like hell now to get headquarters back into line behind us."

"I'd lay it on pretty thick," Carson said seriously. "Tell him it just won't be possible to go on with the operation if he's going to be so panicky and paranoid. Use his first name a lot, since you're playing father."

"You don't think I'll lose him?"

"It's not impossible. But if so, you were going to lose him anyway, sooner or later. Look, in the relations between an agent and his case officer, there's always a crisis at some point. Yours has just come early, and in a way that's an opportunity. The important thing is to meet it head on. That sets the whole tone of the relationship. Otherwise, you're just asking for a series of crises, each one destroying more confidence than the last, until the whole thing blows up or falls apart." Carson was pacing slowly between the sofa and the fireplace. "You can be very helpful to him, George, as well as save the whole operation, if you can meet that need of his to believe that things are under control. Later on, you can be more sympathetic and less authoritarian. But right now, he badly wants to be put in his place. When's your next meeting?"

"Tomorrow evening. We have an arrangement that if one meeting aborts, we'll meet twenty-four hours later at Au Pied de Cochon. His idea," he added, seeing that Carson was about to congratulate him on his tradecraft.

"Good. Excellent. Anything else?"

Her briskness made Inigo look at his watch. He was startled to find it was after midnight. "I didn't realize it was so late, Emily. No, I guess that's all for now."

"Look, I know how it is with men." She gave him another of her grins. "Get a little shoptalk started and they're ready to run on until four A.M., getting more sloshed by the hour. I've opted out of that game. Takes too much energy. And I'd like to see you in good shape for tomorrow too." Her laugh was short, but its pitch somehow reminded Inigo that she was a woman.

Geneva was buttoned up like a nunnery as he drove home. There was a night life here, but it was tiny and had to be searched out. Having found Erika, he had never made the effort. It hit him then that for all his confiding in Carson, the use he was making of her, he was still holding out about Erika. He was suddenly appalled at what he was up to. He was trying to pull off a major intelligence coup, certainly the Agency's biggest in a decade, and at the same time carry on an affair with a beautiful young Eastern bloc national—something kept him from saying "Communist." Was there something in him that courted disaster?

"And you an analyst, George Inigo, a rank amateur of an operator!" he exclaimed aloud. It was like his teenage fantasy of being at the same time a famous, invincible lawyer and a pro football quarterback. And immediately he plunged on. Yes, by God, he was going to do both!

He realized he had just run a red light. He had never felt more foolish. Nor more alive.

22

The restaurant Au Pied de Cochon was nestled under the cathedral, halfway up the steep cobblestoned street leading from the smart shopping avenues along the left riverbank to the Bourg de Four, center of the Vieille Ville. Posters of postimpressionist art exhibitions, none of which had occurred in Geneva, covered the walls. Foreigners were not attracted to it, partly because of its name, which meant "at the pig's foot," partly because of the lure of a classier restaurant a few doors farther up, partly because of a menu featuring animal parts that are usually thrown away in the English-speaking world. The waitresses were speedy, efficient, and incurious. For all these reasons, Inigo found it an ideal place for meeting Smirnov. Even the noise level was just right, high enough to provide a covering buzz of sound but not so high as to interfere with their conversation.

Smirnov was twenty minutes late. It was uncharacteristic of him, and Inigo understood that it was meant to express his fury over the fiasco of their previous appointment. When he entered, he slowly and elaborately surveyed the entire room, then made straight for the table where Inigo sat waiting. He began to speak as soon as he sat down, not pausing as his hands patted the underside of the table, searching for microphones.

"Who was that with you last night?" he hissed.

Inigo answered him coldly.

"Why did you run away?"

"Do you take me for a fool? One who would walk straight into a trap?" His glare was venomous.

"Do you take me for a trapper? And such a crude one at that?"

Smirnov continued to hold his gaze, but the fire in his eyes dimmed a little. Inigo returned his stare and said nothing. After a few moments, Smirnov spoke, in a tense voice that carried more entreaty than anger.

"What did you expect me to think? A total stranger appears at our private meeting. With no warning from you in advance. I didn't know what to think. Of course I was upset."

"Frightened, I would say," Inigo remarked. He ignored Smirnov's reproach about the lack of warning and fell silent again. When his companion looked away, he continued. "Naturally, when you got your nerves back, you were ashamed and angry at yourself. And then, of course, that became anger at me. It's understandable. But we can't afford to lose our nerves again. Here, what would you like to order?" Handing him a menu, he picked up another and devoted himself to it.

It worked. Smirnov's shoulders slumped as he accepted the menu and briefly studied it. He selected an entrecote; when in doubt, Smirnov always found beef the most comfortable choice. Waiting for their orders to be taken, they exchanged appreciative remarks about an attractive young student seated alone against the wall. When the waitress had come and gone, leaving behind a basket of mixed breads, Inigo began.

"My companion last night was a colleague from Washington. He is in charge of the plan to get your daughter out of Moscow and into New York. He wanted to ask you some questions about her."

Smirnov's face fell. He dropped his eyes and began to toy with a piece of bread. Inigo went on.

"Unfortunately, other commitments prevented him from remaining here for an extra day. So he has told me what information I must get from you."

"I may conclude, then, that your agency has accepted my proposal?" Smirnov was regaining his composure; his mind was working again.

Inigo ignored the interruption. Things were moving faster than he had intended. "Washington was also expecting him to supply a second opinion concerning yourself. Now he will have to say that he was unable to meet with you, and why. His report, to say the least, will not be reassuring."

But Smirnov had had enough of the defendant's role. Like a warrior recovering from a wound, he thrust his shoulders forward to fend off the continuing attack. "Nonsense. My reaction was perfectly normal and will be correctly understood by everyone. Except your famous Mr. Shambler, who will be convinced that it was all an act on my part. Has he been informed, by the way?"

"The matter is being kept in the smallest possible circle."

"He is well known to us in the Center, of course," Smirnov went on. "Quite a ridiculous figure. He provides us with a great deal of amusement. One of the requirements in advanced training in our service is to spend a year handling his case. The trainee is obliged to feed him information that will sustain his delusions, from sources he will accept without question. It is not a very demanding task, since he is so attached to these delusions."

This corresponded so completely to Inigo's suspicions that he had to wipe his mouth with the napkin to hide his smile. He was beginning to enjoy the game. It was, as Sloan had told him long ago, full of tension and disappointment, but often full of fun as well.

"Your proposal was positively received in Washington. There was some debate over the amount of money you mentioned. It will depend upon the value of the information that you supply. At worst it will not be far from the sum you requested." His voice underlined the next sentence. "I can personally assure you of that."

"Very well." Smirnov accepted the demand for trust. "And my daughter, how are you going to get her out of Moscow?"

Inigo felt relieved to move onto the solid ground of truth.

"I don't know. My colleagues do not want you to have that information, for reasons that you are sure to understand. So they did not tell me. In addition, I have no need for that information."

"I must confess that I approve." For the first time that evening, Smirnov smiled.

"I can tell you, however, that the task is in the hands of colleagues in whom I have the highest confidence. As you yourself noted, they have already accomplished it in the past."

"Yes. Once only, or more times?"

"Sorry." The wine had arrived. Inigo took a sip and peered over the rim of the glass at Smirnov, who abandoned the subject.

"And the director?"

"I spoke with him at length. He is thoroughly involved in the operation and will follow it closely."

"You don't happen to have a letter from him to me, or anything like that?"

Inigo had heard of such things. The loneliness and guilt of a spy was terrific. No matter how committed he was to his secret purposes, he thirsted for tangible acknowledgment and justification from his new fellow conspirators. Colonel Mayorsky had requested the rank of colonel in the British army and had himself photographed repeatedly in the tailored uniform made especially for him, even though he could not take the pictures back to Moscow.

"No," he replied, resolving silently to find some way to meet Smirnov's need.

"No matter. We are off to a successful start at least."

"Ah yes, the Tyuratam Eighteen."

"General Mardirosian was quite glum about it." Inigo was tempted to report that so was General O'Rourke as well, but reminded himself there was no need to pass on internal delegation matters. Smirnov might well imagine that O'Rourke reacted cheerlessly to every sign of progress, but he was not going to confirm it.

"About your daughter. We need several pictures of her. Height and weight. Her address and telephone number. Her best friends, their addresses. Her course schedule, her professors. Places where she studies, and where she spends her free time."

"She is to contact someone?"

"She will be contacted by someone. She is to know nothing as yet. Later, I will give you instructions to pass to her."

Smirnov looked at him gravely. "I appreciate that some strangers, whom I shall never meet, will be taking great risks for the sake of my daughter. If you could find some way to tell them of my gratitude, I would be most happy."

"Certainly."

"Now there is another matter we need to discuss."

"Oh?"

"Yes. The young woman. Fräulein Hartke."

It was completely unexpected. Inigo's breath stopped. He said nothing.

"You must give her up. It is too risky."

"Oh, do you think so?" He needed time. Ideas careened through his head; he could almost hear his brain whirring. Suddenly a click, and everything locked into place. She was not working with Smirnov!

"You are running too big a risk."

She was not working with Smirnov!

"Really? Why do you say so? And what do you imagine our relations to be?" His words had a supercilious ring to his own ear as he fought for time.

"I shall speak of what I know, not what I imagine. You see her two or three times a week. Sometimes you spend the night at her apartment, sometimes she at yours. You see no other woman."

"So?"

"She is an East German." Smirnov said it with the air of a prosecutor completing his case.

"So?"

Smirnov's exasperation overcame him. "How can you sit there and say merely 'so'? I have put my life in your hands. I don't intend you should put it in hers!" To calm his rising voice, Inigo made a hushing gesture with his hands. A solitary elderly man who had glanced up at them from the next table dropped his eyes to his plate again.

"Control yourself, please. Miss Hartke has nothing to do with you and me." Inigo was in no mood to yield. He had overmastered Smirnov in the matter of Gonzales, and the discovery that Erika was not working with the Soviets swelled his confidence.

"How can you be so reckless?" Smirnov spoke in a low hiss of fury.

"I have not found a single reason to mistrust Miss Hartke. She is from East Germany, true, but she is quite apolitical. Her name does not appear in the records of my service. Does it in yours?"

The moment he spoke, Inigo knew that he had asked a fateful question.

Smirnov, hesitating, also seemed to sense its fatefulness. Inigo realized how easy it would be for the Soviet to lie, as he himself had been lying this evening. "We know her as an agent of East German Intelligence," Smirnov could say. "An experienced agent," he could add to clinch his point. There would be no way under the sun for Inigo to disprove him. Their eyes locked across the table. Could he never be sure of Smirnov? Would doubt always remain? Suddenly the game was not fun anymore.

"Our Soviet records convey a strong possibility that she works for East German Intelligence. They are not conclusive, I will admit to you. And while you may find this strange, I am not in a position to obtain clarification."

"I see." Inigo knew at once that Smirnov was telling the truth. He could feel the lie considered, rejected. Shame invaded him, but he saw no choice except to press on. "I see why you are alarmed. Naturally, you prefer to avoid every risk, however small."

"Precisely. And I would not describe this risk as small."

"Shall we have a cognac while we think this over?" Inigo signaled to the waitress and gave the order. "I can appreciate your point of view," he began. "You perceive a risk, you find it unnecessary, and naturally you wish to remove it. I am in a somewhat different position, with a different perspective. I also have an advantage in that I know Miss Hartke personally. Of course I was immediately concerned, even before you proposed our project, because of her nationality. That is why I checked with my service. And I have continued to keep in mind the possibility you have raised."

He pulled his chair closer to the table and laid his elbows upon it. "She has said and done nothing that has caused me any concern on this score."

Smirnov continued to stare at him.

"Let me tell you, Victor, something I have learned since I embarked on my new profession with you. This new world is full of distrust. I do not like that. Nevertheless, I see that it is necessary. I accept it. But in the end, it is necessary to trust a little. Not too much, perhaps, and never unconditionally. One cannot trust blindly in this new world.

"One must make careful judgments and review them continually. But with no trust at all, with nothing but suspicion and distrust, I cannot work or live. Perhaps from your perspective, you find this a serious flaw in me. Perhaps you find me as unsuitable as Mr. Hickok. If that is so, I shall be very sorry. Because not only do I believe deeply in our undertaking, but I have begun to feel a growing trust of you as well."

Inigo found himself gazing into the far corner. The old man was struggling into his raincoat. He brought his eyes back to Smirnov's.

"So now you will know how I am going to answer you. I do not agree to break off my relationship with Miss Hartke. I will continue to say nothing to her of you, of our work together. I will continue to be alert to the possibility you raise. If I find reason to suspect her, I will break off at once. Not before."

This time it was Smirnov who dropped his eyes.

"You speak of a little trust being needed, but from my viewpoint you are demanding a great deal of trust."

"Perhaps so." For Inigo the intensity was over. It was his turn to pay the bill. Like lovers who have come upon an unexpected crisis, they needed to get away from each other quickly.

"Very well," Smirnov said. "We will go forward. This note contains the resolution of the data base issue that the Soviet delegation is authorized to accept. I count on you to destroy it after you have memorized its contents." He handed a folded paper to Inigo, who put it immediately into his jacket pocket.

In the street, a light rain was falling. Tires hissed softly on the cobblestones, lights cast smeary reflections from the cold stone buildings. Smirnov glanced up and down the hill and then, without looking at Inigo, grasped his upper arm and squeezed it. It was an indecipherable gesture. Then he set out wordlessly down the hill.

Back in his apartment, Inigo tried to make sense of what had happened. Erika was not working for Smirnov; that was the biggest news. He forgave himself his suspicions of her. God knows this new world of his was a breeding ground for them. He would continue to watch for signs that she was working for East Berlin, but at the deepest level Smirnov's words had dissolved a great fear.

Also, he had surmounted the Gonzales crisis. Smirnov had provided another Soviet fallback position, and their understanding remained intact. But Inigo had brought it off with lies. There was no getting around that. His face burned when he thought of how easily, when he first met Smirnov, he had credited himself with a moral superiority over this crass Soviet manipulator. Now it was he who had turned out to be the manipulator. He had made Smirnov into a victim. But there was no fun it it. No fun at all. Nor any victory.

The problem drove him into the night street, where the drizzle had ceased but the lowering clouds still pressed down on the city like a blanket, holding the dampness in. It pursued him out of the Vieille Ville to the Promenade des Bastions, where the grim giants of the Reformation glowered down in cold stone. It drove him on to Place Neuve, where golden lights illuminated the delicate crescents on the conservatory facade. He would have liked to find an open café, but by this time of night only the strip clubs were still operating. I'm being followed, he suddenly thought. Screw you guys. He didn't turn around.

He didn't solve the problem. Instead, it simply dissolved as he mounted the dark stairs to his apartment. Turning his key in the lock, he suddenly realized his mind had reached a decision: I trust Smirnov. I believe he is on the level. And he trusts me. The meaning of Smirnov's grasp upon his arm suddenly became clear. Even the deceptions are part of the bond. The early ones, the lesser ones, were his. The later ones, the greater ones, are mine. Now we put the deceptions behind us. From this point forward, we will trust each other. There's no other choice.

23

TOP SECRET REDBIRD
DIRECTOR EYES ONLY

AT DINNER LAST NIGHT, SUBJECT SAID HE BOLTED FROM RES-
TAURANT ON PREVIOUS EVENING BECAUSE HE FEARED A TRAP.
TO SUPPORT EXPLANATION I PROVIDED, VITAL THAT GONZALES
DEPART GENEVA, AND NOT RETURN.

SUBJECT'S BEHAVIOR SUGGESTS, ALTHOUGH IT DOES NOT
PROVE, THAT HE IS DEALING WITH US IN GOOD FAITH. SEE ALSO
NEXT TELEGRAM.

SUBJECT HAS ASKED FOR INDICATION OF DIRECTOR'S PER-
SONAL INVOLVEMENT AND SUPPORT. RECOMMEND SHORT PER-
SONAL LETTER FROM DIRECTOR PRAISING HIS COURAGE AND
DEDICATION TO ARMS CONTROL.

Inigo pecked away at the second cable. By typing the Redbird cables himself, he could keep the circle of the witting in Geneva down
to himself, Carson, and the commo operators. The commo boys were
silent as mice.

TOP SECRET REDBIRD
DIRECTOR EYES ONLY

SUBJECT HAS PROVIDED FOLLOWING. SOVIETS ARE PREPARED
TO COMPLY WITH US "DATA BASE" DEMAND. THEY WILL PROVIDE
NUMERICAL INVENTORY, AT SIGNING OF TREATY AND EVERY SIX
MONTHS THEREAFTER, ON ALL TEN CATEGORIES OF STRATEGIC
WEAPONS LIMITED BY THE TREATY IF US AGREES TO DROP ELEV-
ENTH CATEGORY, LAUNCHERS OF HEAVY ICBMS, WHICH IS NOT
SPECIFICALLY LIMITED IN TREATY.

PLEASE NOTE HISTORIC CHARACTER OF THIS PROVISION,
WHICH SOVIETS HAVE STEADFASTLY RESISTED SINCE US PRO-
POSED IT TWO YEARS AGO. WHILE ACTUAL DATA WILL BE REDUN-

DANT TO US, FOR THEM IT REPRESENTS FORMAL ABANDONMENT OF SECRECY AND OFFICIAL ACCEPTANCE OF ENEMY'S RIGHT TO KNOW. VALUE AS PRECEDENT SHOULD BE SUBSTANTIAL IN FUTURE NEGOTIATIONS.

Then he called Carson. She was in the morning staff meeting, as he knew she would be. "Just give her a message, Ellie. Tell her everything is all right."

24

Saturday was a noisy day in the Vieille Ville. Especially in the Rue Etienne Dumont, where the high, close stone facades traded echoes of the sounds of housewives shopping for the weekend, clumps of tourists calling to one another, and students warming up their mopeds. Tomorrow would be Sunday-still, but this morning the street woke Inigo before ten. After putting on the coffee, he ran down to the bakery for fresh croissants. With these, plus an egg, he was ready to face the day.

Today, however, there was nothing to face. Erika suddenly had extra work, a deadline to meet, and the idea of getting up in the gray dawn to catch the ski bus without her had seemed too doleful. He telephoned the commo shack to learn that only routine cables had arrived. The whole day was his, to loaf away.

The wide walkway leading down from the cathedral was steep enough to jar Inigo's heels as he made for the river. He skipped across the Rue du Marché just in front of a streetcar, setting its bell clanging. A series of bridges and islands filled the Rhone as it flowed out of the lake and through the city, headed for France. One of Inigo's favorites was the waterworks island, Geneva's original source of electric power. It was still in use, though more out of sentiment than economic necessity. A long series of paddle wheels under the waterworks and the Pont de le Machine leading to it could be lowered into the stream, already running rapidly as the lake water crowded between the narrowing banks of the city. Downriver was a tumult of whirlpools and whitecaps as the water battled its way through the turbines.

The next stop was the Ile de Rousseau, a small wooded park holding a playground and an outdoor café. Dawdling over an espresso, Inigo gazed contentedly at the Jet d'Eau, the world's highest fountain, throwing its plume 460 feet into the air to sparkle stunningly in the sun before falling back in a scatter of spray. Flotillas of swans circled below children who bombed them with bread crumbs, while small brown ducks darted in like destroyers to snatch the prizes from under the bows of the battleships.

It was a beautiful day for a boatride. At the Place du Lac Inigo paid his franc and stepped aboard the little cutter that would carry him upstream to the opposite bank, above the first bridge of the city. The young woman who captained the boat was just about to cast off when a tall couple, shouting, jumped aboard, tilting the craft sharply.

"Mr. Inigo!" It was Pavlovsky and his wife. They clambered forward and sat down beside him. Pavlovsky pulled his coat closed over his broad chest against the lake winds. His wife, a beauty with delicate features that had nothing Slavic about them, tugged at her kerchief to control her thick blonde hair.

"Why are you not skiing?"

"I plan to go tomorrow," Inigo replied. "Perhaps it will clear our damned treaty out of my head. And you, aren't you also a skier?"

"Yes." Pavlovsky flashed his broad smile. "But we cannot leave Switzerland. We are prisoners of the Swiss. But protected," he joked, "by the Geneva Convention. Next week we are filing a complaint with the authorities about the torture you are subjecting us to."

Madame Pavlovsky turned her hazel eyes upon Inigo. "Once we cheated. We took our Soviet passports and trusted to luck. Nobody checked us at the border, and we spent the whole day skiing at Chamonix." She laughed merrily at the memory of the escapade.

"But of course we were found out," Pavlovsky concluded. "We could never figure out how. But our delegation policeman—your Mr. Smirnov—called us in and scolded us. In this city someone is watching all the time. And they call the Soviet Union a police state!"

Madame Pavlovsky was not to be suppressed. "Is it safe for us to be talking to Mr. Inigo, dear? We did promise to behave."

"Just don't let him trick you into giving him the combination to the safe. He's a dangerous man."

"I don't even know it!" And she burst into laughter again.

In four minutes they had reached the Quai de Mont Blanc, where the big lake steamers departed. The Pavlovskys bought tickets for a half-day tour of the lake and its little ports. But when he consulted the timetable, Pavlovsky discovered that the next departure was forty-five minutes later.

"Come have a coffee with me," Inigo suggested. The cold wind was keeping the sidewalk tables empty. Once inside the warm café, Pavlovsky grew even more expansive. He commandeered the menu and read off each offering before they all settled for espresso.

"So, Mr. Inigo, how long will you keep us here in Geneva?" There was something wolfish about his jovial smile.

"I see that you want to put me on the defensive. Let's not have such a combat. Tell me, do you believe that we will eventually succeed?"

"Oh, sooner or later." Pavlovsky spoke off-handedly. "Sooner or later. I doubt that it makes much difference, if you want to know the truth."

"What do you mean?"

"Well, it's not much of a treaty, is it? Our forces will get reduced a little, and yours won't be limited at all, as far as I can see. But you've put so many fine details into it that within a year, you'll be charging us with a dozen violations." He threw his big head back and finished off the espresso in a single gulp. "Then we'll find a dozen counter-charges to make against you. No, a dozen plus one. Just to show we're even tougher than you."

"Darling." His wife laid her hand on his arm. "Don't speak so. Mr. Inigo will think that you are a cynic."

"But I am!" Pavlovsky's roar turned all heads in their direction. "You know that! Everybody knows that, including my friends in the American delegation!"

Inigo, slightly embarrassed for him, was nevertheless intrigued and pushed on.

"So what will happen then?"

"Then I don't know. But I'll tell you what will happen eventually. War. What else? Surely you can see that. Neither side trusts the other, and they are correct not to do so. Our side will hide things. Your side will do as it pleases, hiding nothing, just reinterpreting the treaty as it goes along. Sooner or later there will be war. It doesn't matter when."

"Then what, may I ask, are you doing here?"

"Me personally? My job." Pavlovsky was quiet and smiling again. "Do you think it rests with me to turn aside the course of history? No, I do my job. I like it, in fact, this combat we have here in Geneva. My opponents are worthy, and it's a good way to pass the time."

His wife sighed, as though she knew better than to try to stop him twice. She began staring back at the other customers, who quickly dropped their eyes.

"Oh, there are some idealists on our delegation," her husband went

143

on. "Perhaps even more on yours. But not many in Moscow. Nor in Washington. You think I am wrong? Or perhaps you simply find it disagreeable to listen to such ideas, even though you know I am right."

"To tell the truth"—Inigo grinned at him—"I think you are both wrong and disagreeable."

Pavlovsky threw back his head and roared with laughter, his wife joining in. Inigo signaled for the check and, standing up with them, wished them a pleasant sail. Madame Pavlovsky touched his sleeve and confided in a stage whisper, "We may even set foot on French soil." The ensuing laughter covered what could have been an awkward parting.

The Quai de Mont Blanc was for Inigo the dullest part of town, Geneva at its most antiseptic. The broad walk along the lakefront was broken by tidy flower beds and filled with strollers. Solemn diplomats, deep in conversation, passed equally solemn but silent Genevois. The boulevard was lined with plane trees, cut off precisely at fourteen feet. Their gnarled, mutilated trunks marked them as victims of the Swiss passion for order and conformity. Across the boulevard stood the grand hotels, the Richemonde, the Beau-Rivage, des Bergues, with their splendid lobbies, tiny bedrooms, and steep prices. Here, in 1898, the Italian anarchist Lucheni stabbed Empress Elizabeth of Austria. Inigo could see why. Sissi, as she was called, died in her room at the Beau-Rivage; Lucheni made his way into history.

Inigo paused at a small palace of white stone tracery that symbolized all of this Geneva: the mausoleum of Charles, duke of Brunswick and Luneberg. Run out of his duchy in the nineteenth century, he had taken refuge in Geneva, where he was so royally received and entertained by the local inhabitants that upon his death in 1873 he left all his wealth of twenty-four million gold francs to the city. A grateful populace built his mausoleum on the lakefront; it was, after all, a condition of the bequest. Guarded by a delicate wrought-iron fence and a moat, protected physically and spiritually by surrounding knights, scribes, and angels, the top of the head of Charles's stone effigy was barely visible under the elaborate peak of his forty-foot-high tomb. His nearby equestrian statue was meant to be placed on the very top, but the weight had proved too much. He was Geneva's first Arab sheikh.

Enough. Inigo found a phone booth and called Erika. No answer. He headed on foot across the long Mont Blanc Bridge, letting the lake breeze blow his head empty. Upon gaining the left bank, he called again; again no answer. Tired now, he labored up the hill and through the Bourg de Four, past the statue of the unclad girl on the rim of puberty, strangely androgynous, her expression solemn, almost sullen. He called again from his apartment.

"Hello?"

"Erika! May I come over?"

"Do."

He was there in ten minutes. She opened the door wearing a bright red terrycloth robe, her hair streaming, the shower running in the background. Inigo had never felt so urgent. He pushed her laughing against the wall and strained to press his body through hers.

"That feels like some sort of phallic symbol down there," she teased him. But Inigo was not to be denied; it was his day to be aggressive. When she first curled her fingers around his member, he gasped and froze, but only for a moment.

His blood seemed to be rushing everywhere. In two minutes they lay back, exhausted. "That was lovely, George," she murmured. "What got into you?" Inigo could only growl, "You shouldn't work on Saturdays."

He had nearly dozed off when she rolled out of bed and, gleaming in her damp skin, brought the cigarettes, the ashtray, the Scotch he'd bought at the consulate. Back beside him, she took one of his hands, pressed it onto her breast, and spoke.

"George, you have a lot more ardor than you do curiosity."

Inigo's eyes were closed. "Huh? Oh, I'm sorry, sweetie. What did you say your name was?"

"Stop it, dear. I am serious. You never ask me about myself. We have been lovers for three months now, and what do you know about me?"

"Well, your breasts are perfect globes and you have a lovely hairy place between your legs that—"

"All right, George."

The truth was, he admitted to himself, that he had put Erika and himself into a time compartment. They would have a few months of joy together, and then he would be gone. Later she would go back to East Germany. The present belonged to them, and it was enough. To bring in the past threatened the barriers he had erected in his mind against the future.

But a feeling of fear told him it was more than that. Opening up Erika's past risked discovering something he wouldn't want to face. What if he sensed she was hiding something? Then he would have to turn into an interrogator, cross-checking her story, searching for clues of a secret intelligence assignment. A foolhardy cowardice, he saw, had led him to turn his back to that danger.

He pushed himself up to a sitting position. "Sorry, dear. I guess I figured you'd tell me what you wanted me to know. So who are you, sweet Erika?"

She was silent for a moment. Then, "I do not know, when you put it that way. Somehow that is not the right question."

"Where were you born? What was it like as a child?"

"That is better. In Prussia. During the war. Do you know Prussia? Flat, with forests and a wind from the Baltic. We lived there for generations."

"Anyone still there?"

"Oh no, we moved to Berlin when the war broke out. When I was still very small." Like every German Inigo had ever known, she spoke of the war as an elemental, impersonal force. One day it just "broke out."

"Are your parents still in Berlin?" Inigo lit two cigarettes and gently placed one between her lips. She took it away.

"Mama is. I have not seen my father for over thirty years."

"Missing in the war?"

"Missing after the war." She stared at the opposite wall. "We think he may be in South America. He was a Nazi."

"Wasn't everyone?"

"No. Lots of people were not. And not only Communists. But it was more than that. He was a big Nazi."

On instinct, Inigo turned toward her and began to stroke her belly, but Erika was in no mood to snuggle. She continued to stare straight ahead. "An industrialist. I do not even know his name."

"It's not Hartke?"

"No. Mama never told me what it was. We lost everything in Berlin, between the bombing and the Russians. We took the name Hartke. It was easy in those days. Lots of people lost their papers, with all the fires.

"So we got new papers from the authorities and I started school and she went to work. For the first time in her life. There was not much food at first; we ate a lot of potatoes. It is a wonder I never got fat, but maybe there were not enough potatoes for that."

"I'd love you fat," Inigo murmured.

"No, you would not." She absently put his hand on her breast again. "Mama made herself into a typist, and then a secretary, and then an office manager. And she made herself into a Communist."

"Wait a minute, not so fast. How do you know about your father being a Nazi? Did your mother tell you?"

"Her? Never! For a long time she did not even know that I knew. No, her sister told me. My poor Aunt Hildegarde. She was jealous of my mother, especially after her own daughter died. So she told me about my father's factories and the Ukrainian slave workers and the high death rate. But no Jews; my father never employed Jews. She would not tell me my real name."

Erika was sitting up now, hugging her knees and shivering. Inigo pulled a blanket loose and draped it around her naked shoulders. "And your mother became a Communist to cover her past?"

"Something like that. Even though one could get new papers right after the war, there was always some suspicion of those who did so. It helped to be politically positive and active. Except that mama ended up as a real believer. One of the few who remain. She fed me, clothed me, drummed communism into me, and that was all. I could not wait to get away to the university."

They talked on for an hour. There had been lovers, an abortion, an abortive young marriage. She spent two years in the USSR at Dubna, where Soviet and East European scientists conducted unclassified nuclear research. She had hated living in Russia; it was dirty, uncultured, without style or color. Out of boredom she fell in love with a young Soviet physicist, but a Russo-German marriage was too much to take on. For one thing, where would they live? So it was back to East Germany, to a research appointment in Leipzig, where at last she found her own natural circle of friends. And then to CERN and Geneva.

"Did your mother push you into the Party?" It was the kindest way he could ask the question.

She snorted scornfully. "Mama could not push me into anything. No, it was clear to all of us that Party membership was the only way to get ahead. It would not be possible for me to get to Geneva, for example, without that." She thought a moment, then added wryly, "Or to Dubna either. I paid for Geneva, in advance, at Dubna."

The dusk was beginning to gather outside as she finally ran down. Inigo was listening quietly, eyes closed, his lips lightly touching her scissored hip. It was not bad, she was saying, being in the Party. Two or three meetings a month, a political speech to her cell once a year. "I always make my speech about American imperialism. Perhaps you can tell me of some fresh crimes; my examples are getting stale."

Inigo was lazily cupping his hand under her buttock when she slid down beside him and turned her body to his.

"Now make love to me again. A different way."

So they became slow explorers, languorous right to the end, a long, surging wave like a giant roller moving in at half speed. Afterward they lay beached, with no spot in their bodies where tension might find a hold.

They decided to have dinner in France. The drive to the border, through the drab eastern part of the city, reminded them that Geneva had its lower middle class, even though it lacked a true proletarian quarter. Still dreamy from bed, they had forgotten their passports. It was better to park, wait for a streetcar to arrive at the terminus, and join the crowd walking across the border. One hundred steps inside France lay the Auberge du Foron, with even better food than the Genevan fare and lower prices as well.

"It strikes me," said Inigo as they settled at their table, "that your mother must live in constant tension. Suppose she's found out. Any day someone from the old times might suddenly appear and recognize her."

"True. She could be denounced at any time. Without warning. I have thought a lot about that. But I do not believe it bothers her. In her mind, she has put those former times out of sight. I think she would be honestly surprised if anyone reminded her of what she was.

"When I was a teenager—what a useful American word!—we fought all the time. In my anger, I used to have fantasies about denouncing her myself. But of course I never would. Once I lost my temper so badly that I threatened to go the authorities and expose her. At first she did not know what I was talking about. For her, communism has crowded out everything else."

"And yourself? What would happen to you if they found out your father was a big Nazi in hiding abroad?"

"Just some unpleasantness, I imagine. They would want to know where he was, did I write to him, when we had had contact, things like that. I think they would accept my answers. It is the truth, after all. I might do some extra Party work for a while to reassure them. Nothing more than that. But for mother, it would be the end of everything, job, career, Party membership, respectability, position. You see, she lied to the Party about him. I could always say that I never knew anything but what she told me, that my father was a salesman and then a corporal, who never came back from the eastern front."

After they ordered, he went to the men's room. Returning, he saw a man sitting at their table, talking to Erika, his back turned to the room. Inigo hurriedly threaded his way through the small linen-draped tables.

"Excuse me," he said behind the man's shoulder. When the face turned toward him, it was Gonzales.

"George! How nice to run into you again. I've just been getting acquainted with Fraülein Hartke. Pull up another chair."

Erika was on her feet, fuming. "He simply sat down without a word of invitation! If this is a friend of yours, he is very rude," she told Inigo. Then, turning to Gonzales, "How do you know my name?"

Inigo grabbed Gonzales's arm.

"Rough stuff, George?" Gonzales said calmly. "Not a good idea. Not in here. The border police are just down the road. Brought your passport, I trust?"

Inigo held his grip. "You've got a nerve being back here," he hissed at Gonzales.

"Here?" Gonzales's good humor was unfailing. "Switzerland? But we're in France, old boy. Had you forgotten? And unless I'm much mistaken, two of us have no passports. That's an old trick, walking across the border with the commuters."

"Erika, this man is no friend of mine. He's a pest, whom I thought I'd gotten rid of. Don't answer his questions." He tugged at Gonzales's arm. "All right, get out of here."

Gonzales got slowly to his feet, turning away from Erika to face Inigo. He spoke in a low voice. "One punch and I'll have you on the floor, Inigo. The police will be here within one minute. They won't shoot you for being without a passport, but they won't take very kindly to it either. You could spend quite a few hours in their office straightening it out. So, for starters, let go of my arm."

Inigo dropped his hand. "Gonzales, the lady is not going to answer any questions. That's final. If you have anything to say, you can say it outside to me. Let's go."

Gonzales let his smile fade; his eyes remained hard. "Anything you say, Inigo. But you're making a big mistake. All right, we'll talk outside." He led the way.

The parking lot was covered with loose gravel, invaded by grass and weeds from its ragged edge. The restaurant sign was a little dilapidated; the streetlights gave off a weak glow; one of them was broken. A few steps out of Geneva into France, one could already feel the difference.

Gonzales swung around on Inigo fiercely. "Listen, buddy, you can be a fool all you want. But don't treat me like one. First a month in the Soviet Union, then all those lunches and dinners with your KGB pal. Those stupid cables in which you pretend he's giving you the hot poop on their SALT positions. Meanwhile God knows what you're giving him. And now an East German broad. Did Smirnov fix you up with her? Is that all the payoff you're getting? Or are you headed for Moscow after you've finished selling us out here?"

Inigo tried to bull him up against a dark sedan, but Gonzales was quick. He rolled smoothly along the fender and, free of Inigo's rush, held up a fist of darkly gleaming metal. He must have put on the brass knuckles as they left the restaurant.

"Inigo, I'll hurt you if I have to. In fact, you could say I'd welcome the chance. But Art frowns on that stuff unless it's necessary. Now you listen to me." Inigo stood off away from the car, in the open, his chest heaving. He was silent.

"Shambler thinks you're crossing over. Myself, I'm just about convinced of it. But Art says it doesn't count until we can prove it. He's been to the director on it, but that guy's as big a fool as you are. If we could prove it, you'd have been yanked out of Geneva and put on the box long ago. And now this."

"Screw you, Gonzales."

"Now there's a fine answer. A real high-class answer," Gonzales sneered. "What do you know about this Hartke babe, anyway?"

"What are you getting at?"

"How do you think the daughter of a big-time Nazi gets to come to Geneva? That's what she is, in case you didn't know. And she gets to come here because she's been co-opted into East German Intelligence, that's how. Either she joins up or she's through, with the Party, with the labs, with her profession."

150

"What are you talking about? She's not even in the Agency files!"

"She's in our files."

Suddenly Inigo remembered the rumors. Shambler had been one of the first Americans to get to Berlin after the war. There were stories of files captured and hidden away, stories that Shambler always denied. No, he had turned everything over to the regular Agency archivists. Everyone suspected; no one knew.

"So? Being a Nazi's daughter doesn't prove she's been recruited into Intelligence."

"Granted. But it sure makes it likely. Especially since she's posted abroad."

Inigo's mind was racing, careening. "Look, Gonzales, she told me herself about her father. I could have exposed her. She put herself in my hands."

"Not if she's already in theirs. But it's a nice piece of work, I must admit.'

Inigo leaned against a car. Suddenly all his certainty had left him. Now that he thought about it, the odds were that Erika and her mother had been spotted, identified, reported by someone. Such a prominent family was bound to be known, and to have enemies. And the authorities hadn't lowered the boom; why? To use the information as leverage on Erika?

Gonzales saw his confusion and pressed on. "Yes, a nice piece of work. What better way to get you to trust her? Has the advantage, also, of being true."

But at least she wasn't working with Smirnov. Of that he was certain. Smirnov had been desperate to have him break off with Erika. If she was trapping him, it was a separate operation. Soviet-controlled, perhaps, but outside Smirnov's ken. Still, he wasn't going to expose this evidence to Gonzales's cynical quickness, his double and triple thinking.

"Well, Inigo, think it over. And remember, we're keeping an eye on you. Good luck at the border tonight."

"Wait a minute."

Gonzales, who had already begun to move away, stopped and returned, on his guard. Inigo searched for subtle phrases but found none. Gonzales had been blunt enough; he might as well be the same.

"Somebody shot Allan Hickok. Killed him. It was you, wasn't it?" He was glad his voice was steady.

Gonzales gave him a long, insolent stare.

"Anyone who played the games Hickok played with your buddy Smirnov deserved what he got." They glared silently at each other for a long moment; then Gonzales moved off into the darkness, took shape again under a wan arc light, and faded out into France.

The restaurant was another world, bright, full of low, contented conversation, sparkling crystal, subdued warm odors. Erika had her back to him, the thick hair tumbling at her shoulders. At the sight of her, Inigo refused to believe Gonzales's accusations, the whole Shambler view of life. He had the evidence of joys, of confidences, of long open gazes. One did come truly to know someone. But then why was he refusing to believe Gonzales? Was there something that required to be refused, that had enough power not to be ignored, that had to be consciously opposed and rejected?

"George, what is happening? Who was that man?" She was full of vigorous anger.

"Darling, I'm sorry. He's a pest whom I thought I'd gotten rid of. Let's just forget about him."

The waiter, who had kept their order warming in the kitchen while Inigo was outside, was bringing the food now. But Erika was not to be put off.

"There seems to be a lot that I am supposed to forget about." Her voice rose; the waiter hurried to finish and be gone. "Broken dates. Your silence about what you do, who you are. And now this."

"But you know what I do! I'm on the U.S. delegation. I'm here from Washington to negotiate the SALT treaty with the Soviet Union." He could hear the defensiveness in his own voice.

She simply stared at him, one eyebrow raised.

"Erika dear, it's classified work. You know I can't talk about it. Besides, it's rather boring. A lot of little details. All kinds of technical stuff having to do with missiles and submarines and bomber aircraft. It's only interesting if your work buries you in it, if you can fight with the Soviets about it."

"You mean like my nuclear physics? It is too difficult for nonspecialists? No, George, that is not what I am talking about. I am talking about your Mr. Gonzales. He cannot be so difficult to explain to a nonspecialist."

He looked miserably at his plate. I'm paralyzed, he thought. That damn Gonzales has planted a canker in my soul. To find himself distrusting Erika! He was appalled. But he couldn't help it. There was an implausibility to her story that her mother had succeeded in hiding that whole hideous past. And if she hadn't, then Erika was hiding something else, and Gonzales might be making some very good guesses.

"Look, dear, I don't completely understand it all myself. As soon as it gets clearer for me, I'll tell you everything I can. Until then, please . . ." He was about to say "trust me," but the outrage of that stopped him. "Until then, please wait." Even that was a plea for trust, and it was sickening. He felt rotten.

Erika was brusque. "I have to go to the ladies' room now. Please excuse me. And I am sorry to have bored you with my little story this afternoon." She left the table.

It was a dismal meal, eaten mostly in silence. The return across the border, which at another time would have been a gay adventure, was tense but uneventful. They gave up trying to talk altogether on the way home. Inigo was actually relieved when she told him coldly not to come up to her apartment. On the way back to the Vieille Ville, he suddenly threw off his guilt with a vengeance. "Maybe," he shouted aloud, "you're just the best damn actress that ever came out of Berlin!" But that was the worst thought of all.

25

It was a sparkling morning as the limousine sped down the parkway from Langley to the city. The morning traffic had cleared itself away, and they were going to make their ten o'clock meeting easily. The Park Service mowing machines were making their first spring cut on the highway embankments, their buzzing foretelling the insect sounds that would soon be heard again in the backyards of Washington. The director felt just fine.

When the automobile telephone rang, Blom picked it up, listened briefly, and replaced it. "The office says the president may drop in on part of today's meeting."

"Splendid." The director felt that he was at his best in the Verification Panel. He had mastered nearly all the issues in the SALT negotiations, and his military background was standing him in good stead. Peters, sitting behind him, steadily wrote notes as the session progressed and, when the director faltered in handling a question, silently handed him the correct response. He had even gained enough confidence to be able to say, on the really tough ones, "Well, I'd like to let Guy Peters speak to that one." Peters would begin to lay out the details, and as soon as he recalled the chain of reasoning, the director would smoothly cut in and complete the answer.

Best of all, there was Redbird. This fellow Smirnov was really delivering the goods. All the fallbacks he had passed to Inigo had, in the end, been accepted by the Soviet delegation. It was a lengthy and circuitous route that the information took: from Moscow to Geneva, there from Smirnov over to Inigo, then on to Langley, where he and Blom recast the Soviet fallback into an American proposal, then down to the Verification Panel at its White House meetings, back to Geneva in the form of an instruction to the U.S. delegation, and lastly across the table to the Soviet negotiators. By that time, of course, the actual language had been changed, first deliberately by Smirnov, again by himself and Blom, and finally by the Verification Panel.

The director leaned back expansively, pleased with his coup. It would be an even greater pleasure, he thought, when his colleagues at the panel—the heads of State, Defense, ACDA, and the JCS—found out about Redbird. So far they knew only that the director of CIA was increasingly stepping out of his role as intelligence adviser to make policy recommendations, which was exasperating, and that his suggestions always led to success. That was even more annoying, but impossible to complain about. Besides, the president had made it clear, on his last visit to the Verification Panel, that he regarded the director not only as the head of CIA but a senior policy adviser to himself.

"This fellow Smirnov is really delivering the goods, isn't he?" he fired at Blom as they eased onto the Theodore Roosevelt Bridge across the Potomac. Blom merely grunted; he was used to hearing isolated bits of the director's train of thought. The director retired into his reverie, recalling happily that all the fallbacks that Smirnov had handed over had, in the end, proved genuine. The man's record was one hundred percent so far, and so was his.

Exactly because it was so gratifying, the director was spending more and more of his time on Redbird and SALT. Yesterday he had met again with Marcus, Shambler, and the others to review the operation, not because any decisions needed to be made, but because of the pleasure it gave him. Sloan had assured him that preparations were going forward for the Moscow exfiltration but had been vague on details. Petrocelli had passed on Carson's report that Inigo was in touch with her on Redbird and her opinion that the case was being handled professionally. In no uncertain terms the director had ordered Shambler to pull Gonzales out of Europe. He had ignored Blom's skeptical remark after the meeting that, with Shambler, ordering was one thing but compliance was another.

Redbird's highest value, however, came in the weekly meetings with the president. When he accepted the post, the director had successfully negotiated for a regular Thursday-morning appointment with the president. The only other person present at these sessions was the national security adviser. At the outset the director had used these meetings to present important intelligence conclusions on such subjects as the capabilities of the Israeli armed forces, the likelihood of armed conflict between Nicaragua and its neighbors, the prospects for the Soviet grain crop. When the cancellation rate for these meetings approached fifty percent, he began to include such matters as the sexual proclivities and peccadilloes of a certain European prime minister and an intercepted and decrypted cable containing a local ambassador's sneering comments on the secretary of state. Operational details, such as exactly how weapons and a large amount of cash were secretly delivered to a private antiterrorist group, also got a good response. The cancellations diminished; a discreet single round of drinks began to be served.

Redbird was too good to be shared with anyone but the president. The director had chosen a Thursday when the national security adviser was ill and was represented by his deputy. Fifteen minutes before the session was to end, he had made an unusual request: that the deputy be excused before he presented his final item. The president was surprised but did not object.

"Thank you, sir. This is about a new agent who has begun reporting to us on Soviet positions in SALT. He has access to their fallbacks on all the remaining unresolved issues."

"You don't mean it!"

"Indeed I do, sir."

"Where is he?" The president had jumped up from his desk in excitement.

"That's extremely sensitive information, as you well realize. That's why I asked that the deputy adviser leave the room. He's on the Soviet delegation in Geneva. My personal representative on the delegation has recruited him."

"Wonderful! I'd like to meet your man."

"So you shall, sir, the next time he's back in Washington. Man with a funny name. George Inigo." He went on to underline the extreme sensitivity of the operation. "That's why I'd like not to give you the Soviet's name," he said, forestalling the question. "He's the KGB man on their delegation. Those fellows have a strange affinity for CIA. I guess it's because they know they can trust us." But for security reasons nothing was to be said about the operation. The director would present the Redbird fallbacks to the Verification Panel as his own suggestions, "worked up by my experts." The circle of the witting was to be kept as small as possible.

"Gordon, this is really marvelous!" the president had said, walking him to the door. "This is the best news you've brought me yet. I've been getting mighty discouraged about that treaty, but now it looks like we can get it. Anything I can do to help?"

"Not at the moment, sir. I'll let you know if we need something like that."

"Don't hesitate. And don't spare anything on this, this, Redbird, you said? Discretionary funds, anything. Remember that I want to meet this Indigo fellow too. Give him my personal congratulations."

The director had managed to keep a sober expression until the door closed. Then he flashed a big grin at Blom, sitting against the wall in the anteroom. He said not a word until they were in the hall, beyond the hearing of the secretaries. Then his tension had exploded in one loud burst of laughter. Even Blom had smiled.

The conference room was filling up fast when they arrived. The director was pleased to notice that with the word out that the president "might drop in," no one had sent his deputy. Each panel member brought the usual pair of aides. As chairman, the national security adviser cut the pleasantries short and got the meeting started quickly.

"Let's begin with a rundown on the remaining issues, gentlemen. There are six of them. No, five, since Moscow caved in on the Tyuratam Eighteen. We've signed off on instructions to the delegation in Geneva on two of these—reentry vehicle limits and frods for the Bison tankers. I understand that our experts haven't finished their latest studies on two others—telemetry encryption and the ban on all but one new type of ICBM. That leaves the data base issue for decision today. Defense, you've been taking the lead on this one, haven't you?"

"Right. The U.S. position is that both sides should formally advise each other of the number of strategic weapons they have at the time of signing the treaty and every six months thereafter. Officially, this is to check on whether the SALT counting rules are being interpreted the same way by both sides. Any discrepancy between one side's reporting and the other side's intelligence count would suggest we weren't using the same criteria for counting, and then that would have to be sorted out jointly."

"And unofficially?"

"Unofficially," the secretary of defense went on, "we're using this issue to put pressure on Soviet secrecy. We don't actually need the numbers. CIA can count all the weapons limited by the treaty with great accuracy. But we're trying to establish the principle that the USSR's obsession with secrecy is incompatible with real arms control. If they want to go down that road with us, they'll have to begin to relax and start exchanging data with us. This issue today is the merest beginning."

"We're trying to drag them into the twentieth century," remarked the secretary of state.

"More like the nineteenth. What's the Soviet position?"

"They say it's all unnecessary. The counting rules are clear. Each side's intelligence people can count the other's weapons quite adequately. The U.S. is raising an unnecessary complication that delays the talks."

"They've been stonewalling on this for eighteen months," put in the chairman of the Joint Chiefs of Staff. "The JCS attaches a lot of importance to this one."

"Well, what about it?" asked the adviser. "Do we drop the issue? Press on as before? Anyone got any ideas?"

There was a silence, broken only by a growl, surly and unintelligible, from the chairman of the Joint Chiefs of Staff. The director saw that his moment had arrived.

"We've been looking over the record on this one out at Langley. The U.S. position calls for exchanging data on eleven categories of strategic weapons. As you know, only ten of these categories are explicitly limited in number by the treaty. The eleventh, launchers of heavy ICBMs, is not. These launchers, of which the Soviets have three hundred and eight, are in fact indirectly but effectively limited to that number by other provisions forbidding the construction of new launchers or conversion of existing silos from light to heavy ICBMs. But the treaty contains no actual number for them, as it does for the others.

"It occurs to me," the director concluded, "that if we dropped that category, and just asked for data on the others, the Soviets might go along with it." He leaned back and looked confidently around the table as the criticisms began.

The secretary of defense was indignant. "Gordon, those heavy missiles are precisely the ones we're after. They're the ones that can knock out our whole ICBM force in a first strike. How can we hope to get them reduced in the next treaty if we can't even get the Soviets to put a number on them in this one?"

The adviser was more judicious. "It seems to me, Gordon, that if we drop one category, that will just encourage the Soviets to hang in there and whittle us down, category by category. Although I see what you mean about the heavy ICBM category being different."

The door opened and a new voice intoned, "Gentlemen, the president."

"Please, keep your seats," said a sandy-haired man who bustled in behind the official proclamation. He was of medium height, with a heavy nose, not at all prepossessing. Only the alertness of his eyes as they swept the room marked him out in any way. "No, John, you keep your chair. I can't stay long. Just wanted to see how you're getting along."

"We're discussing the data base issue, Mr. President. That's the requirement to tell the other side officially the actual number of weapons that one has."

"Oh yes, I remember that. Where do we stand?"

"No Soviet movement at all, sir, since we introduced it eighteen months ago. It's one of only six remaining issues. The question is whether to hold fast or drop it."

"No middle ground? No room for compromise?"

"Well, CIA has suggested that if we reduce the number of reporting categories from eleven to ten, the Soviets might buy the idea."

A tense hush filled the room. The issue suddenly threatened to leave the panel's control. If the president actually made a decision, that would wipe out the options of stalling, of commissioning new studies, of standing pat. It was a bureaucratic moment of truth. Someone was going to win, someone was going to lose.

"Let's hear your idea, Gordon."

The director restated his proposal, then forestalled Defense and JCS by stating their objections for them. No one spoke as the president kept his gaze upon the director.

"You know, Gordon," he finally said, "I think it's time to let the others in on our little secret. After all, if I can't trust the members of the Verification Panel, whom can I trust?" His glance swept the table. "CIA has a new source, gentlemen. He's a Soviet official with access to their SALT planning. For some time now he's been telling us their prepared fallback positions, and Gordon here has been feeding them in here as his own suggestions, to protect his source. He and I have kept all this to ourselves, but his man's reporting has proved totally reliable to date. If Gordon says the Soviets will accept something, you can count on it."

Everyone looked unhappy except the director, who hung onto a sober, responsible expression. Silently but unmistakably, the balance of power in the room was shifting.

"So let's drop the eleventh category and collect the other ten. Any objections?" There were none. Briskly, flushed with decisiveness, the president continued. "What's next?"

"That's it, sir," the adviser replied. "The other issues are still out for study. You've finished today's agenda for us."

"Well, glad to be of help." Everyone scrambled to his feet as the president rose. "It's nice to see that presidents are good for something occasionally, after all." Everyone smiled appreciatively. "And remember"—he jabbed the air with a finger—"not a word about Gordon's source. It's not to leave this room. Agreed?" Amid a jumble of assenting noises, he left the room.

The director was nearly ecstatic on the ride back to Langley. He felt as though he had virtually been put in charge of SALT policy. He fantasized pleasurably about the chapter this would occupy when he published his memoirs. "They'll think twice before they buck me again in the Verification Panel, eh, Joe? Though it was fun to pass off Redbird's stuff as our own ideas."

Blom was as laconic as ever. "Leaving out the president, you, and me, I counted fifteen people in that room."

"So?"

"I don't think Inigo or Smirnov would be comfortable if they knew about that number."

26

On the morning after Gonzales's reappearance, Inigo arrived at work in a foul mood. Suspicions of Erika were alternating in his mind with feelings of guilt, both for his suspicions and for his own secretiveness with her. Perhaps new instructions would be in from Washington and he could bury himself in the work of preparing new plenary statements. But the cables on his desk were all routine. Beside them was a note from Jenkins's secretary. The ambassador wanted to see Inigo as soon as he arrived.

He climbed the stairs with a heavy feeling. Jenkins did nearly all his business in the tank. A private summons was unusual, and Inigo's guiltiness toward Erika was seeping into the other parts of his mind, making him apprehensive. Was Jenkins going to chew him out for some mistake in his work? His liaison with an East German? Was he going to be quizzed about Hickok?

When he arrived, the secretary waved him straight in. Jenkins came around from behind his desk and took an armchair at the coffee table. "When I was on the secure phone to Washington last night, George, they told me of a rumor that CIA has a new Soviet agent who reports on SALT. Very hush-hush. Nobody will confirm anything for sure."

Inigo reached for a cigarette, forcing his hand not to tremble as he lit it. Jenkins was watching him closely. He wished that a miracle would give him a ten-minute respite. But the question came.

"Know anything about it, George?"

"Haven't heard a word." Inigo's voice sounded shaky to himself; he couldn't tell whether it did to Jenkins or not.

"The director hasn't said anything to you? Guy Peters?"

"Not a word, Al. If it's true, you know, I'd be the last one to be told."

Jenkins still held him in a steady gaze. "The local station chief. It's a woman, isn't it?"

"That's right, Emily Carson. First rate."

"She's gotten the word, hasn't she? I mean, I presume she knows the Soviet delegation here is off limits to her. Is she the kind who would fool around with recruitment anyway, in the face of that?"

"Emily?" Inigo's poise was returning. "Oh no, I don't think so. She's a pretty balanced type. Not one of your gung-ho, old-time, wild operators. No, I think you can rely on Emily to play it straight."

"Okay." Jenkins stood up. "I just wanted to get it clear. Maybe the rumors are wrong." Moving back around his big desk, he suddenly turned and sat on the corner, facing Inigo. "By the way, you should know that you're not exactly at the top of Walt O'Rourke's list of favorites."

"I'm not surprised. Has he been complaining about me?"

"Nothing specific. Just some growls about being disappointed to get so little support from you in the tank." Jenkins grinned at him. "He didn't expect the CIA rep to join the ranks of the treaty-at-any-price types."

"Al, if I were in Walt O'Rourke's good book, I'd really be worrying about what I was doing wrong." Inigo was relieved to be back on safe ground. "I happen to think we're getting a treaty at a damn good price. It's too bad Walt can't see that and be proud of it."

"I agree. But forewarned is forearmed. Just be aware, George, that he's started to keep book on you. Like he's been doing on me for years."

"Then I'm in good company."

Descending the stairs to his own office, Inigo realized he was badly rattled. He wondered who was talking loosely in Washington. Most likely it was the director, out to impress somebody. But it wasn't out of the question that Shambler was quietly spreading the word in order to sabotage the operation. If Jenkins got firm word that one of the Soviets in Geneva was a defector-in-place, supplying secret information, Inigo knew he would shake the American delegation mercilessly until the truth fell out. Then he'd hand the culprit a ticket on the next flight to the States.

The whole day was a total loss. Jenkins kept them in the tank all morning, listening to a long account from Michaels about semantic battles with Pavlovsky over the meaning of *functionally related observable differences*. In the afternoon session, Inigo found himself in an unexpected duel with the interpreters over the proper translation of *encryption*. The debate carried him beyond the limits of his Russian-language competence. Late in the afternoon, insecurity piled on top of guilt finally got the better of his temper.

"Damm it, we're not going to put a ban on *coding* in this treaty when the real problem is *encryption!*" he exploded.

"But the Russian language does not distinguish between the two!" the interpreter shouted back.

"It's got to! They're two different things!" But for the life of him, Inigo couldn't come up with anything but the simple term *zashifro-vanie*. Finally Jenkins called it off.

"I guess we can't settle this today. George, why not cable your people in Washington and ask them to put one of their linguists on this?"

Inigo agreed sulkily, then felt ungrateful as well. After all, Jenkins was getting him off the hook.

Driving home after work, Inigo maneuvered savagely in the early evening traffic on the Quai Wilson. Abruptly he pulled over and parked. He was shaking. I'm not in a straight way with anyone, he told himself. I'm lying to Al. I'm holding out with Carson and the director about Erika. I'm holding out with her about everything, including who I am. I'm faking it with Smirnov, about Gonzales. It suddenly struck him that Gonzales was the only one who knew the whole story, who had all the pieces of the puzzle. Gonzales and Shambler. It was intolerable that those paranoid thugs should be the only ones sharing all the facts with him. It was as though his enemy were his only friend.

He eased out into the traffic again and headed straight for Erika's. I've got to get straight with someone, he thought, and she's the one I hurt the most about. With everything threatening to disintegrate around him, he could at least make himself whole with one person.

He heard talking inside her apartment as he knocked, but before it registered in his mind, it was too late. When she opened the door and saw him, she frowned. They had not met or talked since that night in France with Gonzales, five days ago. Inigo had been unable to think of a way to heal that evening's wounds, and Erika hadn't called him. He stood now at her doorstep, conscious that he had no right to take her in his arms or even to cross the threshold.

"May I come in, Erika?" It was humbly said.

"All right, George." Her voice was guarded. "I am just now on the telephone." She turned curtly and he followed her in, relieved that no one else was here. What had he imagined?

"A guest has just arrived." She spoke into the phone in German. "No, unexpectedly. May I call you back? Oh, I don't know. In half an hour, perhaps." She was using the *du* form, the familiar form of *you*, the intimate form, but without letting Inigo know the sex of her caller. "Yes, thanks a lot. *Tschuss*."

"Who was that?" He couldn't stop himself.

"George, you're upset. Why did you come? Sit down, please. I will get you a drink."

Normally they went together into the kitchen, where Inigo loved to touch her briefly as she moved from cabinet to refrigerator to counter. Now he sat glumly alone. In the silence, she seemed to be taking a long time.

"Want some help in there?" He worked to manage a sociable tone.

"Nearly ready, thanks," she sang out. "I have been wondering whether you would ring me."

So there was to be no small talk, no social chatter. They were going right to the trouble. Yes, that was best. Erika returned with his drink and hers and seated herself across the coffee table from him. He began.

"Erika, I've felt awful since that evening. I've been trying to think of some way to explain it to you."

"Yes?"

"The truth is, I haven't told you everything about myself. You know that I'm a U.S. Government official."

"And you are on the SALT delegation," she added when he paused.

"Yes. The part I didn't tell you is that I am the intelligence officer on that delegation. I work for CIA. I have for over twenty years."

"And that is your terrible secret?"

"Part of it. I'm an analyst, an expert on Soviet affairs. I do desk work, writing papers, giving briefings, going to meetings. I've never been on the spy side of the house." He stopped again and took a long sip from the glass, grateful that she had made him a strong one.

"And this has what to do with your friend at the restaurant in France?"

"Yes, him. Hardly a friend. Well, since I got to Geneva, I've gotten mixed up with the spy side of the house. I can't tell you any more than that, obviously. That's how that bastard from the other evening has gotten into my life. And I couldn't explain that to you because then I'd have to tell you what—what I just did."

Erika leaned forward across the table and stared into his eyes.

"And why is it you tell me now?"

"Love," he said tonelessly, meeting her gaze. After a while he dropped his eyes. "And misery." He let his head fall into his hands. "I can't stand deceiving you anymore."

"So you love me," she said angrily. "And you deceive me and are miserable about it. And you miss my taking you skiing. And the good meals I cook for you. And my warm vagina, it is so agreeable to put your penis into!"

The words were like a whip cracked across Inigo's face. His head jerked up in fury. But what started as a denial came out differently.

"No! I mean, yes, dammit! That's all true! But that's not all! There's so much—"

But she cut him off and went coldly on.

"And you could not tell me the truth because you thought I might be a spy myself. An East German intelligence officer. That is what you are afraid of?" Her stare was burning.

"Yes!" No turning back now. "I was worried about that. Especially at first."

"And even now you cannot be sure!"

"Erika . . ." His voice faltered. They glared at each other for a long time. Then her eyes softened and welled with tears. Silently she moved toward him, but as he moved to embrace her, she caught his right arm and led him out onto the balcony. At the railing she turned to him.

"Talking here is safer," she said in a low voice. Then, after a pause, "You are right, George. I do work for East German Intelligence. And you are my assignment. As the Americans say, you are my case. I am your case officer."

Inigo shrank back and reached for the railing. Erika took one step toward him, then halted.

"George, we have a lot to talk about. I have much to tell you. But not right away." She reached out to touch his cheek. "First come to bed with me. Please."

Erika wept all through their lovemaking. It was the first time he had ever seen her cry, and it nearly broke his heart. The more tender he became, the more she wept and urged him on. When they had finished, the heaving of her chest slowly subsided. They let calmness flow gradually over and into them. The world seemed safe, safer than ever.

After a while she began to talk, keeping her voice low "for fear of microphones." A man from the Ministry of State Security had approached her shortly after she applied for the Geneva post. He spent a certain amount of time warning her about the dangers from capitalist secret services that an East German working in the West would face. Especially a woman, and most especially a single woman. He asked about her political attitudes. It was easy to give all the right answers, and besides, her Party record was blameless, as he admitted.

In view of her ideological commitment, he went on, she would surely have no difficulty in accepting an additional assignment if she were sent to Geneva. He stressed the *if*. As she circulated normally in the scientific and diplomatic colonies of Geneva, she was to keep her eyes open for persons who would be of interest to his service. Of interest in terms of their sympathy for communism, say, or their personal weaknesses, or the official positions they occupied. If she would simply report on such persons to his colleagues stationed in Geneva, she would be rendering a great service to socialism, and nothing further would be required of her.

"I played along with them," she said. Her voice was quiet, almost dreamlike. "It was not difficult. I knew it was the only way to get to Geneva. And, once I was here, to stay." So she told them about the people she met, their personalities, their likes and dislikes, their political views. "I was rather passive. I did not ask questions of the people, just listened. I felt I was not giving them anything useful, but they did not seem to mind. They just told me to keep on that way.

"Then I met you. I did not say anything to them. I believe I sensed from the start that we might come to love each other." Inigo squeezed her smooth bare shoulder. "Then they asked me about you." She stopped for a while, staring at the ceiling, then resumed in almost a whisper.

"That was a frightening interview. They already knew too much. Claude told them. It turns out that he works for them too. They put us under surveillance and quickly discovered we were sleeping together. Then they confronted me. Why had I not reported, not just the contact, but the whole relationship with you?"

It had been a tough, frightening spot. She had answered that Inigo was entirely unsympathetic to socialism. She had detected no weaknesses in him that might be exploited. Not even your own womanly body, Comrade Hartke? they had softly jeered. Not especially, she had replied. He likes me, but he's not a specially passionate lover, and he could easily be satisfied by some other woman. (In the darkness, Inigo smiled but did not interrupt.) They had not been persuaded, and when she insisted, they became vulgar, suggesting that perhaps she could do her sleeping with someone who would be more useful to the German Democratic Republic. Then she had wept and now, as she told it to Inigo, began quietly to weep again.

"So we are both deceivers, my dear. And both of us are miserable," he comforted her.

"Yes. I was glad when we had that fight in the restaurant after your friend left. I think I provoked it because I felt so guilty. It seemed like the best thing not to see you again. Then you came this evening. And I got angry for the same reason. It was really myself that I was angry against."

After a long, fierce embrace they lay quietly together, sober, drained. Later they would plan, Inigo thought. They would find a story that Erika could tell her East Germans, one that would allow them to go on together. Now, full of trust, they fell asleep.

27

Michaels trotted briskly up the metal circular staircase to the delegates' floor. The elevators always took forever to arrive when you really needed them. He had forgotten that today was the day before a plenary, that new instructions were due from Washington, and that General O'Rourke would be in early to read the cables and be phoning him for support. When he reached the outer office, O'Rourke's secretary rolled her eyes upward and waved him straight in.

"What the hell is this, Michaels?" O'Rourke yelled. "And where the hell have you been?"

"Sorry, sir." Michaels took the cables that the general shoved across his big desk and read them quickly, standing up.

"The first one is a data base instruction, sir. It orders us to table our proposal again, but this time without the launchers-of-heavy-ICBMs category."

"Damn! That's the one where we're going to make them count the Tyuratam Eighteen in their total."

Michaels sat down on the couch. "That's been taken care of, General. Remember? The Soviets have promised to destroy twelve and convert the other six to test launchers."

"Oh, yeah. But we still need to single the heavies out so as to target them for reductions in the follow-on negotiations."

Michaels said nothing.

"I told the Joint Chiefs to hold out on this one. It's just the beginning of the slippery slope. This week we drop the heavies, next week we'll be dropping the MIRVs, while the Soviets sit there laughing at us. Well, am I right?"

But Michaels, studying the second cable, did not reply. "The next one, sir, is about reentry vehicle limits. There's a lot of complicated details, but the gist of it is that no missile can be tested or deployed with more warheads than it's already been tested with."

O'Rourke stopped pacing and gazed out the window, fretfully sipping at his coffee.

"Doesn't that freeze their advantage in ICBM warheads?"

"That it does, General."

"Leaves them with all those big birds carrying four and six and ten RVs and leaves us limited to three for the Minuteman."

"There are no plans to put more warheads on the Minuteman missile, sir. Never have been."

"Wait a minute!" O'Rourke turned excitedly into the room. "Wasn't the Minuteman tested once, years ago, with seven warheads? Yes, I'm sure it was!"

"That's right, sir. The instruction takes that into account. It's in the First Agreed Statement, which states the maximum number of RVs tested on all the missiles of each side. Here it is: ICBMs of the Minuteman Three type—seven RVs."

"Good! So we can go from three to seven warheads, while they're frozen." For the first time that morning, the general looked happy.

"Afraid not, sir." Without thinking, Michaels rose to his feet. He could sense a blast coming. "There's a Common Understanding here that says Minutemen Three won't be equipped with more than three."

"Incredible! They're giving away the farm! I don't care what our plans are; why should we throw this to the Soviets for free?"

"To freeze them, sir." Michaels felt himself getting very tired of his general. "CIA says they have the technology to put twenty warheads on their heavy missile instead of ten."

"Anything in there about when we're supposed to table these proposals?"

"Nothing explicit, General. I assume it's execute upon receipt, as usual."

"We'll see," O'Rourke snorted. "That's all, Colonel. Be at the meeting on time."

As usual, new instructions excited Jenkins. This time, though, Inigo sensed electricity running through the entire delegation. They were nearing the finish line. Even those who were cool toward the treaty, who wanted to press the Soviets for more and more concessions, had to admit that the balance of the present language favored the United States. For many of Inigo's colleagues, it had been a long seven years, frequently grueling, often boring. Now they could smell a success. Home, congratulations, family, satisfaction, then on to a new assignment. All except O'Rourke.

"Let's start with data base," said Jenkins. "Any questions about the instruction?"

Boroz, who hadn't yet read it, asked for time. When he finished, he looked up. "Well, it's just the same position as before, except for dropping the heavy ICBMs."

"That's supposed to be the sweetener, I guess," Rappaport said.

"Anyone think that will do the trick? George, what about it?"

"Beats me," Inigo replied gloomily. It had dawned on him that it could prove dangerous for him to anticipate Soviet concessions to his delegation. Sooner or later questions would be asked. "Smirnov doesn't show me any flexibility on it."

"Well, it's certainly worth a try." Rappaport fingered the cable, made a note. "Pavlovsky hasn't been his usual scornful self with me on this subject lately."

"Worth a try or not, we're instructed. We'll need a draft plenary statement on it that we can review this afternoon." He looked at the aides and assistants seated around the walls of the tank, to select a drafter.

"Wait a minute, Al." It was O'Rourke.

"Yes?"

The general hesitated a moment. "Is there anything in the instruction about when we have to present this?"

Inigo suppressed a sigh. They'd been down this road before. But Rappaport, who had joined the delegation only five months before, innocently took the bait.

"No, there's nothing specific. Walt, you're right. Should there be?"

"The original U.S. position was sound," O'Rourke began, as Inigo and the others settled back for what they knew was going to be a long speech. "Now we have an instruction to change it, true, although I understand that the Joint Chiefs have proposed that it be rescinded, and no decision has been reached on that. More important, however, the delegation is expected to make judgments about timing, about when the Soviet delegation seems amenable to compromise offers or when, conversely, any proffered U.S. compromise would be taken as a sign of weakness and met with rejection. It's we here, not the Verification Panel, who are face-to-face with the Soviets every day and in the best position to make such tactical judgments. The way I read the instruction, we're not ordered to do this tomorrow, particularly if it's our judgment that another presentation of the original U.S. position has any chance of being accepted. For my part, I think the USSR is much more likely to cave in if we hang tough with our original position for one more plenary. Does anyone have evidence that, if we drop the eleventh data base category tomorrow, the Soviets will buy the other ten?" And so on and so on.

Much of this long harangue was addressed to Rappaport, whose initial stumble made O'Rourke think he might be the weak link. But Rappaport was a fast learner. After two minutes, he was paying more attention to the bored or dismayed expressions on the other members' faces than to O'Rourke's oration. When it ceased, he was ready.

"I hear you, Walt, but none of our other instructions has specified the timing. There's certainly nothing in this cable that says anything about further explorations or tactical delays. I think we're expected to go right ahead promptly."

O'Rourke embarked on a repetition of his arguments, but this time Jenkins jumped in at the first pause. "I think Abe's right about the intent of the instruction. Anyone else share Walt's position?" He waited; silence. "All right, we'd better go ahead." He named a drafter, then took up the second instruction.

Paul Boroz spoke up with a problem. The Soviets' heavy ICBM would be limited to ten warheads in all its tests. But suppose they fixed it up to fly to twenty different points in space and go through the mechanical release procedures twenty times even though in half of them the release would be simulated rather than real? Wouldn't they then be in a position to equip all their heavy missiles with twenty warheads without ever testing the full capability, and without our knowing it?

Neither Inigo nor anyone else had thought of that. He scratched his head and pushed his chair back from the table with all the others, their eyes turned up to gaze at the ceiling. Jenkins decreed a coffee break.

After ten minutes, when everyone had straggled back into the tank, Jenkins turned to Inigo. "What about Paul's scenario, George? Could they do it? Would we detect it?"

"Yes on both counts, Al. But according to these instructions, it wouldn't be a violation so long as only ten warheads were actually released in the test flights. However, the warheads would have to be a lot lighter than the ones they're using now, if the missile was to carry twenty of them. Maybe that's our way out."

And so it proved. Jenkins drafted rough language at the table providing that a missile could not be tested with warheads lighter than those used in previous tests. The loophole was closed. Another aide was assigned to perfect the wording and prepare the argumentation for the plenary statement. It was then that O'Rourke laid down his second roadblock.

"There's a kind of contradiction in this instruction, it seems to me. First, missiles can't have more warheads than they've been tested with. Second, Minuteman has been tested with seven. But then third, we promise not to put on more than three. Where's the logic in that? Or the fairness?"

Another prolonged wrangle ensued. In the midst of it, O'Rourke acknowledged the fact that Washington had decided the matter and fell back to his second line of defense. "The entire instruction doesn't have to be presented immediately," he argued. "Why not hold off this one-sided limitation on Minuteman warheads until we see how the Soviets react to the rest of it? Maybe we'll never have to make this unilateral concession. The Soviets aren't matching it, and if it isn't offered, they may not demand it. It strikes me as the sort of inequity that would be very hard to defend before the Senate."

Inigo remained silent. Smirnov had been crystal clear to him on this point. The Soviets would forgo putting twenty warheads on their heavy missile only if the United States were seen to be making some corresponding concession. The Minuteman limitation was symbolic only, but no less important on that score. The seven-warhead version had been tested only once, eleven years ago, but the Soviet fallback expressly included an explicit maximum of three.

O'Rourke was isolated, a lone voice. He turned to Inigo. "What do you think, George?"

"Not my business, Walt. It's a U.S. program. I just want to nail down the limits on their missiles."

O'Rourke gave up. He asked Jenkins to note his formal dissent to the decision to propose all parts of the instruction simultaneously. He grumbled something about "being in a rush" and "patriotic concern for U.S. interests." The other principals let him subside while the aides and assistants looked shocked. Jenkins adjourned the meeting.

Inigo and O'Rourke were the last to leave. At the door of the tank, the general stopped. "I must say, George, I expected a little support from you on that last one. State and ACDA are obviously out to get a treaty as fast as they can, at any price. But I always regarded CIA as a patriotic agency."

At first Inigo couldn't believe his ears. His face began to burn with anger.

"Listen, Walt, I'll discuss substantive matters with you till the cows come home." He was trembling furiously now. "But if you're going to question my patriotism, you can damn well go to hell!" O'Rourke began a string of effuse apologies, but Inigo, his self-control slipping away, marched off without another word.

That afternoon, Jenkins did not appear at the two o'clock meeting. Instead, his secretary brought word that one of his children had been taken to the hospital and that they should get started without him. Leaderless, the delegation drifted on in the desultory conversation that always preceded getting down to business. Finally Boroz said, "Well, hadn't we better get started?"

"Right," said O'Rourke firmly. He began to read. " 'Mr. Ambassador, the United States delegation will address two issues at this plenary meeting. The first is the question known as the data base, under which the two sides will exchange information concerning the numbers of strategic weapons that they have deployed in categories that are limited by the treaty. The second is the issue of limiting the number of reentry vehicles that may be . . .' "

As he spoke, Inigo and the others looked up in amazement. What was going on?

"Wait a minute!" Boroz broke in sharply. "What are you doing, Walt?"

"I'm reading the statement, Paul."

"Why?"

"That's how we've always worked. The chairman reads the statement aloud and everyone comments as we go along. You know that, Paul. And since Al's not here, we've got to proceed without him."

"But Abe's the deputy chairman."

Until now calm and innocent, O'Rourke's expression suddenly turned hard.

"Who says so?"

Confusion ensued. For years, the State representative had served as chairman during Jenkins's rare, brief absences and no one had ever questioned it. Now, confronted by O'Rourke's challenge, no one could produce or even remember a document that established this.

"Really, Walt," said Rappaport, his face beet red, "it's been understood for years that the State man is number two here."

O'Rourke stared him down. "It hasn't been understood by me. Show me the paper that says that." As the only man who had entered the room prepared for confrontation, he pressed his surprise attack. "I've been here seven years. I'm the senior man after Al." And he resumed his reading of the statement.

Rappaport sat miserable. It was Boroz who first gathered his wits. He rose to his feet.

"I can't work in these circumstances. I refuse to stay in the face of this—this coup d'etat." He picked up his papers and left the room. As O'Rourke resumed reading the text aloud, Rappaport followed Boroz, squeezing through the narrow space between O'Rourke's chair and the wall. When Inigo rose, so did the rest of the delegation. O'Rourke's voice trailed off. In silence, the room emptied.

Later that afternoon, Jenkins returned and reassembled the delegation in the tank to review the draft statements. Everyone was subdued and businesslike. O'Rourke's formal objection to the tabling now of the Common Understanding limiting the Minuteman to three warheads was registered without debate. The work was quickly finished.

Next morning an incoming cable informed the delegation that its chairman was Ambassador Alfred R. Jenkins and its deputy chairman was the representative of the secretary of state, presently Abraham L. Rappaport. Morgan filled Inigo in. It turned out that a similar cable had been circulated for clearance in Washington seven years ago when the delegation arrived in Geneva. Only yesterday, after prodding from Geneva, was it discovered that the cable had never been sent. By withholding clearance, the Joint Chiefs of Staff had automatically interrupted the cable release procedures. It was so routine a matter that no one had noticed. Everyone, that is, except O'Rourke.

"Just imagine!" Morgan said to Inigo in the hall. They were on their way upstairs to congratulate Boroz. "Walt waited seven years for his big chance, and then Paul knocked him out with one punch!"

28

Next morning there was a cable from Peters.

THERE FOLLOWS TEXT OF NEW YORK TIMES ITEM PUBLISHED YES-
TERDAY UNDER BY-LINE OF WALLACE KREIDEL. BEGIN TEXT.

TWO INFORMED SOURCES IN WASHINGTON STATED TODAY THAT
THE CENTRAL INTELLIGENCE AGENCY HAS RECRUITED A SOVIET
SOURCE WITH ACCESS TO THE HIGHEST ECHELONS OF SOVIET DE-
CISION-MAKING ON THE VITAL QUESTION OF SALT NEGOTIATIONS.

A HIGH ADMINISTRATION SOURCE WHO DECLINED TO ALLOW THE
USE OF HIS NAME, WHILE NEITHER CONFIRMING NOR DENYING
THE REPORT, STATED THAT SUCH A SOURCE COULD GIVE THE
UNITED STATES A KEY ADVANTAGE IN NEGOTIATING THE FINAL
DISPUTED ISSUES OF THE TREATY, WHICH HAS BEEN UNDER NE-
GOTIATION IN GENEVA FOR THE PAST SEVEN YEARS.

PENTAGON OFFICIALS, WHO ALSO REFUSED TO PROVIDE CONFIR-
MATION, TOOK A DIFFERENT VIEW. SENIOR PLANNERS THERE
NOTED THE POSSIBILITY THAT A DOUBLE AGENT, BY PRESENTING
HIS INFORMATION AS THE FINAL POSITIONS OF THE POLITBURO,
COULD LEAD THE US TO ACCEPT LESS FAVORABLE SOLUTIONS TO
THE UNRESOLVED ISSUES THAN IT MIGHT OBTAIN IN PROLONGED
HARD BARGAINING. THE APPARENT AUTHENTICITY OF A SPY'S RE-
PORTING, THEY WARNED, COULD LEAD TO AN AGREEMENT ON SO-
VIET TERMS.

A SPOKESMAN FOR THE CENTRAL INTELLIGENCE AGENCY DE-
CLINED TO COMMENT. END TEXT.

DIRECTOR DENIED THIS REPORT UNEQUIVOCALLY TO STAFF AT HIS
MORNING MEETING TODAY. YOU MAY CITE THIS DENIAL IN RE-
SPONDING TO QUESTIONS FROM DELEGATION. PLEASE REPORT

PROMPTLY ANY SOVIET REACTIONS TO THIS DISTRESSING EPI-
SODE.

Inigo sat stunned. Before he could recover, his secretary buzzed
him on the intercom. Ambassador Jenkins wanted to see him at nine
o'clock, before the delegation meeting. He was to bring Ms. Carson
with him. There could hardly be any question why.

Emily responded without hesitation. She was in Inigo's office at
quarter of nine. When she finished reading Peters's cable, she was all
business.

"So what about your ambassador? What's he like? Are you on good
terms? Can he be told?"

"We're on good terms. But he wouldn't sit still on this for a minute.
I'd be on the plane to the States tomorrow."

"Thereby pointing the finger straight at Smirnov," she observed
dryly.

"We'll just have to hang in there with the director's denial," Inigo
said.

"For the time being, yes. It's always a bad situation, though, to be
hiding intelligence operations from an ambassador. The usual situation is to get a presidential letter directing him to go along. You
hand that to him just before briefing him into the operation. It makes
bad blood, of course, but success usually cancels that out." She
calmly finished her coffee while Inigo peered at his watch. "Settle
down, George. Let me do the talking. We'll be out of there in ten minutes."

Jenkins was barely civil when they entered his office. He rose, and
grudgingly shook hands. "I'd been hoping to meet you, Ms. Carson,
but under more pleasant circumstances than these. You've read the
Kreidel piece in the *Times*?" He picked up his cable from his home
agency and waved it at her like a criminal indictment.

Unperturbed, Carson took a seat without waiting for an invitation.
"Yes, Mr. Ambassador. George has shown me a copy. His cable also
reports that the director has unequivocally denied it."

"Denied it?" Jenkins's voice rose. "It says here the CIA declined to
comment!"

"In public, sir. That's an ironclad rule with us. The director denied
it internally, at his senior staff meeting."

"And how much can I rely on that?" Jenkins asked icily.

"May I have some coffee?" Carson asked easily. Inigo poured her a cup. "Mr. Ambassador, before I arrived here, both State and my own superiors made it clear to me that under no circumstances was the Geneva station to undertake operations against the Soviet SALT delegation. No surveillance, no audio, no photography, and most certainly no recruitment." She paused to sip but resumed just as Jenkins was about to break in.

"I presume you've asked me up here today to find out whether I've violated those instructions. I have not. If you're not willing to rely on that statement, there's nothing I can do to help you," she finished pleasantly but firmly.

Jenkins retreated behind his desk. "You understand, don't you, that a recruitment effort would be utterly disastrous to the negotiations?"

"That consideration was very clearly explained to me." Inigo noted that she was withholding assent. "Now, if you choose to disbelieve both the director and myself, I would point out that the *Times* piece says nothing abut the locale of this alleged espionage. If the operation exists, it could be in Moscow, or in Washington, where the Soviet embassy undoubtedly has SALT responsibilities and information. I frankly don't know about the Soviet UN mission in New York." She finished and waited for the ambassador to respond.

But Carson's quiet aggressiveness had taken the wind out of Jenkins's sails. He complained of the difficulty the *Times* story would give him, the skittishness it would produce on the Soviet side, the cryptic allusions Lebedev would make to it. Even if the story were false from start to finish, it could not fail to make Moscow pull back, and suspicion and unease would trouble the Soviet delegation. Carson let him go on. Eventually Jenkins talked himself out, ending the meeting on a note of near-apology.

Carson waited until they were back in Inigo's office before she relaxed and grinned.

"Nice job, Emily."

"Thanks. There's one more thing to do. This whole thing may come unglued yet. Before it does, have the director try to get one of those presidential letters for Jenkins so you can tell him the truth and keep the operation running. It's always best to be as square as possible with one's ambassador; you never know when you'll need him. I think you're in a better position than I am to take that up. I'd have to

177

work through Petrocelli, whereas you can go straight to the top. But that's for later. We have a bigger problem than Jenkins."

"Precisely. Smirnov." Inigo sank dejectedly into a chair.

"Precisely," Carson agreed. "How soon can you get the word to him? It's important that he hear it from you first."

"We're having dinner together tonight. God, how I dread it! How about your coming along?"

"Out of the question, George. Never introduce a new colleague into the midst of a crisis. It's a cardinal rule. Weakens the agent's confidence in his case officer."

A dismal bell rang in Inigo's mind. He needed a story for Jenkins, a story for Smirnov, and a story for Erika to tell to East German Intelligence. But just now it was the story for Smirnov, urgently.

"For starters," said Carson, "give him a copy of your cable. He needs the whole truth, in exact terms."

"What about communications security? That cable was encrypted. If the Soviets have my text, couldn't they match it with the *Times* article and break into our cryptographic system?"

"George," Carson said wearily, "screw commo security. You've got a crisis on your hands. Don't leave Smirnov floundering in the dark, wondering about details. Give him the text." She gave him a long look. "And stop looking so miserable and defeated. This kind of thing comes up all the time. That's why CIA is the world's best. It has to be, to overcome the U.S. press."

"So I give him the text. What then?"

Carson leaned back and smiled broadly. "Cheer up, George. What's the worst that can happen? Smirnov reads the text, he panics, demands to be flown out this afternoon. So we fly him out. Simple. His wife too, if he wants her. You get canned from the delegation, but you're the director's fair-haired boy. Promotion, medal, new job. Meanwhile you've solved half the disputes in the SALT negotiations. Not bad for an amateur. You don't really imagine the Sovs will pull out if they find out about Smirnov, do you?"

"Of course not. You make it sound a lot better, Emily. Especially about getting Smirnov out of here. I wouldn't feel right about leaving him in the lurch."

"Of course you wouldn't. And it does you credit. But you won't have to."

Inigo was idly peering through the drapes, searching for the glint of a camera. Now he turned back to the room.

"How so?"

"Moscow doesn't know whether to believe the *Times*. Who can figure out these crazy Americans? And when they start to investigate, why focus on Smirnov? His record's impeccable, isn't it? Moreover, as I was telling your ambassador, it's not just Geneva, it's Moscow and Washington too and maybe New York. You two have a little time, if you'll just calm down and realize it."

"Calm down and do what?"

"Well, that's pretty much up to him, I should think. Basically, he has two choices. He can bolt, in which case we'll rescue him and keep our end of the bargain. Or he can hang in there and try to finish the negotiations together with you according to the original plan. My guess is he'll try the second."

"Why?"

"You're forgetting something, George. If you weren't so upset, you'd remember."

"Don't tease, for Christ's sake. What?"

"His daughter."

The Soviet mission lacked a tank, but there was no need of one. No outsider could get within two hundred yards of the conference building, which sat in the middle of a five-acre compound surrounded by a chain link fence. The fence was pierced by a single entrance controlled day and night by a guard post. A housing settlement, cafeteria, and movie theater helped to discourage the lower and middle ranks of the Soviet colony from going into town very often. Only five hundred yards away, open to any casual stroller, stood the Palais des Nations, proclaiming a different ideal.

Smirnov was having trouble keeping his mind on the discussion. Pavlovsky was showing off again, boasting how he had discomfited Rappaport at the last meeting of the Drafting Group. Aggressiveness was a much prized quality in a Soviet diplomat; it forced the enemy onto the defensive and made him excessively grateful for small concessions. Pavlovsky's deputy, Starovsky, was learning the technique rapidly in his discussions with Morgan. But Smirnov was getting tired of their playing the same role in their own delegation. He smiled to himself as he recalled how his operation with Inigo was beginning to undermine his colleagues' loud arguments. However mightily they protested at the post-plenaries that the USSR would make no further concessions, Washington would know better.

What was chiefly on Smirnov's mind, however, was his women. The pestering letters from his daughter were increasing. His next assignment absolutely must be in the United States. Washington, New York, the consulate in San Francisco, anywhere, so long as it was in America. His replies were always truthful. There was not a chance of another U.S. assignment for him just now. Irina, however, refused to understand. Daddy, she believed, could arrange anything.

Then there was Vera Mikhailovna.

Smirnov had not yet found the courage to tell his wife of his plans. He knew that he must do it soon, now that his work with Inigo was promising to bring the talks to an end. But he dreaded the arguments, the scenes. Never to see her dear parents again! Never to see Moscow again, never to stroll along the river embankment under the Kremlin walls. There would be endless tears, fresh weeping with each thought of another loved one, another beloved spot. She could adjust to America again, he knew, but he could never make her wholly happy there.

"Do you agree with me, Victor?" With a start he realized that General Mardirosian, directly across the table, was addressing him.

"Usually, Pyotr, usually. But not yet this time. I don't know what you said. You see, I was daydreaming."

His frankness won him a round of tolerant chuckles. No one expected him to be an expert on the details of the treaty. American politics, especially the politics of SALT ratification, was Smirnov's specialty. He was responsible, along with the general, for advising his colleagues on what information on Soviet military programs could be passed to the enemy. He directed the delegation effort to obtain classified information from the Americans, particularly on their intelligence capabilities. It was understood that he reported on the negotiations through his own channel to KGB headquarters. But he himself became involved in the negotiating issues only when he chose to.

The talk moved on. Smirnov returned to his brooding. Should he tell Inigo that his wife did not know of his plans, that she might balk at the last moment? Actually, he was confident that she would give in, as she always had to him, on everything. But there would be a scene. Better to put it off as long as possible. In the meantime, better not to share the problem with Inigo.

Now there was an interesting man. The American was a strange combination, calm and yet headstrong. Smirnov liked his temperament. One could not be confident of someone who took direction too easily or allowed himself to be bullied. He had watched carefully the signs of struggle within Inigo over whether to trust him. The man had performed what tests he could and then, confronted with the question of whether to commit himself, had accepted the uncertainties and decided. It was how Smirnov saw himself: careful but willing to act. At some point, one had to trust another person, or fate, or both. Or else opportunity would fade and vanish; in this case, the chances for arms control would sink lower and lower. But it was hard, this trusting. It was as much a forced necessity as a choice. Or rather, having checked and tested and thought and finally chosen to act, now he was forced by that choice to trust. No wonder he felt love for Inigo at times, hated him at others.

As Lebedev's low, rumbling voice rolled out across the table, Smirnov forced his attention back to the meeting. The ambassador summarized the discussion and directed Starovsky to revise the draft plenary statement in the light of its conclusions. The American proposal on the exchange of data—the data base issue, as they called it— was to be accepted as provided in the fallback instructions. With the eleventh category dropped, no more time was to be wasted on seeking further deletions. It might be true, as some members had argued, that further resistance would succeed, but the time for action had arrived. Various suggestions from the delegation to alter words and phrases in the American language were rejected. It was clear to Smirnov that Moscow had ordered Lebedev not to prolong the resolution of this issue.

The meeting broke up and the delegation moved from the bare conference room through the equally undecorated hall and anteroom. Why is it, Smirnov wondered for the thousandth time, that Soviet offices are so resolutely plain? It was the same at home and abroad. In the beginning we were a poor country, and besides, rejection of the ostentations of czardom had had a positive political meaning. But that was over sixty years ago. Our apartments are full of plants and pictures, but at work we think everything must be dreary. Would a little color and beauty make us think we were no longer Bolsheviks?

He joined Rublov and Mardirosian on the steps. They looked at him oddly.

"Is the KGB really ready to begin dismantling Soviet security?" the general asked him bitingly. "I was surprised not to have your help today."

Smirnov put on a glum expression. "I was surprised at our instructions, General. If we had held out, I feel sure the Americans would have dropped this data base business. I assure you I did not recommend acceptance. But Moscow has decided." He gave an unhappy sigh.

"Yes, we failed to persuade Moscow," Mardirosian answered gloomily. "I fear it is a serious mistake. It can only encourage the Americans to demand more secret information in the next negotiations. A bad precedent." He shook his head and moved off.

Rublov gave Smirnov a helpless smile and followed the general. That old rascal doesn't fool me, Smirnov said to himself. He wants a treaty as badly as I do, I'm sure of it. But you'll never catch him admitting it. I hope I hide my desires as well as he does. I'd like to survive as long as he has.

29

The Café of the Philosophers lay beyond the Vieille Ville, two miles from the river. It was Inigo's choice, but according to Smirnov's prescription. The Soviet had asked for a "bourgeois" restaurant outside the fashionable parts of the city. Inigo had been intending to try out the restaurant ever since he had noticed its small sign while wandering beyond the Plainpalais the weekend before. "We philosophize regularly on all the usual subjects." Among the Swiss, even such a mild touch of humor deserved to be investigated.

Inigo was early, out of nervousness. The restaurant was sparsely occupied. No philosophizing tonight, he told himself grimly as he sought once more to grapple with the coming crisis. He had known instantly that Carson was right, that Smirnov must be told immediately about the *New York Times* leak, in all its details, and above all that he must hear it from Inigo. After that was done, there was no way for Inigo to plan his next move. He was in no position to adopt an attitude of independence, as he had when Smirnov had challenged him about Erika. Still less could he take the chastising position that he had used in the crisis over Gonzales. Carson made sense, but it was cold comfort.

"Times come along, George," she had said, "when you just can't control events. No matter how much you try, how hard you plan. You have to go into a meeting with no idea how it will turn out. Play it by ear. Hope for the best. It's hell, isn't it?"

Inigo ordered a glass of white wine, which arrived just as Smirnov entered the restaurant. The Soviet seemed to fumble awhile at the coatrack, and Inigo wondered whether he knew, whether he too was preparing himself for a difficult encounter. But when he reached the table, Smirnov was all smiles.

"You will enjoy the next plenary, George," he greeted Inigo. "The data base issue is resolved. On the expected terms."

"Good."

Smirnov burbled along happily while they made their selections and discussed them with the waiter. Then Inigo drew a silent breath and plunged in.

"I have some unfortunate news to share with you, Victor." Instantly Smirnov's face turned serious, even frightened. "I suppose the best way to do it is to tell you everything I know." He handed over a copy of that morning's cable.

As Smirnov read, his face turned white. Once he looked up at Inigo in terror, then returned to the text. He read it a second time. A passing waiter started as he tore the cable in half.

"I knew it! I knew you Americans couldn't be trusted!" His low hiss of fury was like scalding steam. Then a grim look came over his face.

"I must have the pictures back!"

"What pictures?" Inigo was bewildered, but Smirnov had already pushed himself out of his chair and was heading for the door. Inigo caught up with him at the coatrack, where Smirnov was scrabbling madly through the four or five raincoats that hung there.

"What are you doing, for God's sake?"

Smirnov swung around on him. He seemed to have gone mad, but his words were suppressed and terrified.

"I put the photographs of my daughter in your coat pocket. And all the other information about her. I didn't want to be seen passing them to you at the table. Now your coat is gone! What have you done with it?" he demanded.

The enormity of the mistake dawned upon Inigo. He took Smirnov's arm and began to propel him through the door. He was afraid that at his next words, the Soviet might lose control altogether. They reached the street.

"Victor, I didn't wear a raincoat tonight. No coat at all."

Smirnov stared at him, then began to shake silently in his grip.

"You put them in someone else's coat," Inigo said slowly and firmly. For a moment he was not sure Smirnov understood him. Inigo tightened his grip. "You put them in someone else's coat. It's early. Whoever it was can't have left long ago. Was it a tan raincoat, like mine, with tabs on the shoulders?"

Smirnov nodded, unable to speak.

"You go this way, I'll go that. He can't be far." Without a word he set off at a run down the street. He didn't look back. Either Smirnov would search the other direction or he would stand paralyzed on the pavement. It was out of Inigo's hands.

Parking was not allowed on this street, so Inigo swung rapidly to the right as he reached the corner. The pavement was empty. Nothing to do but go on.

Down at the far end of the block, Inigo heard a starter sputter and an automobile engine catch. He broke into a run. Headlights came on and moved across the rear of a parked Mercedes. The fit was tight, the driver had to maneuver back and forth twice to work his way clear. As he turned his wheels for the last time, Inigo appeared at his window and tapped upon the glass.

The startled driver, a balding Genevois, peered up at him and in almost the same instant he flipped the door handle into the lock position. Inigo could see in the dim interior light that he was wearing a coat of indeterminate color. On the left shoulder, a tab was barely visible.

"Monsieur!" Inigo spoke loudly in French. "Please do not be frightened. A mistake has happened. Roll down your window for a moment!"

The man stared at him in alarm through the glass, then began to inch his car into the street.

"Monsieur! I beg of you! Roll down your window a few centimeters. I will stand away from your car." He moved two steps into the street, ready to fling himself upon the hood if the car moved.

Cautiously the driver put the engine into neutral and lowered the window a crack.

"Stand back, monsieur! What do you want of me?"

"Did you just leave the Café of the Philosophers?"

A careful, searching look, then—

"Yes."

"I believe that an envelope belonging to me was put into your pocket by mistake." Inigo did not move. "While your coat was on the rack."

Still idling the engine, the man looked hard at Inigo, then rolled up the window. He leaned over to lock the streetside door. Then, reaching into his coat pocket, he pulled out a long envelope. After staring at it for a moment, he returned his gaze to Inigo and opened the window partway again.

"Is this your envelope, monsieur?"

"It is."

"May I ask what it is doing in my pocket? And who put it there?"

Inigo was thinking of making a dash and grabbing for the envelope, calculating the distance and the window opening, when a deep voice spoke behind his shoulder.

"Is there trouble, messieurs? Can I be of assistance?"

He turned to see a uniformed policeman. The Swiss driver, who had seen him coming up behind Inigo, spoke first.

"Officer, I think this man may be drunk. He is also a foreigner."

"Yes, but what is the trouble?"

Inigo broke in. "Officer, an envelope belonging to me was placed in this man's coat pocket by mistake. I need to have it back."

The policeman stared at him quizzically. "And what is in the envelope?"

"Pictures. Of a young woman. And some private notes."

"Perhaps I had better have a look at them." With ill grace, the driver handed the envelope out the window. The policeman produced a flashlight, put the contents on the car hood, and began to study them.

"A most attractive female. But surely rather young for you, monsieur?"

Inigo was glad to feel embarrassed; it fit.

"Some might say so, officer."

"And this writing. What is it?"

Inigo peered closer and saw that Smirnov had written his notes in Russian. The Cyrillic script must have seemed like code to the policeman.

"Her letters to me, officer. She is Russian."

"But you are not, I think. Let me see your passport, please."

Inigo carried his passport regularly since the fracas with Gonzales in France; now he handed it over humbly. Examining it carefully, the policeman made notes in a little book. The driver, hoping to witness an arrest or at least a lecture, waited expectantly.

"Mr. Inigo, this seems to be a private matter. Please be more careful of your possessions in the future." He handed over the envelope and sauntered away.

Inigo leaned down to the open window.

"Screw you, you bastard," he whispered fiercely. Flustered, the driver slipped the clutch and his car lurched forward, striking the Mercedes hard. As the policeman turned and started back, Inigo walked off in the opposite direction.

Twenty feet away, watching from the shadows, he found Smirnov.

Silently Inigo handed over the envelope. They walked back to the restaurant without a word.

"That was well done," Smirnov remarked when they were seated again at their table.

"One can't be unlucky all the time." Inigo, still tense, signaled for a Scotch. "Now what?"

Smirnov was a model of composure. "I've been thinking," he said. "This little excitement has helped to clear my mind. Can you get my wife and me from Geneva to New York on short notice?"

"Tomorrow, if you like."

"Good. But if we leave tomorrow, we will never see our daughter again. We cannot depart until she is out of the Soviet Union. How quickly can that be arranged?"

"I don't know." Carson was right, Inigo thought. "I'll find out as soon as I can."

"As soon as possible," Smirnov insisted. "In the meantime, that newspaper story said nothing about Geneva. So the Center will have to investigate in Moscow and Washington as well as here. There is nothing in the story that points at me or my service, either. So we have some time." He looked steadily at Inigo.

"True." Under the influence of Smirnov's calmness, he was beginning to relax. "But if you leave Geneva"—he didn't say "defect," it was too harsh a sound—"before the negotiations are finished, what will happen to the treaty?"

"Ah yes, the treaty. I don't know. We will simply have to play the song by ear, don't you say?" He smiled his first smile since the evening's crisis. I'd forgotten, thought Inigo, that he's a professional. "Perhaps it will finish at the right time. If not, we will have to make choices, won't we? In the meantime, when the Center begins its investigation here, I may be able to divert it in interesting directions." A second smile.

For the remainder of the dinner, they tried to help each other forget the crisis of the evening. Smirnov gave a long description of the Caucasus as a vacation spot, the towering mountains, the pure hard lakes, the villages tucked away in upland valleys. Inigo spoke sadly of his own childlessness and even recounted some of the story of his wife's early death after an auto accident. Smirnov, sympathetic, responded by telling of his brother's disappearance from the partisan unit in which they both had fought; he went out on a three-man mission from which no one returned. Over cognac, they fell into a comfortable quiet.

Between the dining room and the street was a small vestibule, sheltered on all sides. As they passed into it, Smirnov stayed Inigo with a hand on his arm.

"Don't forget your envelope."

Inigo took it with a weary smile. On the street outside, they parted on foot in opposite directions.

30

"How did the briefing go?"

"Not too bad. Not too good either." Inigo crooked the receiver between cheek and shoulder as he lit a cigarette. "You sending any more professional athletes my way?"

Jenkins's chuckle came low over the line. "George, he's a United States senator now. And far from the worst. Athletes, actors, astronauts—the Senate is a representative body, as they say. But what I say is that some of these new types are as good as the small-town lawyers we used to have in there, and a few of them are a damn sight better."

"When they elect a game show host as president, that's when I'm emigrating. Maybe even to Switzerland. But I figure that's at least a decade away yet."

"Was there anything he was particularly interested in?" Jenkins asked.

"Well, he pushed me pretty hard on those monitoring stations in Iran that we've just been kicked out of. Argued that the treaty wouldn't be verifiable now."

"We can expect more of that. The shah sure picked a great time to fold, didn't he?"

"I gave him what I've gotten from headquarters about alternative sources of data. I even hinted that the Chinese might take up the slack. He was rather underwhelmed."

"Anything else?"

"Yes indeed. His main problem was telemetry encryption."

Jenkins groaned. Telemetry encryption was the major issue remaining unresolved and, they both knew, by far the most delicate. Inigo had tried hard to convey that to the senator, but he wasn't at all sure he had succeeded.

"Now let me see if I've got this straight, Mr. Indigo," the senator had said, leaning his massive frame forward over the conference table. "You say every Russian missile has a little broadcaster on board that sends back to them signals on how it's doing?"

"That's right, Senator. It monitors the performance of every component, variables like pressure and temperature, and radios the numbers back to earth. Those radio signals are called telemetry. It's a stream of numbers. They need the information to tell how the missile is performing in flight. Particularly if there's a failure, so they'll know what went wrong and needs to be fixed. We intercept those data and analyze them to see whether they're testing something that would violate the treaty."

They were in the tank, just the two of them. Inigo was giving his "crown jewels" briefing, taking the senator through the intricacies of CIA's capabilities to monitor all the provisions of the draft treaty. Maps, charts, and pictures were spread out on the conference table. It was what was called an all-source briefing, with no secrets withheld, right down to the orbital characteristics of intelligence satellites and the locations of radar stations. For most visiting senators, it was their first lesson in the complexities of SALT verification, on which they would ultimately have to make a judgment when the treaty was presented to them for ratification.

"So if they encrypt those numbers, why don't you guys just break the code? That's what you're supposed to be good at, isn't it?"

"No one can decrypt high-level Soviet encryption systems, Senator. Sorry. They've already put a small amount of their telemetry into those systems, and short of stealing the systems themselves out of Moscow, we haven't a prayer."

The senator grew indignant. "But they have no right to do that! Not if they want arms control! Haven't you put something in the SALT treaty to forbid it?"

"Precisely. That's one of the major fencing matches going on right now. You see, it's like pulling teeth to get the Soviets to acknowledge our right to information. Secrecy is an old habit with them, going way back beyond the Revolution to centuries of czarist rule. They've always used it to hide weakness, but now that they're strong they can't give up the habit. That's one of the side benefits of SALT, forcing them to become more open. But it's slow going."

"Mmm."

The senator turned thoughtful. Inigo was alarmed. Once before, when a delicate issue was being worked out in intricate language, a visiting senator had bulled his way in, wrecking weeks of patient effort.

"The language is complicated, Senator, no doubt about it. But we're getting there. You're free to raise anything you want with the Soviets at their reception tonight, but I'd suggest that this one is best left alone for the moment. They're quite sensitive to pressures right now. And as I say, we've just about got what we need."

"Mmm."

Inigo, making a mental note to tell Jenkins to reinforce his warnings, had gone on to complete his briefing.

"And when we finished, Al, he asked for a copy of the draft treaty to study."

"That's always a bad sign." Jenkins's sigh came heavily over the line. "The damn treaty's unreadable to a layman."

"Yes, I made that point. Told him that, what with closing all the loopholes we could imagine, we'd produced a highly specialized document. Warned him it wasn't intelligible on first reading. He just stared at me and asked again for a copy."

"Well, you could hardly withhold the text from a United States senator. I see I'll have to talk to him. Thanks, George. See you at the reception."

The Soviets had put out a good spread. They had a preference for shellfish, which suited Inigo perfectly, and the hors d'oeuvres featured shrimp and baby oysters. The caviar was more plentiful than usual, as it regularly was when the guest list included a U.S. senator. Vodka flowed in quantity, of course, including the brownish Strelka, but Scotch as well. The table was even nicely decorated; if only the room weren't so bare.

There was a new Soviet, Inigo noticed. Tall, rough looking, sociable, he seemed to be making a point of chatting with each member of the U.S. delegation, although he ignored the senator. He was particularly attentive to Inigo, whom he approached at the refreshments.

"Maltsev," he said in deep tones, pressing Inigo's hand hard in his enormous paw. He had not waited for an introduction.

"George Inigo," Inigo replied. The man's great size and even more his face, swarthy and heavily jowled, struck him as somehow out of place at a diplomatic reception. More like a thug than a negotiator, he thought.

"I come from Moscow," Maltsev said with a big smile. "To observe here the talks. How do they go, in your opinion?"

Inigo decided to try a pleasantry. "Slowly. But I'm sure they will go much better now if you have brought concessions with you from Moscow."

Maltsev's face darkened.

"Mr. Inigo, there is no use to wait for that. We make no more concessions. It is America who must change her positions now." He glared fiercely. If we were sitting at a table now, Inigo thought, he would pound it.

"Then what does bring you to Geneva, Mr. Maltsev?" he asked.

"I come to observe. Yes, to observe." His body seemed to relax, but the eyes remained hard and cold.

There was an awkward pause. The Soviet stopped speaking, but his expression remained unchanged, his eyes fixed on the American's. It's that goddamn Soviet bullying again, Inigo thought. Lebedev and the other members of the Soviet delegation had dropped that look of menace after they had gotten to know Inigo, but this newcomer reminded him of those first encounters. He thought of Churchill's withering remark about the Germans: They are either at your throat or at your feet.

"Will you be attending our next plenary meeting?" he asked.

"Perhaps." Maltsev suddenly turned sociable again. "But I think I learn more from observing the delegation members. I talk to the Americans and ask their impressions. I would like to hear more of yours. And of course," he added oddly, "I observe the Soviet delegation also."

Inigo looked sharply at him, but Maltsev was all smiles now, including the eyes.

"The Soviet delegation is very able, as I'm sure you know." He felt a need to be careful. "As for my impressions, it is as I said. I am optimistic about our prospects here, but that is because I assume that Moscow will soon make the reasonable concessions needed to complete the treaty. Ah, have you met Colonel Michaels?" Michaels had wandered idly up to them. Inigo performed the introductions with relief and moved away.

Smirnov was nowhere to be seen. The drift of the party brought Inigo up against Starovsky, the number three representative of the Foreign Ministry after Ambassador Lebedev and Pavlovsky. They

resumed a discussion, half joking and half serious, which they had
pursued through the two previous receptions: Would you lie for your
country? The conversation, both men seemed to sense, moved on
three levels. On the first, which was explicit, they agreed that lying
was a sin, not to be countenanced, and especially pernicious in international diplomacy. On the second, each knew—and knew that the
other knew—that each would lie endlessly and shamelessly to gain
advantage for his government. On the third level, only half sensed,
never even hinted at but somehow communicated, was a feeling of
being trapped in one's nationality, condemned to lie by the badness
of the world, a knowledge that their lying was deeply harmful to both
sides but that they were helpless to do otherwise. Inigo liked Starovsky. Tonight they concluded the discussion wryly; yes, they would lie
for their country, but only very sparingly, and only for the most important of reasons. It was the best they could manage, and they were
relieved to put the subject behind them.

"... no right to put that stuff in code! We need it for verification!"
It was the senator, standing behind him. Inigo's heart sank.

He heard General Mardirosian's interpreter clumsily putting English into Russian. A difficult conversation was going to become even
more difficult, he foresaw, through botched language.

"Testing information is needed by the testing side for its own purposes," Mardirosian's deep voice rumbled slowly in Russian. "It is
not the property of the other side."

When the interpretation was finished, the senator responded rapidly. "You mean that if you wanted to you could record all those numbers on a tape recorder on the missile and parachute the recorder to
the ground before the missile landed? Without broadcasting them at
all?"

Mardirosian and his interpreter turned slightly away, and Inigo
missed overhearing their exchange. It would be just as well if they
didn't understand the senator at all, he thought. But the interpreter's
English answer dashed that hope.

"Yes, the testing side would be in legal right to do that, what you
say."

"Well, then!" The senator's tone grew wrathful. "Suppose the observing side sent in an airplane at the end of the test to recover the
tape recorder. Under the SALT treaty, wouldn't that be legal? If the
information was needed for verification?"

Behind him, Inigo heard a gasp, then silence. After a few seconds, Mardirosian's voice firmly instructed in Russian, "Proceed. What did he say?"

The interpreter, putting it into Russian for his general, gave it his all. "In that case, the United States would have the right to invade Soviet airspace and steal the tape recorder if it could find it first. Does the general agree?"

Inigo, watching Starovsky eavesdrop with him, saw an expression of horror come over his face. It must have mirrored Mardirosian's reaction.

The general took a long time to reply, but even so, his voice was shaking as he slowly said, "I think that would be very dangerous. Tell the senator extremely dangerous."

Inigo turned to see the senator looking at Mardirosian with a puzzled, angry stare as the interpreter delivered the response. Firmly Inigo took him by the arm and said loudly, "Senator, I think you haven't met Academician Rublov. He is quite anxious to talk with you. Let me introduce you to him." With a discreet tug, he got them under way.

"Touchy fellow, that Russian general," the senator grumbled as Inigo anxiously searched the party for Rublov. "Are they all that way?"

Inigo withheld a reply until they came upon Rublov chatting with Paul Boroz. Then, "Only when provoked, Senator. Excuse me, Paul. Academician Rublov, may I present Senator Brightson?"

Escaping immediately, he looked around for Smirnov, but without success. He left Boroz to baby-sit the senator, found Jenkins, and pulled him aside. The senator's exchange with Mardirosian took only a few seconds to recount. "God knows what he's saying to Rublov now, Al. I think you'd better take him in tow." Jenkins hurried off. A minute later, Inigo spotted him and the senator deep in conversation with Madame Pavlovsky, who was being charming.

Halfway across the room, he finally saw the familiar short, round shape. Smirnov looked up and they exchanged the briefest of glances. Each began a slow circuit, nodding here, exchanging a word there, until they came together on the fringe of the party. Surreptitiously, Inigo thought, like secret lovers.

"Ah, good evening, Mr. Inigo. Are you enjoying yourself? I hope so."

"Thank you. It's a fine party. Have you met our senator?"

"Yes, we had a few words. And General Mardirosian told me of an amusing conversation with him." Smirnov permitted himself a smile. "He seems not to know our treaty very well."

"Perhaps not. But he has a good grasp of the principle that secrecy and arms control are incompatible."

"Only at certain advanced levels," Smirnov replied. "You must be patient with us, my friend. Rome wasn't built in a day."

"But now Rome and the rest of the world can be destroyed in an hour and a half."

"Well put." Jousting in the old way was a safety measure that they used in public. Besides, they had come to enjoy it.

"I would like to invite you to join me at lunch the day after tomorrow," Inigo said.

Smirnov ignored him. "And our side also has a new face. Have you met Mr. Maltsev?"

"We spoke briefly."

"Briefly," Smirnov repeated. "His spoken English is perhaps not impressive. But he reads the language very well. He is a devoted reader of the American press."

"Ah?"

"Yes, the *New York Times* and the *Washington Post* are flown to him daily here in Geneva."

Inigo understood. He lifted his head to scan the crowd. At the same moment Maltsev, standing tall in the middle of the room, lifted his head from his conversation with Michaels and glanced around. Meeting Inigo's eyes, he held them and smiled. Inigo looked down at Smirnov.

"I see. Will he be here with your delegation for long?"

"I do not know. He has a special task, I believe, and has brought two helpers. But I cannot say when he will finish his work."

Morgan joined them and inquired after Madame Smirnov. His wife was well, the Soviet replied, but she did not care very much for large parties. She was working on her translation. If he might ask on her behalf, did either of his two companions know the meaning of *a miss is as good as a mile?* What did a young girl have to do with distance?

Driving home, Inigo recalled with foreboding that Smirnov had not responded to his luncheon invitation. His fears were confirmed in the tank next morning when the delegation compared notes on the reception. Three colleagues reported that their Soviet counterparts had declined invitations to dinner or lunch, pleading the press of work. It was plain enough. The USSR delegation was confined to quarters.

Maltsev had cut his line of communication to Smirnov.

31

"Do? George, there's nothing you can do," Carson told him. "Surely you see that."

Inigo couldn't sit still. He paced Carson's office restlessly, unmindful of the brilliant day outside the windows, the sandwiches that she had had sent in still untouched.

"But surely we're not just going to sit here!" he exploded.

"Well," she answered cheerily, "you can stand up if you like, or go on with your caged-tiger routine. Myself, I'm going to sit. What have you told headquarters?"

"I sent Peters a cable that the Soviet delegation was campused and that a stranger had arrived from Moscow. Possibly KGB. I asked for traces."

"There won't be any. If he's Counterintelligence, chances are he rarely travels abroad and uses a fake passport. Or that his name's not Maltsev at all."

"Well, that doesn't matter." Inigo, who had lit for a moment on the arm of an easy chair, jumped up again. "Actually, that cable is just to keep Peters from the truth. Anyway, Smirnov made it pretty clear that Maltsev has brought a team here to investigate the *New York Times* story. I put that in a Redbird cable to the director. For what it's worth, I added that at this point, a second leak would almost certainly be fatal."

"What it's worth is exactly nothing. The director's lost control over that."

"I know, I know." He finally sank into an armchair, leaned back, and closed his eyes. Carson watched him silently for a while.

"I can see you're not prepared for crises. How was Smirnov taking it last night?"

Inigo opened his eyes and stared at her thoughtfully. "By God, he was cool as a cucumber. And it's his neck, isn't it?"

"Sure is. And you'll just have to leave matters to him for now.

You've already told him we can take care of him whenever he feels he has to bolt. That'll be when he feels Maltsev's breath on the back of that neck of his. Nothing you can do but stand ready to receive the fugitive."

She was right. Inigo stared glumly at the carpet awhile longer, then rose wearily to his feet and set out for the door.

"Thanks, Emily."

"Right. And remember, there's one thing less to worry about now."

"What's that?"

"Whether Smirnov has been straight with you."

"Oh, yeah." Inigo was not cheered. He had accepted Smirnov's genuineness long ago.

The Britannia was crowded by early evening. As they pushed their way in, their ears were assaulted by more raucous English shouting than Inigo had ever heard in a London pub. The place was filled by the kind of British who did not bring their decorum with them when they went abroad. Code clerks, secretaries, junior travel agents, security guards, Australians; perhaps the pinched manners of the Swiss released a coarseness that they kept corked at home. Here they had created their own world, complete with steak and kidney pie, Guinness Stout, and darts. The sounds of French and German were as absent as if they had been forbidden.

Inigo was not fond of the place. Its loose loudness got on his nerves. But tonight was not an evening to spend alone, and Erika was committed to a professional dinner among the physicists. When Michaels had told him that two or three of the boys were stopping for a drink after work, he had been glad to tag along.

Morgan battled his way back from the bar to their table, gripping four big steins of beer. As the senior man, Inigo had claimed the honor of buying the first round. It seemed oddly out of place to be paying in Swiss francs.

"Don't look so down-in-the-mouth, George," Michaels told him. "Cheer up. We'll all be going home soon. With a signed treaty in our pocket."

"Not signed," Morgan put in. "Initialed. Once we have an agreed text, Jenkins and Lebedev initial it for authenticity. Later the two presidents throw themselves a big summit meeting and sign it. Then it finally goes to the Senate for testimony, debate, and ratification.

All that could add up to six or eight months more after we've finished the text here."

"Aren't you forgetting the Supreme Soviet?" It was an Army major from O'Rourke's shop.

"Ah yes, the dear old Supreme Soviet. Scene of many a stormy debate and close vote. The most dangerous obstacle of all."

"SALT's greatest test, no doubt about it," said Michaels. "What's your guess, George? When do you think we'll be getting out of here?"

"Beats me. I've been wrong half a dozen times already."

"Well, I can tell you that O'Rourke's expecting it soon. He's already done three drafts of his resignation statement. 'I cannot in good conscience associate myself with a treaty that . . .' Or should it be 'My seven years of service on the delegation have convinced me that this treaty constitutes a grave danger to . . . blah, blah, blah.' Me, he asks me! I tell him to use all three drafts, one after the other."

"When's he going to take this noble stance?"

"Right on the eve of the summit meeting. He figures he'll get maximum media attention that way. Dramatic dissent within the U.S. delegation, general challenges president on SALT, veteran U.S. negotiator repudiates treaty. That way he'll get a running start to be key witness for the opposition in the Senate hearings."

The crowd was thickening; they were lucky to have gotten a table. Ten feet away, an incautious shove transmitted itself through the standing drinkers like a shock wave. A chubby English girl received the end of it and toppled into Inigo's lap. "Sorry, love." Plain and sassy, she grinned at him and made no move to get up. Morosely, Michaels pinched her bottom, which did the trick. He stood up with her, grabbed her arm, and began to pull her behind him toward the bar.

"Friend of his?" Inigo asked.

"Once or twice, I think," said the major.

Inigo finished a second beer and excused himself. Michaels had not returned, nor did he spot him or the girl as he made his way through the crowd toward the men's room. Just before he entered, he half-glimpsed a familiar face in the next-to-last booth, but it happened so fleetingly that it only registered as a vague puzzlement in the back of his mind. Upon emerging, he saw with astonishment that it was Pavlovsky.

The big Russian spotted him immediately and got to his feet. "Mr. Inigo! How nice to see you." There was a girl with him; he unceremoniously dismissed her. "Please sit down and let me buy you a beer."

Nonplussed, Inigo lowered himself into the girl's chair. "Do you come here often?" he heard himself foolishly say.

"Now and then. When I want to get away from both Russians and Swiss." He gave Inigo a broad smile. "It's a nice friendly bar; I rather enjoy the noisy crowd. Moreover, I get to practice a different kind of English than I can use with your delegation."

Inigo leaned around to look over the crowd, wondering whether his companions could see him. The room was much too crowded for that, and getting smoky too. Buttocks pressed against their table.

"We are as good as invisible here, my friend." Pavlovsky joked. "Are you alarmed to be seen here with me?"

"Not at all. Surprised, however. I had heard that the Soviet delegation was working overtime these days and had no time for social pleasures."

"Where did you hear that?" Pavolvsky snapped. "Did Smirnov say that to you? Ah well, it doesn't matter. Yes, we are quite busy. But one must know how to get away from it all occasionally and take time to relax. Don't you agree?"

Inigo did agree. Furthermore, he told Pavlovsky he had the impression that the Soviet delegation permitted itself less relaxation than did the American. True, he had once encountered Mr. Pavlovsky on a boat—recalling the girl Pavlovsky had sent away, he thought it tactful not to mention Madame Pavlovksy's presence as well—but in general he almost never saw members of the Soviet delegation abroad in Geneva, enjoying the weekends. His colleagues reported the same. "What do you do inside that compound all week long?"

"Ah, we are very busy. The Soviet government never sleeps. We reread Marx and Lenin. We plot the downfall of capitalism. We devise clever plans for secretly violating the SALT treaty after it comes into force."

Inigo fell into the bantering style. "And we for our part enjoy the blessings of free enterprise and democracy that are daily undermining Soviet totalitarianism."

"Admittedly, the material temptations of the West are tremendous. Particularly as our work draws to a close and one begins to think about going back to Moscow. Have you met our new member, Mr. Maltsev?"

He said the last sentence with no change in tone, as though continuing the idle teasing, but the language was suddenly Russian.

"We spoke briefly at your reception the other night," Inigo answered noncommittally, also falling into Russian.

"An interesting man. I understand that he has a Chinese wife. Most unusual for a man in his profession."

"Oh? And what profession is that?"

Pavlovsky's eyes roamed over the crowd.

"I should like a whiskey now, but I suppose there's no chance of catching that waitress." He filled his glass again from the pitcher of beer. "Yes, Mr. Maltsev also has an interesting task."

Inigo made no reply. Let him talk.

"Yours is a strange country, Mr. Inigo. It speaks with many voices." Pavlovsky was speaking slowly. "If one knows the truth, then it all makes sense, I'm sure. But for those who are not insiders, it is difficult to know what to believe. Or what is going on."

There was a long pause while he toyed with his glass. Still Inigo remained silent.

"Take Mr. Maltsev, for example," Pavlovsky finally said. "He reads a strange story in one of your newspapers. Is it true? he wonders. But if it is not true, then what is its political meaning? What lies behind its appearance? With *Pravda* it is much simpler. *Pravda* contains both truth and lies, but the difference is clear to all, as are the meanings of the truths and the lies."

Both men smiled, relieved by the little joke. Inigo kept his eyes on the other's face as they drained their glasses. Pavlovsky spent a little time lighting a cigarette.

"That is Mr. Maltsev's problem. He is befuddled by your curious newspapers. He needs to separate truth from lies. He thinks that perhaps Geneva is the place to do that." The big Pavlovsky smile appeared again, but a little forced this time. Inigo decided it was time to help him along toward whatever it was he was getting at.

"And you? Do you think he can find his answers here in Geneva?"

"I think perhaps you can answer that better than I."

"I see. But I don't understand your concerns in all this."

"Ah yes, my concerns. You see, it so happens that I am acquainted with Mr. Maltsev. From years ago."

Pavlovsky held his gaze for a long silent moment, then rose, knocking against the table. "I see I'll have to get that whiskey myself. May

I bring you one?" Inigo nodded and his companion disappeared, pushing roughly into the mob.

When he reappeared, he set four drinks on the table. "I've called in the reserves," he said cheerfully. "Now"—wedging back into his seat—"we were speaking of Mr. Maltsev." He drained the first glass in a long swallow. "He is a spy hunter. Counterintelligence, I believe you say. And I believe also that you know why he has come to Geneva."

"I do follow the American press," Inigo said carefully.

"Exactly. We are beginning to communicate." Pavlovsky began, more slowly this time, on a second whiskey.

"But I know nothing more than what I read there."

"Of course, you have no choice but to say that. I realize that if there is no spy, there is no one for a spy hunter to find. And if there is a spy, he could be somewhere else than Geneva. And if there is a spy in Geneva, you are certainly not going to tell me about it."

"Are you a spy, Mr. Pavlovsky?" Inigo smiled calmly at him.

"Of course not." Pavlovsky grinned back. "That is another thing I know: I am not a spy. But Maltsev does not know that."

"Surely you can convince him of it."

"I must give you some more information." Most of the second whiskey was gone; so was the smile. "I first met Maltsev when we were fifteen years younger. He was a hunter then, but a different kind of hunter. There was some trouble. A big party one evening in Moscow. Many people went home, but a few stayed into the early-morning hours. A great deal of vodka was drunk. An unpleasantness broke out. It was very unfortunate. A young woman died."

A drunken murder, Inigo found himself thinking, I wouldn't put it past you. Then, to his astonishment, Pavlovsky crossed himself.

"I was innocent, I swear. Nothing could be proved against me. But Maltsev was convinced otherwise. He lost a good deal of face, never solved the case. Since that day, he has carried a mortal grudge against me. He has brought it to Geneva with him."

"And you think he will arrest you here as a spy?"

Pavlovsky, the glass halfway to his lips, nodded glumly and finished it off.

"But if you are not a spy?"

"The accusation itself would be most disagreeable. After such a charge, vindication is never complete. A suspicion always lingers, even after total exoneration. Besides, there is the interrogation. It is much more—how shall I say it—vigorous for treason than for murder. Maltsev would have the opportunity to reopen the old case under new circumstances."

"I see." What Inigo saw was that Pavlovsky was going to request asylum. He could have no other reason for telling the story.

"You will guess by now what I want. Let us talk about what I can offer your country in return." Coolly, Pavlovsky ticked off his areas of information. Current Soviet policy on SALT. The organization of the Foreign Ministry. The policymaking process in Moscow, particularly policy toward the United States. Political information (mostly gossip, he confessed) about the Politburo and Central Committee. Suspected intelligence officers operating under diplomatic cover. Defense Ministry policy regarding the preservation of loopholes in the SALT treaty and their subsequent exploitation. "And whatever else you care to ask me about," he finished grandly. His composure was superb. No observer who did not understand Russian would dream that the man was facing a life-or-death crisis.

"And if you were to disappear here in Geneva?" Inigo put it as delicately as he could. "What effect would that have on our treaty?"

"Positive," Pavlovksy replied immediately. "There would be displeasure, of course. Ambassador Jenkins would have to experience some bad temper from Ambassador Lebedev. Soon, however, the talks would move forward again. As it is now, Moscow has frozen them until it catches your spy. You Americans sometimes do not realize, I think, how much my government desires a treaty. For political reasons, as well as arms control.

"Furthermore," he added, "if you really have a spy, my plan would save him. When they noticed I was gone, they would stop looking further."

Only later did it occur to each of them, separately, that with this last remark Pavlovsky had sealed his fate.

"I'll have to consult with my superiors," Inigo told him. "You have some plan of how we can be in contact again?"

"Of course. I will be in this bar each evening from seven thirty to eight. I live not far from here. If I see you here, I will not speak to you, but I will meet you elsewhere at eight thirty. I suggest the monument of the duke of Brunswick."

"Fine." Inigo started to rise. Suddenly he saw Pavlovsky's face start to crumble before his eyes; his knuckles whitened on the table-top.

"For God's sake, hurry!" he implored, all composure gone. Tears stood in his eyes. "I'll be here tomorrow evening. But even that may be too late. Go now, send your cable, go!"

He brushed past Inigo and pushed away through the crowd.

He had not, Inigo realized, said a word about his wife.

32

When foreign service officers spoke of an "old hand," Prewitt was the sort of man they had in mind. Tall, big-nosed, broad-shouldered, he had a totally plebeian appearance that resembled not at all the stereotype of the socialite-diplomat. He had done his time in the trenches, replacing lost tourist passports in the lesser consulates, learning two languages well and two more passably, running the political section in Warsaw. He had kept the London embassy on an even keel as number two to a naïve, flighty ambassador whose only qualification was his wealth or, more precisely, that portion of it he had shared with the Republican party. Now he was at the peak, ambassador to Moscow, presiding over a dump of an embassy and a jewel of a personal residence. There was no competition from the politically faithful here; from corporation presidents to automobile dealers, no contributor to either party had ever asked to be paid off with a post behind the Iron Curtain. If he kept his nerves healthy, Prewitt could expect his next assignment to be near the apex, perhaps number three man in the department.

Keeping his nerves healthy was exactly what Prewitt did best. He was known for his toughness, but also for his unshakable composure. This morning, for example, a less canny bureaucrat might have actually lost his temper. When Prewitt read the cable, however, he recognized immediately that he was in the presence of a *fait accompli*. Since he could not undo the decision, he at once set himself the objective of making himself a part of it.

EYES ONLY FOR AMBASSADOR FROM SECRETARY

YOU ARE REQUESTED TO PLACE THE AMBASSADORIAL AIRCRAFT AT THE DISPOSAL OF THE CIA STATION CHIEF FOR THE NEXT THIRTY DAYS. THE MISSION FOR WHICH HE MAY REQUIRE IT IS OF THE UT-

MOST SENSITIVITY AND HAS THE APPROVAL OF THE HIGHEST AU-
THORITY.

Despite the testiness that this message produced, Prewitt had to
smile once again at the euphemism *highest authority*. The department in its cables and documents still clung to the fiction that if the
president was not explicitly cited, he was somehow protected from
formal responsibility. Moreover, some careless reader might make
the gratifying assumption that the highest authority was the secretary of state.

He knew the knock on his office door to be Jorgensen's; his secretary had told him the station chief was on his way up. Prewitt liked
Jorgensen. CIA assigned to Moscow quiet, competent men, able to
stand the rigors of a confined life in a bleak environment and cope
with more than the usual run of operational emergencies. Jorgensen
was fifteen years younger than Prewitt and stood to gain, in career
terms, as much as his ambassador from a successful Moscow tour.
Except that for Jorgensen, the risk of black marks or even disgrace
was incomparably higher.

"What the hell is this about, Vince?" Prewitt's bark had enough
bite to show he was aggrieved, not enough to commit him to a confrontation. He tossed the offending cable across his desk, where it
skidded over the smooth walnut veneer and fluttered to the floor. Jorgensen picked it up and put it back on the desk; he didn't need to read
it.

"Yessir," he said easily. "I got my version of it late yesterday, after
you had left. It's entirely a headquarters show. Nothing to do with
our cases here. We're to fly someone out black. They don't say why,
just a lot of contact instructions."

Prewitt knew he'd been told nothing an amateur couldn't figure
out. Why else would his air force plane be handed over to CIA, if not
to exfiltrate a Soviet citizen, secretly and illegally? He also knew Jorgensen well enough to accept his disclaimers of knowledge.

"Vince, I won't pretend I like it. Frankly I have more confidence in
the operations you run locally than on some mysterious big deal that
your masters lay on you. All I can say is, you keep my airplane out of
trouble, dammit!"

"I think we can manage that, sir." Jorgensen settled into a chair.
He figured that Prewitt was entitled to a lengthy complaint and that

absorbing it was part of his job. He also knew that the ambassador was due at the Foreign Ministry in twenty minutes to lodge another formal protest against Soviet violations of the Human Rights Convention. This wouldn't last too long.

"You know, don't you, that that plane is supposed to fly a pregnant embassy wife out to Frankfurt in two weeks?"

"Yes, indeed. It's Mary Fitts. She's a good friend of my wife's. I'm working to get things timed right."

"Vince, I know you're instructed to keep the details secret. But let me remind you that I'm going back to Washington for consultations in two weeks. I expect to have my usual short session with the president. He may make a reference to this, and I don't want to look like a damn fool, not knowing what's going on in my own embassy."

Jorgensen got to his feet. "I quite understand. I'll request permission to cut you in. If that fails, I'll request that you be briefed in full when you get to Washington. In fact, that would be even better. You'd learn a lot more there than I know myself."

"Good. Got to run now. Get on it right away, please."

Jorgensen got on it right away. Within thirty minutes a cable was drafted and typed.

Before the commo boys had begun to transmit, Jorgensen had driven off to collect his wife and take her to the Tretyakov Gallery.

33

It was too late to catch Erika on the phone; she would already be on her way to his apartment. He would have to hurry to get there before her.

Pavlovsky's a fool, he thought, gunning away from the curb with a slight nick against the bumper of the car parked ahead. A shout pursued him through the evening's drizzle. It was dark, but if they got his license number, he'd pay, diplomatic immunity or not. At the first red light, Inigo took himself in hand. It was no good cracking up the car now, putting himself out of action. He made good time on the long bridge across the Rhone, which beckoned like a racecourse straightaway, but he took the rain-slick cobblestones of the Vieille Ville in second gear.

A light in his apartment told him that Erika had arrived and let herself in. It was too bad, but she would have to understand. He knew she would understand. Just now it was imperative that he find Carson.

But Erika was on him before he could begin.

"George, something is happening! What is it? I am frightened!" She pressed against his wet raincoat without a kiss.

"Erika!" He gathered her in his arms and squeezed her hard, long, and wordlessly. When she stopped shaking, he looked into her tear-wet face.

"A man," she sobbed. "On the street outside. He stopped me. In German. Gave me a letter for you."

"What did he look like? Short? Fat?"

"No. Tall. All bundled up in black. A broad brim on his black hat. And terrible eyes peering out from under it."

He shepherded her into the tiny kitchen to make her a drink, keeping his left arm around her as he poured. "When did it happen? Could it have been that Gonzales?"

"No, not him, I would recognize the smell of evil from him." Erika was steadying down. "Not a German, either. He had a slight accent." Inigo put the drink in her hand, but she remained motionless. "It was just a few moments ago. You could have passed him in the street. My God, he may be watching the house right now!" She leaned hard against him and took a sip. "It was so sudden! And his terrible look!"

"You'd better show me the letter." The name Maltsev flew through his mind like a black crow.

She fetched it out from her purse. "Herr Inigo," he read silently. "Please meet me on the north side of the cathedral at 8:30. It urgently concerns your work. I cannot come again." It was unsigned.

Inigo took a deep breath, then a sip of the drink Erika offered him. "Darling, I'll have to go." He handed her the note and got her coat from the hall as she read it. "I told you I'd gotten mixed up in the spy business here. I never meant for you to get involved, never dreamed you would. But now things have gotten a little off the track." She looked at him in puzzlement. "Out of control, that is. I'm afraid I'll have to go find out who this person is and what he wants."

"Is it safe?"

"Oh yes, I'm sure it is."

"You would say that anyway."

"Yes, I suppose I would. But I really do think so. Now you'd better go home."

"I want to stay here. Until you come back."

Inigo began to protest, then checked himself. Why not? She would be as safe at his apartment as at hers, and less frightened here than there. He would have to return to deal with her immediately, but hell, he thought, I want to deal with her! She's in my life so deeply already. He hugged her passionately.

"All right. I want you to stay too. Try not to worry." He looked at his watch. "I've got a few minutes to get there. Don't know when I'll get back. Shouldn't be too long, but it is a mystery, isn't it?"

He hadn't taken off his raincoat. At the door Erika kissed him hard. "Be careful. I love you."

"Right. Me too."

Reaching the pavement, Inigo suddenly wasn't so sure. The fine rain hung in the air. His street was slick and deserted. Abruptly, he felt watched. He looked up to see Erika waving from his lighted window and hoped that was all it was. As he set off down the street, he saw a man staring into a shop window a hundred feet ahead, dry under the little red roof of overhang above. When he was nearly upon him, the man gave him a quick glance and moved toward the window to give him space to pass on the narrow pavement. He was a stranger: one of Rudenko's watchers? When Inigo reached the Bourg de Four, he glanced back and saw the man, still standing in front of the shop window, looking at him.

The square was deserted as he crossed it; only a couple of restaurants showed signs of life. He patted the sullen preadolescent statue on the rump. "Wish me luck, little girl." He recalled the first time he had encountered a lone Genevoise late at night, on a dimly lit street. She had passed him with neither cringe nor glance, as if it were broad daylight. He had realized then the sense of safety within which the Swiss lived. Did that go for spies too? He left the square by the Rue de l'Hotel de Ville, a stately procession of lighted shop windows containing gleaming silver, elegant crystal, Persian carpets, old masters, antique desks. He had never seen a purchase being made here and had to imagine Swiss bankers and Arab sheikhs discreetly signing contracts in some handsomely paneled rear office.

When he turned downhill at the first right-hand street, the cathedral loomed blackly, its base below him but its towers reaching high above. On the far side, the south side, where the main entrance lay, it was set off by a floodlit plaza overlooking the city and lake below. Here on the north side, all was darkness and a jumble of construction materials for the never-ending work of restoration. The south front was plain but open. It was the healthy face of Calvinism, which had stripped the cathedral of its Catholic baubles when it conquered the Genevois, leaving them humorless, sound, and diligent. The north front was the darker face, the face that thundered condemnations and handed down edicts of death to the frivolous and the sinning. It lay black, empty, open to the rain.

Thirty feet from the pile, Inigo stopped in an errant patch of street glow. Nothing could be seen in the dark crannies and folds of the cathedral's rear wall. He checked his watch: 8:32. He would go no farther.

"*Guten Abend*," he said in a low, clear voice. "*Herr Inigo hier*."

After a moment a shadow detached itself from the darkness ahead and moved forward. It too spoke in German.

"Please come forward. I am quite alone." Even in the wrong language, the voice was unmistakable.

Ambassador Lebedev.

The terrible eyes that had frightened Erika. Eyes of an iguana.

Inigo cried out softly as he barked his shin against a pile of building stone. He peered around but could see no one but Lebedev, who had retreated into near-invisibility against the wall. As Inigo approached, he spoke quietly.

"It is good of you to come. I have very little time. I am supposed to be at the opera. *Lohengrin* is so long that I was able to slip away," he chuckled.

"Unusual rendezvous," Inigo muttered.

"Yes, but an important one. I will get directly to the point. Nevertheless I cannot help being a little amused. I have done many things in my life, but I have never played secret agent before." And he chuckled again.

Inigo remained silent.

"Yes. To the point. You have met Herr Maltsev. He is here with two co-workers from Moscow to discover whether we have a traitor in our delegation. Because of that wretched story in your newspaper."

"I read it."

"All of us are under suspicion. We are all being watched. Even me. My entire delegation is demoralized."

"My director denies the story. Not in public, of course, but to his colleagues."

"He does? That is interesting. But we can hardly trust that, can we? At any rate, Moscow will not."

"I'm sorry you've been put in difficulties."

"Yes, it is too bad. But one endures such things. The worst of it is that our negotiations are frozen. I am instructed to make no further moves in our negotiations until this matter is settled."

Inigo peered into Lebedev's face, two feet from his own. The humor was gone, the fierceness was also absent; Lebedev simply looked extremely grave.

"Then I hope it is settled quickly."

"Perhaps that is up to us. In particular, to you, Herr Inigo."

Inigo said nothing, so Lebedev continued.

"If there is a spy on my delegation, you are the person who would know."

"If."

"Yes, if. I realize it is possible that he is in Moscow. Or Washington. Or that he does not exist, except in the mind of a deceived newspaper reporter. But Moscow is serious."

"Then it will have to continue its investigations. When they are over, we can resume our negotiations."

"It is not so simple, Herr Inigo." Lebedev stepped away from the wall, peered intently in both directions, then came back. "The idea of spies throws Moscow into a panic. If they don't find him soon, they may break off the talks altogether. Some members of the Politburo, I believe, would not be unhappy with that outcome. At any rate, my instructions are clear: No further movement until the traitor is in our hands."

"Maybe yes, maybe no. Anyway, why should I help you, even if I could?" Inigo fought to keep his voice calm. He was more tense than he had ever been with Smirnov, with Gonzales, with Pavlovsky earlier that evening.

"Yes, why? To save our negotiations, of course. I assume that you desire their success. Herr Smirnov has assured me of this." At the mention of Smirnov's name, Inigo felt his fists clench in his pockets.

"That is correct. But I am not sure the Soviet side desires it also. Desires it enough, that is, to meet our minimum requirements."

Lebedev gave him a long look, the fierceness flared briefly in his eyes, then died away. "I understand. You require reassurance. Very well. I shall select the issue of telemetry encryption, in which I believe you have a special interest."

"It is a critical question."

"Moscow has decided that it can go no further in the treaty than it already has. The Second Common Understanding to Article Fifteen already provides, as the Americans wish, that neither side shall engage in deliberate denial of telemetric information, such as through the use of encryption, whenever such denial impedes verification."

The quote was nearly word-perfect. Like many members of the two delegations, Lebedev carried most of the treaty in his head.

"But the force of that is seriously undermined by your insistence in the same Common Understanding that each party is free to use various methods of transmitting telemetric information during testing, including its encryption." Inigo's quote was letter-perfect.

"Yes. One can feel the tension between the two versions. But I repeat, we can go no further here in Geneva. They are complaining in Moscow that we are making it illegal to preserve military secrets. The line has been drawn." He peered about once more into the darkness.

"However, I am informed by my minister that at the signing of the treaty, the Soviet president is willing to go further. He is prepared to make an additional statement that, while it will not appear in the text of the treaty, will have the full force of a formal commitment by the Soviet government. I have been requested to prepare such a statement."

"And what have you drafted?"

"I have not yet written a draft. I expect that whatever I submit will be accepted."

"An interesting idea," Inigo mused aloud. "Yes, I imagine that the United States could accept that solution of the problem. Depending, of course, upon the exact language."

"Depending, of course, upon the exact language," Lebedev repeated. "Perhaps the best thing would be for you to draft that language."

"The statement of the Soviet president?" Inigo was astonished.

"Exactly. You are in the best position of anyone in the two delegations to know what will satisfy American requirements and at the same time not be unacceptable to the USSR."

Inigo considered for a long two minutes. He could stall, demand a day in which to think the matter over. Lebedev could not refuse him that. And in that day he could put Smirnov and his wife on an airplane to the States. Smirnov could even bring the remaining Soviet fallbacks with him. But Lebedev had said that Moscow had frozen the talks "until the traitor is in our hands." If that was meant literally, merely learning of Smirnov's treachery after he was beyond Soviet reach would not suffice. At the least, surely Lebedev's offer on the issue of telemetry encryption would be null and void.

And, it suddenly struck him, there was the question of Irina. Could he expect Sloan and his people to spirit her out of the USSR on short notice, before the Soviets discovered that Smirnov was gone? Could he persuade Smirnov of that? Irina's escape was a vital part of their bargain. Surely it would be a betrayal to force Smirnov's defection in a way that might strand his daughter in the USSR, never to be reunited with her parents.

Lebedev showed no signs of impatience. Once he moved slightly away to conduct another brief reconnaissance. When Inigo finally turned to him, he was instantly alert.

"Yes, I believe I could work out the necessary language. How would I get it to you?"

"I have given that some thought. I frequently attend the German Film Club here in Geneva. There is an informal reception, then the film, then some more social conversation. Someone could pass me a note during the showing of the film, for example."

"That seems workable. But how can you guarantee that your president will make the statement?"

The fierceness jumped into Lebedev's eyes. "I can't, Herr Inigo. But I can tell you that I have not spent seven years of my life here in Geneva just to see all my work destroyed by some stupid spies! I refuse to let this treaty be destroyed!" In the darkness he seemed to grow larger.

Inigo looked away. So once again, he thought, we're brought up against the question of trust. There's no way around it. Yes or no.

"Very well, I agree."

"Good!" Lebedev seized his hand and gave it a solemn, strong shake. Then, "And the man?"

Inigo took a deep breath.

"Pavlovsky."

"But George, you've sent that man to his death!"

"My God, have I?"

After the first shock came a second, when Inigo realized that, there with Lebedev in the shadows, it had crossed his mind only in one brief flash that he might be condemning Pavlovsky to execution. He had been so anxious to protect Smirnov, to divert Maltsev from him, that he had pushed away all thought of the consequences.

"I don't think so, Erika." It was another shock to see how quickly his mind came up with rationalizations. "Once the real defector disappears, they'll know Pavlovsky is innocent. Besides, he as good as told me he got away with a murder years ago, in Moscow. And he's not really for SALT at all. It's just a job to him." He told her about how cynical Pavlovsky had been about the treaty when they had shared coffee at the lakeside café.

"But still."

Inigo looked at her helplessly. Once this treaty is signed, he swore to himself, I'll never get mixed up in this espionage stuff again. I won't go near it. Something swelled in his throat as he pulled Erika toward him, hoping that her eyes, like his own, were closed.

It had been, Carson told Inigo afterward, quite a scene. At seven fifteen in the morning, when the consulate was empty, save for one marine guard at the reception desk and another making rounds on the upper floors, a car had careened in from the Rue de Lausanne, jumped the curb, and almost rammed the building.

"Then this big guy jumped out and started hammering on the door. It was unusual enough for the corporal to call his buddy on the walkie-talkie and to take his time releasing the door lock. When the man got into the lobby, he was in a frenzy. He was in a panic to see you, George, but of course your name meant nothing to the marine. Then he started asking for me, for the CIA, for the consul. Said it was an emergency, he wanted asylum, he was being pursued, he was a political refugee. Kept slipping from English into something the corporal couldn't understand; Russian, of course.

"Well, by this time the other marine had arrived. They couldn't see any pursuers. They asked for his passport and sure enough, it was Pavlovsky."

They were in the consulate cafeteria, eating pastry and drinking the coffee-and-cream combination that the Swiss call *renverser*. Carson had arrived early for work, just in time to see the marines shove Pavlovsky out onto the street and lock the door behind him. He had looked wildly around, then jumped into his car and headed toward the railroad station, banging a lamp post as he bounced over the curb. As soon as Carson got the story from the corporal, she had phoned Inigo to come in. It was still early; they were the only breakfasters.

"So it was a damn good thing you rang me last night, late as it was. Right after your call I phoned the guard desk and told them to keep a certain Pavlovsky out if he tried to get in, no matter what he said. You know, those kids look like they couldn't handle an Eagle Scout, but they did a nice job on your boy. And no excesses."

"What'll happen to him now, Emily?"

"Oh, he'll be picked up before noon, unless he's got a hole to hide in somewhere. Obviously the Soviets are cruising around after him, but it'll probably be the Swiss police who nab him. At the border, maybe, or perhaps right here in Geneva, on a speeding charge. He'll ask for asylum and Chief Inspector Durkeim will call me to find out what I know, and to offer me first choice."

"And then?"

"I'll say that we're not interested, thanks. That we know of no grounds for political asylum. So after a day or so they'll telephone Rudenko and tell him to come down and pick up his lost property."

The night before, as Inigo was drifting off to sleep, Pavlovsky had suddenly jumped into his mind, bringing him upright and wide awake. Taking care not to wake Erika, he had gotten out of bed and called Carson to tell her of Pavlovsky's approach to him in the Britannia. The man might bolt at any time, he said. Could Emily arrnage to keep him out of the consulate?

She could and she would. Right away. No, don't apologize for the hour. Part of the game. Goodnight, George, sleep well.

"So now Smirnov has some time to breathe."

"Yes," said Inigo. "He'll be a happy man in an hour or so, when he gets to work and finds out what's happened." He had explained last night, though it was hardly necessary, how Smirnov would gain a reprieve if suspicion fell on Pavlovsky.

He had said not a word about his rendezvouz with Ambassador Lebedev.

34

Inigo was in a box.

Fidgeting in the tank, he tried to follow the "new-types" argument. Both parties had agreed that the treaty would permit each side to develop and deploy only one new type of ICBM. But what would be the definition of a new type? Missiles were being improved all the time; the ingenuity of engineers was phenomenal, frightening. Could one side substitute more efficient propellant to increase the range of an existing missile? A new gyroscope to improve its accuracy? If so, by how much, before the missile would be so different from the initial version that it would be classified as a new type? The problem had not been clearly foreseen when the only-one-new-type provision had been adopted; now it was evident that the complexities were enormous.

The threads of the argument, however, all led back to telemetry. What kinds of improvements could CIA be confident of detecting? With what margins of error, what ranges of uncertainty? The intelligence capabilities would determine the definitions of allowable and forbidden changes, and these depended on the telemetry. If the intercepts were encrypted, the Soviets could radically upgrade their existing ICBMs in secret, leaving the United States none the wiser.

The delegation pulled and tugged at various suggestions for the language of the definition. But Inigo was preoccupied with a totally different problem. Back in his office safe, he already had the key language, the promise that the Soviet president would make at the summit meeting, to leave telemetry in the clear. The problem now was how to pass it to Ambassador Lebedev and get his reaction. The plenary and post-plenary meetings were much too open and formal for Inigo to chance handing over a note. To go himself to the German Film Club was unthinkable; anyone might be there, watching. Perhaps one of Carson's people, fluent in German and unknown to the Soviets, could carry it there. But that would require cutting her in

217

about Lebedev, and she would be obliged to report it to Washington. Then matters would be entirely out of his control. He could imagine the headline over the leaked story: Soviet SALT Chief Conducts Secret Negotiations with CIA Officer.

No, there was no one but Erika.

Each time Inigo fought off the idea, the facts drove him back to it. She was German; there was no link between her and Lebedev (unless someone had observed their brief encounter in the street outside his apartment); she even visited the German Film Club occasionally. He could not tell himself that there would be no danger for her. If a slip-up occurred, she as well as Lebedev would be under interrogation, by their separate services, within the hour. But the risks would be minimized; a note silently passed to a stranger in the next seat of a darkened theater.

That decided, Inigo threw himself into the delegation meeting. It was nearly over, with everyone exhausted. Their job was to figure out what kinds of limitations could be put into treaty language. Not every idea could. It was painstaking work, and everyone felt its futility in the absence of instructions from home. Jenkins pushed on for another quarter of an hour, then called a halt.

Morgan fell in beside Inigo as the tank emptied.

"What do you think, George?"

"About the new-types rule? We'll get one eventually. It'll be a nightmare policing it. Bound to generate a lot of charges and countercharges."

"Is it worth it?"

"Sure." Inigo stopped and faced him. "The Soviets have at least four new ICBMs under development, short of the testing stage. If we can knock out all but one of those projects, the chances for the next treaty will be a lot better. If we can just halt the momentum, those people may start to think differently about the arms race in a few years."

"But what about our side? There's a loophole in this treaty for every weapon the Pentagon wants."

"True. It's a long haul, Morgan. This is SALT Two; I'm counting on some real arms control in SALT Four or Five. In the meantime, don't forget that while the U.S. *has* a military-industrial complex, the USSR *is* a military-industrial complex. Even a minimal treaty is going to affect that psychology."

Morgan had been in Geneva for five years. Arms control was his profession and his passion, and he was subject to depression about it. "And what about you guys? Is CIA going to block the treaty if it doesn't get its precious telemetry?"

"You bet." Inigo replied cheerfully. "No verification, no treaty."

Morgan sighed and started toward his office. After a few steps he turned and came back. There was an angry urgency in his voice. "You fellows will have it on your conscience forever if we fail here!"

"So let's not fail." Inigo smiled and walked away.

The proposal filled Erika with excitement. She accepted too readily for Inigo's liking.

"Please think about the risks, dear. You don't have to do it. I'm sure I could find another way."

"Risks, pah! I have to have some real life here before going back to Leipzig next year. Is it for the Russians I am doing this? The Americans?"

"Both of us. All of us, really. To start stopping the arms race."

"All the better. It will be a slap in the face of my father, that Nazi bastard! Maybe it will make up for some of what he did. To all of us."

She gripped his arm eagerly. They were strolling by the lake. It was a conversation that Inigo wanted to conduct in the open air, far from possible hidden microphones. He tried to keep her excitement from infecting him.

"You may have to watch a lot of movies before he turns up."

"I do not mind, I will go tomorrow night. And he will be there. You will see; I feel it."

So it was agreed. Inigo gave her the text, typed out in Russian on a Cyrillic typewriter from the office of the interpreting staff. Erika read it and laughed.

"So this is what world peace hinges upon!"

"We diplomats speak in strange tongues."

"Give me your strange tongue."

"When we get home."

"No, right now."

Her kiss was savage. Inigo forgot all thoughts of dinner. In the taxi that he hurriedly hailed, they tore at each other's clothing. The buttons of her blouse ripped away. Once in his bedroom they devoured each other, she more ravenous even than he.

219

The lobby of the German Film Club was depressingly bright and bare when Erika arrived. It was an unofficial organization, started by West German diplomats to amuse themselves and shunned for the first two years by their East German counterparts. Gradually, however, détente had blossomed here too, and now the vice-president was an East German, scheduled to succeed to the presidency next year. In principle, films from both countries were shown on an equal basis, but in practice there was little demand for the Eastern products.

Erika picked up one of the glasses of white wine set out on a card table for the early arrivals. She recognized a couple from the International Labor Organization and went over to chat, looking out all the while for an older man, large, barrel-chested, bald-headed, with deep-set eyes. When she found him, he had already spotted her. They both looked quickly away. His younger wife, talking gaily in German to another couple, seemed to notice nothing.

Erika and Inigo had talked about how to get the note to Lebedev. They had discussed half a dozen little schemes before giving up. She would simply have to improvise, they decided. If no good opportunity could be found, she was to abandon the plan and bring the note back for another try later. Now, as the audience began to file in, she disengaged smoothly from her companions and let the Lebedevs enter first. Staying close enough, she saw them turn into a row halfway down the aisle of the small theater. Lebedev went first and stopped at the next to last seat. Was he leaving the last seat for her?

A foursome followed the Lebedevs in, but when she reached the row, the last seat was still empty. The foursome stood noisily as she maneuvered past them. Madame Lebedev reamined seated and gave her a curious stare as she bumped along her knees. A single woman was unusual here. Lebedev ignored her. The space was narrow, and she held onto the back of the seat ahead of her as she pushed past his heavy legs. On an impulse she murmured softly in English, as if to herself, "In I go."

Erika heard Lebedev cough softly as the lights suddenly went down. Glancing sideways, she saw that he has placed his hand on his knee, palm upward. Quickly, before eyes had adjusted to the darkness, she placed the folded note in his hand. When she looked again, his hands were in his lap.

It was a revival, *The Cabinet of Doctor Caligari*, a movie that she had already seen once, and that by mistake. The grainy black-and-white film, the ludicrous painted faces, the Gothic eyes had no appeal for her. After ten minutes she began to feel caught between Lebedev's bulk on one side and the wall on the other. Was anything else going to happen? Should she leave? Did Lebedev want anything further of her? On the screen, a trembling victim was entering Caligari's consulting room. Was she herself in a trap that was about to be sprung, perhaps by the two stolid, heavyset men sitting in front of her?

The film was half over when Lebedev, with whispered excuses, heaved himself up and made his clumsy way to the aisle. One of the men ahead of her turned his head for an inquiring look. Erika fought the impulse to follow him out; she must stay where she was. The emptiness of the seat beside her felt like an abandonment. Five minutes later she glimpsed him returning at the end of the row, muttering apologies and scraping noisily back toward her. Again a glance from ahead, this time from the second man.

As the Russian sank into his seat, Erika opened her hand on her knee. For two minutes nothing happened, and her turned wrist began to ache. Then a small piece of paper dropped into her palm. She closed her fist around it, turned her hand over, and waited another three minutes before slipping the paper into her bag.

The film seemed endless. Finally, after coffins, knives, ropes, terror-stricken faces, it flickered to a close. As the crowd moved slowly up the aisle, a young man spoke to Erika.

"Did you like it?"

"Not at all." She was startled, and the words jumped out of her.

"Neither did I. Can't think why I came. Actually, I thought they were showing a different film, a Fassbinder." There was no question about it, he spoke in the Saxon accents of a Dresdener.

"Would you like to condemn it with me over coffee?"

"No, thank you." Erika forced herself to face him with an angry stare.

"Perhaps a drink, then. My name is Horst Goerigen." He smiled and offered his hand.

The crowd was thinning now. Erika could stand it no longer. She marched rapidly across the lobby and broke into a run when she reached the sidewalk. When she reached her car, the key and the lock seemed entirely unfamiliar. Her fumbling seemed to take a full minute.

Safely locked in at last, she scanned the sidewalk. The Lebedevs were nowhere to be seen, nor the importunate East German, nor the two men from the row ahead. Two couples lingered talking in front of the theater entrance, that was all. Erika started up and turned toward the Rhone and the Vieille Ville beyond and above it. A car pulled away from the curb in the same direction behind her, although in the traffic she soon lost track of it in her mirror. On the bridge of the Rue de Mont Blanc, the headlights of a vehicle hung a constant thirty feet behind her bumper, but there was no way to know whether it was the same vehicle or not. As she turned along the ramparts of the Vieille Ville, it closed to a nearer distance and stayed on her tail. Ignoring the stop sign, Erika coasted fast into the Bourg de Four and turned right, where the main police station stood fifty yards down the hill. She halted and jumped out of her car just as her pursuer drove up. It was Inigo.

"Oh God, I frightened you, didn't I?" he shouted as he ran up. But Erika was too exhausted to reply. She tripped as she turned toward him and he barely caught her.

Creeping back through the square, they got their cars into the parking lot and themselves into the apartment. In a minute or two Erika stopped shuddering and told him the entire story.

"The note! The paper he gave you back."

She fished it out of her handbag and uncrumpled it. On the paper they made out a single universal word.

"Okay."

35

"There is no further room for compromise," Smirnov assured him, "in the Soviet position on the encryption of telemetry."

It was a day of brilliant sunshine. Across the sparkling lake, Inigo gazed at Le Dôle rising in the distance; behind it loomed the true Mont Blanc, broad-shouldered and magnificent. The restaurant courtyard, almost empty of diners, ran straight down to the shore where a family of brown ducks paddled placidly, providing a homely foreground for the grandeur of the Alpine horizon.

The curfew had been lifted from the Soviet delegation, but Smirnov still seemed uneasy. His invitation to the lakeside restaurant had been on short notice, with a hint of urgency. Now he was earnestly telling Inigo that while Moscow had instructed the Soviet delegation to accept the modified American proposals on new types of ICBMs and functionally related observable differences for Bison tankers, it was refusing to budge on telemetry.

"I never told you that the USSR would meet all the American demands. I promised only to supply you with the fallbacks." His nervousness made him petulant. "You have gotten your way on the last six issues. This is the only one that remains unresolved. You must tell Washington that now it is its turn to compromise."

Inigo leaned happily back in his chair and looked out over the waters, flecked with ten thousand points of jiggling light, at the lake steamer setting out on its cruise to Lausanne. For the moment, his mind was as cloudless as the sky. The night before, when Erika had finally calmed herself, she asked him to take her back to her own apartment. There they fell immediately into bed. She wanted to talk.

"Now I will tell you the real reason why I did it," she said.

"The real reason?"

"Yes. All that business about world peace and the arms race and my father, that counts for nothing." She paused, and he could feel her staring into the darkness. He waited.

"Ach, you men are so stupid. I did it for love." He was about to protest, but she stopped him. "Be quiet now. You want me to have fine ideals, noble aims. You want me to want to risk myself for mankind. But it is much finer to do something out of love. Simple love."

She groped in the dark, lit a cigarette, and handed it to him, ignoring his gasp when she placed the cold ashtray on his bare stomach.

"You men are so difficult. You always want to make things so complicated, so abstract. Right now you are upset with me, that I did not do it for the good of mankind. You will not let me do it just for you. But that is what I wanted, and that is what I did. Why can you not accept that?" She sighed. "Ah, it is a sad thing for women, that there is not something better in the world to love. But we have to love, and men are the best thing available."

Inigo silently held her naked body to his. Then she had turned away so that he could cup both her breasts and they had fallen asleep, without making love.

Inigo pulled himself reluctantly out of the remembrance. Smirnov was still talking.

". . . returned to Moscow. It happened quite suddenly."

"Oh, yes, what a shame."

"A shame? Why is that a shame? I find it a relief that Mr. Maltsev has gone."

Inigo opened his mouth, then shut it. Smirnov, he realized, was speaking of Maltsev, while he had been thinking of Pavlovsky. If Smirnov knew that Maltsev was gone, he would also know that Pavlovsky had gone with him. Inigo hoped his slip had gone unnoticed. To cover his confusion, he leaned down to the gravel floor of the courtyard and lifted his briefcase to the table. Smirnov watched him steadily as he opened it and took out a large manila envelope stiffened by a cardboard insert. He was not to get off so easily.

"A nice piece of work, George," he said slowly. "A very nice piece of work."

"What? I don't know what you're talking about."

Smirnov smiled at him. "I expect we'll have a lot of things to tell each other when this is all over."

"Yes, I'm sure we will." Inigo opened the envelope. "Look here, Victor, I have something for you." He pulled a sheet of white paper out and handed it across the table. It bore the presidential seal.

Smirnov read it silently, his face solemn. He read it again, then looked up at Inigo, smiling broadly now, with tears standing in his eyes.

"Let's hear it aloud."

Softly, huskily, Smirnov began to read.

" 'Dear Mr. Smirnov. Please allow me to express my deepest admiration for your great courage in making a vital contribution to the cause of arms control. Your services in the search for world peace are of inestimable value. I look forward to expressing my sentiments more fully in person in the near future.' "

Below, in a bold, open hand, was the signature of the president.

"Very nice, isn't it?"

Smirnov was too moved to reply. He took a napkin and wiped his mouth, then his eyes. He read the letter again. Finally he was able to speak.

"You'll come with me, won't you, George? When I meet him?"

"If they'll let me," Inigo answered cheerily. "After all, you're the hero. Shall I keep that for you?"

"Yes. Please do." Smirnov turned his head and gazed at Mont Blanc while Inigo put the letter back in the envelope and returned it to his briefcase. A long moment passed. Then, still looking away, he said quietly, "I thank you most deeply."

"And I thank you." Inigo was brisk. "Now about my telemetry. Is there nothing to be done?"

Smirnov sighed deeply. He shook his head.

"Nothing."

They drove away in their separate cars. Inigo suddenly found it odd that for all the times they had met, all the time they had spent together, they had never sat together in the same automobile.

Back in the office, he laboriously typed out a cable.

TOP SECRET REDBIRD
DIRECTOR EYES ONLY

SOURCE REPORTS SOVIET MILITARY IS ADAMANTLY OPPOSED TO FURTHER COMPROMISE IN TREATY ON TELEMETRY ENCRYPTION AND THAT POLITBURO HAS ADOPTED THIS STAND. HOWEVER, PO-LITBURO AGREES THAT SOVIET PRESIDENT, IN FORMAL STATE-MENT AT SUMMIT, WILL UNDERTAKE THE FOLLOWING:

THE SOVIET GOVERNMENT STATES THAT THERE MUST BE NO EN-CRYPTION OF INFORMATION INVOLVING PARAMETERS COVERED BY

THE TREATY, THAT THERE IS AN UNDERSTANDING BETWEEN THE PARTIES ON THIS ISSUE, AND THAT IF ANY MISUNDERSTANDINGS ARISE, THEY CAN BE CONSIDERED IN THE STANDING CONSULTATIVE COMMITTEE.

SOURCE FURTHER REPORTS SOVIET DELEGATION IS INSTRUCTED TO ACCEPT LATEST US PROPOSALS ON NEW TYPES OF ICBMS AND BISON TANKER FRODS, LEAVING TELEMETRY AS ONLY UNRESOLVED ISSUE. IF SOVIET SUMMIT STATEMENT ACCEPTABLE, SUGGEST YOU SEEK DIRECT PRESIDENTIAL DECISION TO CLOSE ISSUE OUT ON THIS BASIS.

SOURCE DEEPLY MOVED BY PRESIDENTIAL LETTER, WHICH HE RETURNED TO ME FOR SAFEKEEPING.

It was only a mildly deceptive cable. He had neglected to mention that more than one source was involved.

36

"So what's left?" Morgan asked. "Just the new-types rule for ICBMs and the frods for Bison tankers, right?"

"Don't forget telemetry encryption," said Inigo. Morgan frowned.

They were standing with Rappaport and Michaels in the basement of the delegation building. Even with voices lowered, their words echoed weirdly off the undressed cinder-block walls. Four black limousines had been pulled out of their parking stalls and were waiting to take them to the Soviet mission.

"Could be the last plenary, except for that." Rappaport nodded at Inigo.

"I've got the same feeling," put in Michaels. In recent weeks, as the list of unresolved issues dwindled, he had begun to drift toward his civilian colleagues and away from his boss. O'Rourke stood twenty feet away beside another car, chatting with his interpreter.

It was an unenchanting place to wait, ugly and bare. When the United States was hosting the plenary, four black Soviet Chaikas were parked there. While their masters struggled with the capitalists upstairs over the world's fate, the chauffeurs played a Soviet version of poker on the hood of their ambassador's vehicle.

Boroz came bounding out of the elevator, bustling with his usual lateness.

"Not to worry, Paul. Al still hasn't showed up." Not till Ambassador Jenkins was ensconced in the lead car would the cavalcade rumble across the floor, wait for the automatic door to open, then move slowly up the ramp into the sunlight and the uphill drive to the Soviet mission.

"Got any Washington scuttlebutt?" Rappaport asked Boroz.

"I was on the secure phone to the Pentagon last evening," Boroz answered. "The secretary's people seemed to feel it's all nearly over but the shouting. Except for telemetry," he added. "The president's got that under consideration personally, along with your boss, George."

"Hope he doesn't fold," said Inigo, smiling mischievously at Morgan.

Again the elevator door: This time it was Fairchild, Jenkins's personal assistant.

"Gentlemen. There's been a delay. Ambassador Jenkins has a phone call from the president. They're on the line now. I've notified the Soviets that we'll be late." The rising young foreign service hopeful was enjoying the spotlight. "The ambassador would like to meet with you all in the tank when he's finished."

O'Rourke moved up beside Inigo as they headed for the elevator.

"Funny business," he muttered.

"You think so?"

"I'm worried about a sellout. That phone call is too pat."

They were still milling about in the tank when Jenkins joined them. His expression was grave.

"I guess you've been told that the president called. We've phoned the Soviets to let them know we'll be late. I wanted to meet with you first."

The silence was total. It's like a funeral, Inigo thought. With a wake to follow.

"The president asked me where I thought we stood. I said we were right on the brink with respect to new-types and frods. I rather thought the Soviets might buy our latest language today. And he said, 'That leaves telemetry encryption, doesn't it?' And I said, yes."

Rappaport, O'Rourke, Morgan, and Boroz were all looking at Inigo. Michaels gazed at the ceiling.

"He said he'd been closeted with your boss for two hours, George. They went through it from start to finish. He's made a decision."

Inigo leaned back and shut his eyes.

"The president instructed me that if the Soviets accept our wording on new-types and frods, I am to include in the treaty their language, along with our own, on telemetry encryption."

The silence held and held. Inigo remained motionless, imagining behind closed lids his colleagues' eyes upon him.

"Damn!" It was O'Rourke, softly, fervently. Now he could open his eyes.

"I know it won't please everyone," Jenkins said soothingly. "But there it is."

O'Rourke pulled himself together. "I want to see the cable," he snapped.

"Cable? There is no cable, Walt. I told you, it was a phone call."

"We've never done business like this before!" O'Rourke's hands gripped the table edge. "We operate from official cables, signed off on by all our home agencies and available here for everyone to study!" Nervous anger crackled in his voice.

"True enough." Jenkins was conciliatory. "But now we're directly instructed by the president himself. There wasn't time for the usual coordination in Washington. He wants it wrapped up today if possible."

They stared at each other, O'Rourke glaring and Jenkins holding steady. Michaels found something to watch in another corner of the ceiling.

Boroz broke the silence. "Well, we'd better get going." He nearly gagged on his glee at O'Rourke's discomfiture.

"Wait a minute," O'Rourke ordered. "Are we all going to go up there and sell the farm on the basis of a secondhand report of a telephone call?"

"Do you think I made it up, Walt?" Jenkins asked quietly.

"I've got no basis for saying that, no. But it's damn funny all the same. I can't see finishing up this treaty on the basis of the first instruction we've ever had that didn't come in a cable cleared by all the agencies."

"It is unusual, I agree," Jenkins replied. "But it's happened."

"What's the matter with holding off for a day? If the president's decided, they ought to be able to get the cable out in a few hours. We could meet with the Soviets tomorrow. Anything wrong with waiting twenty-four hours?"

This time Rappaport spoke. "It might be a little embarrassing for Al to explain to the president that we doubted his authority, Walt."

"Precisely." Jenkins smiled thinly. "Thank you, Abe."

"George?" O'Rourke turned fiercely on Inigo. "What've you got to say? It's your issue, after all."

"It's also my president." Inigo spoke calmly. "He's the guy who got elected. He's given us our day in court. Now he's decided. That's the way it's supposed to work."

"But I don't agree!" O'Rourke roared. "The Joint Chiefs don't agree! I spoke with them last evening. They made it clear—hang in there on telemetry encryption!"

"Well, I guess that's the president's problem. He's their president too, God give him strength." Jenkins rose to his feet. "We'd better not keep the Soviets waiting any longer." Morgan stared quizzically at Inigo, who rolled his eyes and shrugged his shoulders. The delegation moved toward the door of the tank.

"Oh, by the way," Inigo announced, "I almost forgot. Smirnov tells me that Pavlovsky has suddenly gone back to Moscow. Some sort of illness. Maybe someone can find out in the post-plenaries."

As the guest, Jenkins spoke first. Starovsky sat in Pavlovsky's seat, his own place occupied by a junior diplomat. Maltsev was nowhere to be seen.

The U.S. statement on new types of ICBMs was mainly a reiteration of the previous American position. It contained a slight revision that would allow for the testing of existing types of ICBMs with lesser amounts of fuel and fewer reentry vehicles, without this being counted as the one new type permitted to each party. That put the wording squarely into line with Smirnov's last fallback. On the Bisons, he had told Inigo that one more repetition of the U.S. frod provision would do the trick.

As Jenkins read his way through the seventy-eight lines of technical proscriptions that constituted the new-types rule, there was no mistaking the rising tension on the Soviet side of the table. Mardirosian tracked the interpreter's words against his own text through the thicket of Agreed Statements and Common Understandings. Starovsky drummed his fingers silently on the table before him. Rublov kept a fixed gaze of attention upon Jenkins's face; Lebedev refrained from his usual shuffling of papers. Smirnov, who knew where the key revision would appear, could not bear to look at anyone, keeping his eyes unfocused and straight ahead. When Jenkins finally reached the new language, he gave it no emphasis at all, but a faint collective sigh from across the table told him that his labors were nearly over.

The Bison tanker statement was boiler plate, an unchanged reiteration of the U.S. demand. The Soviets, whispering to one another and allowing themselves tiny smiles, paid no heed.

When Jenkins finished, Lebedev played it to the hilt. He put on heavy black-rimmed glasses and searched among his papers in front of him. Then while everyone waited, he leaned over and held a long whispered conversation with Rublov on his left. There followed more fumbling through documents until at last he put his glasses away, fixed a sober gaze on Jenkins, and began.

"Mr. Ambassador. The Soviet side has no prepared statement to make today. I am authorized by my government to accept the proposals that the United States delegation has presented this morning."

Those on the American side who understood Russian grinned and whispered to their neighbors, waiting for the interpretation into English. When it came, Inigo could not resist poking O'Rourke's arm, which lay on the table. There was no give, he suddenly realized; O'Rourke had gone rock-rigid.

Now it was Jenkins's turn.

"I welcome the agreement of the Soviet side as a major contribution to the success of our endeavors here." He paused, then put on an enigmatic smile. Lebedev and the Soviet delegation waited, caught in fascination.

"In the light of this action by the Soviet side, I am instructed to make an additional statement today. I am authorized to accept the language that has been proposed by the Soviet delegation for the Second Common Understanding to Paragraph Three of Article Fifteen of the Joint Draft Treaty."

Lebedev knew exactly what this meant. The issue of telemetry encryption was resolved. The last disputed issue was agreed. The treaty was complete. Without batting an eye, he searched through his text until he found, or at any rate pretended to find, the Second Common Understanding to Paragraph Three of Article Fifteen. Silently he read it. Thus, thought Inigo, must elephants frolic and hippopotamuses disport themselves.

"I believe, Mr. Ambassador"—Lebedev raised his head—"that you have spoken in error. You spoke of the Joint *Draft* Treaty. At this moment it would be more correct to speak of the Joint Treaty." Finally he broke into a broad grin.

As Jenkins smiled in return, Inigo heard a rumble on his right and felt O'Rourke coiling like a spring.

"I think it only fair to tell the Soviet delegation," the general spoke up in a choked, dry voice, "that the chairman of my delegation has spoken without the usual confirmation of instructions. I suggest that we might be wise to postpone the celebration of our success."

The effect was electrifying. No mere member of a delegation had even intervened in a plenary session before, much less challenged his own ambassador. Even the American interpreter blanched, then dutifully proceeded to repeat O'Rourke's words in Russian. Lebedev, the calmest man at the table, raised an eyebrow at Jenkins.

"You may be assured, Mr. Ambassador, that my statements were made upon instruction and represent the official position of the United States government. I apologize for the untoward remarks of my colleague."

Lebedev paused politely, but the American side was silent, so he went smoothly on, as though O'Rourke had never spoken.

"Then as chairman of today's plenary, it is my privilege and pleasure to declare this treaty agreed, complete, and ready to be submitted to our respective governments. Gentlemen, let us congratulate ourselves upon our historic accomplishment. I declare this meeting adjourned and invite our American colleagues to join us in refreshments." He smiled broadly. "No tea or coffee today, if you please, but champagne. Neither Russian nor American, but French champagne, long reserved especially for this magnificent occasion."

Chairs scraped. For the moment, everyone on both sides of the table was too drained to speak. As they filed out, there were a few silent, heartfelt handshakes within and between delegations. Inigo and Smirnov exchanged the briefest of glances, then drifted in diverging directions. When the two delegations reached the door of the lounge, O'Rourke proceeded straight past it, down the hall, and out of the building. General Mardirosian watched with a philosophical air as he disappeared, then turned and took Inigo's elbow warmly, steering him to the celebration.

"Do you believe in God, Mr. Inigo?" the general murmured quietly.

"Yes, I do."

"I, of course, do not. But if you should like to thank Him, on behalf of all of us, I should not object."

Inside, a decorous pandemonium was under way. The colonels were toasting one another and exchanging gay salutes. Rappaport was shaking the hand of every Soviet he could find. The aged Rublov, tottering slightly, was embracing everyone in the two delegations, one by one. When his turn came, Inigo saw tears in the old man's eyes.

"Do you know, Mr. Inigo, I have spent twelve years at these negotiations. Twelve years! Five on the first treaty, and now seven on this one! Now my work is finished. I can retire, play with my grandchildren for a while, and then die happily." He held Inigo by the shoulders, then kissed him on the cheeks. For a moment his grip tightened and his eyes winced, then he recovered and moved away toward Boroz, who was holding out two glasses of champagne.

Inigo found Smirnov chatting with Morgan and Starovsky.

". . . about another ten days, I'm told," Starovsky was saying.

"Ten days?" Morgan was incredulous.

Starovsky turned to greet Inigo, pumping his hand warmly. "George! Let us congratulate each other!" It was the first time he had called Inigo by his first name. "Yes, I was just telling everyone about Izhov's disgrace." He gestured toward Izhov, the executive secretary of the Soviet delegation, who joined them at that point, his expression hapless.

"Disgrace? Mr. Izhov?"

"Ah yes," Izhov sighed. "I had to send our best typist back to Moscow. Her baby is arriving early."

"Oh, but it's worse than that," Smirnov chimed in. "He forgot about the treaty paper."

Inigo turned to the little Russian. They joined in a heartfelt double handshake.

We did it, their eyes said.

That was all. Back to business.

"Treaty paper?" said Inigo.

"Oh yes," said Starovsky. "You didn't know? All nations use a special grade of paper. It's for nothing but treaties. Very heavy, very beautiful, very expensive. And Izhov forgot to order it."

"I suppose that's needed for the summit, when the heads of state sign it."

"No, no, George, you've got it wrong." Morgan took him through the formal steps. First, each side prepared two versions of the treaty, in Russian and English, on treaty paper. Then each side had to proofread the other side's versions, with the interpreters certifying the correctness of the translations. Then the two heads of delegation hold a solemn ceremony to initial each page of each version.

"Sort of like a marriage," Inigo offered. "If any here present know any reason why these two may not be joined in lawful wedlock . . ."

"Okay," said Morgan. "All this is what's going to take ten days, because our friend Izhov here lost his typist and forgot his treaty paper."

"Or two weeks," Izhov added mournfully. "Moscow does not like to be hurried."

"Then," Morgan went on, "the heads of state schedule a summit, sign the damned thing, and submit it for ratification to Congress and the Supreme Soviet. God knows how long that will take."

Inigo glanced at Smirnov, who was following the conversation closely. "But at least the delegations have finished their work," he said. "We can all go home now."

"Not us," Starovsky replied. "Ambassador Lebedev has ordered the entire Soviet delegation to remain in Geneva until the initialing ceremony."

Inigo and Smirnov looked at each other. Ten days. Ten days in which Maltsev would continue to work Pavlovsky over. Ten days for Smirnov's daughter to go through the paces of her routine without being observed.

Or two weeks.

37

"Two weeks, eh? That's not good. Want a refill, George?" Carson poured herself another half cup of coffee.

"Please. Black and bitter. Fill it to the rim. Got a slug of whiskey to go in it?" Inigo flopped back on Carson's office sofa.

"As a matter of fact, I do. For crisis use only, but I guess this qualifies."

Inigo was exhausted. Leaving the celebration early, he had made a date with Smirnov for dinner the next evening and come straight to the consulate. He needed some consolation.

"Yes, too much can happen in two weeks. I'll have to cable the Moscow station to stand down till further notice. But there's no reason to get down in the mouth and quit, George. We'll think of something."

Inigo was in no mood for encouragement. The exhilaration of actually completing the negotiations, followed by the disastrous news of delay at the post-plenary, had been too much of an emotional roller coaster. His mind was invaded by black fantasies of Smirnov's discovery and arrest, of furious Soviet reactions, of Moscow's repudiation of the treaty. Izhov's disgrace was nothing compared to what awaited him. But personal disgrace could be borne; it was the disintegration of SALT that would be truly appalling.

Carson was pacing her office. "Belknap? No, that's not right. Beauchamp? I've almost got it. Beaucamp! That's her name!"

Inigo sipped his coffee and ignored her. The whiskey was weak; it didn't help.

"George, never underestimate the resources of the CI of A! Our judgment maybe, but our resources, never! In the present instance, Miss Lydia Beaucamp."

"What the hell, Emily?"

"Lydia Beaucamp, a strangely gifted woman. Started in the typing pool, straight out of high school. Someone left a Russian grammar around, so she learned Russian. Someone left a Cyrillic-alphabet typewriter around, so she learned to type Russian. At incredible speeds. Then came Arabic, three or four European languages, then Chinese, for all I know; do the Chinese use typewriters? Yes, they must. Anyway, Lydia's our man."

Carson's energy was beginning to infect Inigo. He sat up, collected the coffeepot and whiskey bottle, and poured himself a small half-and-half. Carson waved his offer away.

"Lydia Beaucamp pretty much writes her own ticket these days. She's in plenty of demand at headquarters, but what she really likes is the overseas emergency. Flying to Israel to forge a letter of resignation in Hebrew. To Jakarta to transcribe some nifty Russian documents on the spot. Have typewriter, will travel, that's Lydia."

"And she's going to type the treaty for the Soviets? How do we work that?"

"Dunno. But let's get her out here first. I'll send a cable off right away."

"And the treaty paper?"

"Oh, we'll leave that to Petrocelli. That's the sort of thing he's good at. Judgment, maybe, resources, yes. Off you go, I've got a cable to write."

Inigo shook his head doubtfully and started for the door. Suddenly he remembered something.

"Say, you'd better tell the marines to let Smirnov in if he shows up on the run. We don't want him to be locked out like Pavlovsky."

"Sure, and it's like a real spy yer thinkin', Georgie me lad." Carson was full of happy energy. "Off with you now. Just leave it all to me for a while."

At six in the evening, the alarm woke Inigo from a deep sleep. After the turbulent final plenary at the Soviet mission and the session with Carson, he'd gone straight to his apartment and let consciousness slip away. If he'd missed an afternoon staff meeting, too bad, but he rather thought Jenkins had declared a holiday. Now he was going to have what he needed most: dinner with Erika.

Her embrace was loving but tired. "Please, let's go eat," she whispered when he glanced toward her bedroom. "Someplace quiet. But first give me fifteen minutes to shower. Fix yourself a drink."

Inigo got ice from the kitchen, Scotch from the dining alcove, and settled down on Erika's balcony, twelve stories up. All across his view, modern apartment buildings jutted up through the canopy of foliage below. It was a still May evening; the Swiss were not noisy. A few people appeared on the opposite balconies, moving quietly about as they watered a plant, adjusted a chair, sat down to chat. Children were an oppressed minority in this well-to-do neighborhood, rarely seen or heard. Inigo supposed that in the pre-dinner hour, they were planted in front of the television.

He heard the shower go on inside the apartment and immediately saw Erika in his mind's eye, her rounded upper arms, the flare of hips below her waist, her face under the shower cap squinting against the water. It was the sweetest body he had ever taken in his arms. How could the same person be both so comforting and so exciting? But it had come to be much more. Now that the negotiations were over, there was a parting to be faced, and he didn't know how he was going to manage it. Or even whether he could. Washington, where he'd lived for twenty-five years, suddenly seemed a cold and lonely place.

She was fresher when she joined him on the balcony, a yellow dress fitting her slim body closely, but still subdued and a little sad. Nothing to do but talk about it, thought Inigo. But first a restaurant, a drink, and some nourishment.

When they had ordered, however, it was Erika who began.

"I went to the German Film Club again last night. Your friend was not there."

"Ah. So you wasted an evening on my account. I'm sorry, and grateful to you."

"No, that was all right. They showed a marvelous film. Heartbreaking. *The Great Dictator*, by Charlie Chaplin. Do you know it?"

Inigo nodded, not taking his eyes off her.

"Who else would have thought to make Hitler so ridiculous? Just a funny, warped little child, frightening the grown-ups and then going off to play by himself with a balloon made to look like the world, all shyness and silly dreams. And that stupid ally of ours, that pompous Italian Mussolini."

"Our ally," Inigo heard. He had never talked to a German about Chaplin's classic.

"Actually, it was quite courageous of the club to show it. We Germans do not like to be reminded of those times. East and West both."

"How did people react?"

"They were entranced. They roared at the comic scenes. But the ending—it was *so strong.*" Erika put down her glass; her voice became intense. "Do you remember? On the screen there was nothing but a beautiful sky and lovely clouds. And while we stared at that, Chaplin made a speech. About peace and brotherhood and love. It was like a little sermon. It was so simple. Short and simple and true. No one would dare to film that sort of thing these days. We are all much too clever for that."

"Did people like it?"

"It was not a question of liking or not liking. We were moved, deeply moved. We walked out in a silence like church, no, like the grave. Except for the sniffling, and not only women. I got through the lobby and to the sidewalk, then I burst into crying."

"It sounds very deep."

"It was. And very good too. I felt good all day, even though I was also so tired. And now my eyes are wet again."

Inigo handed her his napkin. She dabbed at her face, then emerged from it with a smile of relief. "So, what has happened to you these last days?"

"Last days, yes." Inigo gazed out across the quiet dining room, the local customers, the party of Third World diplomats. There was such calmness. Was everyone else really living such well-run lives? Were they the only ones in anguish?

"It's time to talk about that, Erika. Today we finished the treaty."

"Oh." Her eyes dropped to the plate before her.

"We'll be here—I'll be here two more weeks at the most. Perhaps less."

She used her napkin again. There was a long silence.

"George, something else happened yesterday too. The intelligence people called me again."

"Damn! Oh, darling."

"They wanted to know how it was coming along between us," Erika went on. "You remember we were going to think of something to tell them. But we never did."

It was true. They had never gone back to that. There's always something, Carson would say, that gets forgotten till the last minute. Inigo covered her hand with his.

"What did you say, Erika?"

"At first I could not think of any answer. Then I told them that you seemed to be more and more attached to me—I did not speak about myself—and that you wanted to take a long holiday with me when your treaty was finished. A vacation trip to Italy, Spain, the south of France." She was clenching and unclenching the heavy crumpled napkin. "They said good. I should make my proposal to you on that trip. They would teach me what to say, how to do it."

"That was brilliant. And to think you invented it right there, on the spot, under all that pressure."

"Actually, I did not." She put the napkin down and faced him. "I have been thinking about it for a while. A long trip with you, at the end. Before you leave me."

"Erika."

"And yesterday it just suddenly fitted in as something to tell them, to keep their pressures off." She was solemn and dry-eyed now.

"Before I leave you. Erika, it's an absolutely beautiful idea." There was no way to avoid the next. "But I can't."

"I was afraid you'd say that."

"Darling, I have to take my Mister X back to the States. The minute we're finished here."

"Yes, of course. Two weeks, you said."

"Two weeks. At most. It's even worse than that. This will be the most dangerous time. I have to try my best to make everything finish earlier. Can you believe it? I have to try my hardest to leave you sooner!"

They gazed at each other a long time, in pain. God, it's hard, Inigo thought, loving someone. He hadn't imagined these wrenching feelings when he had climbed aboard that ski bus, a few short months ago, looking for a woman. He had found one, and it was terrible.

Finally she smiled. "May we spend your last night together? It would help me to remember your body. And you."

"Of course."

Their order had not arrived. They left the restaurant.

38

Inigo arrived late at work next morning. Even so, the delegation offices were practically empty. Fairchild had organized a small crew of typists and interpreters and was supervising the production of the official SALT treaty, English and Russian. He had ordered and received his stock of treaty paper weeks ago and kept it under lock and key. He was too busy to talk to Inigo. The Soviets might be two weeks behind, but Fairchild was going to finish his treaties in record time. You never knew what might strike the eye of an Officer Evaluation Panel.

Morgan drifted in and found Inigo reheating yesterday's coffee. They sprawled on the two couches in the ambassador's office. It was a liberty they would not have taken earlier, but today morale was high and feelings were unbuttoned. Living alone in a small hotel room, Morgan had nothing but a hangover to keep him away from work. Inigo missed a great party, he said. The delegation practically took over La Diligence for dinner. Rappaport did some hilarious imitations of the Soviets. Michaels kissed three giggly waitresses, and Jenkins had been the drunkest man there. O'Rourke was the only absentee. "Except for you, that is. Where were you, George? Sulking over your telemetry?"

"In bed," said Inigo with a wink.

"Aha! Having your own celebration, I see. Okay. But you were missed."

"When do you think we'll be out of here, Morgan?"

"God knows. Damn that Izhov anyway. The way Fairchild's going, our side will be ready to initial tomorrow. Al's given everyone administrative leave. I'm off to Florence on the night train. I'll just plant myself in the Uffizi and call in every day. Want to come along?"

"No thanks."

"O'Rourke's already off to Brussels. I imagine he wants to warn all the NATO commanders about what a terrible piece of work we've done here. But he did do one decent thing. Sent word to the air force to hold that transport he'd laid on to take us all home. I wouldn't have been surprised if he'd canceled the flight out of spite, to make us all fly commercial."

"Well," recalled Inigo, "you remember Michaels saying that O'Rourke wouldn't resign from the delegation until the eve of the summit. Now he can revise his speech and tell about yesterday's valiant, last-ditch effort to avert catastrophe."

"I still can't believe that," Morgan exclaimed. "He practically called Al a liar to the Soviets."

"Now don't exaggerate. It was pretty stunning, though. The man's a true believer, you've got to give him that."

Jenkins's secretary appeared in the doorway, put on an expression of mock disapproval, then came in to join them. "The ambassador won't be in till after lunch," she said.

"That sounds like about three-thirty," Morgan answered. "Shall we dance, Lily? Take a nap together? While the cat's away, you know."

The phone rang. Lily gave Morgan a light cuff on the back of the head as she went to answer it. It was for Inigo.

"George? It's Emily. There's someone down here at the consulate you would enjoy meeting."

"Right away." He hung up and gulped the last of his coffee. "You guys go on goofing off. The silent service is still working, protecting your liberties."

"That sounds encrypted, George," Morgan called after him as he left.

Lydia Beaucamp, as Carson had warned Inigo, was a character. Nearly six feet tall, her height was accentuated by a fuzzy yellow wig, raggedly spherical. Overhanging a strongly painted mouth was the biggest nose he had ever seen on a woman. Her pink pants suit bulged with a busty figure about forty pounds overweight. Merry, shrewd eyes were crouched at the bridge of that monumental nose.

"Hi, Georgie," she said in a gravelly Tennessee twang as an amused Carson introduced them. "Understand you're the guy who needs a rush typing job."

"That's right."

"I read your blessed treaty on the way over. Awful sludge. Did you write any of that?"

"A bit. The worst parts, I'm afraid."

Beaucamp reclined full length on Carson's couch. Like a monstrous Marlene Dietrich, Inigo thought.

"Well, no problem. Fifty pages, one in English, one in Russian, error-free. I figure about twenty hours, working straight through. When do you meet your contact?"

"At dinner tonight. He—"

"No names that I don't need, please. One of these days I'll end up on some hot seat, and I'll want to know as little as possible. So tell him this." Beaucamp was in full charge. "You've heard of a Genevan document center that does rush international jobs. You forget the name, but it's written down somewhere. You'll get hold of them tomorrow and have them call the Soviet mission. Find out whom to ask for." The "whom" didn't fit with this rawboned moll.

"That'll be Izhov," said Inigo.

"Okay, Izhov, whoever. Meet me here at ten tomorrow morning and we'll get started. Put this stuff in the vault for me, okay, Emily?"

"What is all that?" Carson asked.

"Behold," said Lydia Beaucamp, heaving herself to her feet. "Here we have,"—opening a black case—"the finest Cyrillic typewriter in the world. Made to my own specs. Ten times better than anything the Soviets have. And here," she went on, opening a brown package, "is your treaty paper."

It was lovely stuff, cream-colored, trimmed in gold, with a gray inner framing line hand-drawn an inch inside each edge.

"Marvelous," said Carson. "Where'd you get it?"

"A modest feat by Petrocelli. He sent a lock picker over to the State Department last night. The guy came back with this, disgusted. Seems that State doesn't even lock its supply cabinets. Once Petrocelli finds out who makes the stuff, we can replace it before they even know it's missing."

Inigo fingered a heavy page. It put him in mind of Jefferson and Madison and the Bill of Rights. "Seems a shame to type on it," he said.

"You want high-class calligraphy, you've got the wrong babe," Beaucamp growled at him. "So where am I sleeping, Emily? No hotels, remember."

"There's a safe house six blocks from here. My deputy will drive you over."

"Great. Gotta go sleep off the jet lag now. See you in the morning, Georgie. Don't be late." And Lydia Beaucamp marched out the office door.

"What did I tell you, George?" Carson was delighted. "Judgment maybe, but resources, yes!"

It was, they both understood, their last meal together in Geneva. Inigo had chosen Au Pied de Cochon, where he had never seen another member of either delegation. Smirnov, however, was nervous, scanning the other diners and checking the underside of the table for microphones.

"Anything special troubling you, Victor?"

"It's the wait. Damn that Izhov! If I were going back to Moscow, I'd make sure that his career stood still for a while."

"What do you hear from Moscow?" The question was open-ended; Inigo wanted to see where his mind was.

"From Irina? Nothing. I instructed her not to telephone. All the international lines are monitored. Our letters go through my service's pouch, inside the Foreign Ministry's pouch; they have never been disturbed. Today I had to send her a note about the postponement."

"How will she react to that? What sort of nerves does she have?"

"She's only nineteen, you know." Smirnov threw him a quick direct glance. "She trusts me. I hadn't yet told her about—about the actual trip, just that she must follow my instructions without asking questions. She may have guessed, of course; she's a bright girl. But today, in telling her about the postponement, I thought it best to let her know."

"Was that wise?" Inigo kept a calm voice.

"I think so. If only she doesn't decide to say good-bye to some friend."

"Precisely." Too late now to do anything about it. "And Maltsev? Pavlovsky?"

"Oh no. I would not expect to hear anything about that in Geneva. Nor would I inquire."

"And Madame Smirnov, how is she?"

Smirnov tensed, but Inigo, moving his wineglass to let the waitress set down his food, missed it. "She's fine. Quite calm. She continues with her translations." They ate for a time in silence.

"A possibility occurs to me," said Inigo after a while, "that we might not have to stay here another two weeks."

"You mean," Smirnov asked eagerly, "we might leave right away, before the initialing?"

"No. That risks too much. But I seem to remember a place here in Geneva that does diplomatic typing. They specialize in rush jobs, I think." There was no point in putting Lydia Beaucamp at the slightest risk.

"But in the Russian language? On treaty paper?"

"I've no idea. I think a friend in the American consulate told me about it. I could ask him tomorrow. It would be a good idea, don't you think?"

"It would be wonderful. Izhov is dying to escape his disgrace."

"All right, I'll check. If they do that sort of work, I'll tell them to telephone Izhov tomorrow. You might let him know in advance."

"I will. I see no danger in that. But I doubt there is a place with Russian typists and treaty paper."

"Perhaps not." Inigo returned to his plate.

When the coffee arrived, Inigo went over the plans for the last time. The initialing ceremony, whenever it occurred, would be at the United States delegation. A reception would follow. They would leave early, Inigo first, with Smirnov following him to the basement garage after three minutes. From there they would drive straight to Smirnov's hotel, pick up his wife and baggage—no more than two pieces each—and head straight for the airport.

"There will be an airplane there. We will not have to pass through Immigration Control. We can go straight on board. It is all arranged."

Smirnov asked no questions. Nor did Inigo tell him that they would be boarding the delegation plane. It would only be one more thing for Smirnov to worry about. They decided on a cognac and waited for it in silence, each lost in thought. It was Smirnov who spoke first.

"You asked about my daughter and my wife. May I ask about Miss Hartke?"

Inigo was surprised, but somehow the question seemed natural and right. A period of their lives was ending.

"Yes, I fear I made you very nervous by continuing to see her."

"You certainly did. But," he smiled, "in the end nothing happened."

"That's right. And now? It's a problem. Parting will be very painful. It's been a long time since I was in love, Victor."

"Yes, your wife's death." Smirnov spoke gently. "And you carry a torch for her, as they say?"

Inigo stared at his glass. "Not at all. I've mostly forgotten her. I seem to be made for solitude. That's my character. My wife was the only one who ever broke through that. Until Erika now."

Even with his face averted, Inigo could feel Smirnov's thoughtful gaze. Finally, quietly, "George? Is there no more room on that airplane?"

Inigo turned slowly to face him. "You're right. I do have to decide, don't I? I've been refusing to think about it."

"And when you do think about it?"

"Scary. Not that I know what she would say. She has a career, after all. A country. And a mother. But it's still scary."

"It is always difficult, in the end, to act."

"Yes, you would know about that, wouldn't you? And yet, you know, I really trust her. I suppose that's the rare thing."

"Yes, that is rare," said Smirnov. He pushed away his empty glass. "It is as rare," he finished, "as trusting oneself."

39

Inigo arrived ten minutes early at the consulate next morning. Carson's secretary told him to go right in. Miss Beaucamp would be along shortly; the car had already left to pick her up.

Carson sat at her desk, drafting a cable. "Nothing to do with you, George. You know, I do have other things to do than help out your little operation."

"And I write treaties in my spare time."

This would be another parting, of a different kind. He would miss Emily. Oh, there would be a lunch or two when she finished her Geneva tour of duty and got back to the States. They would talk over old times. But there wouldn't be the shared problems, the sense of shared danger. He didn't know her husband. Eventually she'd go overseas again, and they would lose each other.

"Going to miss you, Emily."

She looked up from her desk and gave him a warm smile. "Me too. We should keep in touch." Then she went back to her work.

Lydia Beaucamp sailed in on the dot of ten. "Much better today, thanks. I feel like I could type a whole dictionary. Did you make your meet last night, Georgie? Good. Now let's have friend Izhov's phone number. I always like to dial my own calls. Is there an extension for you to listen in?"

There was. Inigo heard her work her way through the switchboard of the Soviet mission in faultless, unaccented French. Izhov came on the line.

"Monsieur Izhov? This is Mademoiselle Beaucamp at the Geneva Documentation Center. What language shall we employ?"

Izhov was alert and wide awake. "Russian if you please."

"Certainly. My partner has left me a note to telephone you. She understands that you are in need of some emergency service."

"You have Russian-language typists?"

246

"We have one Russian-language typist. It is myself. I am quite experienced!"

"Very good. Yes, we do need some work. But it requires special paper. Treaty paper."

"Of course. That will be no problem."

"But I thought that only governments possessed such paper." Inigo, his hand on the mouthpiece, thought he heard a faint note of suspicion in Izhov's voice.

"Mr. Izhov! This is Geneva! How could we not have treaty paper?"

There was a flustered silence on the other end of the line. Then Izhov took the bait.

"Very good. You will have to work here at our mission."

"Certainly, Mr. Izhov. How many pages have you? Is the text clean and legible?"

"Fifty pages. It must be done in Russian and in English. The text is typed, and the revisions are clear. How long will it take?"

"Let me consult my appointment calendar." Lydia Beaucamp put down the phone, walked over to Carson's sideboard, and poured herself a cup of coffee. She gave Inigo a silent wink, then returned to the desk.

"Mr. Izhov! I can begin immediately. Here are my conditions. I require a private room with toilet facilities and a key that I can lock from the inside. Also a telephone. My time is limited, so I shall work without interruption until I finish. I estimate twenty hours. My fee is one hundred fifty francs an hour, payable in cash upon completion. You must supply meals every eight hours, which I shall eat in the room. I shall provide my own typewriters. Are we agreed?"

"Excellent. It shall be as you wish, Mademoiselle Beaucamp."

"Mr. Izhov! One more thing. I will arrive in half an hour. You must meet me personally at the entrance to your mission. I will not put up with delays and questions from your security people. It is too unpleasant."

"Of course, mademoiselle." Izhov was eating out of her hand. "I shall be there myself. In thirty minutes."

"Good-bye, Mr. Izhov." She hung up.

"Bravo!" said Inigo.

"You gotta know how to handle these boogers." The Tennessee twang was back. "So I'm off to the lion's den again. Not for the first time, so don't you fret, Georgie."

"Anything I can do?" Carson asked.

"Sure is, Emily. When I come out of there tomorrow, I'm gonna be worn to a frazzle. I'll need your safe house, two big steaks, a half gallon of Scotch, and a man. Make sure he's clean and strong. Tell him I may not be a raving beauty, but things'll go fine when the lights are off. Then I'll want a flight out to New York the next morning."

"All of that, huh?" Carson was grinning.

"All of that, Emily. Don't let me down. No other station chief ever has. Don't you be the first. You gotta be a credit to your sex."

At four-thirty the next morning, telephone calls began to crisscross Geneva.

The first was from Beaucamp to Izhov. She had to let it ring twelve times before he answered. The work was completed. Would Mr. Izhov kindly come to take her home? He was there, rumpled and sleepy, in ten minutes. He insisted on proofreading both documents from start to finish. It took over an hour, during which Beaucamp pretended to fume, declaring that all errors had been corrected. Privately, she approved of his thoroughness. Moreover, Izhov looked clean and strong. But that was a nonsensical idea; she would rely on Carson.

She asked to be taken to the railroad station, where she unloaded her typewriters into a cab. Had Izhov followed her then, he would have discovered a CIA safe house. But Izhov was speeding back to the Soviet mission, where he placed the morning's second call, to Lebedev.

"Mr. Ambassador! Pardon me for telephoning so early. But I thought you should know that the work is completed . . . yes, English and Russian . . . yes, I checked it all myself . . . no, I was able to locate local resources . . . Thank you very much, Mr. Ambassador."

It was six-thirty, early for Lebedev, but he did not go back to bed. Leaving his wife undisturbed, he fixed a breakfast for himself in the kitchen of the ambassadorial apartment. At seven-thirty he decided he had waited long enough. The sky was cloudless; it was going to be a famous day. He rang Ambassador Jenkins.

"Mr. Ambassador. Lebedev here. Forgive my early call, but I wish to inform you that the Soviet delegation is prepared to proceed with the initialing ceremony . . . yes, whenever you like . . . certainly, eleven o'clock today . . . Thank you also . . . good-bye."

Then the calls came thick and fast.

Jenkins to Fairchild: Notify the delegation that the initialing ceremony will take place at eleven today at our building. The delegation plane departs directly after the reception.

Fairchild to Inigo: conveying the above.

Inigo to Carson: This is it. Get word to Sloan's people to move today.

Carson to the duty officer, CIA headquarters, Langley, on the secure phone: Patch me through to Hugh Sloan . . . yes, I know it's two in the morning there . . . yes, I know it'll be an open line . . . Hugh? Emily Carson . . . in the field . . . listen fast, Redbird has to fly today . . . that's right . . . get the word to Jorgy . . . tomorrow will be too late . . . yes, they'll be home tonight or tomorrow . . . right, good-bye.

Sloan didn't make a phone call. He raced into work down the empty, dark parkway, scrawled a handwritten cable, and ran down to the main commo office. It was to Moscow, top secret, top priority.

EXECUTE OPERATION REDBIRD TODAY. REPORT RESULTS IMMEDIATELY.

It was noon in Moscow; half the day was already gone.

In Geneva, Erika had begun to stir. Inigo looked at her sadly as he dressed. Remember my promise to spend the last night with you, dear? We didn't know it, but I just kept it.

As he watched, she opened her eyes and smiled at him. Inigo sat down on the bed and took her shoulders in his hands.

"Erika, I just got a phone call. We're leaving this afternoon."

Her eyes widened. Quickly, before she could speak or he could think further, he blurted out, "Will you come with me?"

As she silently pulled him down onto her shuddering body, the telephone rang again. They clung to each other silently for eight long rings, then Inigo picked up the receiver.

"George? Emily. You'd better get down here right away. A friend of yours is sitting in my outer office right now, quietly going to pieces. He won't leave. He says Maltsev is back."

40

Lots of people swore they loved the Tretyakov Gallery. Squatting on flat ground halfway between the Kremlin and Gorky Park, a castle of red brick piled in a helter-skelter of elevations and projections, with a dozen random arches picked out in yellow, it was touted as the essence of Muscovite culture. Of course the same people exclaimed over old icons and black madonnas and wood-shingled country churches. Essence of Muscovite culture indeed it was, thought Irina Smirnov, in all its graceless ugliness. Besides which, there was scarcely a decent painting in it.

Irina had become an expert on the Tretyakov collection. For the eighth consecutive day now, saving only last Monday, when it was closed, she had come to the gallery directly after her last class at the university. Faithful to the instructions of her father's letter, she took up a position in front of Repin's *Murder of the Son of Ivan the Terrible* at exactly three-thirty. After exactly four minutes, she would turn away to the left and enter the women's room, where she was to receive instructions from a stranger. Except that it was already the eighth day now, and no stranger had yet approached her. What had started out as a great adventure was becoming a great bore.

Irina Smirnov knew that she was a strikingly pretty girl. At fourteen she was already taller than her parents, neither of whom she resembled. The next two years filled out her figure, and the last three saw her shed the baby plumpness in her face, changing her from girl into young woman. She acknowledged that a certain lack of delicacy in her features marked her off from true beauty, but her thick black hair and flashing black eyes attracted attention everywhere, particularly when the Russian winter suffused her perfect complexion with a rosy tone.

Irina herself considered her legs to be her best feature. Just now her legs were proving bothersome, since they seemed to have caught the notice of the old pensioner who took tickets at the main entrance. Irina knew that this was a time for inconspicuousness.

What made it worse was the outfit she was wearing. Again, following her father's instructions, she had gone to the GUM department store and bought a blue dress, a short tan raincoat, a scarf, and sunglasses. All these items, he had stressed, had to be ordinary and of common taste. After three days, Irina could not bear to wear them to classes any longer. The time required to change at the university forced her to take a taxi each afternoon. But to be deliberately plain for eight days in a row was almost more than her vanity could bear.

Irina had guessed by the first day that she was intended to next see her parents in America. Her father's last instructions, that she should carry only her jewelry to the Tretyakov every afternoon and should say good-bye to no one, left little alternative to that conclusion. She was delighted, both with the prospect and with the adventure. As the daughter of a KGB colonel, she did not really believe in danger.

Irina had never been to Geneva; the KGB was inflexible on that point. She saw her parents only when they returned to Moscow during the infrequent recesses of the negotiations. Except for those times, she lived in the apartment of her mother's brother and his wife. They were an amiable couple, themselves childless. Her aunt drank herself to an early bedtime every evening. One night, shortly after she had turned fifteen, Irina came home from a party to find her uncle nursing an ill-hidden erection. In the end, after a certain amount of labored intergenerational conversation, she had taken care of him with her hands. That set the pattern. In return for periodic ministrations of this nature, both manual and oral, she was given her freedom. She used it to become intimately acquainted with a number of students and quite a few junior officers of the KGB. In the process, she had become skillful, priding herself as a seductress and despising her mother's empty flirtations. But American men, she was sure, were different. With them she would find not only virility but consideration, gallantry, even tenderness. Perhaps with a TV producer, or the director of a New York modeling agency. Women were appreciated in the United States. She would have to find a way to get her own apartment. Her father would be difficult about that.

Gazing once more on Czar Ivan staring madly at the agonies of his son and heir being put to death, Irina thought about the good-byes she had not said. Her aunt would scarcely notice. Her uncle would simply have to find someone else. There were a few girl friends to whom it would be delicious to send a letter postmarked Manhattan. And Pavel Golubov would recognize, when he learned the truth, that she had given him a proper good-bye.

Sweet Pavel! She could still remember the day when, big and shy, he had joined their third-grade class. His father was an admiral, but that seemed to mean nothing to him. Dreamy, clumsy, he had been there when she had first joined the Pioneers, when she had graduated to the League of Young Communists. When she had discovered the world of males, Pavel had remained devoted only to her, worshiping from whatever distance she allowed.

Never once had he dared to touch her, not even on the long summer afternoons of mushroom hunting in the woods outside Moscow. So last night it was Irina who had had to take the initiative. Eager, frightened, inexperienced, he stabbed blindly at her crotch until she took him in her hand and guided him in. Afterward, he suckled at her breast like a baby and cried a little. Clumsy, shy, sweet Pavel.

With a sigh, Irina turned away from the czar and entered the women's room. It was empty at first, but immediately a young woman emerged from a stall. She was dressed exactly like Irina, in the same new, ordinary blue dress, short tan raincoat, scarf, and sunglasses. The woman spoke to her.

"You are ready to leave." It was not a question. The Russian was accented but easy and correct.

Suddenly, unexpectedly, a wave of nervousness enveloped Irina Smirnov. She tried to speak, but her mouth was too dry.

"It's all right." The woman smiled and switched to English. "No one will question you. Here is a diplomatic passport. Speak only English after you leave this room, and say as little as possible. Leave here and walk straight out the main entrance of the gallery at a normal speed. On the sidewalk a man in a green shirt will address you in English as Helen. Get into his car. He is your father and will go with you as far as Frankfurt. There another man will accompany you on to New York. You will meet your parents in Washington. Are you all right?"

Irina nodded dumbly. She was still holding the passport in front of her, like a ticket that she must present to someone.

"Put the passport in your bag," the woman said sharply. "I will leave first. You sit in that stall for two minutes, then go out by the main entrance. Speak to no one but the man in the green shirt, and to him only in English. The car is waiting. There is no danger. Goodbye." And she left.

Alone, Irina entered the stall, shut the door, and sat down. She took out the passport and examined it. Helen Jorgensen, age eighteen, address 3214 Bradley Lane, Chevy Chase, Maryland, U.S.A. The passport photo, taken several years ago, even looked a little like Irina. She stuck it back in her bag.

Suddenly it was impossible to leave. Her mind was flooded with pictures: all her childhood friends, the Moscow River, the towers of the university, herself as a bridesmaid at a brilliant wedding. The secret hours with her uncle, who had begun lately to stroke her breasts. Ivan the Terrible watching his son's agonies. Pavel everywhere, always at a little distance, gazing at her in adoration.

But it was all gone, of course. Her father and mother were en route to Washington, perhaps already there. She would be an outcast if she remained. Everyone would shun her. There would be only Pavel, one or two clumsy, shy children, a small apartment in Novosibirsk or Sverdlovsk, a boring job.

Irina rose and tugged down at her skirt. Outside the stall, she heard the door open and two sets of footsteps entering the room. Whoever it was, they did not speak. After a few seconds, the footsteps stopped. Silence.

Two minutes! She had no idea how much time had gone by. Was the man in the green shirt still waiting? She threw open the stall door and marched out. Two peasant-looking women were absorbed in studying their faces in the wall mirror. She left the room and, forcing herself to stroll, made her way through the crowd and out the main entrance into the sunlight.

"Irina!"

It was Pavel's voice. What in God's name was he doing here? She marched blindly on. Where was the man in the green shirt?

"Irina!" He caught up to her and grabbed her arm in his big fist. "I've been looking all over for you! Where are you going?"

She managed a few more paces before he forced her to stop. The ticket taker looked up and was watching them curiously. Forty yards ahead stood a policeman, his back to them, looking at a crowd of children clambering out of a school bus. She turned to face Pavel from behind her sunglasses.

"Irina! Last night! I'm so sorry! I mean, I'm so happy!" His big eyes were fixed on her, anxious and pleading. "Irina, are you angry? Why don't you speak? You're angry with me!"

"Excuse me, young man." Someone slid smoothly between them. Pavel let go of her arm helplessly. "Please do not make difficulties here." The stranger's voice was low and calm, with only a trace of accent. Putting his arm around her waist, he urged her forward toward the curb, where a black American car stood with its motor running.

"Get in quickly and lock the door," he whispered. "Do not speak." She didn't even notice what color shirt he was wearing.

Pavel was recovering. He came up to her closed window and began beating on it with his fists. "Where are you going, Irina? What is happening? Are you angry with me?" The policeman turned around as the man slid into the driver's seat. He gave them a long stare as they accelerated slowly past him down the street.

The man handed her a note. She saw that the cuff of his sleeve was green.

There may be hidden microphones in this car. We must speak normally, in English, as father and daughter.

He shot her a quizzical look. Irina gulped and nodded.

"Who was that young man, Helen?"

"Oh, just a student. He thinks he's in love with me."

"But he called you Irina."

She stared out into the flowing traffic, trying to think of a reply.

"Yes, he has given me a Russian name. It seems more romantic to him that way."

"I see. I was almost ready to call that policeman for help."

In desultory chatter, the man established for her that she was leaving the university and Moscow for the summer, that she would spend her holidays with her uncle and aunt in Vermont, and that he would fly as far as Frankfurt with her. "I have some business there," he said. "Mother wanted to come along to see you off, but Jerry's running a fever. She sent her love." Irina kept her replies to a minimum. She was terrified of the microphones and unsure of her accent. In New York she had spoken pure Americanese, but her university courses had contaminated that with British.

It was incredibly simple at the airport. Her "father" parked the car and took three new American suitcases out of the back seat. "The luggage is a holiday present from both of us," he said. When she lifted them, they had weight; she hoped there were clothes inside. They walked without incident to a small room where a dozen Americans waited. Three Soviet officials were there, but the passport check was cursory and there was no customs inspection. A young man in an American sergeant's uniform piled their bags onto a cart and they all followed him out to the tarmac.

There stood a high, shining transport emblazoned with the words *United States Air Force*. To Irina, it loomed above like a silver chariot. Her "father" was the messenger of the king. She threw her arms around his neck and kissed him on the mouth. No one was near.

"You must never tell anyone how you managed to leave," he said in a low voice, pulling away. "We may have to bring others out this way later on."

They had been the last passengers to arrive. Tension mounted in Irina as they taxied down the runway. Even after the takeoff, her muscles refused to relax. Desire suddenly swept over her, an impulse to find some corner of the airplane, perhaps the lavatory, into which she could pull her "father" and have sex with him. But of course, it was out of the question. She wouldn't even dare to ask.

41

Bursting into Carson's outer office, Inigo's first sight was of Smirnov huddled in a chair, his face in his hands.

"Victor!"

Smirnov looked up in despair. His round, chubby face was streaked by tears or dirt, Inigo could not immediately tell which. He made no move to rise.

"What's happened? Tell me!"

Carson appeared at her door. "Perhaps you should both come inside and we'll talk in here." Two young women came through the door by which Inigo had entered, looked curiously at them, and went on back into the warren of station offices.

Smirnov gave Inigo a harrowed look.

"Maltsev is back. I saw him. He's after me."

Carson walked over and took his arm. "Come inside, Mr. Smirnov. We all need a cup of coffee." Inigo followed as she walked the Soviet into her office and led him over to an armchair. Inigo poured black coffee for them all.

"I was out for a morning stroll," Smirnov began shakily. Hearing the tremor in his own voice, he took two slow sips of coffee. "On my way back, just as I turned into my street, I saw him getting out of a Chaika. There was another man with him. They went into my hotel."

"Did they see you?"

"No. Of course not. If they had, I would not be here. I stood frozen until they went inside. Then I walked over here."

"And Vera?"

"She is in the hotel."

In the long silence that followed, first Smirnov, then Inigo and finally Carson drank solemnly from their cups. At last Inigo spoke.

"The treaty will be initialed today. Starting at eleven o'clock. Then we leave." The handsome little clock on Carson's end table read nine-thirty.

"I cannot go to the ceremony!" Smirnov burst out.

"Of course not. You are safe here. The question is how to get your wife out of the hotel."

"Where that monster Maltsev and his thugs are now sitting," he answered in despair.

There was another long silence, this time broken by Carson. "I can't see any way to trick Maltsev out of there. He's got a hostage, and he'll just sit there till you finally turn up."

"So?" Inigo asked.

"So we'll have to use force. I've got two good men I can send. They'll have the advantage of surprise. Resources, George." She smiled thinly.

"Will there be shooting?" Smirnov asked anxiously.

"I can't guarantee against it."

"But my wife!"

"She could hide in the bathroom," Inigo offered.

"Yes. But she'll have to be warned."

They decided that Madame Smirnov would have to be telephoned. Her best friend in the delegation was Madame Lebedev. Someone would have to phone, impersonating her, and give her instructions. Someone who could speak both Russian and French, which Vera knew but Maltsev, Smirnov assured them, did not.

"I know someone." Inigo looked straight at Smirnov. "Erika Hartke."

Despite himself, Smirnov gave a small smile.

"Trust put to the ultimate test? I seem to recall an English expression: 'a strange twist of fate.' "

"But would Miss Hartke run such a risk?" Carson asked. "She would be deeply implicated. The Soviets could tell the East Germans."

"The East Germans? How do you know she's East German, Emily?"

Carson did not smile. "You mentioned her the first time you were in here. So we've been doing some checking and some watching. I've been waiting for you to mention her. Not very good judgment, George."

"So you say." Inigo was angry. "It's worked out fine, hasn't it?"

"Granted. And we could use her now. But will she help? Is it fair to ask her?"

Inigo picked up the phone and dialed his apartment.

"Erika?"

"George! Are you all right?"

"Yes."

"George, tell me. Is there room for me on your airplane today? Do you have an empty seat?"

The tension inside Inigo's chest finally broke. He felt that he might cry; as it turned out, laughter engulfed him. He struggled to regain control.

"Yes! Of course, Erika, yes!" He avoided Carson's inquiring look. "Listen, I'll pick you up in ten minutes! Don't move. Don't open the door to anyone. I'll be right there!" He hung up, jumped from his chair, and headed for the door.

"She'll do it!" he cried.

"But you didn't even ask her!" Smirnov objected.

"Nevertheless!" Then he was gone.

Smirnov turned to Carson in bewilderment. "Nevertheless?"

"We'll just have to wait and find out," said Carson soothingly. "You look like you could use another cup of coffee."

"George," Erika murmured from inside his embrace, "you are a lucky man. If I were a sentimental Italian, I would insist upon a day by ourselves here first. To say good-bye to the lake and the Bourg de Four and the rest of Geneva. But fortunately I am an efficient, well-organized German. Do we leave now?"

"Now."

"I'll just need a few things from my apartment."

"Not even that, darling. Much too risky. The only safe place for us for the next few hours is the American consulate and then a U.S. Air Force plane that's waiting out at Cointrin Airport."

"Then you are even more fortunate that I am not a materialistic person. But I do not even have a toothbrush."

"Tonight we shall both buy new toothbrushes. Together." Inigo hugged her tightly. "In Washington, D.C."

He grabbed his passport as they went out the door, which locked automatically behind them.

When they reached the parking lot, Inigo led her over to a parapet that overlooked gardens below. "There's one last task, Erika. I couldn't talk about it on the phone or in the apartment, and we can't talk about it in the car."

Quickly he told her everything. The identity of Mr. X, the work they had been doing together, Maltsev's investigations, and the catastrophe of his last-minute return. Would she make a telephone call from the consulate to help get Madame Smirnov out? Of course she would, gladly. He told her what to say.

"So I am to be Madame Lebedev. It was her husband with whom I exchanged notes in the film club, was it not? And who stopped me in the street that night also? I begin to feel like a member of their family."

They drove to the consulate, saying little for fear of microphones. "Good-bye, Vieille Ville," Inigo whispered to himself as they passed out through the walls. Erika heard him, and they began a series of covert farewells.

"There's the river."

"And the lake."

"Isn't that the flower clock we're passing?"

"Yes. Here's the Mont Blanc Bridge. Did you know that the Jet d'Eau is the world's highest fountain?"

"I love that funny monument of the duke of Brunswick."

"Look, Erika! You can see Mont Blanc today. The true Mont Blanc." Sure enough, there it rode on the far horizon, silent, awesome in breadth and height, like nothing but itself.

"Remember," he whispered to her in the consulate elevator. "None of these people knows anything about Lebedev being mixed up in this."

"You mean I'm the only one who knows the whole story?" Erika was delighted. "But no. You still have to tell me about your friend Gonzales."

"So I do, so I shall." He grinned happily. And about little Irina too. Soon all the deceptions and evasions would be over.

Inigo performed the introductions in Carson's office. Now that Erika was here, and was coming to the States with him, his spirits were up. They faced a challenge, not a disaster. He ran through Erika's instructions again. Smirnov supplied the first names of Madames Lebedev and Smirnov. Carson reported that her men would be at Madame Smirnov's door in exactly eighteen minutes. Smirnov dialed the number and handed the instrument to Erika; he was keeping a firm hold on his fears.

"Good morning, Vera! Lebedev here." Inigo, crowded around the extension with the others, had never heard her speak Russian before.

"What?"

"It's Tanya. How are you dear?"

"Fine. I guess."

"Have you heard the news? The treaty is to be initialed today."

"You sound funny, Tanya."

"So do you. Perhaps it's a bad connection. Is someone else on the extension?"

"Yes, Mr. Maltsev."

"Oh, Mr. Maltsev, you are an impossible man! Get off this line instantly!" There was a click. Brilliant, Carson mouthed silently to Inigo.

"Has he hung up?"

"Yes."

"Listen, Madame Smirnov, we will speak French now. I am calling from the American consulate. Your husband is with us. He is quite safe. We are coming to get you. Listen carefully now. We will be there in exactly sixteen minutes. Check the time on your watch now. In fifteen minutes, go into the bathroom and stand in the shower. There may be a little violence, and that is the safest place for you. Stay there, no matter what happens, till we come in for you. Do you understand?"

There was a long pause. Smirnov's breathing stopped. Then, "*Oui.* Fifteen minutes."

"Good, now pretend to arrange lunch with Madame Lebedev." They switched back into Russian, chatted for a minute or two, and hung up.

"Bravo!" Inigo shouted. Smirnov, rushing across the room, reached Erika first and kissed her hand. Carson turned quietly to Inigo.

"She was superb, George. I hope she doesn't have to pay for it. Now let's get moving."

Vera Smirnov glanced surreptitiously at her watch. There were still three minutes to go, but she couldn't stand it any longer. Those two men watching her. She got up and started toward the bathroom.

"Where are you going?" Maltsev asked hastily.

"I believe that I am allowed to use my own bathroom," she sniffed.

"Wait." Maltsev crossed the carpet and checked the bathroom. Satisfied that there were no windows, he came back. "All right. But if Madame Lebedev arrives for your lunch before your husband returns, you're not going, remember? You can think up some excuse while you're sitting in there," he added harshly. In Maltsev's mind, she could see, her husband already stood convicted.

She shut the door and sat down on the closed toilet lid. Immediately she got up to run the water, washing the tears out of her eyes. Now she would have to make up her face again. Peering into the mirror, she sighed at the lines running from the corners of her eyes. She was too old to be put upon so badly. To be torn away from her country, her Moscow, her parents. Last night when he told her, she had stared at her husband in horror and disbelief. He had appealed, argued, cajoled, even begged. There had been a terrible scene, her tears and his shouts. It was just like him, she had yelled, to decide this by himself and to wait until the last minute to tell her.

She had never yelled at him before. Even now she remembered how his eyes had grown small and steely as he delivered the final blow.

"Irina is coming too. From Moscow. She may already have left. You will never see her again except in America."

She wept through the night, falling asleep only at sunrise. When she heard her husband get up and dress, she had pretended to be asleep. He went out, and twenty minutes later the door suddenly burst open without a knock and there stood a black giant, Maltsev.

The time had come. With a last dab at her lipstick, Vera stepped into the shower stall. She had a crazy impulse to turn on the water and stand there, fully dressed, drenching herself into some different reality.

It all happened so fast. She heard the outside door bang open. There was a shout, she thought from Maltsev's partner, then a running of feet and a crashing of furniture. A shot rang out, surprisingly soft, followed by the loud sharp report of another gun. She clung in fear to the shower handles and the water suddenly came on over her head, cold and strong. As she worked to turn it off, the muffled noise of wrestling bodies came through the bathroom door, along with a stifled cry of pain.

Abruptly the uproar subsided. Vera took a towel and rubbed madly at her red hair, wet but not soaked, the ringlets flattened against her temples. What is going to happen next? she thought, and how I must look!

When the bathroom door handle turned, she cowered in a corner of the shower. A big strange man came into view, his hair mussed, breathing heavily. There was a long tear in his jacket sleeve. He looked ferocious, but his face softened into a smile at the sight of Vera Smirnov, frozen like a terrified rabbit in the shower, a few last drops of water falling onto her head.

"It's all over, Mrs. Smirnov." He spoke to her in an unmistakably American English. "Everything is fine now. My name is Lark. Come with me quickly, please. Your husband is waiting."

Overwhelmed at last by panic, Vera slipped past the American swiftly and ran into the bedroom. Opening her handbag, she began thrusting jewelry into it, a framed photograph of her parents, some Swiss francs on the dressing table. The American, who had followed her, stood smiling in the doorway.

"Not much time, Mrs. Smirnov."

"But I need some dry clothes!"

"Just one dress. There'll be plenty of new clothing at the other end." He took a midnight blue dress—it was entirely unsuitable, much too formal—off the rack in the closet and, gripping her firmly by the elbow, propelled her out into the living room.

It was a shambles. Maltsev lay on the floor on his stomach, a second large American sitting astride his back and making the last knot in a gag at the back of his head. Maltsev's partner, bleeding from the shoulder, was already trussed and gagged. Gently but firmly, Lark guided Vera through the wreckage of furniture and bodies. When she got to Maltsev's body, she stopped to lean over him.

"So, Mr. Maltsev. You thought you could outsmart my husband, did you? Not in a thousand years!" She spat suddenly upon him, then marched out into the hall without turning back.

The Americans led her down an old iron service stairway and through a large steel-plated fire door. They hurried down a long basement corridor, paralleled by piping overhead and punctuated by huge valves set in the concrete walls. It was gray, silent, cool, and very frightening. If I'm ever to be murdered, Vera thought, it will be in this kind of place. At the far end, through another fire door, they came out into the hotel's underground garage. Two dark Fords were parked near the door, one with the engine running. Smirnov stood by it and opened his arms. She ran across the echoing concrete floor and threw herself upon him, her little fists beating on his chest.

"You are such a stupid fool, Victor!" she kept repeating. Finally the tears came. Even through them, she noticed with surprise that it was a woman who organized their departure.

At the airport fence, Inigo showed his delegation card and the small motorcade was waved through. They drove straight up to the air force transport and he got out, telling the others to stay in the cars.

"Yes, sir. Can I help you?" It was the same sergeant who had brought the drinks and steaks on the last delegation flight.

"I need to see the captain. My name is George Inigo."

The pilot broke off his cockpit checking and met Inigo down on the runway.

"Mr. Inigo? May I see some identification please, sir?"

Again he showed his delegation card.

"Fine, sir. I have an order concerning you, signed by the chairman of the Joint Chiefs."

So Blom and the director had done their job. "May I see it please?"

"Certainly, sir." Inigo read it quickly. The commander of the aircraft was ordered to make available to Mr. George Inigo, on a personal and exclusive basis, the VIP cabin of the plane. Inigo noticed at the bottom that a copy had been routed to Gen. Walter O'Rourke.

"Has the general seen this yet?"

"Not yet, sir. Colonel Michaels picked up his copy ten minutes ago. I'm just as glad not to be around when he reads it," the pilot grinned. "Here's your key."

"I want your key too."

"Negative, sir. Can't be done. Regulations require that one key be outside the cabin at all times."

"Well then, Captain, once I lock that door, I don't want it unlocked by anyone, under any circumstances except fire."

"Or nuclear war, sir." The captain smiled. "Also in the regulations."

Inigo went back to the cars, where everyone was standing around, a light wind whipping coats and hair. Carson was watching Erika with an appraising look.

"Okay, everybody. All aboard for Andrews Air Force Base."

Smirnov shook hands with Carson and her men. Taking a deep breath, he put his arm around his wife's shoulder and set off for the loading steps. Inigo took Erika's arm and followed them.

"George."

Carson was standing by the car, beckoning to him.

"Be right back, Emily."

"No, George, now." She moved toward him, trailed by her men. "The girl can't go."

"Don't try that, Emily."

"I'm drawing the line here, George. The covert admission of illegal aliens is strictly controlled by Washington. The director has a very small quota. I can't send anyone in without authorization."

"Then don't. You never saw her."

"George, you've broken a lot of rules here, and I admit it's worked. But now you go too far."

Her voice had become loud and high-pitched. The flight crew stopped work to look, and Erika came up to link her arm through Inigo's. Behind his back he could feel Smirnov, who had stopped on the ramp, returning to watch the scene.

"Goddamnit, Emily!" he shouted. "You've got nothing to do with this part! The director can always ship her back if he wants to." He felt himself at the edge of control. "I know you've got the resources"—he nodded toward Lark and his companion, now close beside her—"but this time I'll make the judgment. Don't pull this on me, Emily! Not now!"

Carson returned Inigo's furious stare for a full fifteen seconds before a slow smile spread over her face. "Well, George, it's like I always say. Give a rookie case officer one big success and he ends up thinking he owns the world." She turned to Erika and extended her hand. "Good luck, Miss Hartke. You did a beautiful job this morning. I'm grateful."

All tension gone, Inigo was moving to embrace Carson when an agonized howl spun him around.

"Vera!"

It was Smirnov. Vera had disappeared.

Carson drove like a stunt driver. She took charge immediately, ordering her men to lock Smirnov and Erika in the plane's cabin and stand guard till relieved. Then she had raced toward the first car, taking the driver's side, moving so unexpectedly fast that Inigo barely tumbled into the passenger seat before she gunned the vehicle across the runway.

"Last-minute cold feet," she snapped as they careened through the airfield gate. "Happens a lot of the time. Where would she go?"

"Not back to the hotel, certainly. Maybe to her friend Tanya's. I don't even know where that is. Probably to the Soviet mission."

"It's the only home she's got left here," Carson agreed. "She must be in a cab. See if you can spot her."

"We should have brought her husband."

"By no means. Much too risky. Our first responsibility is to get him out safely. There's no death penalty facing her."

Traffic was light, and Carson was skillful. Inside the third taxi they passed, Inigo spotted a small, hunched body and a head of red hair. Amid furious honking from the cabbie, Carson forced him over. Inigo jumped out, opened the cab door, and slid into the back seat. Vera, exhausted and disheveled, let out a fresh stream of cries.

"Always he does this to me," she sobbed when he had taken her into his arms. "From the beginning. He never asks me. 'We're off to Tokyo, Vera dear, next Thursday; start packing.'" Her Russian flowed in a broken stream. "'We're transferred, Vera. You'll love it in Tbilisi. In Geneva. In New York.'" Inigo pressed her to him and said nothing, letting the sobbing wear her out. "And I love him!" she exclaimed furiously. "A traitor to our country, and I love him! He kidnaps me, tears me away from my parents, my homeland. But this time I do not agree!"

"What will you do, Madame Smirnov?" Inigo put it as gently as he could.

"I go back to Russia. To disgrace, yes. My husband gone forever, our daughter too, our name blackened. But at least I will have my parents, my relations, my friends, my Moscow. No, this time finally I do not agree." She calmed down, pulled away from Inigo, smoothed her skirt, touched at her hair. "Please, Mr. Inigo. You mean well, but let me go now."

He got out and joined Carson at the roadside. The fresh morning breeze tugged at their clothing. The cabbie stood some distance away, silenced by a fifty-franc note.

"Well?"

"She wants to go back." Inigo stared at the sky.

"She understands the situation?"

"Completely. Including the daughter."

"So?"

"How can I take her back to him now? It would be kidnapping.

She's a person, after all. We all have to make our own decisions. Smirnov, Erika, me, you, why not her?"

After a pause, Carson said softly, "I think that's right, George."

"But I feel so much for Victor. And for her too, suddenly."

"That's right too." Carson let him wander a bit about the shoulder of the road, while a low moaning resumed inside the taxi and the driver whistled in unconcern. Then she quietly reminded him of the initialing ceremony he still had to attend. He sighed and got into the back seat again.

"You're quite sure?" he asked in Russian. Vera nodded silently at him, tight-lipped. "I'm sorry." She touched his cheek, tried to smile, failed. "Good-bye, Madame Smirnov."

"Good-bye, Mr. Inigo. Tell my husband I love him still. Try to make him believe it." She straightened up on the seat. "And now you will please let me go."

42

Coming out of the elevator, Inigo ran into Morgan.

"Ah, there you are, George. Just in time for the drinks."

"What's going on?"

"The two ambassadors are up on the eighth floor initialing." Morgan was excited and not trying very hard to hide it. "They've been at it for an hour, but the word just came out that they're nearly finished. The Soviet delegation is on its way now for the reception. Then it's straight to the airport, and home at last. Got your bags packed?" He pointed to a big pile of luggage in the corridor.

"Mine are in there somewhere." Little lies, big lies, soon it would all be over.

"Jesus Christ, George, what have you done now?" It was Michaels, coming up from behind. He grabbed Inigo's arm and pulled him into an empty office.

"Something about a cable, is it?" Inigo said lightly.

" 'Something about a cable,' he says!" Michaels's face was flushed. "I've been looking all over for you! The general is wild. Absolutely wild. It's a bad enough day for him as it is, and now you steal his VIP cabin!"

"You surprise me, Bert. I thought you'd see the humor of it."

Michaels calmed down a little. "All right. I suppose it is funny. In fact, when I tell my wife tonight I'll be roaring with laughter. But right now I've just been chewed out for an hour, all because we couldn't find you and I was handy. What are you going to tell him?"

"Don't know. Got any ideas?"

"None."

"Fine. That's what I'll tell him."

"Huh?"

"Nothing. I'll tell him nothing."

Michaels looked at him enviously. "God, what I wouldn't give sometimes to be a civilian."

"Well, I guess it's about time to mosey on up to the reception," Inigo told him. "That'll be a good place for Walt to find me. He'll have to keep the decibel level down."

When he entered the eighth-floor conference room for the last time, the Americans had begun to gather. They were clustered around Lebedev and Izhov, who had accompanied his ambassador to the initialing. Fairchild was handing out engraved commemorative pens to the members of the U.S. delegation; Jenkins had taken the time to sign his initials with as many different pens as there were members, past and present. O'Rourke accepted his graciously.

Inigo walked up to the group and touched Izhov on the sleeve. When the Soviet turned to him, he tapped him playfully on the nose with his closed fist.

"You did it, Mr. Izhov. Congratulations."

Izhov grinned broadly. He was full of accomplishment, and besides, tomorrow he would be in Moscow.

"George, a word with you." O'Rourke had him by the arm.

"Sure, Walt." Inigo led the way ten paces toward the door, then stopped.

O'Rourke's voice was low and menacing. He was working hard to control his anger. "What's this about my VIP cabin?"

"Oh, that? Can't tell you, Walt."

"What the hell does that mean?" O'Rourke's voice rose, and one or two of the negotiators glanced in their direction. "You know, don't you?"

"Sure I know. And if we wanted you to know, we'd have told you."

" 'We'? Who is this 'we'?"

"Oh, me and the chairman of the JCS."

O'Rourke squeezed Inigo's arm and thrust his face forward. "Listen, Inigo, I won't forget this!"

"Neither will I, Walt. In fact, the whole experience of working with you has been quite unforgettable. Now let go of my arm."

O'Rourke's color rose, his face almost apoplectic. At that moment, the door opened and the Soviet delegation walked in. Rublov, in the lead because of his seniority, stopped short when he caught sight of them, immobile, glaring at each other. Gently, Inigo removed O'Rourke's hand from his arm.

"We have guests, Walt," he murmured quietly. Then he turned to Rublov and extended both arms. It was the same gesture, he suddenly recalled, with which Smirnov had first greeted him, months ago, in this same room.

Delegates from both sides began to circulate around the room, pumping hands, delivering toasts. Boroz and Rublov paired off one last time for a final tête-à-tête. Izhov, who had gotten an early start, became a little tipsy. The interpreters were madly overworked, but no one minded much if they left out half the words. Everyone had lived so long by words, had struggled so hard over them, that now meanings and feelings were all they needed.

Inigo caught sight of Jenkins and Lebedev standing together, glasses in hand, near the middle of the room. The two ambassadors seemed inseparable in this hour of triumph. Various members of the two delegations came up, chatted happily, then drifted away. Inigo wondered whether he should approach the Soviet ambassador. Lebedev might know by now that he had been deceived, and Inigo was uncertain how he would take it. Still, it was important to find out whether the agreement on the Soviet summit statement about telemetry held good.

As Inigo stood undecided, Lebedev noticed him and waved him over.

"Mr. Inigo! A historic occasion! Let us congratulate each other! In honor of this day, I try to speak English, but Ambassador Jenkins will not speak Russian to me." With a huge grin, he raised his glass in a toast. The omens seemed good, so Inigo ventured delicately ahead.

"It is unfortunate that Mr. Pavlovsky is unable to celebrate with us today."

"Yes, most unfortunate." Lebedev didn't bat an eye. "But the news from Moscow is good. They say he makes a full recovery."

"I'm happy to hear it." If he's taking it this well, Inigo thought, he deserves a little forewarning of the next surprise.

"I don't see Mr. Smirnov here today."

Lebedev opened his mouth, then closed it abruptly and stared at Inigo. Finally he spoke.

"Yes, it is strange that he is absent. I do not know where he is."

"Ah well, I assume that he has some good reason," Inigo smiled lightly, "that will become evident in due course."

Without taking his eyes off Inigo, Lebedev accepted a fresh glass of champagne from Jenkins.

"Today the important thing," Inigo went on, "is that the treaty has been completed and initialed. But now we have the next steps ahead. The signing by our presidents, and then the ratification by our parliaments. So we are not finished yet."

"And, of course," Lebedev said slowly, "the observance of the agreements." He was in Russian now.

"Naturally."

"It is necessary that all agreements be honored."

"Yes indeed. I am sure they will."

"I also am sure."

Jenkins was beginning to look strangely at the two of them. But Inigo had what he wanted. The promise of a Soviet statement on telemetry at the summit held good.

"Good-bye, Mr. Ambassador. It has been a great pleasure to share this work with you and to achieve such a splendid joint success."

"Good-bye, Mr. Inigo." Lebedev turned slightly away from Jenkins, lowered his voice, and said, "I value your contribution. You have been most resourceful." They shook hands gravely and Inigo moved away.

He left early. He had birds in a cage at the airport who would need food before the long flight. As he waited for the elevator, a secretary came running down the hall.

"Ah, Mr. Inigo, caught you just in time. Someone in the consulate telephoned an urgent message for you. It sounds terribly exciting. They told me to find you right away and tell you. It says: 'Irina is in Frankfurt.' "

43

Inigo slipped into the cabin and quickly locked the door behind him. Inside it was airless, windowless, and hot. Smirnov and Erika, weary, imprisoned there without news for over two hours, clearly had exhausted their supply of small talk. Smirnov, he knew, was far too careful a professional to talk with Erika about either the past or the future, while she herself could be counted on to keep silent. Each wondered what the other knew, but knew better than to ask.

Smirnov stared fearfully at him. Inigo had wondered, all the way back to the airport, whether it would be kinder to lie. He could say that they had never found Vera. Or, to remove the uncertainty, he could say they were too late, catching up with her cab just as it entered the Soviet mission. No, he thought, in the end we all have a right to the truth. And to our own pain.

"Yes," Smirnov murmured when the whole story had been told. "I do believe she still loves me. The question is whether she believes that I love her." He put his face in his hands. "I do, you know, George. But I was never very good at it. She's right, I did order her about and treat her like a child. Perhaps I loved her as one loves a child." A sob escaped him, but his round body seemed to forbid Inigo's approach. "Perhaps that's all I was capable of."

Inigo stood motionless awhile in the hush, then went on with his report.

"There is more news. First of all, I received a message fifteen minutes ago. Irina is in Frankfurt."

Smirnov let out a tremendous sigh. "My daughter," he explained to Erika. "She was in Moscow."

"How wonderful."

Inigo smiled. "Second, the treaty has been initialed. They finished about an hour ago. The reception should be ending just about now. Everyone is coming straight to the plane. Then we will get some air-conditioning."

271

"Later on, we must drink to the treaty." Smirnov managed a wan smile.

Before long they began to hear the sounds of boarding, first a few footsteps in the corridor outside, then a sentence or two exchanged, rising to the excited chatter of a happy group of men and women going home to their families. Finally Inigo heard Fairchild shouting a name count. His own name was followed by a silence, then questions and a little consternation. But the pilot, who knew where Inigo was, took off anyway.

Erika was the first to fall asleep. Ten minutes later Smirnov stretched out along the length of the couch, turned his face toward the wall, and fell silent. Inigo, slouched in the other armchair, watched him silently for two hours. It was impossible to know whether the man was awake or asleep, whether the occasional twitches and shruggings of his body came from nightmares, misery, or simple cramped restlessness. There was no sound but the low throb of the engines and, when he listened for it, Erika's light breathing. Vera's absence was palpable.

"It's as though you are sitting up with the corpse of a dead friend." Smirnov's remark startled him; he must have been beginning to doze off.

"Is that how you feel, Victor? Dead?"

"Not really." Smirnov hoisted himself into a sitting position. "Well, partly, I guess. Certainly most of my past has died in the last twelve hours."

"Were there ever any other women?"

"Never. I married her when I was twenty-six. Twenty-four long years ago. Before that, nobody. After that, nobody else. I had no gift for attracting women, and I never learned how." He got up and stretched. "Besides, I had my work. It suited me perfectly. I never lost interest, I gave it all my time. Papers, reports, endless meetings— how I laugh when I hear American diplomats complain about the meetings they have to attend. They should spend a year inside our bureaucracy. It took all my energy. I suppose you could say that Vera has been a widow for many years. A political widow."

"She didn't seem too unhappy."

"No, I don't think she was. And we did love each other, in a comfortable, routine sort of way. But it never became very deep. I was buried in my work. She had her translating, but it wasn't enough, and she always had to follow me everywhere. Too much alone, not needed enough. I think her heart shrank. I should have paid attention."

"Will you be blaming yourself forever?"

"Oh yes. Later on, probably not so much as now. But right now it is very strong." Smirnov stared at the ceiling, and they sat without talking for a while.

"She was right, you know," Smirnov resumed. "There's nothing for her in America. Just me, whom she loves mostly out of habit, and a daughter who has never been very kind to her. In Moscow she will have family, warmth, attention, love. She could never be at home anywhere else."

Inigo said nothing. Smirnov gazed for a long time at the sleeping Erika, then turned to him with his first smile since Vera's flight.

"I envy you, George."

"Yes, I'm very lucky."

"I think not. I notice that each of you has a serious attitude toward the other. That is not luck, it is better than luck. And there is another difference between us.

"You are going home. With a new woman, but to your old life. Your friends, your job, your country."

"Yes."

The rest went unspoken. How was it, Inigo wondered, to leave one's country forever? To become a defector? To go over to the enemy, forsaking one's entire past? He imagined that he could not imagine it.

"It is very frightening," Smirnov said, as if answering the silent questions. "Several times I have thought about turning back. I will miss my country. Not so much as Vera would. I am not so much a Russian as she. But still." He got up and stretched. "So much is unknown. So much uncertainty. I am old for such a new beginning."

"We will help you."

" 'We will help you?' Who is this 'we'? Oh yes, I know, the CIA will help me find work, a place to live, perhaps even a new identity. Money until I can earn my own. But I will need other help too."

Inigo looked at him wordlessly.

"When I am sad, I mean. When I am depressed. When I forget all that we have accomplished in the cause of arms control. There will be such times, I feel it now. You Americans have a way of putting it: when I have the blues."

"When you need a friend, you mean."

"Yes, that is the meaning of the blues, I believe."

"Right." Inigo felt the demand and met it. "I'll be there, Victor. Don't worry. I'm good at chasing the blues away. Erika is even better."

Refilling their glasses, Inigo felt an impulse.

"To Allan Hickok," he proclaimed. "A foolish man with a good heart."

"To Mr. Hickok," Smirnov joined him. "A good man with a foolish heart."

Epilogue

A great deal happened in the next two months.

Erika and George got married in the first week. It was a quiet affair. He asked Smirnov to give the bride away. Victor was delighted as well as moved.

"Besides being an honor, George, it gives me a chance to redeem myself. For the time when I tried to force you both apart."

Sloan stood up as best man. He had asked Erika, in his gentle way, whether she would care to furnish information on East German nuclear programs, physicists both established and rising, the organization of Party cells in the scientific community, and so on. She thought it over for a day and then declined. She did not feel like an enemy of her country, where her mother still lived and perhaps suffered as a result of her defection. Besides, after her taste of the intelligence world in Geneva, she really didn't care to be further involved. Sloan did not persist.

Three days after that conversation, she got a letter from her mother, addressed to Inigo at CIA. It was a bitter, cold repudiation of her daughter.

"She had to write it, you know," Inigo tried to console her. "To protect herself."

"Of course. I know that. But I cannot escape the feeling that even without that, she might have written the same thing."

Erika had not yet found a job, but the prospects seemed good. Although there were no references from East Germany, her boss at CERN, Chandaree, had written a most positive description of her work and abilities. More important, she got in touch with three or four American physicists who had been temporary colleagues in Geneva and who were happy to give her suggestions and recommendations. There was a prospect developing nicely in Washington and another in Baltimore. In the meantime, she began to attend professional conferences and to spend time in local technical libraries.

"You have a strange country, George," she told him. "Everything can be bought here, without waiting, good quality and decent prices. I like almost everyone I meet, they are all so friendly and helpful. But your newspapers are so critical and aggressive. Perhaps because I am German. And how can one grow up and learn to enjoy sex here, when it bombards one from every side of public life?"

"I don't know. I did. But it took me a long time."

Smirnov made the same complaint when Irina had her abortion. He was bitter about it, blaming this "pornographic American society" for his daughter's corruption. She did not tell him that it was the third time for her. It was by another student, also big and clumsy but not so shy as Pavel. She soon realized it was a mistake; he might become well off, but never rich. It was not so simple to assess American men and their prospects. She was learning that while family connections counted here, they did not count nearly so much as in Moscow.

At the State Department, she went through the obligatory interview with a representative of the Soviet embassy. The first secretary was suave and reassuring.

"Moscow understands the difficulties one falls into sometimes. Anyone can be misled once in their life. There is actually sympathy for such persons as yourself, facing the possibility of never seeing your relatives and friends for the rest of your life, of never treading again on Russian soil. There will be no recriminations, I can assure you, if you return now. Explanations certainly exist and can be given. Especially by those who are passive victims of recent unfortunate events. You are a Soviet citizen, and it is my task to inform you that you cannot be deprived of your rights. If you do not wish to exercise these rights today, specifically the right to return to the homeland, you can telephone me at any time, day or night." He gave her his card.

"You say this, do you?" she spat at him when he finished. "You speak for a government that blocks my telephone calls to my mother, that intercepts our letters! I know very well this homeland you speak of. It is not my homeland any longer. You and your fellows have made it a hellhole!" She tore up his card, threw the pieces on the floor, and marched out.

Victor was extremely busy. After an initial three weeks of intensive oral debriefing, Sloan set him to work writing monographs on the topics on which he was best informed: role and structure of the KGB, the apparatus of arms control policymaking in the USSR, Soviet means of influencing Western peace organizations. With Vera still preying on his mind, the pressure was good for him. Initially, of course, he was subjected to the lie detector and other tests by Sloan's people, to the disgust of Shambler, who maintained forever afterward that Smirnov's information could not be trusted. It only bolstered Shambler's suspicions when Smirnov steadfastly refused to name his colleagues overseas. Meanwhile, Smirnov's defection remained a closely guarded secret; he agreed with Inigo that his public career should be delayed while the SALT treaty was still under debate in the Senate.

"And speaking of SALT, your treaty seems to be in some trouble," Sloan remarked to Inigo as they met to compare notes on Smirnov's adjustment problems and the information coming from his debriefings.

"Yes, it looks bad. It's a crazy world, isn't it? We discover a Soviet army unit that's been in Cuba for three years, or Moscow sends troops into Afghanistan, and suddenly we decide the Russians are the world's untouchables. They're not even fit partners for an arms treaty that works in our favor. I hear the president has decided to put off a Senate vote until after the election."

"By which time," Sloan put in, "he may not be president anymore."

Smirnov was right, thought Inigo. The treaty was a fragile structure, vulnerable to every passing difficulty arising in Soviet-American relations. Inigo had not expected the fatal difficulty to arise out of American politics. But with the election less than a year away, a powerful opposition candidate was attacking the treaty as a giveaway, a new form of appeasement that conceded some sort of strategic superiority to the USSR. Right-wingers of various stripes were playing upon the latent distrust of Moscow that lay deep in popular opinion.

"I see where Walt O'Rourke, with all that inside expertise, is making a name for himself these days," Inigo remarked. "I even hear him touted for a big job in the next administration."

"It's tough to be beaten by your own side."

"Sure is." Inigo slowly walked to the window. "Well, it'll come sooner or later. If not in SALT Two, then in SALT Six or SALT Eleven. Patience, Hugh. It's got to happen eventually."

"And in the meantime?"

"In the meantime, we can all love our wives. How's Sue these days?"

"Just fine. And Erika?"

Inigo looked at his watch. "Three-thirty. She should be home about now. I think I'll take off early today. Just in case the world blows up tonight."

Sloan walked him out to the parking lot and, on a sudden impulse, went home himself. His wife was surprised to see him, and pleased.